PROM *Perfect*

EDITED BY: S.E. REED &
DEMI MICHELLE SCHWARTZ

All content is protected by the individual copyright.

All rights reserved. No part of this publication may be

reproduced, distributed, or transmitted in any form or by

any means, including photocopying, recording, or other

electronic or mechanical methods, without the prior written

permission of the publisher, except in the case of brief

quotations embodied in critical reviews and certain other

noncommercial uses permitted by copyright law.

Wild Ink Publishing LLC

wild-ink-publishing.com

Editors: S.E. Reed and Demi Michelle Schwartz

Design & Layout by: Abigail Wild

All references to historical events, real people, or real

places are used fictitiously. Names, characters, and places

are products of each author's imagination.

CONTENTS

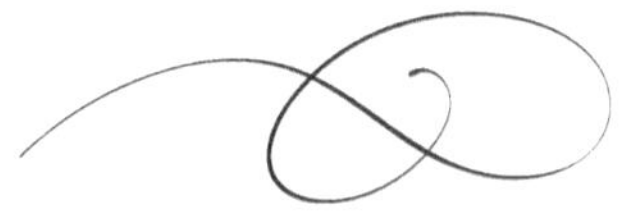

Dear Reader,

I CAME UP WITH the idea for The Prom Perfect Anthology after dress shopping with my teenage daughter. It wasn't Junior Prom, it was her Sophomore Homecoming and her first big school dance. Homecoming, as you may know, is not as formal as the Prom—but it's still a dressy night full of glitz and glam.

While walking around the mall, I noticed so many teenagers with parents, friends, and other loved ones, all doing the same thing... shopping to find the perfect dress, the perfect shoes, the perfect jewelry. Their youthful faces are a mix of joy and apprehension for this huge milestone high school event.

Later that night, I couldn't get the idea of 'perfect' out of my head. What exactly did that mean? Was any school dance ever really perfect? I wasn't entirely sure since I had never gone. It was the late 90s, and I was living in the suburbs of Seattle. My focus was more on drama, choir, and writing politically charged poetry than worrying about going to dances.

But that never stopped me from enjoying the idea of the "Big Formal" and wanting to explore it further through writing, music, and film. Some of my favorite movies are teen-centered flicks where they have the magical, or maybe horrifying, Prom Night. It's a universal American teenage experience, whether you attended or stayed home. Every Prom (or anti-Prom) experience is a rite of passage.

With those feelings in mind, The Prom Perfect Anthology was born. We had an incredible outpouring of submissions across genres. And it's been such a pleasure working with each highly talented author to bring this book to life.

So, without further ado, welcome to The Prom. Make sure you're home by midnight, don't drink the punch, smile, get on that dance floor, and above all, HAVE FUN!

xo

S.E. Reed

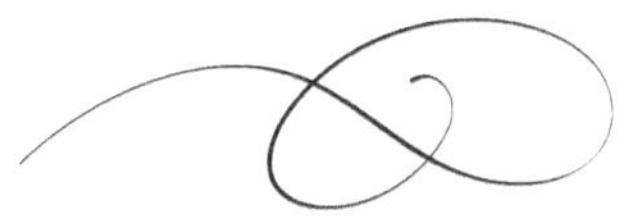

A Brush with Sisterhood

By Andie L. Smith

Chapter One

BEATRICE

If a poster could change someone's life, this would be the one to do it.

I stare at glossy paper on the wall, the silhouetted couple dancing the night away under a thousand twinkling lights. A boy spins a girl, her dress billowing out at the waist while her hand extends toward the sky—or in this case, the sparkly letters across the top of the flyer, marking the special four words in a silver glow.

Reach for the Stars.

The committee decided on the theme at the beginning of the school year, and it's the only thing I've thought about since.

"Bea! Can we get your opinion on the projector set-tings?"

Clutching my clipboard, I take a deep breath and offer the beautiful poster one final glance as I call over my shoulder, "Be right there!"

The smile on my face has been permanently affixed for weeks, but it wavers as I approach the light booth of the auditorium. The drama club volunteers have been kind to lend their expertise, but prom is five days away. I can't afford any last-minute mistakes.

"What's up?"

"We think we figured out the electromagnetic spec-trum configuration and were able to manipulate it alongside a specific set of coordinates."

I look from the girl who spoke—Ava, I think—to the brown-haired boy sitting next to her. Despite the million thoughts running through my head, my brow furrows. "What does that mean exactly?"

Ava smiles, nudging the boy to her left. "Let's show her, Jasper."

I glance at the clipboard, the unchecked to-do items screaming at me from the page. *I don't have time for this*, I want to say. "Let's just—"

My words are cut off as Jasper flips the switch of the auditorium, and the entire room around us shines in iridescent light. Not just light—*stars*. Every inch of the space is covered in blinking, bright, sparkling stars.

I have no idea what to say. No, that's not true. I know exactly what to say. "It's beautiful."

Ava and Jasper smile, sharing a fist bump before the latter goes to turn the lights back on. For a moment, my heart aches at the sudden brightness—the shock of reality breaking into my dream.

Because that's what this is. For me, for every senior this year, and every rising one anxious to witness this same moment when it's their turn. Prom is a dream. It's pure magic, encapsulated for one night only. A chance for us to dance under the stars—literally now, thanks to Ava and Jasper—and reflect on the past few years of our lives while feeling hopeful for the many to come.

It's the night that changes everything, and it must be perfect.

"It took us longer than we wanted, but overall, I'm happy with the result," Ava says, pulling me from my trance.

There's nothing wary about the smile I offer her now. "It exceeds expectations. Thank you both so much."

I stare back out at the newly lit auditorium, watching groups of students work on different tasks for the dance—set pieces are being stained, light colors undergoing tweaks, decorations glued together by careful hands.

It's happening. My perfect prom, one last chance at freedom and an opportunity to leave my mark on this school forever. One final night for all of us to be together before we go our separate ways into the unknown.

I won't let anything ruin it.

Chapter Two

Tristan

There's a certain place in Hell for whoever decided school dances were a good idea.

The decorations, the dresses, the fake niceties of peers you've never spoken to suddenly knowing your name—it has never sat right with me. Which is precisely why I've chosen to spend my last period anywhere but my assigned seat in Leadership Studies, where the class is helping the prom committee with final preparations for the dance.

I'd rather chew on my own toenail.

Blowing out a breath, I reach up to tie back my dark brown hair before slipping out into the hallway. Now ten minutes past the late bell, the path to the art room—and my freedom—is clear. Steel-gray lockers take up either side of me, bordering the infamous bulletin board encouraging students to *Pick Up Your Yearbook! Get Your Prom Tickets Now! Celebrate Our Seniors!*

In two strides and one final breath, I open and close the door to room 207, my one and only favorite place in this entire school. The room is dark, save for the stream of light filtering through the paper-thin blinds. It'll have to do. I'm not dumb enough to risk getting caught from flicking on the fluorescent bulbs.

Making my way to the back corner of the room, my unease finally settles. I flip over the thick sheet, a barely filled canvas on a wooden easel greeting me.

This is why I come here every day. This is what's important.

My art—the words I can never express but somehow flow freely with a paintbrush in hand—is the only thing keeping me going.

Except for when Mrs. Freiss assigns prompts I have no idea what to do with.

Staring at the whiteboard, I wince at the words, the bold black lines mocking me.

Paint your perfect day.

We've had two weeks to work on our final project, and all I've got is a light blue sky and imperfect white clouds that lean a little too much to the left. In all my life, I've never had an art block, always itching for any excuse to feel my brush stroke against a canvas. Haunted house? Fields of flowers? You name it, I can paint it.

Except for my perfect day.

As a junior, everything is riding on this final grade for art class. Before she had assigned the prompt, Mrs. Freiss shared the exciting news that whoever gets a straight one hundred on the assignment will receive the opportunity to interview for the RSID Fellowship. The summer intensive program is my one shot at getting into the Rhode Island School of Design, a school I've dreamed about ever since Mom gifted me an oil set for Christmas.

And the only thing holding me back is a stupid prompt that should be the easiest thing in the world to paint.

Just as I'm about to dip the brush into a glob of dark green dye, the doorknob rattles, and I freeze in place.

"Ms. Williams? There is no art class this period. What are you doing in here?"

I flinch as Principal Brennan flicks on the light, bright spots clouding my vision and emptying any reply I could muster.

"I—"

"Not another word. Skipping class is inexcusable, especially with so little of the year left. Come with me." Principal Brennan widens the door, extending his arm to wave two fingers towards me.

A sigh escapes me as I grab my bag and follow him into the hallway. One glance back at the now closed art room door, and I know I'll be back. I need to finish my project. My future depends on it.

I won't let anything get in the way.

Chapter Three

Beatrice

One hundred and twenty.

That's how many hours there are until the dance, not counting the seven I'll need for sleep every night until then.

Everything's coming along, but it also feels like nothing is happening at the same time. Today's the last day in the auditorium before we start moving decorations into the gym, and I can't help but feel like something's missing.

But I'm Bea Williams—I don't forget things.

Watching the crew assemble one of the last set pieces for the dance, my quiet moment in the auditorium stalls is interrupted by an onslaught of questions.

"—can I put this?"

"—go over here?"

"—think will work?"

I look up, meeting several eager and smiley faces I'm unfamiliar with. Freshmen—I can tell by the way they're bouncing on their heels, dying to play some role in a dance they won't attend for two more years.

Taking a deep breath, I nod toward the stage where the crew is still building the final rung in the makeshift fence.

"Give it to Simon. He's the one in the dark gray shirt pounding frantically into the plank of wood," I say to the girl with braces.

"Yes, that's fine," I tell the boy in a fedora.

And finally, to the girl with eyes so glossy, they could be part of the decorations, I challenge, "What do you think?"

She stares back at me, jaw open after not receiving a quick dismissal like her friends. "W-What?"

I bite my cheek to hold back my grin, seeing so much of myself in her. Where my hair is pin straight and blonde, hers is black and curled tightly around her dark face. I wasn't much older than her when I got my first taste of the prom committee, my desire to be something *more* born so early.

"What's your name?" I ask, ashamed I don't know it. The Prom-Queen-To-Be should know the names of her constituents.

"S-Sarah."

I turn in my chair, blocking out the sounds of whacking tools and shouts of teenagers. "Sarah, what do you think of the piece you're holding?"

She faces the painting, though I'm hesitant to call it such. It's a swirling mess of blue and purple, as if the artist simply poured two bottles of colors together and hoped they worked.

"I can't tell what it is," Sarah says.

A small grin teases the corners of my mouth. "Now, do you think the opening painting—the first thing guests will see when they enter the gym—should be something unrecognizable?"

Sarah shakes her head, and my grin widens. She'll be Fairview High's Prom Queen in a few years.

"Exactly, we can't use that. Is there anything—"

"Sorry to interrupt, but Principal Brennan is here, Bea. He's asking for you, specifically."

I grimace and rise from the seat, facing my committee co-chair. "Thanks, Lara." Exiting the row, I tell Sarah to go back to Mrs. Freiss and find another painting for the welcome piece.

It's not until I reach the back of the auditorium that my smile falls, seeing our principal standing next to my sister. Before I can open my mouth to question them, Principal Brennan is speaking.

"Bea, just the girl I was looking for. I think I've found a solution to your little art problem."

Chapter Four

Tristan

"You've got to be kidding me."

Principal Brennan ignores me, continuing to talk to my sister. "Tristan heard the committee was having trouble securing a welcome piece, and she jumped at the opportunity to be of service." He turns to me with an all-knowing grin. "Isn't that right?"

No! I want to scream. If there's anything I'd hate doing more than painting a picture for prom, it's helping my sister. From the disgusted look on her face, I can tell Beatrice is thinking the same exact thing.

But for whatever reason, Principal Brennan is giving me an out. He could write me up for skipping class, or worse, suspend me. Then, I'll never have a chance to finish my project. I could kiss the fellowship goodbye.

"That's right," I say through clenched teeth.

Beatrice sees straight through the lie. "Thank you for the offer, Principal Brennan, but I'm confident the committee will find a wonderful piece for the opening painting."

"You heard her—" I start.

"Enough." Principal Brennan's gaze is menacing. "You will help the committee with whatever they need to paint the welcome piece, Tristan. Understood?"

Students around the auditorium are staring now. My skin itches underneath my clothes. I hate being the center of attention. To take their gazes off me, to get back to my project, I'll do anything.

Even if it means working with my uptight sister.

"Understood."

"Great," he says, heading for the auditorium doors. "I'll leave you both to it."

At his departure, my sister crosses her arms across her chest, one eyebrow raised. I've always hated how one look can contain so much disappointment.

"What?" I ask, nervously tugging at the sleeve of my sweater. Can everyone stop *staring*?

Beatrice shakes her head, her tongue clicking the roof of her mouth. "What did you do this time?"

"Nothing."

"What are Mom and Dad going to think?"

I shake my head, twisting the fabric of my sweater between my fingers. There's no need to respond, not when we both know the answer.

Our parents won't care, I want to say. *Not when you're there to shine in the spotlight.*

"Fine, be that way." Beatrice turns on her heel, but not before spitting back over her shoulder, "But we've got work to do."

Aye, aye, princess. I offer a mock salute to my sister's retreating form and try not to bite my tongue when I notice something glittery on my boot. *Are you kidding me?* I've only stepped foot in the place, and I'm already covered in sparkles.

I've heard it all before—prom is special, magical, a once-in-a-lifetime experience, as Beatrice claims. What I don't understand is why? Why people like my sister care so much about one night. As chair of the planning committee, she has spent the entire year gearing up for this dance. For months, it's all she has talked about at the dinner table—squealing over the perfect dress, how the posters she designed were going viral, even crying over the star decorations arriving in the wrong shape. I'm talking full-on waterworks over a flimsy piece of paper that no one is going to glance at for more than two seconds. Watching her plan this dance has been a roller coaster of emotions, the leading one being anger.

If she paid half as much attention to me as she did her glitter-infused rite of passage, maybe things would be different between us.

The impossibility makes me laugh. The only thing Beatrice cares about is herself.

"Tristan?" she calls from the stage, solidifying my punishment.

Ugh. Better get this over with.

Chapter Five

Beatrice

Moving the set pieces from the auditorium to the gym goes a lot smoother than I anticipated. Two guys are on a ladder, hanging string lights from the ceiling rafters. The techies are at their booth by the makeshift stage, pushing buttons and tapping into microphones. Freshmen giggle and drape navy tablecloths over the small round tables at the front of the gym. And there, in the corner, my sister sits with a sketchbook in her lap.

In another life, my sister and I could be planning this prom together—gossiping about boys, shopping for dresses, and sharing a special night of memories.

But that isn't us.

Emotions churn in my gut. I wish things could be different between us. I can't pinpoint when everything changed, but somewhere along the way, we stopped being close, stopped being anything—the most we say to each other is "pass the butter" at dinner.

For some reason, my feet carry me forward, and I'm walking toward her. She doesn't even glance my way as I approach, probably hoping no one could spot her all the way over here.

"Hey," I say.

Tristan looks up at me, brows pinching together. I've always wondered if the lines on her forehead are from doing that too much.

"Hi."

It's not much, but it's a start.

I peek at my clipboard, clicking the matching fuchsia pen with my thumb. "How are things going over here?"

One of the guys on the ladder thinks I'm talking to him and chimes in. "We're solid, Bea! Almost done hanging these lights, then we'll work on the disco ball."

I try not to laugh when Tristan's eyes roll to the back of her head at the mention of the most iconic prop for a school dance.

"Oh goody," she says through clenched teeth.

Why are you so miserable all the time? I want to ask her. *Is spending time with me really that bad?*

Focus, Bea. There are still fourteen unchecked items on the list. Your psychoanalysis for why your sister hates you will have to wait.

"Great," I reply to the guys on the ladder, nodding at Tristan in my redirection. "And how's the painting coming?"

"It's...coming." She glances between me and the blank page of her sketchbook, worrying her bottom lip. *I never should've agreed to this.*

I glance down at my clipboard, pretending to review the catering menu one last time instead of panicking over the welcome piece that's still not done, when it hits me.

"I need to run an errand," I tell my sister. "Can you come with me?"

After a pained expression crosses her face, Tristan nods and tosses her pad into her backpack before flinging it over her shoulder. It's not until we've crossed the parking lot and buckled the seatbelts of my white Corolla that she asks where we're going.

"Trust me," I tell her.

We ride in silence, and every so often, I can't help but notice how Tristen fidgets with the sleeve of her sweatshirt. It's always been a habit of hers, not being able to sit still. A smile fights its way to my face, and I wonder if maybe Tristan hasn't changed that much after all.

After fifteen minutes, we arrive at The Pointe—a cliffside edge our family used to have picnics at. Now, it's usually overrun by high schoolers looking for a place to hook up.

Recognition dawns on Tristan's face, but she stays quiet as I put the car in park.

"I come here every so often when I can't think straight. When my thoughts race a million miles an hour. It helps to take a step back from it all."

Tristan follows my gaze over the edge of the mountain. For that one moment, she lets go of her sweater.

Chapter Six

Tristan

My sister was right.

If anyone ever heard me say that, I'd plead insanity. I'd say an alien abducted me and took over my brain, because that's the only way I'd ever agree with Beatrice.

But sitting here now, staring out at the hills and valleys of our hometown, I can't help but feel at peace. Like for a moment, everything will be okay—my art project, the summer fellowship, the prom painting, these unresolved feelings about Beatrice leaving for college in the fall—all of it seems so far away.

"Sometimes, things are too much for me. Between finals, prom, and graduation, it all feels so..." Beatrice blanks, searching for the word.

"Heavy," I suggest.

She turns to me, her bright eyes glossy. I've always been jealous of the color she got from our mom, wishing I could trade my dad's browns for her blues. Something tugs at my chest as I stare into them now, a feeling of similarity.

"Exactly," she says with a small smile.

The moment feels too intense, too serious for us to be present in. I never thought about it—if my sister struggles as much as I do. She's Beatrice—popular and beautiful and perfect. She has no idea what it's like to be me, to live in her shadow.

"I didn't realize being Prom Queen came with such a downfall."

Beatrice's smile fades. "Can I ask you something, Tristan?"

My eyes find the floor of the car. "Go ahead."

"What did I do?" She sniffles, and out of the corner of my vision, I see her wipe her cheek. "What happened for you to hate me so much?"

A lump forms in my throat, my face burning from embarrassment.

Tell her, the voice inside me urges. *You may not get another chance.*

"I don't hate you," I say, eyes still trained on my feet. "You're the one who acts like I don't exist."

Ever since my first day of school, Beatrice made it known I wasn't welcome in her high school world.

"What are you talking about?"

My gaze snaps to hers, fury boiling low in my gut. "Freshman year, Beatrice. Lunch period. I walked up to your table, hoping I could sit with you. I heard what you said about me."

Her mouth gapes, eyes blinking rapidly as it all comes together for her. She was a sophomore and dating the captain of the wrestling team at the time—Jack or Jake or whatever his name was. I had come from journalism class and was looking forward to lunch all day, just to have someone to sit with. But when her friend, Lara, asked her how she felt about her sister being at the same school, I heard Beatrice's answer loud and clear.

What sister? she had said. *I have no idea who you're talking about.*

Their laughter followed me all the way to the bathroom, where I cried over my lunch tray. That was the day I knew nothing would be the same between Bea and me again.

"Oh, Tris," my sister says now, placing a hand on my arm. "That's why you stopped speaking to me? Because of a dumb thing I said to my friends?"

My brow furrows, and I toss her hand away. "It wasn't dumb to me. You made it very obvious you wanted nothing to do with me. God forbid your little sister ruin your perfect princess image."

"Tristan," she scolds. "That's not what I meant. What happened that day, it's not what you think. The girls at that table were ruthless—I knew if they found out who you were, they'd never leave you alone."

What? The thing I've held onto for so many years—the words she used that hurt me so much—was her way of protecting me? That doesn't make any sense.

"I'm so sorry." Her voice catches in her throat, and I know she's crying again, but I refuse to look at her. "I wish you told me sooner."

Chapter Seven

Beatrice

Prom is in two days, and the only thing I can think about is my sister.

"It was tight, but we did it, Bea. Everything looks amazing!"

I turn to Lara, forcing a smile as we check off the remaining tasks on the list. Disco ball. Photo booth. Balloon archway. The only thing missing is the welcome piece, the painting my sister is responsible for.

Her admission at The Pointe has turned my brain into one, giant, unhelpful lump. For years, I've wondered what happened that caused her to stop talking to me. I chalked it up to Tristan wanting space or needing to distance herself from me to land on her feet at a new school.

Never in my life would I have thought the reason was me—something I said because I thought I was looking out for her, when I only hurt her instead.

"Do you think your sister will have the painting done by Saturday?" Lara asks me.

I have absolutely no idea, I want to say. Tristan could completely flake on us and leave me flailing my arms on the most important night of my life, and I'd deserve it.

"I'm sure she's putting finishing touches on it now," I tell Lara. Satisfied with my answer, she skips away to finalize the playlist with the DJ—aka the sound guy from the drama club.

With nothing left to do in the gymnasium, I head to the one place I know my sister will be.

Pushing open the art room door, I can't help the smile that grows on my face at seeing Tristan in her element. She's nodding along to whatever music fills her ears through the headphones adorning her head, her arms covered in paint splotches and face scrunched in concentration. I almost feel bad interrupting, but this is too important to ignore.

"Tristan," I call as the door closes behind me.

She doesn't hear me, and I think about how Mom would yell at her right now to turn her music down.

You're going to burst an eardrum! she'd say.

Finding the switch near the door, I flick the classroom lights off and back on.

Tristan looks up, her stare questioning as she removes her headphones. "Hey."

"Hi," I say, suddenly nervous. *You can do this, Bea.* Be the bigger sister. "Can you take a break?"

She nods and places her brush on the easel before coming to sit on top of a desk. I take a seat at the one in front of her.

"I wanted to talk about Tuesday," I start.

"Bea—"

"Don't." I hold up a hand to cut her off. "I haven't been able to stop thinking about what you said, how I'm the reason we've been so bitter to each other."

Tristan shrugs, her fingers finding the end of her black cardigan. "It's fine. It's not like it really matters, anyways."

I tilt my head. "What does that mean?"

She looks up at me, and for a moment, I wonder if she's going to cry. I can't remember the last time I've seen Tristan cry. "You're leaving soon."

"I'm going to college, Tris. Not enlisting in the military."

"Is there a difference?" she asks, her thumb scraping at the paint chips on her wrist. "You'll be miles away, but nothing will change. We won't see each other. We won't talk."

I may not have had my heart broken by a boy yet, but my sister has done the act with her words alone. My eyes water, and I reach out to grab her hand, to take it away from her stupid sweater.

"Listen to me, Tristan." I clear my throat. "I'm so sorry for what I said, for making you feel less than, simply because you're my sister. I've never thought that. For my entire life, you've always been my favorite person. If you'll let me, I'd like to be that for you, too. Even when I go to college."

Her eyes never leave mine, even when a single tear falls down her cheek. "Okay."

"Okay," I say. "Now, how's that painting coming?"

Chapter Eight

Tristan

I fumble with the zipper on the tight black pantsuit, already regretting my agreement to go to the dance. I couldn't wait to show Beatrice my piece, but I didn't think I'd have to attend the prom to do it.

"You girls look so beautiful!" Mom screams.

Beatrice and I wince at each other as we pose for another picture outside of our house.

"I can't believe you talked your sister into going to prom, Bea. And look at you both. A sight for sore eyes," Dad calls.

"All right!" Beatrice holds up her hands, the lavender gossamer gown flowing with every movement. "That's enough! We need to leave before we miss the whole thing."

"Would that be so bad?" I ask.

Beatrice rolls her eyes but grabs my hand and pulls me toward the car. After shouting goodbye to our parents, we head off to the dance.

Tristan Williams is going to prom, who would've thought.

I squint at the sun as we arrive at the school and step out of the car, tugging on the end of my jacket sleeve. Beatrice smiles and offers her hand. Still not used to the sudden touching, I loop my arm in hers, and we walk inside the lobby of the gym, where my painting hangs to welcome everyone to the night of their dreams.

"Tristan..."

My eyes are squeezed shut, my grip on my sister's arm tight as I prepare for the outburst. I knew it was different, but I really thought I had created the perfect opening piece.

"I'm sorry, I can take it down if—"

"Tristan!" Beatrice screams. "Open your eyes!"

I do, and I gasp so loudly, I swear the entire school can hear me. All the students standing around us don't seem to mind as they stare at my painting.

"Gorgeous," a girl to my right says.

"Breathtaking," her date adds.

"Tris." My sister captures my attention. "It's perfect."

I peel my gaze from her face to look at the final product, hoisted high above the entrance doors for all to see. A mountain range in the distance, a night sky with twinkling stars. At the bottom, a car's parked on the cliff's edge, the silhouette of two figures inside.

Paint your perfect day.

I haven't had many perfect days with Beatrice over the years, but that's okay. I have a feeling there are so many more to come.

"I'm glad you like it." I blush and tug her along, ready to see what all the hype for this night is about.

When I walk through the doors, I'm speechless. Though I saw most of the set pieces when I was working on my painting, I was not prepared for the scene before me.

The walls are covered in deep blue paper, hiding the broken slabs of concrete of an old gym. A dark, thick carpet covers the floor, which is decorated with several tall tables adorning celestial-themed flower bouquets. The room spins under the glow of the disco ball, and somehow, the entire space is covered in bright, illuminating, silver stars. For a moment, it feels like we're outside, not in a cramped gym filled with too many bodies.

"Is it too much?" Beatrice asks. I know she's doubting everything—every choice and decision she's made about this night.

"It's beautiful," I say, and I mean it. Her starry night goes beyond words, and watching the pure awe on the students' faces as they file in behind us has me wondering why I went so long without supporting my sister more.

She tries so hard to be perfect, to do everything right, but it's never for herself. It's for everyone around her. And we'd all be fools not to appreciate every moment of it.

"Come on." Beatrice grabs my hand and leads me towards the open floor beyond the tables. "Let's go dance."

A Charming Night on the Flipside

By Michael Joseph Tharnish Roby

For the second time in as many weeks, Carter Wilkerson stood stock-still in his bedroom while his father fussed over getting a bow tie around his neck.

"A simple clip on would have done you just fine, I think." His dad chuckled as he struggled to secure the knot around his own neck. "You'd think last weekend would have made me better at this. Okay, think I've got it. Bring your head down."

Carter lowered himself. Having a tall, broad, quarterback's frame, he stood more than a head taller than his father. With a pinch on the inside of the bow tie to maintain the knot, his dad slipped the tie over his own head, slid it over Carter's neck, and cinched.

"Hey, hey, there we go." Carter beamed.

"You look good, son, very good." His father raised a hand, and they shared what was a high five for him, a down low for Carter. He looked at the alarm clock next to his son's bed. "And with twenty minutes to spare before Skylar arrives."

"It's a lot easier than last week," Carter said. "But thank you for taking all those pictures. Everybody online thinks they turned out great."

"Sure, sure." His father reached into his pocket, produced a wallet, and slipped out a few twenty-dollar bills. "Here, let me pay for some of dinner, too."

Carter raised his hands and tried to push back. "You seriously don't have to."

"I seriously want to. You paid for dinner yourself last week. Most boys your age only have to cover one fancy pre-prom dinner. Let me help on this one."

For a moment, Carter considered further pushback, but then, he smiled wide and accepted the money. "Well, all right, if you insist. Thanks."

The two stood quietly for a few moments, as if each thought of what they might say next.

Eventually, the boy's father said, "I want just a word with you about this dance tonight."

"Dad, I don't think that's necessary—" Carter started to speak.

"No, this is important. You know your mom and I like Skylar a lot, and we're happy the two of you are together. But this is the first time you're going to be around a lot of her peers. And I think it goes without saying, well, the people on the Flipside of town are pretty different from here."

Carter blew a breath up at his face. "I know, Dad. Trust me, I've been thinking about it more than you have."

"Just remember you're a guest. That means a lot of respect is going to be expected of you." His father placed a hand on his shoulder. "But it also means a lot of respect and grace should be extended back toward you. Don't forget it, and don't let anybody get away with treating you any differently than that."

A silent few moments passed between them, as if Carter struggled with how to respond. Before he could come up with a decent reply, there came a call from the kitchen downstairs.

"Carter!" his mother shouted. "I think Skylar just pulled up."

"What?" Carter grabbed the suit jacket he had draped over one of his bedposts. "No, crap, I could swear she said five fifteen! She wouldn't have said four fifty-five. That makes no sense."

"Well, her culture values punctuality." His father patted him on the back as he turned around. "Hurry and answer the door. You got ready early too, champ."

Carter pulled on his coat and adjusted his tie as he walked downstairs. He took in a deep, stabilizing breath as he crossed the foyer and reached for the front door.

Prom at Skylar's school was sure to be intense—he'd never been there, and a lot of rough stories always floated around. But how bad could it be? If Carter was the football team's quarterback and prom-royalty material at his own school, that would surely translate into some kind of cool at Skylar's.

He also braced himself for her dress again. True, he'd seen it just a week ago, but Skylar made every time he beheld it special.

He opened the door and flashed his biggest, brightest smile. "Hi, Skylar."

A young, dark-haired woman in a backless, wine-red dress smiled back at him. The six teal-scaled serpents that extended out of the sides of her spine shifted about and stuck out their tongues. Maybe Carter always imagined it, but he figured they knew his scent by now, and he liked to think they started to smile too.

"Hi, Carter. Ready to party?" She extended her slick black tentacles toward him and wrapped him up in a tight hug.

"You know it."

A swirling vortex of luminescent magentas and deep, blood orange sat behind Carter's Jeep in the driveway. Carter and Skylar took a few steps toward it before a cry of "Wait just a minute!" rang out from inside the house. Carter groaned and Skylar smirked as the boy's mother came rushing out, an old-fashioned, Polaroid camera in her hands.

"Let me just get one more picture of my special little man and his lovely friend before you go out tonight."

"Aw, Mom, you guys took, like, a hundred photos last week." Despite his protests, Carter stood up straight and dutifully smiled as she snapped a few shots.

"All right, Mandy, let the boy go," his father said as he joined them outside.

"You two have a wonderful night." Carter's mom tightened her stare on her son. "And you come home as soon as the after-prom is over, you hear me?"

"I will, I will. Good night." Carter waved with his free hand, his other still clasping Skylar's tentacle, and the two stepped into the swirling portal together.

After their reservation at Skylar's favorite restaurant for roast jackalope, Carter and Skylar arrived at Scylla Academy. Carter heard time and again that he should temper his expectation around the academy in the title—Flipsiders just had a taste for the old fashioned and theatrical.

"Is that also why you have those round, castle-looking things on the corners?" he asked as they approached.

"The parapets? Oh yes, strictly tradition." Skylar blew an embarrassed breath up at her face. "Like the statue of great grandma over there."

Indeed, a towering thirty-foot statue of a tentacled woman, also with snakes sprouting from her back and a trio of yowling dogs jutting from her midsection, stood in the middle of the school lawn. Carter had looked up the visage of Skylar's ancestor once and asked about the dog thing. She insisted since her father was a kalku, the dogs probably skipped a generation for her. Carter only got a C in biology, so he didn't question that any further.

As they approached the front door, Carter squinted at a couple that walked in ahead of them. "Hey, I thought you said I was probably going to be the only human here. What about those two?"

"Hm?" Skylar glanced at the boy in a high-collared suit and the girl in the hijab. "No, no, Ben is a vampire, and Aisha is a jinn."

"Oh, sorry."

Skylar gave her best approximation of an elbowing, no mean feat when her tentacles lacked the anatomy. "I told you, you gotta be careful about that around here. Some people take a lot of offense to misidentification."

"I'm sorry. They're not all easy like those centaurs over there."

With a cringe, Skylar said, "The one without any skin is a nuckelavee, actually. Don't let Kendra hear you call her a centaur. She's top of the class in bloodline curses this semester."

Arm in tentacle, the young couple entered the school. A twinge of nervous energy ran through Carter as a few of Skylar's classmates double-took at the sight of him. But after a moment's consideration, the two nearest to them—trolls of some sort, if Carter had to guess—looked away from him and resumed their own conversation. It seemed the students of Scylla academy would treat him as his classmates did Skylar. They'd perhaps never seen a creature like her in a school dance context before, but it wasn't something that would alter reality as they understood it.

"The gym's over this way." Skylar ushered Carter toward a line of other students that led to a set of long wooden tables. On the opposite side of one, an enormous manticore sat on all fours. Her scorpion tail rose up to her side, her great lion's paws remained planted firmly on the floor, and with the bespectacled, pinched face of a sour-feeling human grandmother, she scrutinized every ticket presented to her.

"Everybody slow down. Everyone with a legitimate ticket will get to go inside." There was nothing lion-like in her voice. Carter thought she sounded like every cranky substitute teacher he'd ever had.

For a minute after, she punched tickets at a quick clip. Eventually though, a tall figure in a Knights jersey with skin the color and texture of grass and hair like hundreds of vines sprouting from his head approached.

The manticore took an extra few seconds to scrutinize his ticket before she slammed it down and glared upward. "Nice try, Basil Greene, but maybe next time you try making a forged ticket, you could allot some better material than crayons."

The big, green figure raised a hand to his forehead and swooned. "Oh, but madam, there must be some mistake. No party is ever complete without a green knight in attendance."

"You tried to make that excuse back at Homecoming, too. At least then, you had the decency to paint your forgery." The manticore crumpled up the slip he gave her and stuffed it under the table. "You want to participate in school events, then you pay your way inside like everyone else."

"But Lady Morrison—"

The manticore cut Basil off with a throaty, leonine roar that shook her mane. A few other students in line cringed and held hands over their ears. Carter stiffened for a moment in terror before the strange green student ran off.

As Carter pressed at his ringing ear, he asked, "What was that all about?"

"Oh, Basil Greene is a prankster," Skylar said. "He shows up where he's not welcome and tries to make trouble. Sorry you had to hear all that."

A tiny laugh cut through the air behind them. "Oh yeah, he's a real piece of work. Hey there, Skylar!"

Carter and Skylar turned around. No more than two feet in height but flying three and a half feet off the ground was a sprite. Next to her, towering over all of them, stood a creature in an enormous tuxedo, what must have been at least size fifty shoes, and a delicately manicured face of apelike fur.

"Hey there, Jessie." Skylar opened her tentacles and the two embraced. It was like a girl hugging a teddy bear. "Jessie, this is Carter, my boyfriend. Carter, I know I've told you about Jessie before."

"Oh yes. Hello." Carter smiled at the sprite, but with her tiny size, he felt awkward trying to go in for a handshake or hug.

"Hi, Carter," Jessie said. "Skylar and I have been besties since second grade, but I'm sure you knew that already." She gestured to the giant at her side. "This is my date, Lincoln."

Carter quickly racked his brain to recall if Skylar ever mentioned a Lincoln. Then, he remembered a few details—yes, he dated her friend, Jessie, and he was a sasquatch.

"It's a pleasure." Carter extended a hand toward Lincoln.

The giant hesitated a moment before he reached out and took the hand with the gentle care of someone handling a bunny. "Yes, good to meet you." Then, he frowned and looked toward Skylar. "Sky, I thought you said he was on the football team, though?"

Skylar blushed. "He is. He just—you know—average sizes are a little smaller on the Flipside."

Lincoln squinted down at Carter and eventually grinned, not quite honest, not quite unkind. "Of course. I'm on the football team myself, took us to the championships." The grin morphed into a wide smirk. "Glad our conference is just inter-state and not inter-dimensional, huh?" He burst out laughing.

Carter put on the best smile and let out the best chuckle he could muster, but the implications of the sasquatch's words troubled him. As his father advised him, he just nodded until the manticore called, "Next." The four had their tickets punched, and they were ushered into the gymnasium.

From a simple observation, Scylla Academy's gymnasium looked much the same as any other school gym decorated for prom, but the finer, magical details made Carter's eyes go wide and his mouth open in joyous wonder. In one corner, a bubbling cauldron of potion sat where a punch bowl would have been, and little glass jars that hung from the ceiling held tiny, dancing faeries instead of fairy lights. In place of a DJ, three kiddie pools were lined up side by side, and a dozen water possums floated on the surface. Carter had read about these creatures, maybe the coolest he'd ever heard of. They were ahuizotl, Aztec creatures that could perfectly emulate any noise. The dozen possums recreated the sounds of instruments and singers as they performed all of the music. Carter enjoyed his own dance well enough, but his heart soared with the rare chance for a simple human to behold just how awesome prom on the Flipside could be.

After his uncomfortable run in with the sasquatch, Carter felt grateful to follow Skylar's lead to the middle of the floor and show off his moves. The young man was quick on his feet and kept an impeccable rhythm, and whenever slow songs came along, Skylar's tentacles allowed for multiple pirouettes from a single raise of the hand.

Carter needed to speak up to be heard over the singing. "Are you having a good time?"

Skylar yelled back, "Absolutely!"

A moment after she did, a shrill, reverberating laugh cut through the music and nearby conversation. "Skylar, is that you?"

Skylar's face fell to a frown as she and Carter turned toward the questioner.

With a sigh, Skylar said, "Hi, Javier."

Carter did a little internal flinch and took a hard swallow at the sight of him. The young man with the shrill laugh stood just a little taller than he did, wore a masterfully tailored white suit and hat, and his tanned brown face had the shape and perfection of a marble sculpture. Even as someone whose interests only ever laid with the opposite sex, Carter couldn't resist the thought this was the single most attractive young man he'd ever seen.

"Boa noite, senhorita," Javier said. "Are you going to introduce me?"

Skylar looked to barely suppress a groan as she raised a tentacle toward Carter. "Carter, this is Javier. We used to date. Javier, this is Carter, we're dating right now." She said it with the kind of forced intonation that suggested Javier go away.

"A pleasure. Any amigo of sweet Skylar is an amigo of mine." The whole time he spoke, Javier swayed perfectly to the beat of the music, both as if he was possessed by it and intended to capture others with his movements. "You're certainly a looker for a Flipsider."

Carter hesitated before he said, "Uh, thanks."

"Don't make it weird for him," Skylar said. "He's the only human here."

With another shrill laugh, Javier said, "Oh no, he isn't. Didn't you see? Erla brought a human with her, too. In fact, I think that's them over there." He motioned to a corner just behind the musical kiddie pools.

"What? Erla?" Skylar went red in the face.

"What's wrong?" Carter squinted as he looked for whatever Javier was talking about. "Who am I looking for?"

Skylar pulled Carter out of the middle of the dance floor, so they wouldn't have to yell. "Erla is only the most popular girl in school. She's an elwetritsch."

Before Carter could ask what one of those looked like, he caught sight of something else that made his whole body go stiff. Under his breath, he muttered, "Holy crap. Gene?"

Skylar raised her voice to ask, "What?"

"That guy. I know that guy."

Carter referred to a short, curly-haired teenager wearing glasses and an untucked shirt. His face was reddened in a few spots, probably by attempts to clear away some acne. The elwetritsch that Skylar motioned at stood in a cleavage-baring, short-skirted dress that showed off a pair of thin, yellow chicken legs, and she spoke using her beak to the boy at her side. The two leaned against the wall, as if they were waiting on something.

Skylar asked, "Is he from your school?"

"No, but we were at the same one when we were younger." Carter looked down and scratched the back of his head. "He was kind of a dork back in middle school, and sometimes, I could be a jerk to him. I feel bad seeing him here."

"Aww." Skylar wrapped her tentacles around one of his arms. "Well, he must be doing okay now. Erla is everyone's favorite girl around here."

Carter opened his mouth to respond, but was cut off as the last beat of the current song ended and one of the ahuizotl said, "All right, everybody like that last one? I've got a classic coming at you next."

The sound of modern dance music was supplanted with the quick strings of fiddles and the beats of a frame drum. All across the gym, Flipsiders cheered as Carter wondered what this was. If he had to guess from movies and TV, some kind of Irish jig, maybe? Faerie folk always went in for that in the stories. Maybe he shouldn't be surprised, but the old timey stuff made him feel like he was trying to move around on two left feet.

At a dash, Gene and Erla rushed from the outside to the center of the dance floor. Gene slipped off his jacket in a smooth motion, revealed a pair of bright red suspenders underneath, and started throwing his ankles about in quick dance moves. Carter averted his eyes. He still felt bad for making fun of his old classmate years before, but this was, without question, the dorkiest display he could possibly imagine.

The cheer that followed was even louder than when the song began. Carter turned back, dumbstruck, as dozens of Skylar's classmates clapped to the beat while Gene and Erla performed. When he looked to Skylar, she too smiled broad and beat her tentacles together.

After a few moments to take in the sight and a swallow to push down the dryness in his throat, Carter wondered aloud, "What am I doing here?"

Skylar asked, "Huh?"

Carter shook his head. "Never mind. I gotta use the bathroom."

"Okay. Hurry back." She pushed up on her equivalent of tiptoes to kiss him on the cheek.

With a distant look in his eyes, Carter carefully navigated his way out of the gym. Skylar's sasquatch friend was bigger and stronger than him, her ex was more attractive than him, and even the nerdy kid from middle school was cooler than him. Did he have anything he could claim here? When he finally found the bathroom, he had to walk past several large urinals intended for creatures two or three times his size, and he felt like he needed to stop at the shorter one for little kids when he finally found a normal-looking one at the end of the line.

"Having a good time out there?"

Carter jumped when he heard the voice, just after he'd pulled up his zipper. "What?" The stall door next to him opened, and the big, moss-colored knight, Basil Greene, stepped out. "What? What do you mean? Weren't you kicked out?"

"I have others serving as my eyes in there." A conniving grin crossed the big knight's face, and he flashed a mouth of wooden teeth. "And I wanted to give you the chance to not be the lamest mortal inside."

In his heart, Carter knew he should turn around and leave. But in his gut, he wanted to hear what Basil had to offer. "... I'm listening."

"Here in just a bit, my boys are going to distract some of the chaperones and let me in through one of the gym exits," Basil said. "I wanna take the human down a couple notches. I just need somebody to get that little dork over by the punch cauldron, I'll handle the rest." He reached into his jersey and produced a small vial.

"What is that?"

"Little curse I've been working on. It's a two-left-feet enchantment," Basil said. "I'll just have one of my boys put some of this in the punch, splash that nerd with it, and nobody will be cheering for his dancing skills the rest of the night."

Carter's hesitant heart picked up a few paces. "Why me? What if I don't even know that guy?"

"You do, because you didn't just say, *I don't know him*." Basil smirked and shrugged his shoulders. "I'm just trying to do you a favor, little man. The dweeb's gonna take a cauldron bath and start tripping over himself no matter what. I can get somebody else to help make sure it happens. I just thought you might appreciate the boost." The two held stares with one another for a few more seconds before Basil crossed his arms. "You don't even need to say anything. Sensing people's nature is just another one of my gifts. Give me fifteen minutes. I'll see you by the witch's brew." He departed and left Carter alone in the bathroom.

After a moment of contemplation and washing his hands, Carter let out a long breath and returned to the gym. Skylar waited just on the other side of the entrance. She flashed him a smile, but Carter felt there was something wary in it.

"Hey there," she said.

"Hey." Carter slid up to her, and the two shared a kiss. "I'm still a little burned out from the dancing. Can we sit for a couple minutes?"

"Sure thing."

Carter scanned the room, and after a few seconds of searching, picked out an unoccupied table. Unbeknownst to Skylar, he had chosen it specifically for a good look at the clock up on the wall. Basil said fifteen minutes. Maybe two or three had probably passed already.

After a few more minutes without conversation, Skylar asked, "You sure you're doing okay? You seem tense."

Carter inhaled a deep breath and blew it out. "It's just... This place is so cool to me, you know? All the magic lights and the singing guys in the pools and all that stuff. You gotta be a special kind of person to ever see these things when you come from my part of the

Flipside." As he spoke, Carter caught sight of a pair of large, stony creatures—gargoyles, maybe—as they approached the parents that stood by the exit doors.

"Okay, sure," Skylar said. "But, what, is it making you feel self-conscious?"

"Yeah, maybe," Carter said. "Everything that makes me special back home, somebody's doing better here."

Skylar frowned. "That isn't true."

"I saw the size of the footballers you guys have. I saw how good looking that ex-boyfriend of yours is."

"What, Javier? He's not that good looking. Besides, you wouldn't be saying that if you saw the blowhole under his hat."

"Wait, what?"

"Yeah, a blowhole, all boto encantado do."

"Well... still." For both his next point and another thought, he scanned the room until he saw Gene again. "Around here, I'm not even as beloved as the guy I used to pick on."

With one tentacle resting on top of his hand, Skylar gave him a gentle squeeze. "Well, how much of a jerk you used to be aside, you're not competing with any of those people. You don't have to compete at all, because you're already here with me."

Carter saw the exit doors cleared of their protectors and looked down just as Basil slipped inside. "Why, though?"

"Why? I don't know, Carter, because I think you're really sweet. And I think you look great, and you don't have an awful laugh. If you don't get along with any of these people tonight, you'll probably never see any of them again." With one of her other tentacles, she lifted his chin. "But you get to keep seeing me. And tonight is just supposed to be about having fun with me, isn't it?"

Slowly, Carter raised one hand and shared in another tight grip. With Gene still locked in his periphery, he said, "Yeah, that's a good point... but I think there's something I still gotta do."

"Well, go do it then." Skylar kissed his forehead. "Just hurry back after."

Carter gave her a last, nervous smile, then started to slip around the many chatting or dancing couples on his way to the wall. A collection of harpies, furies, and tengu formed a semi-circle around Gene and Erla.

As he approached, Carter called, "Yo, Gene! Gene Fitzpatrick!"

His fellow human frowned and squinted into the crowd, then his eyes went wide with recognition. "Carter Wilkerson? No way, what are you doing here?"

The girls all gathered around and uttered, "Ooohs," at a second human in their midst. One of them asked, "Is he a friend of yours, Gene?"

"Not as good of one as I always should have been," Carter said. "But I saw you were really tearing up the dance floor. Good for you, man."

Gene slipped his thumbs into his suspenders. "Well, thank you."

"My girlfriend's waiting on some punch. Why don't you come with me?"

From the look on his face, the offer seemed to confuse Gene for a moment. But then Erla gave him a *go on* poke with one of her talons, and he followed Carter as he began to cross the gym.

"Crazy seeing someone even a little familiar around here," Gene said.

"Yeah, tell me about it." Carter saw Basil a ways off with a close watch held on the two of them.

"Has your night been good?"

"Hm? I mean, yeah, pretty good," Carter said. "I, uh... look, I guess you're wondering why I'm leading you over here."

"Maybe a little, yeah. What's up?"

Carter sighed. "I dunno. I didn't want to say it in front of all those people, but I know I was a jerk to you back in middle school sometimes." Out of the corner of his eye, Carter saw a werewolf raise a clenched paw over the punch cauldron and slip something inside. "And I thought maybe I oughta say I'm sorry for that."

To Carter's surprise, Gene let out a big laugh. "What, you? I mean, yeah, you could be, but I could be back to you, sometimes. A jerk sometimes, yeah, I guess, but you weren't ever a bully or anything."

As they reached the punch cauldron, Carter asked, "I wasn't?"

"Believe me, I wouldn't have come over here with you if you were," Gene said. "But, you know, thanks for saying so." He leaned over the cauldron. The punch inside swirled and bubbled in shifting, phantasmic rays of pink, orange, and blue. "Man, that's so cool, isn't it?"

Carter just stared at him, then looked back behind them. The green knight was picking up speed. The prank would go off any minute. With a sink in his heart,

Carter struggled for what to do. Could he even do anything? Basil towered over him. There was no way he could fight him off. Should he just let it happen?

All at once, Carter put out his hands and fell forward with all of his weight. The sudden impact jarred the table, Gene shouted in confusion, and the cauldron of punch spilled all over the front of Carter's suit. As soon as it did, Carter felt magic seep into his legs, and he lost whatever balance he still clung to as he fell to the floor.

Basil came to a stuttering stop. Gene stepped back and asked, "What the hell?"

Carter looked down at the hundred-dollar rental he wore and imagined how much more the suit shop would charge him for all those stains. Moving strokes of pink, orange, and blue, no less.

Still, he smirked at Gene and tried to push off the ground. "Oh man, was that clumsy or what? Some days, I just don't know my own strength, I guess." He then let out, "Whoa," as he started to fall again, but Gene caught him and raised one arm over his shoulder for support.

Basil glared at him from across the dance floor until his face twisted in pain. The sour-faced manticore who was taking tickets stood at his side. Her stinger tail thrust into his waist, and a weak but paralyzing poison ran into him.

"Nice try, punk." She dragged him toward the exit. "Party's over for you."

As Basil was forcibly removed, he cast a last look toward Carter while he stumbled to his table. Green knights, in the stories of old, tested the character of those they came upon. His scowl turned to a satisfied smirk as Skylar first fussed over Carter, helped him dry off, then pulled him into an embrace. The mortal rediscovered his worth to the person it mattered to most. And, since he was in no shape to keep rhythm otherwise, Carter and Skylar were destined to dance slow and close for the rest of the night.

A Perfect Order

By Jenni Howell

IN EIGHTH GRADE, I gave my eyes a boy named Kurt. He stood three steps away, his blue eyes bright and his arms covered in fuzz. The sun painted the small hairs gold.

"Move, fatso," Kurt said.

His eyes looked strange, dragging my chin down with their weight. *Strong legs*, my mother called them, but those eyes saw mud-splattered tennis shoes crowned by round, sagging knees and thighs that trapped sweat between them. I moved.

In tenth grade, I gave my tongue to a girl named Clarice who danced down the halls dressed in flannel and ripped denim.

"Are you serious?" she asked, her words tripping over her laughter as fast as her feet stumbled toward our lockers. "Of course Brantley doesn't like *you*."

"Of course," I said, rolling the muscle in my mouth into a shape that felt familiar and the note from him into a ball small enough to eat.

She closed her locker, biting into an apple. The eyes in my small locker mirror traced the round softness of my chin.

"Of course not me." The words settled under my skin. I left the sandwich in my locker, chewing on my thumbnail instead.

In twelfth grade, I gave what was left to a boy named Kai as I lay beneath him, arms and legs held together by the silver stitches of my prom dress. His tongue was wet against my skin. The windows fogged as his shoulders hunched up and down. My legs clung to the wet polyester of his seats when he sat back, red-faced and sighing. I tried to match the look on his face.

He tugged my dress down. "Are you hungry?"

I picked a bobby pin off the floor and pinned back a curl his fingers forced loose. He smelled like cheap beer and cheaper body spray when he leaned across to buckle me in, his hand lingering on my thigh. I waited to feel free. I waited to feel like this had been my choice. He turned up the music, moved his hand to his phone, and drove us to the diner.

The waitress slid a blue-rimmed plate containing two sunny-side-up eggs and a piece of wheat toast in front of me. The eggs wobbled, round and lopsided like the breasts I hid beneath wire and gel padding. Kai smiled at me from across the table, his cheek already round from a mouthful of his waffle.

"Everything okay, sugar?" The waitress shoved a pen in the pocket of the apron tied around her waist. "Are the eggs not done right?"

My cheeks flushed. "No." I gripped the fork and knife, so my hands wouldn't wipe at my smudged eyeliner. Its zipper pressed against my spine, the wetness where my legs squeezed together. "They're perfect."

Kai reached across the table and stabbed a piece of toast in one egg, ripping the yolk open. He winked at me as he bit the messy edge off the toast. "Let me have some then."

Two booths down, another couple laughed. They sat on the same side of the table, ankles intertwined, hands touching where they rested on the green plastic seat cover. He hid behind a menu while she kissed his cheek. The yolk hemorrhaged.

Kai saw them too. He moved to chain my hand with his. I dipped my finger in the yolk instead and dragged it across the plate, drawing a curving line and two sightless eyes. He chewed and watched me, his smile twisted with uncertainty. I licked my finger. I looked up at the couple again, watching their lips fasten together, realizing that the person in my body didn't want that. Not with Kai.

"These are mine." I picked up an egg and closed my mouth around the bleeding white the way I'd closed my mouth around him.

His smile tightened, screwing down until the look in his eyes morphed into the opposite of need. What did my face looked like? For once, I hoped it mirrored his. In the car, he hadn't bothered to reach inside my bra. I did it for him now, pulling two gel-filled pads out and throwing them onto the table where they lay shimmering, ideal, and dead.

I picked up a fork and gently skewered this fake part of me, bought and pressed against my body to make it look the way someone else wanted it to. I twisted, ignoring the yolk on my lips and the look in his eyes. My dress hung loose from my shoulders, made to fit his expectations and not my own.

"Those are yours," I said, and for the first time in years, it sounded like me.

A Promise on Prom Night

By Kristen Argyres

Prom. Isn't that short for something? Right, promenade. Of course, these parties were originally low-key etiquette lessons wrapped up in pretty bows, dancing the night away like lords and ladies in a fairy tale.

Despite the night brimming with the magic of possibility—the spark of a first kiss, the bitter taste of heartbreak, and whispered vows of eternal love while shuffling in a slow dance—not all princesses donned a gown this evening.

You're wearing a tux when I know you wanted us to have matching dresses. If it weren't for the bullshit you'd have to deal with, we'd pull it off. You're always beautiful in my eyes.

They don't get you like I do. I'm grateful for that—I'm your girlfriend after all—but on a night like tonight, I wish they would.

If only they could see you genuinely happy, like when we sneak up to my room to swap clothes.

I smile at you.

You grin back, but it doesn't touch your misty blue eyes. You're trying so hard to make tonight normal, but it's killing you a little inside. It's legitimately devastating.

I caress your cheek, and you lean into it like a lifeline. Maybe it is. I tilt forward, catching your mouth in a kiss. There's desperation in your soft lips, your touch. You want to lose yourself in something else.

The bass cranks up, like a second heartbeat in my chest.

"I love you," I whisper into your ear. "We'll get you that dress someday."

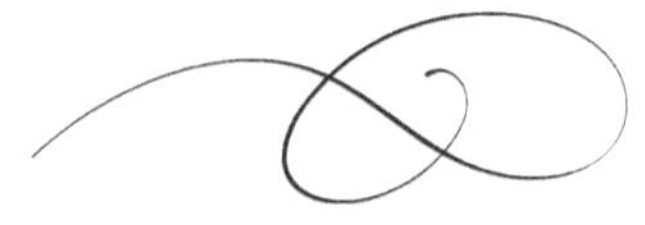

And Even After

By S.R. Hartley

As I FIGHT MY way through thick, thorny branches and step over sticks and mud puddles to avoid twisting my ankle in my heels, the scents of smoke and fire burn their way through my lungs while I glance back at the pile of bricks that remains of Freedmont High.

My school is gone due to a faulty electrical panel and a brand-new pottery kiln Miss. Harper knew we'd enjoy using for our ceramic projects, and students who weren't supposed to be using it until the electrician gave the okay, but who decided to try it out anyway. Miss. Harper was sick that day, but she always left her door open for us.

No one should ever be deprived of art, she'd say.

I'm not sure I'll ever be able to step foot into an art classroom again.

I follow Aiden into the clearing of the woods, and we head toward our waiting friends. His icy blue eyes glance my way but look right through me. He hasn't spoken much since that day. Neither have I. Both of us saw the worst of it, witnessed the other seniors in our class frantic, screaming, and struggling to breathe as dark smoke billowed into the room and deprived us of oxygen. Memories like those don't leave easily. They haunt your mind and cling to your soul, leaving you wondering why such bad things happen to innocent people.

The fire took so much from us already, so we agreed we shouldn't let tragedy steal this night from us, too. It's not what any of them would have wanted. Prom is meant to be enjoyed, a rite of passage to bring hope for the future and for friendship and love. Hope for a better future is all we have left after our high school crumbled into a pile of ash as it stole the lives of so many only weeks ago. Our small town in Ohio doesn't have buildings to hold celebrations or parties, so the prom committee's only options were setting up in the middle of a cornfield or in the woods. Here, behind the school in the clearing where the trees whisper of sadness and the moonlight shines false happiness, is what we all agreed would be best. Tonight, we'll be close to the ones we lost, close to our ghosts of the past who will forever haunt us and remind us how quickly everything can slip away.

I would rather not be here. Pain and torment slice through my heart anytime I'm near this place. The panicked screams ring through my ears when I close my eyes, and I dream of their smiling, hopeful faces every night when I lay down to sleep, though anymore, I can't sleep. We should still be mourning. I am. I'll never be able to stop. Tonight, I'll force the screams and faces of ghosts away and be here for my friends the way they need me to be.

Pushing my shoulders back, I force a smile as I lift the bottom of my velvety black dress, a sharp throb building near my temples already as music blares through the speakers set up around the opening between trees. I step next to Maya and Lilly as Aiden wanders off to where the rest of the football team lounges. He closes the lid of a cooler full of icy drinks before sitting on top of it. His shoulders sag as he brushes his dark hair away from his face, shifting his gaze toward his friends as they place their hands on his shoulders and watch him with eyes full of worry. His eyes, once sparkling and full of light, are dim and pained and swimming with hopelessness. Watching the one I've loved since I was a child become so lost and broken shatters my heart.

"Oh, my goodness, Ellie! You look so beautiful!" Maya's blue eyes sparkle as she tosses her blonde locks over her shoulder. She pulls me into her and squeezes me tight.

Closing my eyes, I wrap my arms around her, my head on her shoulder. The warmth of her arms around me reminds me why I caved and decided to show up. Maya and Lilly have been my best friends since kindergarten. We go everywhere together and have been through so much, and this is just another thing we'll eventually find our way through. We've always said we have to find ways to carve our own happiness, but to do that now might involve carving out tiny, barb lined shards from our hearts.

"You guys look great, seriously." I pull back and smile at Lilly, who beams back at me but doesn't lean in for a hug.

Lilly isn't a hugger. She pats my shoulder, and I laugh, returning the gesture. At times, that's the best I can get from her, but I'm used to it. Hugs make her feel awkward and always have.

"I love that you chose matching dresses. The pink is amazing." I smile at Maya as she crosses her arms, her eyebrows scrunching up in the way they do when she has lots she'd like to say. "I'm sorry I didn't come shopping with you like we'd planned. I just…" I sigh. "I couldn't handle much at the time."

Maya's face softens, and she swallows as her eyes glisten. "We know. I'm sorry."

Moonlight trickles in between the canopy of trees overhead, dancing across the hazel specks within Lilly's eyes. Her dark wavy hair shines like velvet as she tucks it behind her ears. "How have you been, Ellie? We haven't heard from you in days."

I glance over at Aiden, and his eyes meet mine. Just as I raise my hand to wave, he turns away. I wish I could read his mind to know exactly what he's feeling or force him to talk to me, even for just a moment. He needs to let out the pain.

I focus my attention on the long table set up in the center of the party where punch and snacks are laid out neatly over a tablecloth. The golden letters running up and down it read, *Best Prom Ever*. It's a lie, but we're making do with what we have, which I suppose is all we can do now. I turn and head toward the table, and Maya and Lilly follow me. We fill glittery plastic cups with punch and melted sherbert, and I smile as our classmates twirl and spin and jump to the music, the sound of their laughter echoing like ghosts howling in the night.

"I'm okay, I think. We'll all be okay, right?" I sip on the overly sweet punch as my eyes meet Maya's, and then Lilly's.

They both nod, their gazes drifting toward each other and then snapping back to me.

Lilly smiles, her lips tight and her eyes narrowing. "If you say you're fine, then we're glad. Just know that we understand if you're not."

"We're here if you want to talk about it, you know? You don't have to avoid us or pretend you're okay if you aren't." Maya sighs, rubbing my arm and tilting her head. "Best friends until the end, remember? You're stuck with us forever."

I shake my head, forcing out the screams and the smoke-filled coughing and strangled gasps for air that invade my mind when I think of that day. I get why they're worried, but everyone is mourning and some people more than me—the ones who lost their childhood best friends, the ones they told all their secrets and dreams to over the years. I'll be okay. As heartless as it might sound, I know it could have been much worse. We could have all died.

"Best friends until the end. I know. Don't worry about me. I'll be fine, I promise. I'm here for you, too, if you guys need to vent or cry. God knows I've done enough crying the past few weeks." My hand trembles, the red liquid in my cup spilling over the edge and sloshing onto the ground.

Lilly grips my cup, her eyes widening as she takes it and sets it on the table behind me. "Yea. You're totally fine, I see." She shakes her head. "Lying to yourself will get you nowhere, Ellie. It's okay to not be okay. Neither of us are." Her smile is full of sadness as her eyes gloss over.

"I can't mourn forever. We have to move on eventually."

"Yes. We do." Maya loops her arm through mine, and then Lilly's. "I have the perfect solution. Let's forget about this for now and enjoy our time here together, okay? We've been excited for prom for years. Let's not let this night pass without finding a way to enjoy it just a little. We deserve this."

We head toward the twinkling lights wrapped around hanging branches of trees, the place our classmates have turned into a dance floor. They squeal and laugh as if escaping death has brought new meaning to their lives. Maybe it has. Sometimes, death has a way of opening the eyes of those who sleepily let each day pass as if life lasts forever. Death is never a good thing, but it does serve as a reminder to live each day as if it's your last. In the blink of an eye, one day it will be.

As the three of us dance and laugh, it's like no one else exists. Nothing else matters except for living and breathing and refusing to let memories of tragedy weigh us down, as if an inescapable anchor is tied to our feet.

I close my eyes as the warm breeze brushes against my cheeks, pushing strands of my braided hair loose as I lift my arms and become one with the wind and the earth and the perfect prom, no matter how imperfect it might actually be.

Just for tonight, we're invincible. Just for tonight, we're free.

The music cuts off abruptly, and a high-pitched squeal erupts from the speakers as Jessica, the head of the prom committee, steps onto the make-shift stage made of wooden pallets wrapped in lights and soft pink flowers, and clears her throat into the microphone before speaking.

"Hi, hello there." Her bright white teeth flash as she smiles and lifts the bottom of her dress gracefully and walks to the front of the too wobbly stage. "I'm thankful so many of you made it tonight. Prom is something I know many of us have been excited to experience for years. This might not be the perfect prom we all dreamed of, but at least we're here, right?" She shakes her head as tears fill her eyes. With trembling fingers, she brushes the one sliding down her cheek away. Taking a deep breath, her chest quivers unevenly as she works to compose herself. "Without further ado, we all voted for king and queen tonight, and it's time to announce the winners." Her smile returns as the crowd gathered in front of her cheers and claps while Phoenix, another committee member, hands her an envelope before carefully shuffling off the stage.

I glance over my shoulder toward the coolers, the spot Aiden was before, but he's not there. Stretching my neck and shifting on my feet, I search for him in the crowd, but I don't spot him. Most of our class had already told us months ago we'd have their vote when this night came, so I have hope we might win. I'd like us to walk up hand in hand if we're the lucky pair chosen. As Lilly and Maya take my hands in theirs, we huddle in closer, their shoulders warm and comforting enough to distract me. The crowd is silent as Jessica opens the envelope and gasps softly, the thin paper slowly floating to the ground after it slips between her fingers.

Whispers fall over the crowd, and people hush them until the forest is as quiet and still as a graveyard and all eyes are back on Jessica, waiting impatiently as she stares down at us with bloodshot eyes full of tears and an apologetic smile.

She sniffles, using one hand to pull her curly red hair over one shoulder as she raises the microphone back to her lips. "The prom king and queen for this year are..." She swallows, blinking in slow motion before speaking. "Aiden Forester and E-Ellie Wade." Her voice cracks, and her hand shoots to her mouth as sobs rack through her body.

My mind is a mess of confusion as Jessica rushes off the stage. She hands the microphone to Phoenix before disappearing behind the trees as her best friend, Sarah, hurries to catch up with her. I can't understand why she's so upset. We aren't best friends, but we've always gotten along well. We've been to many sleepovers together and shared typical teenage gossip in the cafeteria every day, and we never once had a fight.

The whispers return as Aiden comes into focus, slowly making his way up the stairs without looking through the crowd to find me or waiting to take my hand and help me onto the rickety stage. His head hangs low, and he keeps his eyes pinned to the ground.

"Aiden, wait..." The silence that engulfs the forest in this moment could be heard or maybe even felt for miles, the way the air seems to shift to make room for an invasion of heavy energy.

It's the type of silence that falls right before a storm crashes on land and reminds people how fragile life truly is.

I rush to the stage and follow him up as he faces the crowd, slowly raising his head and meeting the eyes of one tearful student after another. Why won't he look at me? Why aren't any of them looking at *me*? All eyes are focused only on him. I know today is a sad day for us all, but this is our moment, a moment we've talked about so many times before, a moment we'd hoped would belong to us someday.

Phoenix slips the microphone into Aiden's hand, and he inhales deeply, closing his eyes. He raises the microphone as if it's almost too heavy to hold.

"I don't know what I'm supposed to say right now." He shakes his head, lifting his arm and wiping tears from his cheeks with his suit sleeve. He huffs a laugh. "This isn't right. It doesn't...*feel* right without her here."

Sobs break out from the crowd, and our friends wrap their arms around each other, all of them leaning on the one next to them as I stand in shock and watch.

"Aiden, I'm here. I'll always be here…" My voice is loud but strained as I position myself directly in front of him.

He doesn't look at me. "The only reason I'm here tonight is because I know it's what Ellie would have wanted. She'd want me to be here. She'd want me to continue living. She'd want all of us to." Tears spill over, and he closes his eyes.

I watch as the salty beads trace lines down his cheeks and reach up to wipe them away. No matter how hard I try to, they remain, continuing their path down and splashing on the wood near my feet.

Lilly and Maya step up next to me and grip my hands in theirs, sobbing as they gaze out at the hopeless, broken faces of the ones whose eyes look right through us.

No. This isn't happening.

"Aiden, please. Look at me… *see me*… I'm here with you."

"She'd be so happy to be named queen, and I'm sure she's looking down on us and smiling at her friends who still chose her, even now she's gone. I'm sure she's thankful for each and every one of us who played a part in her life, although it wasn't for nearly long enough." He pushes his shoulders back and straightens his spine. "Let us celebrate tonight for all of them. For Daniel and Kent for always leading us to victory." Football players cheer loudly in the back of the crowd as he mentions their teammates. "For Jenn, Cassie, and Rebecca, who were at times annoyingly too cheerful even for cheerleaders, but whose light will be missed by us all." His laugh is short and full of sadness. "And for Ellie, Maya, and Lilly, who were the best friends any of us could have asked for. May they all live on within us forever. Let us never forget their faces or their names. If we never forget, then they will be infinite. They'll never truly die."

The crowd explodes in cheers, and Aiden smiles as Phoenix places the crown on his head and hands him the one that's meant for me. He rubs his fingertips across the diamonds and sharp points as his eyes drift to mine, the iciness within them cracking open and revealing the light he's been unable to grasp onto for weeks.

"I love you," I whisper, though I know he can't hear me. "Be happy now. I'm okay." Tears glide down my cheeks as I reach up and place my palms on the sides of his face, wishing I could feel the warmth of his skin on my own, but I feel nothing but the icy chill of death as my hands pass right through him.

He turns and leaves the stage. I face Lilly and Maya, their pink dresses sparkling much too brightly for what darkness was just unleashed into reality. Looking down at my dress, it now matches theirs, and my best friends smile as I meet their gentle gazes.

"It's not so bad here. We can be who we want to be. We can do whatever we want to do. It's sort of magical. We're happy." Maya reaches for my hand, and I grip it, thankful to feel her and have something real to cling to.

"This moment isn't real. Look around." Lilly turns to the crowd, and slowly, one after another, our classmates fade away, along with the twinkly lights, the loud music, and the lingering joy in the air left from Aiden's speech. "You've been reliving the night of prom over and over for weeks now because you refuse to accept the truth. It's time, Ellie."

Daniel and Kent in their blue and yellow letterman jackets wave as they lean casually against trees. Jenn, Cassie and Rebecca, still in their cheerleading uniforms, sit in a circle, giggling and slapping at each other's hands. They're all here with me. I'm not alone.

But Aiden... He has been my best friend and neighbor since I was in preschool. We started dating in eighth grade and have been inseparable ever since. We were meant to be together forever, and now I'll never get the chance to hold his hand again or go to another dance with him. My parents and little sister must be crushed. This isn't fair. None of this is.

"This isn't real. I- I don't remember dying. I remember..."

"They couldn't save any of us in time because the fire grew out of control. They tried so hard to get to us, but the art room had no windows and no other way to escape, except through the fire, and it was impossible. We passed out from smoke inhalation, which is a blessing, really." Maya rubs my shoulder and smiles. "At least we have each other."

In the afterlife, we have each other. I died. We all died. There's no coming back. The fire destroyed our hopes and dreams, and yet somehow, they're happy?

"Why are you so okay with this? This isn't okay. We're not... okay." I shake my head as I back away from them, focusing instead on the cheerleaders and football stars whose eyes are locked on me. "We're ghosts who will haunt them forever. They'll never get over what happened this year. They won't be okay." I take a seat on the edge of the stage, my feet dangling and brushing against the wet grass.

Lilly and Maya sit next to me, staring off into the distance, into the dark that we now live in.

"How many times have I been here? How many times have I been through prom night already since we...?" I swallow, closing my eyes and forcing back the tears that prickle in the corners of my eyes. "Since we died?"

Maya faces me, pulling one leg up and letting the other dangle off the stage. "Every night for two weeks, at first. But this time, it had been a few days since your pain forced us all back here again." She reaches over and tucks loose strands of auburn hair behind my ear. "We knew you were getting closer to accepting the truth, but for the rest of us, it took no time at all. We knew we were dead almost immediately. We knew during the fire we weren't going to make it out alive." She folds her hands in her lap as she watches me. "You held onto hope that all of this was a nightmare you'd wake up from soon. You hoped we'd all be okay, and we are, Ellie. We're together."

Lilly takes a deep breath and stands, offering her hand to help me up. "We told you you're stuck with us forever." She smiles, and I can't help but smile back at the irony of it.

I pull myself up, and Maya does the same. As we stand here together, all fear and pain cease to exist in my heart, slipping away until the panicked screams no longer play on repeat in my mind.

I will heal.

Together, we will.

"Best friends until the end and even after," I whisper, wrapping my arms around Maya and holding her tight.

Lilly leans her head on my shoulder as she encases us in her arms. "And even after," she says, squeezing us tight for just a moment before stepping away.

We interlock our fingers, knowing with each other, things can't possibly be so bad, despite having to leave everyone and everything else we've ever loved behind. Even in the afterlife, we will carve our own happiness the way we always have before. The shadows of our old selves will live on in this new life we've been given, and our souls won't be stolen the way our lives were in the end. We will find peace.

Those we love will never forget our names or faces.

We will never truly die.

BLINK THREE TIMES

BY HANNAH BROOKS

IT'S THE MORNING OF junior prom, and I'm invisible. Literally. I've always been sort of invisible, figuratively.

I peer into the vanity mirror, but my reflection doesn't stare back. I look down to where my body should be, and there I am. But when I look in the mirror again, I'm not there.

I live a mundane life. I'm your average Jewish, gay New Jersey teenager. Obsessed with Broadway musicals and horror movies. Annoyed that I had a Bat Mitzvah instead of a Sweet Sixteen. Brown hair, brown eyes, average height, chubby, boobs that make it impossible to run without fear of getting smacked in the chin. Completely ordinary. But now I can turn invisible.

The only thing I did before turning invisible was wake up and blink, so that must be how I did it. I attempt to reverse my invisibility, then recreate the magic. I blink so many times, my vision blurs. Dizzy, I sit down. I repeat this a few more times until I figure it out.

Blink three times quickly to become invisible, twice quickly to reappear. I want to sit in bed and brainstorm ways to use my superpower, but my little sister, Shai, has a dance recital. So instead, I pad over to the hall bathroom and turn on the shower.

Later, home from Shai's recital, I grab a soda and two string cheese from the fridge. I jog up the stairs to my room before anyone can talk to me. I've had enough family bonding today. My perfect little sister, Shai, is a thin, thirteen year old, middle school popular kid with a serious boyfriend. At the recital, he watched her dance, his eyes filled with awe, and my stomach churned. No one has ever looked at me like that. And then, I felt even more sick for being jealous of the way my little sister's boyfriend looks at her. When the recital ended, we stood in the lobby, flowers in our arms, waiting for Shai. I felt out of place in my dad's old graphic tee and denim shorts in a sea of moms and daughters in matching sundresses.

I shut the door and sigh, comforted by the pale blue paint my parents let me choose when we remodeled my bedroom last year. I spot a commotion in the backyard across the way from ours. I amble past my wall of signed, framed Playbills, over to the window. Plopping down in the cushioned seat that I call my nook, I crack open the can of soda and carefully set it on the ledge. The perfectly manicured backyard my window looks out onto is filled with beautiful teenagers in bright dresses glittering in the sun. I peel the wrapper off my string cheese and squint. I can't make out all the faces. But that's Jackson Williams's house, so I use my imagination to guess who's there.

I don't need to see Vivian Cook's face to spot her in the crowd. Her fierce, red hair immediately catches my eye. My memory takes over from there. Vivian has a heart-shaped face with wide, blue eyes, unblemished skin, pronounced cheekbones, a dainty nose, and Cupid's bow lips. Her thick hair cascades down her back like a waterfall. A dark green gown hugs her curves. Thin straps line her chest, and flimsy criss-cross strings sit at her shoulder blades. She has stilettos on, and I love that she wears heels despite being tall for a girl. I briefly consider turning invisible to get a closer look, but I decide that sneaking onto someone's property would be going too far.

I peel a long piece of string cheese and toss it in my mouth as I watch the popular kids flounce around in their dresses and suits, posing for photos. All the girls, then the boys. Now each of the couples. One looks like it might be soccer girls, then boys on the football team. I wonder what it's like to have a friend group with so many possible combinations. My only friends are Bram and Isa. That's four combinations at best, if we went to prom. I snort a laugh. Bram and Isa would never go to prom. They're perfectly happy in Bram's basement, watching trash horror movies and pretending the outside world doesn't exist.

Nobody asked me to junior prom. I guess that's not a surprise. I'm a sophomore and a loner, after all. But until the deadline to buy tickets, I held out hope that someone would show up and notice me, notice how much I wanted to go. I would've even gone with a boy, if he had asked me as a friend. But no one did.

I don't know why I'm not popular. Not everyone can be, I get that. But why not me? I've spent years trying to understand. I'm a gay art nerd, but it's not the early 2000s. Popular people come in all shapes, sizes, colors, and sexualities now. Just not me. I wish someone would tell me what to do. I'm great at following directions; I just need an instruction manual.

I'm not ashamed to admit I Googled it. Okay, I'm a little ashamed. But the answer it spit out was useless, anyway: *Show an interest in others, smile in the hallways, and make others feel included.* I can't show an interest if no one talks to me, and what's the use of smiling in hallways if no one's looking?

I peel off another section of string cheese and pop it in my mouth. Laughter floats from Jackson's backyard. I sigh. Am I condemned to a high school experience sitting in Bram's basement while he and Isa pretend they're not in love? Is watching dumb eighties movies with a belly full of popcorn the closest I'll get to a high school party?

An idea forms in my head slowly, then all at once. I can make myself invisible. Literally. I can go to prom and linger near the popular kids to find out what they're interested in and what makes them popular.

I chew on my bottom lip. Is it morally okay to spy? And if I use my newfound power for personal gain, will it be taken from me? Is it better to wait until Monday and go invisible at lunch or something? I don't know if that's any better, morally. Plus, what if this magic is a one-day-only deal?

This isn't just for personal gain. This is for science. If I become popular, I can help other kids. I'll do it for free. The universe can't punish me for trying to do something nice just because I also benefit, can it? I shift my gaze to Jackson's backyard. Vivian and two other girls film a TikTok dance, laughing every time one of them messes up and they have to start over. I swallow hard. I have to do this.

I text Bram to let him know I'm not feeling well and won't be making it to movie night. I feel guilty for lying and for ditching him and Isa, but they might be secretly happy for alone time. Besides, I don't want to spend the next two years in Bram's basement wishing I was out there, in Jackson's backyard, having the time of my life.

I bike over to the Maywell Hotel around seven and lock my bike in the back of the venue on a rack that's probably meant for employees. Then, I blink three times. I walk to the front of the venue and stop. I've thought about how it would feel to walk through these doors for weeks. I never expected I would do it invisible or in ripped up jorts and a big t-shirt. But here we are, I guess.

The Maywell Hotel is the perfect prom venue. Inside, I gape as I take in the ballroom. Evening light shines through its enormous all-glass walls. Like a kaleidoscope, it bounces off the chandelier hanging in the middle of the room. Decorations are sparse, probably because this venue cost the prom committee a fortune.

There's just a balloon arch at the front and greenery on the large, round tables. Worth it, though. This is magical.

I make a few laps around the room. None of the popular kids are here. Prom started at six, and it's after seven. What gives? I take my phone out of my pocket, open the notes app, and type, *Be late.*

Bored, I glance towards the buffet line. The food looks decent, but I don't dare grab a plate. I'm not sure how this invisibility thing works yet. Anything I have on me becomes invisible when I do, but if I start loading food onto a plate, will people see nothing but a plate hovering in mid air? I can't take that risk.

My heart thumps wildly when Jackson, Vivian, and the rest of the group walk through the double doors. It's game time. I need to make sure not to blink twice and suddenly appear next to them. I hover close and follow them to their assigned table. When they sit, I stand behind Vivian and gape at her, very glad to be invisible. She always looks beautiful, but nothing compares to how she looks this close up. I'm convinced she's perfect.

Nobody gets up to dance. I grab my phone and note, *No dancing*, before shoving it back into my pocket. I can't hear what they're talking about from here. I have to move closer. List of reminders: do not, under any circumstances, blink twice, do not cough or sneeze, do not breathe loudly.

I don't dare hover near Vivian, for fear I'll run my hand through her hair. I'm dying to know if it's as soft as it looks. Instead, I stand next to her date, Noah. I don't care about his hair. Noah was friends with Bram and me back in Hebrew school, but we diverged in high school. He's the starting wide receiver on the football team, while Bram and I are art and theater nerds. We didn't have a falling out; we just ran out of things to talk about. And now he's at prom with Vivian. It infuriates me how close I was to being friends with a popular kid. So what if we were bored to tears when we hung out? I was so close.

Vivian and her best friend, Astrid, talk about soccer. I roll my eyes. That doesn't give me anything to work with. I don't have an athletic bone in my body or an interest in watching sports. Every once in a while, though, one of them interrupts the other and whispers a number. I carefully avoid blinking more than once as I watch them, trying to figure out what these numbers mean. I realize, after a few minutes, that they're rating what other girls are wearing. I purse my lips. That seems mean. Then again, if I looked like Vivian and Astrid, I would probably judge other people's outfits, too.

During a lull in conversation, Vivian leans over and whispers to Noah, her lips softly brushing the shell of his ear. My eyes widen at the intimacy. I take a step back.

Shit, did I just blink twice? I was so distracted by Vivian's mouth, I have no idea what my face has been doing. Someone would've noticed me by now, right? I can't be sure. Like I said, I'm pretty invisible most days, even without magical powers. I slowly retrieve my phone and turn the camera to my face.

Nothing.

I'm still invisible.

I return the phone to my pocket and press my index and middle fingers to the sides of my head. I need to keep it together and be more careful. If I appear next to them out of thin air, I'll not only never be popular. I'll get shipped off to a government lab.

I turn back to Vivian and Noah. Vivian whispers in his ear again, leans her hand on his thigh, runs a hand through his hair, then entangles their fingers together. It's torture. As far as I know, he's not her boyfriend. But she wants him to be. I try to quell the disappointment as it rises in my chest. I know Vivian likes boys because she had a boyfriend last year. She could like girls too, though. Either way, it's obvious she likes Noah.

I frown and walk a few steps over to Jackson and Astrid, who actually are boyfriend and girlfriend. This is much less painful. I don't want Astrid, I just want to be her, so I can watch her and Jackson without a pit the size of a watermelon forming in my stomach. Jackson can't keep his hands off of her. It's kind of cute, actually, and a stark contrast to Vivian and Noah. From farther away, it's even more obvious. Vivian is all over Noah, and he is barely paying attention to her. What an idiot.

"Astrid," Jackson whispers sharply.

I snap my gaze back to them. Jackson wraps an arm around Astrid, holding her steady. She looks like she might faint.

"Astrid, you need to eat," Jackson says, his voice low. "This juice cleanse shit has gone too far."

I stare. Juice cleanse? Astrid is so petite. She doesn't look like she has an ounce of fat on her. And she's an athlete. Why would she do a juice cleanse? I wrinkle my nose. Something about this isn't right, and a pit opens in my stomach again. I don't think Astrid is okay. Jackson grabs a roll from the center of the table and drops it on

Astrid's plate. I walk away as he coaxes her into eating it. The moment is too intimate for me to watch.

I stand behind Noah again. He's still ignoring Vivian. I want to shake him. The most beautiful girl at Fairsbury High is sitting there, begging him to notice her, and he just won't. The injustice threatens to swallow me whole. I've quietly liked Vivian for years, and she's never so much as glanced at me. He has her full attention, and he's blowing it. I sigh a puff of frustrated air.

Noah swivels his gaze to exactly where I'm standing. I freeze and, holding my breath, step back. He runs a hand through his hair, then faces the table again. I turn away from him to breathe out. That was close. This invisibility thing is harder than I thought it would be. I seriously need to be more careful.

"I'll be right back," Vivian says. She walks to the bathroom. It's odd that she doesn't notice Astrid's crisis. I glance at Astrid, who has taken maybe two bites of her bread roll. Jackson watches her warily.

I turn back to Noah. His face looks funny, like he's spotted something interesting. My brows knit together. Is he looking at Astrid? Does this idiot want to be here with Astrid instead of Vivian? I mean, Astrid is pretty, too. But then, why ask Vivian to prom?

I follow Noah's gaze all the way and freeze. It's not Astrid he's gazing at lovingly. It's Jackson. I look back at Noah, his expression equal parts hurt and desperate. Why is he doing this? It's 2024, and he lives in a liberal state. He shouldn't hide. I went to his house every other weekend for a year, and when his mom found out I was gay, she hugged me so hard, I thought I might break.

My heart sinks. Is it different for gay men? Maybe. It's probably different for a football player too. I'm grateful I've never had to witness locker room talk, but if it's anything like the movies, I understand Noah's hesitation.

Vivian has been gone for a while. What if she's sick? Isn't anybody going to notice her absence? Noah's focusing on Jackson, Jackson's watching Astrid, and Astrid's trying not to pass out. I guess it's up to me. I walk to the bathroom, inhale, exhale, and walk through the door. I wander down a row of black stalls and stop at a closed one. Vivian's green dress peeks out from the bottom. She sniffles, then whimpers, then sniffles again. I inhale sharply. I can't stand here listening to her cry—it's too intrusive—but I have to do something.

I wet my lips with my tongue. "Hey, are you okay?"

The sniffling and whimpering stops. It's silent other than a dress rustling. "I'm fine."

The first words she has ever spoken to me.

I get a burst of courage. "Noah is an idiot, you know."

A small laugh floats from the stall. My stomach does cartwheels.

"I know," she says. "He's just, like, distracted or something."

"Well, you look absolutely gorgeous. The only thing he should be distracted by is you." Is invisible me smooth with girls? That's unexpected.

"Thanks," Vivian says. "I'm sure you look gorgeous too, whoever you are."

I blush. I know it's on a technicality, but Vivian Cook just told me I'm gorgeous. I'll be replaying that in my head every day until I die.

"Thanks," I tell her. "You should get back out there. You can have a good time without him."

"Yeah, I will."

I walk back over to the sinks and pump my fist in the air. I just talked to Vivian Cook. Even if the only thing I learned was "cool kids are late" and "don't dance," the night is now a success. Maybe next time I talk in class, she'll recognize my voice. Maybe she'll want to be friends. Maybe more.

A lock snaps behind me, and Vivian emerges. Her eyes are ringed red. I wish I could be her shoulder to cry on. She almost walks into me, but I get out of her way at the last moment. I turn and watch her take a small makeup kit out of her purse. She puts some eyedrops in, then takes out a tube of mascara. Then, she stops what she's doing, turns around, and looks right at me.

"What are you staring at?" she asks.

My heart stops. I was distracted. I must have blinked twice.

"S-Sorry." I swallow hard. "I didn't mean to scare you."

Vivian stares at me. "That was you before?"

"Yeah," I respond brightly. This is it. This is when my friendship and maybe eventual relationship with Vivian starts. I wonder if anyone calls her Viv. Maybe I'll be the first.

Vivian reapplies mascara, then looks back at me. Her eyes travel from the top of my head to the tips of my toes. "Why are you dressed like that?" Her Cupid's bow lip curls. "Don't you know you're supposed to look *nice* for prom?"

She stares at me, waiting for a response that doesn't come. The connection between my brain and my mouth is fried. I don't know how to react to Vivian's tone, so full of venom for someone she barely knows, someone who just told her she was gorgeous while she cried in a bathroom stall, someone she has no reason to dislike.

"Freak," Vivian mutters. She gives me one last withering look, then turns around and leaves.

My eyes well up with heavy tears. I knew so little about Vivian before today. I was so desperate to know her, my brain filled in the gaps with qualities I hoped she had. I know Vivian's beautiful, athletic, smart, and popular. I guess I also hoped she was kind, but she's not. I know that now.

Everything about this night is wrong. Astrid might have an eating disorder, Noah's in the closet, and, God, Vivian Cook is a huge bitch. Jackson seems okay, but who knows what I'd find out if I lingered around him? And I'm no closer to knowing how to become popular. If anything, I'm pretty sure Vivian, the most popular girl in school, actively dislikes me now. I look in the mirror and wipe the tears from my eyes. I blink three times. I'm invisible again. Though, to Vivian, I guess I always was. And maybe it was better that way.

I walk back out into the ballroom. I don't want to leave, but I can't stand near that table again. I don't trust myself not to cry. I look at the dance floor for a moment. Two girls and a guy are dancing together in the corner of the parquet floor. Their arms flail wildly, as their torsos sway side to side. Vivian and Astrid would probably give them threes or fours. But they don't care about Vivian and Astrid. They're looking only at each other and having a blast. There's a pang in my chest that feels like homesickness. Suddenly, I know what I need to do.

I rush out of the Maywell Hotel, bumping into a very confused teacher on the way. When I get to my bike, I blink twice and jump on. I can't put my finger on why I so desperately wanted to be popular. Do I really want to be friends with these people? At worst, I would starve myself, hide from who I really am, or become a raging bitch. At best, I would be Jackson, putting up with all that craziness. I don't want any of it. Whatever I thought before, popularity has lost its appeal.

I pedal hard, racing to Bram's house.I want to sit in the basement with him and Isa, eating sour candy until my mouth burns, watching horror movies that scare the crap out of us. And later, when Bram's parents are asleep, sneaking up to his mom's library and taking turns reading aloud the dirty passages from her romance novels, suppressing our laughter so we don't get caught.

When I get to Bram's, I toss my bike on his front lawn and race up the steps as fast as my legs will carry me. I knock on the door furiously. A moment later, Bram appears.

"I thought you were sick." He stares at me, his face lined with confusion.

"I was," I say. "I mean, I thought I was. It was just an upset stomach, I'm all better now."

"Why are you out of breath?"

"I biked here. Can I come in?"

"Yeah, of course." Bram steps out of the way.

I'm always welcome where Bram is. I walk through the door and wrap him in a tight hug.

He laughs, squeezing me back. "Are you okay?"

"Great," I tell him.

He shuts the door behind me, and we walk toward the basement. I race down the stairs and throw myself at Isa, landing in her lap.

"Goldie, I'm so happy you're here. We desperately need someone else with taste on this couch." Isa squeezes me around my middle. "Convince Bram that horror movie sequels are always trash, I *beg* of you."

I let go of Isa and beam at my friends. I'm so happy to be here. I will happily spend the rest of high school on this couch with these people who don't rate outfits or call me a freak, real friends I wouldn't dream of not being myself around.

"You guys are going to flip when I show you what I'm about to show you." Grinning, I stand in front of them and blink three times.

Carousels and Cotton Candy

By Lorie Wackwitz

Good. The rides at Idlewild hadn't changed much since he'd last been to the olde time amusement park. Not much at all. Perfect. He reached for her hand. His soul thrilled at the touch. Not to mention his body. But he wasn't there for that. At the close of her hand, he swung their arms high in the air and pulled her toward the Carousel. He'd like to take her on the little turtle roller coaster, but without a child under seven, he knew the attendants wouldn't let the two of them ride. They could borrow children, he supposed, but then they wouldn't be riding together. And he needed them to be together. Close. No, not close. Tight. He needed them to be tight together. Not just that day, but all days, all day every day, each day. Forever.

Pink cotton candy. Elephant ear. Popcorn. He knew they wouldn't likely eat this way again. Not here. Not ever. Those days were over. Well, almost over. First, he'd ask the question. Then she'd answer "yes." Of course she'd answer "yes." He hoped so, anyway. Wouldn't she? Maybe not. It was a big ask. If he earned the ask—the yes—they'd dance close. Together. Tight. Under the disco ball. There would be a disco ball, wouldn't there? Probably. Probably under the disco ball. Sparkly lights. White satin. Bows. Disgusting punch. The perfect place to pop the question. His real question. The "marry me" question.

He could ask that question first. Skip the slow ride on painted wooden horses, go straight for the... What? What could be better than a carousel? Story Book Forest, perhaps. There was that climbing rope thing on the way over. No. Focus. He needed to focus on the question. The question of prom. P–R–O–M. Prom. The two of them. Together. Tight. Just past the Ferris Wheel, they could hear the music of the carousel. See the Depression-era horses come to life in the light of laughter. He smiled with her, arms still swinging. The question swirling in his head.

The horses rose and fell. The music whirled and tilted. Once the ride began, he'd snuck on behind her. Two bodies. One horse. Tight. Together. Against the rules. He found her ear and into it asked his second-most-precious question. The first question of the series. The launch of their new lives together. Would she go to prom with him? She answered with a neigh, or was it a whinny? Whinny, yes. Neigh, no. Which was it? He had to know. She was laughing. Laughing? Unsure if that was good or bad, he dismounted the steed to perch next to her. The horse ground its body against his chest. The same chest that was aching with desire. Desire for her and him to have been together for always. Backward and forwards, not just to the future. Sixth grade dances, seventh. Dates with parents waiting up angry. PDAs in the hall. Prom. Everything before. Everything after.

Would she go with him now? Marry him later? They'd never been to prom. Not separately. Not together. She thought proms were stupid. So what? Then they'd be stupid together. If only she'd say "yes" once he got her down off the horse. Yes to prom, to roses, to sparkling lights. Then a second "yes" to follow. Yes to him, to eggs for breakfast, to broccoli for dinner, and everything in between. He'd propose as they danced. Close. His lips to her ear. His heart to her heart. Tight together.

The horse finally slowed, and he thought how good she looked at eighty. So good. With flowers in her hair and a sparkle in her soul. A sparkle he knew was just for him. A sparkle charged at their wedding fifty years ago.

CINDERELLA SHOULDN'T EAT THE PROM QUEEN

BY PINES CALLAHAN

I NEEDED ONE NIGHT, just one, when I could be a princess instead of a monster. I wanted to be Cinderella, changing herself into someone else and dancing the night away with her Prince Charming.

It almost happened. I'd been so close, I could taste it. I shut my eyes as my fingers drifted over a flier I'd spent an hour designing for a dance I'd spent months organizing: Cinderella Goes to Prom. I was head of the Prom Committee, but this Cinderella would be home with her monthly curse on the big night.

"Such a lame idea," Quinn said, tapping the laminated paper with her too-sharp pink acrylics. "No one wants to pretend it's the 17th century for prom, even the Disney version." She dropped her voice to a whisper and pushed a lock of perfect, ripe-wheat hair off her shoulder. "My mom says it was awful enough to live through the first time. Why would we want to pretend there's no electricity or running water? Do you know how badly people stank back then? I'm sure your nose would have loved it, Dog Water."

"Don't call me that," I hissed, slapping her hand as she tried to pat me on the head. "Historical accuracy isn't the point. Cinderella's story could take place anywhere, and she could be anyone. We just happen to be centering her in a perfect, imaginary past. It's candlelight, elegance, and magic. How hard is that to understand?"

She snorted, and my ears burned. Yes, it was completely cringe to be seventeen and still love fairy tales, but I'd never be too old for Cinderella. After all, I could relate. The poor girl finally got her chance to show out and win her man, and her big night was cut short by a clock. For me, the problem was a phase of the moon. This month, it happened to fall on May 1st. Prom. The gym doors opened at seven, but come sunset at exactly 7:52 p.m., I'd swap my gown for a dishwater blonde, full-body fur coat. Definitely a dress code violation.

"Candlelight, magic, and elegance? Oh, my God, really? I guess we'll see." Quinn's smile was poisonous. "Oh, but that's right! You won't. A little bit too much magic for you that night, isn't there? But that was the deal, one of us picked the time, the other picked the day. Prom Committee rules."

She'd peeked at the underside of the cards before we drew them, faster than the teacher's eyes could track, and cheated me out of my hard work. I fought for weeks to get the date moved—I even took it to the principal—but I lost. Everyone always sided with Quinn. It was probably mind control. I pulled in a deep breath through my nose and exhaled slowly through my mouth, just like my therapist taught me. I owned my wolf, not the other way around. "Go away, Quinn."

"So rude! Careful, Lydia. Can't get too...bitchy...in public." She tapped the tip of my nose with her tiny claw of a nail and spun on her heels, swaying down the hall as the bell rang for second period.

I wanted to rip out her throat. Stupid, nasty vampires. Bloodsuckers were one of the reasons why my parents fought to homeschool me until senior year, but I was desperate to be part of a real gymnastics team after years of practice and pushed until they caved. One other supernatural creature at my first real school, and it had to be a freakin' vampire on the student council. Everyone fluttered around her like sycophantic moths, too dumb or under her spell to realize she was a threat to more than their class rankings. Everything about her filled me with rage, and the feeling had been mutual since homeroom on day one.

I caught a whiff of Peter's cologne before he wrapped his arms around my waist, and as sudden as sunshine peeking out from behind clouds, my mood started to lift. He wore a bit too much, but I wasn't going to say anything. My nose was too sensitive, anyway. I leaned back into him and tried to breathe through my mouth.

"I know that look," he said. "She got in your head again, didn't she? Don't let her do that, babe."

The pulse in my ears ebbed away. I turned my head and pressed a kiss to his cheek, running my hand through his chestnut curls. "I can't help it, she's so awful!

She knew that night is my cousin's graduation. All this, because the rest of the committee liked my theme more than hers. 'In the Air Tonight'? What does that even mean?"

He lifted a shoulder. "No clue. It's so weird that your cousin's school is having their graduation at night, and like a month before school lets out. Aren't all their volleyball games at night, too? And softball? Is this a boarding school thing?"

I shrugged and kissed his button nose. Keeping up excuses for monthly absences would have been a lot harder if Peter wasn't cuter than he was bright. "It must be."

"I still don't get why your parents won't let you skip it. You only get one senior prom."

"You could still go stag."

He scrunched his face, but he couldn't hide the disappointment in his eyes. They were so big, brown, and puppy-like, you'd swear he had a werewolf in his family tree. "Not a chance. If you can't go, I don't want to."

How did I get lucky with such a perfect guy? For the millionth time, I wished I could tell him the truth, but that dream was more far-fetched than Quinn swearing off evil and turning civil towards me. Peter deserved better, he deserved to go to prom. I had to find a way to make it happen. 7:52 p.m. wasn't holding this Cinderella back.

"Tell your daughter there's no reliable way to stave off a transformation," my mom said over her shoulder as she carved into the brisket.

"There's no reliable way to stave off a transformation," my dad parroted, not looking up from the movement of her knife through meat. "Not news to you, kiddo."

"But it's not true!" I slammed my fist on the table, making them both jump. Baby Jackie started crying.

"Lydia, now look at what you've done." My mother scooped Jackie out of her highchair and kissed her on the top of the head.

I grabbed my phone and looked for the secured link. "LycanKing's latest video says you can use Wolfsbane microdosing to delay transformation."

My dad snorted. "A video? You want to risk exposure based on advice from the internet? I don't even know who this Lycanking is, and we're supposed to take his word over something we've all known for a millenia? You're smarter than that, Lydia."

There it was—that line again. Any time I wanted more for myself than a secret double life, *You're smarter than that, Lydia*. Maybe I was *too* smart for that. "Have you ever considered that new information becomes available over time?" I snarked back at him.

"That's it." He pointed towards my closed door. "Go to your room."

I slammed the door behind me and flopped onto my bed.

"No phone!" my mom called from the dining room.

Groaning, I turned it off. She'd hear me if I used it, even to text. Stupid wolf ears. I bet Peter could text in his room without anyone knowing. "Fine!"

I sat down at my computer instead and put in my earbuds. The Lycanking video was already cued up on my screen. I'd watched it a dozen times, but I hit play again. Lycanking's tanned, smiling face filled my screen.

"What's up, pack?" he asked, striking a pose. "Get ready to have your minds blown! Now, Big Magic doesn't want you knowing about this—"

"Turn that off!" Dad hollered.

Growling, I closed the link. It didn't matter, I already had my answer. The tincture LycanKing used was easy enough to find, even if I skipped buying it through his sponsored link; I ordered it online and had it shipped next-day from a human Etsy shop.

I opened my chat with Peter. *Hey, change of plans. We're going to prom.*

Three dots flash for way too long. *Your parents changed their minds?*

I couldn't lie to him any more than I already did on a regular basis. *Not really.*

I don't know if I'm comfortable with this. They're a little scary.

Please, Peter. I don't want to miss prom. Be my Prince Charming?

Three flashing dots. *Ok. Tell me how I can help.*

Was I really going to try this? I didn't have time to test it out, but Lycanking filmed himself staying human during the full moon until almost midnight. Nearly as cool, when he did transform, he was practically in control of himself. All he had to do was keep the moon out of sight. I could manage that. There were no windows in the gym. As long as I didn't see the moon between home and there, I'd be fine. It couldn't be that hard. All I had to do was close my eyes when I went outside. The hardest part would be getting out of my house.

I'd never snuck out before, and the idea terrified me a little, but as far as I could tell, I'd never get a better opportunity. Normally I'd have two sets of hyper-sensitive ears listening in on my every move, but we all spent the night of the full moon chained up in individual, sound-proof cells. Even family wasn't enough to prevent our wolves from attacking each other. Only Jackie was small enough not to trigger mom's rage. Normally, it felt isolating. Now, it was going to be the key to getting Cinderella to the ball. Mom normally tucked in with Jackie by five—the moon was harder for babies and old people—and dad went to read a book in his cell at around the same time. All I had to do was leave my door unlocked and slip out once they were settled. It was so simple, I didn't know why I hadn't thought of it sooner. Part of me felt bad betraying my parents' trust, but like Peter said, there was only one senior prom.

~ele~

Sneaking out went off without a problem. Mom and dad tucked themselves in by 5:15, and by 5:45, Peter was outside in his old Toyota Corolla. His parents worked nights, so they were already gone by the time we drove to his house. Their BMW was still in the driveway—I guess they carpooled.

An hour of primping later, and I was strutting into prom in a sparkly, Cinderella-worthy navy gown that I snuck off campus during lunch to buy. The look on Quinn's face would have made the whole night's preparation worth it, but seeing my vision brought to life stopped me in my tracks.

The gym had been transformed. It even smelled better than usual. A long navy carpet led to the gym doors. The first stop was a photo booth shaped like Cinderella's pumpkin coach, and the photographer was dressed as a footman. Peter and I beamed for the camera, but I felt another twinge of guilt as I took the photo ticket. My parents could never see the picture.

The rest of the gym buried my guilt in gilt. There was so much gold, it sparkled. LED pillar candles in glass slipper arrangements topped every navy and cream covered table. The bleachers were hidden behind tapestries the theater kids painted for extra credit. Some idiot drew a toilet in the corner of one, but we'd set up the buffet table in front of it to block the view. Even the ceiling looked different. Metal beams had been replaced by twinkling lights suspended in gauze. The space was everything I wanted it to be. I'd arrived at my court.

The other girls (and Randy) on the Prom Committee swarmed me as I walked inside, practically vibrating with excitement. We all took a picture together in the coach, and Randy told me he'd written me in for Prom Queen. The group fell silent. We all knew who would win. Half of them voted for her. It wasn't really my court, it was Quinn's. Still, the sour look on her face as she watched the rest of the school enjoy the dance—and watched me watching the other students enjoy it—almost outweighed my disgust when she won. Almost, but physical disgust was catching up with me.

"Hey, Lydia, you ok?" Peter squeezed my hand as Quinn swaggered up to the DJ booth so Principle Marry-at could put the gold tiara I'd picked out on her head. "I know this isn't what we wanted, but you look like you're going to be sick."

My skin crawled like it was covered in fire ants, and my stomach rolled. "No, I'm fine. I just need to use the bathroom."

He nodded and let me stagger towards the far side of the gym. "Ok, I'll wait here."

There was a line. Of course. My stomach heaved, and I swallowed vomit. My skin itched so much, I wanted to scratch it off. I'd messed up. My body needed to transform to the point of nearly being painful. Lycanking hadn't mentioned pain. It made holding off a transformation even more difficult, and there I was in a gym full of humans, plus one nasty vampire Prom Queen. I needed privacy, so I ducked out of the gym and headed for an empty classroom. All the doors were locked. Again, of course.

"Looking for someplace to hide, Lydia?"

Quinn!

"Don't you have Prom Queen duties to attend to, your majesty?"

She slunk towards me in a disgustingly pink dress. Vampire Barbie. "A queen's first duty is to her people.

I'm going to make this dance a little safer for them. Leave now, or I'll make it impossible for you to stay."

"And how are you going to do that?"

I should have walked away. Instead, I leaned on the lockers next to us, challenging her.

She smiled that poisonous smile again and took a similar position against a classroom door. "Last chance."

"Bite me."

"I don't eat dogs." Faster than I could track, she grabbed me by the back of the neck and spun me towards the classroom, pressing my face against the glass panel on the door. I knew why in an instant. The moon was up, and it hung full and bright outside the half-wall wide classroom window, directly in my line of sight.

No one really understands why a certain amount of reflected light from the moon triggers acute lycanthropic episodes, but there's no denying its pull. It was all I saw. The color drained from my vision like chalk washing off the sidewalk during a storm, leaving me with primal canine grays. I couldn't even see my color scheme. My cream, gold, and navy court was gone. Fur sprouted on my face, sopping up tears, and I shot up another two feet. The top of my dress stretched and tore around my tall, lanky new form, hanging off my shoulders by a single strap. I couldn't go back into the dance. My prom was ruined. Rage surged up my spine and poured out my mouth in a feral howl. I knew exactly who to blame.

"Quuiiinnnn!" I slurred out as my muzzle stretched.

I threw her off of me and flung her backwards into a row of lockers. She hit them with a resounding thud, bending one nearly in half. No, no, no! Too loud! Someone was bound to investigate. I'd have to kill her in private.

I grabbed her by the hair and dragged her down the hall towards the exit, then threw her out the double doors and followed in her wake. Lifting her over my shoulder, I grabbed on to a drain pipe and scaled the school, more like a pathetic King Kong than Cinderella.

It was a beautiful night, and the music filtered up to us on the roof. It should have been lovely. I dropped Quinn next to me, closed my eyes, and howled again, long and mournful. Why couldn't I have a normal prom? Why couldn't I have a normal life? I knew why. Because of people like Quinn. My mouth watered at the thought of tearing into her. When she was gone, I'd rule Steinbeck High.

A flood of too-cold water cascaded over my head. It burned like frostbite and had a musky, herbal smell to it. Wolfsbane? My rage melted away as droplets rolled down my ruined dress. What was I doing?

"Lydia?" Peter's voice cut through the fog of cold and muted emotion.

I opened my eyes. Normally, he had a few inches on me, but now, he was looking me right in the face...Because he was floating.

"Are you ok?" he asked softly, holding an empty bucket with a few tell-tale Wolfsbane blossoms sticking to the sides. "Sorry, I know it's intense, but you were about to do something you'd regret. Well, I think you'd regret killing Quinn."

My boyfriend was inches away from a werewolf in a dress, and he chose to throw a bucket of mildly toxic water on me as opposed to running. He was fearless. And he was floating? "What the hell?" I growled, my voice raw and gravely. I put my hands over my snout, embarrassed.

"Hey, don't hide."

"What's happening? Why aren't you scared of me?"

He chuckled, and I caught a glimpse of a fang. "You have the cutest wolf form I've ever seen. You're like a ragey stuffed animal, why would that scare me?"

"You're a vampire?"

"Yep."

"But..." I didn't know how to finish my thought.

Peter sighed and landed next to me. "Look, Lydia... I liked you as soon as I saw you, but it took me a while to work up the courage to ask you out. Before I could, you and Quinn started fighting. You both believe the whole vampires versus werewolves thing, and I was afraid you wouldn't want to be with me if you knew what I really was." He laughed. "Did you honestly think I was dumb enough to believe you had something important to do every full moon?"

I blushed under blonde fur. "I guess I did, sorry."

He raised a shoulder. "It's ok, you're pretty new to keeping secrets. You'll get better at it, now that you're in public school."

Quinn moaned next to us, starting to come around. I probably wasn't going to kill her. I'd get expelled for sure. "So, vampires and werewolves are normally fine with each other?"

Peter bit his lip and shrugged. "I don't know if I'd go that far, but it's not outright hate. My parents are cool with me dating a werewolf. They'd like to meet you soon. For the record, they do work nights, but they were still home when we left. At my age, sunlight annoys me, but it's too much for them. They were still in their coffins for the day."

"Oh. Wow. Wait, how long have you known about me?"

"The whole time! Why do you think I wear so much cologne? I had to hide my scent." He cocked his head as an overly-cheerful pop song ended and a slow ballad began. "Dance with me?"

"Up here?"

"Why not?" He held out his hand. "We've got a gorgeous sky, good music, and your fallen rival at our feet."

My tail wagged under my dress, and I pressed my snout to his cheek.

"Screw you, Peter," Quinn grumbled.

"Not on your life, Quinn. But if you don't leave my girlfriend alone, I might tell my mom you tried to out her in front of humans. Pretty sure that's still illegal. You know how much our moms love to chat at Book Coven. You'll be grounded for a century before they're done with their charcuterie boards."

She snarled at us and pulled herself to her feet. Flipping the bird, she hopped off the roof and headed back into prom. "I still win. Enjoy the rest of the night up there, Dog Water."

Ok, I wasn't going to kill her, but I was totally scratching her car later.

Peter put a hand on my waist and adjusted the ruined straps of my gown. "Navy is still a good color on you, Lydia."

"I can't tell anymore."

He smiled sympathetically. "Then you'll have to take my word for it."

A gentle breeze caressed my fur as one slow song faded into another. We rocked in place, his head pressed against my chest. The height switch was...interesting, but Peter didn't seem to mind.

He followed my gaze towards the moon. "Well, you did it. Kind of. Let's not try anything like this again."

"Agreed. Peter?"

"Yeah?"

"Thanks for helping make tonight happen, even if it got a little crazy."

"No problem. Guess that makes me more of a fairy godmother than Prince Charming, huh?"

"I guess it does."

"Good. Prince Charming was kind of useless."

I giggled. It sounded more like a growl, but Peter smiled and kissed me on the nose. "Happy prom, Cinderella."

Dress Code

By Marianna Palmer

Oh, my dearest lord, as my mother had said on her good days. I have died. Truly. I couldn't be standing here right now and seeing this poster.

Prom Night

"Prom night," I whispered in reverent tones. I had dreamed of this day, watched millions of movies and television shows. The perfect night. The time to glitter, shine. The night. It was coming.

Here at my high school, it had been rumored to be canceled as a safeguard. I thought it was a punishment.

But it was here, staring at me.

Then...

I almost swallowed my tongue.

No dress code, it read on the bottom.

None? The perfect pink dress in my mind with lots of ruffles and diamonds—well, rhinestones—drowned in a pool of my sorrow.

No dress code. C-c-casual, it read.

"Get out of the way," a voice said behind me, and I felt the harsh nudge.

It was my own fault. Anybody standing and staring for too long here in the warzone of the school's hallway would be singled out. And I usually did stand and stare, forgetting where I was.

I looked up to see The Bubbles, the ones who floated around the hall, never had any patience, and were already halfway out of here on their way to being somebodies.

Having already forgotten the person in their way, they all looked at the poster.

"Wow. Boring."

"You gonna go?" the guy asked.

My heart skipped at beat at his tones. I couldn't get enough. I wanted to look at him, but he wouldn't look back. At least staring at the floor, I could imagine he was checking me out, swooning over my beauty. I almost responded, but before I could make a great big ass of myself, who he was actually talking to answered.

"Of course. It's just going to be boring."

The third member of the Bubbles made a noise in her throat. "Yep. My mom did prom. My grandma, too. What's the point?"

I wrinkled my nose. She didn't say *she* had done prom.

"Are you going to wear a dress?" Danielle asked.

Again, I was almost the fool.

"Nah. I'll wear jeans. A shirt. Maybe some sparkly sneakers, but that's it."

My heart whined. Jeans? Shirt? SNEAKERS?

"No dress code, love it," Dennis answered. "You wanna meet there?"

I couldn't keep my silence. "Aren't you going to rent a limo? Wear beautiful dresses?"

That got three sets of eyes on me. Ouch. Stake me and burn me. I was dead.

"Why?" Freda asked.

"It's prom..." I lost my nerves. I didn't talk to people. What was I thinking?

"Prom is an excuse to waste money, be trapped in an area with the same people you see every single day, and watch them dance, while idiot chaperones make sure you don't enjoy yourself. Besides, it's been done. So done. I have seen it on so many movies."

"But you haven't done it," I said.

Shut up, I ordered myself. *Shut up. Shut up.*

"Pamela, that *is* your name, right?"

I nodded.

"So hard to tell. Anyway, Pamela, as you get more mature," Danielle said, dripping sarcasm and dew. "You realize getting excited about anything sucks. That dance will be boring, useless, and pathetic. You know that."

Because I was boring, useless, and pathetic.

"But who knows," Dennis continued, leaning against the poster, ripping it a bit. "You may like those kinds of things. Wanna go together?"

I gaped. Did Dennis really just ask me out? Oh, eep. Eep. "Yeah. I'd love to."

He bit his lip and snorted. Danielle smacked him on his back, giggling herself. "Don't be mean. Pamela, he doesn't mean it. He's my boyfriend. We'll go to prom."

Oh, stupid. Didn't I tell you to shut up? I asked myself. At least if I shut up, I wouldn't remove the doubt that I was an idiot. It was clear as the three walked away what they thought I was.

I stared at the prom poster, now wrinkled and pathetic on the floor. I picked it up, smoothed it, and returned it to its proper place. My dreams had been stomped on. Of course the prom would be useless. Everything in my life was.

I turned to walk home. Mom had the car today, so that meant I could take the bus or use my own two feet. I'd rather walk. The bus was torture—enclosed in one place, forced when to get on and get off, trying to find a seat, wondering if the end was a one way trip to Hell.

I wore only a simple shirt under my coat. I breathed in the spring air, feeling the promise of rebirth. Life. Spring was the time I felt the most hope. Silly.

As I walked across the parking lot of the apartment building, I looked at the word. *Promise. Prom.* Prom had been a promise to me, a special thing that would mean the world. It'd change my life.

But my life stubbornly resisted change. I passed the row of cars and saw...

Oh no. Our car was home. Mom was home. She hadn't gone to work today. I climbed the stairs to the level our apartment was on, closing my eyes as I heard the pounding music. The neighbor had gotten an early start today.

I unlocked the front door. I could hear her crying before I even got to her room. A bad day. I lived for her good days. I died on the bad.

"Mom?" I asked.

Her cries suddenly stopped. "Oh," she called out, her nose stuffed up. "I just...got home."

I followed her voice to her dark room. She was by the side of her bed, a box of tissues in her hand.

"Didn't work?" I asked. That paycheck would be abysmal.

"No. I told you."

I closed my eyes and pulled her up. "You're a great woman. A great mother. I love you."

A useless mantra. But it helped. Maybe me more than her. Truth was, she was a great mother when she wanted to be. But there were moments when she disappeared. And all she was was a crying ball of tears who hated herself. Who hated me.

"I'm a useless nothing who deserves to die," she responded.

I changed the subject. Best thing was to distract her. "Prom is on after all."

That stopped her. She looked up, surprised. "But I thought Karson banned it after those kids blew up the bathroom."

I nodded. "She swore she would. But I saw the poster." I didn't want to put the nail in the coffin, but I never could lie to her. "No dress code. Casual encouraged."

Mom's face wrinkled. "Yeah. Nothing worthwhile in this damned world. Every minute is another useless ticking to the ultimate destruction of the world and the people in it."

The same sentiment as the three in school. I narrowed my eyes. "No. It will be special. It will be worthwhile. I'll make the best prom ever."

Mom stopped crying. She looked me up and down. "You on the prom planning committee?"

I shook my head. "No. There were others on it. That's why it's casual. It was kinda sprung on us too. I don't have much time."

I felt more and more determination coming over me. I wouldn't let Mom or the others decide how special it'd be. I'd make it my own.

I caught Mom's eyes, and for the briefest second, a glimmer appeared.

"How? You don't even have any money for a dress. Unless you've been squirreling the money away from that job," Mom said.

I wouldn't call getting yelled at by customers or spit on a job. But it gave me money to help out around the home. She was right, though. I couldn't get a dress.

"I'll figure it out."

"Thousands," she said.

I looked at her. "What?"

"That's how much it costs to attend prom. The tickets. The dress. The ride. Face it. You have nothing. You'll go casual. See the stupids from school. Wonder what the point in life is, as you drink punch that tastes like someone already barfed it up. Stale music. Disgusting food. It won't be anything."

I stood. "Yes, it will. I'll figure it out."

"Okay, Ms. Moneybags. Good luck with that." She stood and walked out. She slammed the door to the bathroom.

If she had agreed with me, I probably would have given up. But almost like I needed to prove her wrong, I started planning.

Dress. Not an ugly department store dress. A magnificent pink diamond ball gown with a train. Yes. But I paused. I imagined too well walking into the gym with all the people wearing jeans.

"Casual," I said like I was chewing on sour rocks. "Not on my watch."

Prom committee. Yes. It was time I had a few words with them.

***

I walked into my apartment the next day defeated. I was mentally bruised and beaten.

Some of us, I heard Janine Bellow's voice in my head like an annoying song you want to go back in time and destroy the creation of. *Some of us want to just relax on prom night. Wear sweats. Who really cares? Besides, it's been done.*

Not by me, I wanted to scream. But they had been unbudging.

I was surprised to see Mom pop her head out from behind the kitchen wall, looking a lot better than yesterday. She had dragged herself out of bed and had put on her makeup. "How'd it go?" Bright eyes. Hopeful eyes. No matter what she had said yesterday, she wanted it to work.

"Casual prom. Talking to them was about as useful as wearing high heels on my head and doing a headstand." I fell on the couch with a moan.

"Oh." The depression fell. She moped and went back to her room. I could hear her springs sag as she sank again.

Great. She really wanted me to go to this prom in jewels. So did I. But what was I going to do? I had no money. No chance. And every single person would be wearing sweats or jeans.

I groaned.

I didn't want to sit around listening to Mom cry, especially when I started to feel like it was my fault. I had to get out of this place.

The mall around the corner from my apartment was a nice place to walk, safe with indoor trees and lots of color. I could go there and pretend. I reached it without any problem, and I breathed in the displays. Of course, it only took me a few minutes to realize that without money, the mall was depressing.

It was worse now. There was a new store. And it sold dresses. Amazing dresses. Prom-worthy dresses. Lots of faux diamonds and laces. Ruffles and color. Crowns and tiaras. Trains and buckles.

I could have spent years inside that store.

But I wouldn't be able to afford or wear anything inside.

Today I couldn't pretend. Everything was in cold glass that blocked me from the dresses. I was poor. There was no prom.

I went to buy a cone. As I waited impatiently, the squeaky girl behind the register informed me, "Ice cream maker is broken."

I groaned. "Soda then."

She nodded and told me the total.

I ran my card, but it blinked, *Card declined.* It was all I had. I must have forgotten I was over my limit.

A vice of sadness grabbed my heart, and I ran. I couldn't even buy a soda. I bolted outside and walked past an elderly woman with slow steps. She looked as if every movement was agony. As I walked ahead of her, I heard a loud, "Oof!"

I turned to see an ugly woman shoving her, grabbing her phone, and running toward me. Her expression dared me to do something, say something. I could have let her go, I guess. But suddenly I was angry all over again. Angry at jerks who acted like they could force others to do what they wanted.

As the woman ran past me, I stuck out my ankle, and she went down. I managed to catch the old lady's phone before it dropped. The woman glared at me but was on her feet running like a rabbit.

I sighed. It was good that I saved the old lady's phone. But misery didn't want good feelings. It wanted me to wallow with an ice cream cone, but guess what? I couldn't. I had nothing.

"Here," I said. Sullen. Angry. My petulance was petulant.

"Thank you so much," she said as I helped her up. She gave me a tight hug. Maybe it was a little okay that I saved her. "I know I could get a new phone, but I have all these pictures stored on here."

I tried to step back, show I was on my way home, but she wouldn't let me go.

Her eyes were bright with tears. "All my granddaughter's pictures. She's dead, you know? Ran over by a driver under the influence. Life swiped away."

Okay, so maybe I didn't have the exclusivity on pain. "I'm sorry."

"Me, too. We're all sorry." She blinked as she tried to block the tears. "I want to give you a reward. Come with me inside."

Well, okay. That wasn't so bad. Maybe I could get my cone after all. I followed her, and was about to say what she could get me when she gestured to… Oh my dearest lord. The store. The one with all the dresses. Surely, she'd only give me some money out of the cash register or just a necklace. A cheap one.

"Choose any dress. It's on me. Unless…" She suddenly looked worried as we passed rows and rows of pink satin. "You don't have anywhere to wear it."

I didn't. But suddenly, I said, "Yeah. My prom is coming up. I could use a cheap dress. Don't—"

I couldn't get another word out. She screamed, making everyone in the store look over at us, but she was grinning. "It's her *prom*. Fantastic. Come here. You'll need jewelry. Beth! Beth!"

A nice looking person ran up, giving us a zesty grin. "Oh, prom, Rachel? That's exciting."

Everyone else walked around me. The next few minutes were madness. I didn't know how, but the stuff in my hands grew and grew. Necklaces, a wonderful tiara. A dress with train that fell all the way behind me. Nylons. Heels. An ankle bracelet. A thigh bracelet. Who'd see it—who knew, but I had one.

"Hair?" Rachel asked me, patting my messy waves.

"I have no—"

Rachel squealed, holding Beth's hands and dancing. "I know someone. Beth, get Adam."

Beth yanked me toward the other side of the mall, and we had a freaking entourage. Everyone in Bellisimi Brocade who had been buying a dress or jewelry or just had to use their bathroom was following me. They rushed me into the salon and introduced me to Adam, who said he had wonderful stuff that could help my hair.

I never had felt this much in the center of attention before. My bad mood was gone.

But Rachel had to bring it back.

"You'll shine like a star," she declared.

No. I'd stick out like a thumb. I frowned.

"Ah, what's the matter?" Rachel asked.

I shrugged. "It's casual."

Rachel raised an eyebrow. I didn't like that look. Somehow, I felt like I was Cinderella, but *my* fairy god-mother was more like the godfather. "Casual. Hm. And you don't like that?"

I exploded. "No! Prom's not supposed to be gotten over with. It's supposed to be magical. A time you can look back on and know that it was amazing. It's supposed to shine, not be a casual prom. The problem is, it's been done before. But not by me. Not by us. Why can't they see it?"

Rachel hugged my shoulders. "How many tickets are left?"

I shrugged. "A lot. Not many are going. It's too much trouble for a lot, even as pathetic as it is."

"Do they take credit cards?" she asked.

I narrowed my eyes. "Um, yes. But why?"

Then, she surprised me and handed over a credit card. "Buy the tickets. All of them. Whatever's left. Knowing the casual type, they'll buy their tickets at the last minute. Beth!" Rachel shrieked again. She handed over another credit card, but it wasn't to me. Beth ran out, on her way to some weirdness.

I was pretty sure I had fallen asleep, and this was a dream.

"Your hair will be great. Do you have a car?"

I shook my head.

"Limo. Of course."

I stared at her. "This is way too much. I only helped you a bit. You're...well, going overboard."

Rachel sobered and stared at my expression in the mirror. "Honey, my granddaughter would be in this chair, on the way to the prom. But someone ended her life. Her future. You're here. I can do this through you. Please let me."

I couldn't say no.

The next few hours were a blur. I got the perfect feathery haircut, and Rachel promised me I'd have a personal hairdresser the night of the prom. She brought me to a limo place where she set up a driver.

By the time I had gotten home, I was out of breath. I rushed to my mom's room and started screaming my words. Scared her witless. But I saw the spark appear in her eyes.

The rest of the time to the prom, I couldn't see straight. I was being fit for my dress. I tried on everything, and Rachel decided which she loved the best. Mom helped, until I was watching her eyes sparkle. I grinned as she did.

Finally, the night came. I stepped out of my house, Mom trailing me and taking hundreds of pictures.

I walked down, smelling my light perfume, and feeling the wind move the tendrils of my hair around. I felt the thigh bracelet. And I knew I was wearing it, which gave a bounce to my step. My ankle bracelet jingled. My train had to be carried over the roses. I was light on my feet, and I smiled at Rachel, who also needed hundreds of pictures.

My stomach started to sour as I slipped into the limo, though. What was I going to do, walk in like Cinderella? The only problem was, Cinderella was walking into a lovely place with lovely people. All I had was sweats-wearing people who wanted to get it over with because prom had been done.

I almost asked the driver to turn around, but it was too late. Well, whatever. I would stand out, but I would remember my prom. I would do it.

I stepped out, only to be helped by the nicest looking guy I had ever met. Oh dearest lord. He sported a sharp black suit with a red collar, and his hair was perfectly cut and styled. His eyes were shining brown, and his face... Gorgeous didn't cover it.

"Wow," he said. "I owed Grandma a favor. But she did me one more."

I blushed. "Stop. You have to say that."

"No, I really don't. Name's Andrew. You're Pamela, right?"

I nodded. His name was good. Very, very good. He guided me in. At least, I wasn't alone with my super dressed up appearance. Andrew had a cummerbund and a floral boutonniere. He even wrapped a pink carnation chain around my wrist.

As I walked through the double doors, my heart stopped. Gone was the gymnasium. Stars existed here. Trails of shiny gems. A red carpet that spilled out right up to the dance floor. It was shined and buffed to perfection. Tables of white silk were all around with the red from the punch screaming contrast. Dishes were crystal, and gold chains spilled out. Vases as tall as I was showed a collection of flowers.

"My grandma does good work," Andrew said, squeezing my hand to keep me from fainting.

As I looked around, there wasn't a pair of sweats to be found. No jeans. Nothing but poofy dresses and handsome suits. Reds, greens, and more echoed around me. Some were dancing the freaking waltz, while others leaned against walls with the perfect looks. I was in Heaven.

"Want to dance?" Andrew asked with his hand outstretched.

I nodded, and he whisked me across the floor where the soft, wonderful music of a live band melted my back. He held my hand, and we moved. I didn't know the waltz. But me just shuffling to the music was good enough.

"What the actual fuck?" Danielle's voice was enough to break the fantasy. But everyone turned on her, looking surprised at her wearing jeans and a halter top. She blushed crimson and ran the other way.

Andrew and I moved across the dance floor under fantastic lights. When the dance ended, he offered to get me punch, and I grinned.

"Hey, this is impressive," a voice said near my ear.

I turned to see Dennis looking sheepish. He wore shorts and a shirt. "Was this your doing?"

"Not really, but kinda."

"It looks amazing. I do have to admit, I wish I had dressed up. Still, you look absolutely amazing."

I grinned.

Dennis took my hand. "Can I have this dance?"

I watched Andrew approaching, glancing back and forth between us. He looked amazing. Dennis looked like, well, Dennis.

I stood, took my punch, and glanced back. "Sorry, Dennis, but I have a dress code."

I left him gaping as I took Andrew's hand.

If anyone came after that, it didn't matter. We had taken over the casual prom and turned it into a magical night. One I'd never forget.

Finally, I had done prom. And I had done it right.

Fairy-Tale Ending

By B. Wheeler

THIS IS IT. THE big day.

I've become a cliché, a girl so consumed by an end-of-school party that she struggles to see past it. I want to shower again and rinse away all this teen protagonist energy.

But there isn't time. Instead, I shimmy into the prom dress Carla chose for me.

We've been best friends since she moved in next door, her life carried in boxes to sit snugly beside mine as we made friendship bracelets on my front lawn.

Smoothing out layers of midnight-blue chiffon, I sternly remind myself for the hundredth time that Carla isn't interested in girls in general, let alone me specifically. I'm going as her supportive best friend, helping Carla to survive prom and break her curse.

Of all the things that could have happened our senior year, my best friend gradually becoming a hag wasn't something I saw coming. But I've witnessed her symptoms with my own eyes—gnarled fingernails, excessive leg hair, bushy eyebrows. If she doesn't kiss a prince—however superficial his title—she's doomed to stay a hag for all eternity.

Flaunting my finery, I waltz from Carla's bathroom into her bedroom.

She gasps. "Em! You look beautiful."

Roses bloom on my cheeks. "So do you." My gaze traverses the emerald green of her bodice, the flowing satin of her skirt, and the glistening silver rhinestones that bedeck her like stars. "I'm speechless."

Her eyes twinkle more brightly than the gems on her dress. "Will you do me up?"

Whereas my dress fastens with a sensible side zipper, Carla's corset-like lacing exposes the smooth curve of her back. My fingertips brush her shoulder blades as I tighten ribbons criss-crossing her spine.

Then, I swallow my attraction and bury it deep within the chiffon folds of my skirt.

"Thanks," Carla says. "Oh! I nearly forgot our accessories."

Ugh, right, because prom is fairy-tale themed and we're supposed to work a little fairy-tale magic into our outfits. Luckily, Carla's got me covered. She picks up a ring from her nightstand and slides it onto my outstretched finger. It's a gold band with a round, green bead. It looks just like—

"A pea. Good job."

"You're the princess and the pea," she confirms. "And I'm the princess and the frog." She grabs Snapper the TY

Beanie frog from the snuggly regiment atop her chest of drawers. No wonder everyone voted her the Fairy-Tale Princess of the prom. She thrives on creativity, on performance. She'll do great things at college. Without me. At the end of the summer, we'll be torn apart, and my heart will shatter like a broken mirror.

I manage a wobbly smile. "Perfect." My voice catches in my throat. Carla doesn't notice as she presses a kiss to Snapper's fuzzy lips.

She tosses Snapper onto her bed. The fluffy little frog lands beside a silver tiara and a plastic gold crown. It's absurd that this cheap accessory possesses the power to break Carla's curse when placed atop the head of any random, undeserving boy. The thought tenses my stomach and solidifies it into stone.

Oblivious to my discomfort, Carla descends on me, a glint of mischief in her eyes. "Time for your makeup."

Oh, God.

My stony stomach crumbles into a ruinous heap as Carla applies and blends. This close, I see black stubs around her eyebrows, hairs recently plucked but growing back at an inhuman rate. Strands of gray thread through limp, dark hair that used to bounce around her shoulders.

Carla's breath warms my cheek before she draws back to admire her work.

Her lip curves, pleased with her success. "You'll do."

Then, she takes her eyebrows, hair, breath, and lips away to apply her own makeup. I gather our cosmetics along with my senses, popping the products into my purse in case either of us needs to reapply.

Carla nibbles nervously on her lip as she scrutinizes her reflection. "I'm a wolf in sheep's clothing, a hag hiding in plain sight."

"You're completely beautiful," I say. This curse has really knocked her confidence. "Even with yeti legs and muppet eyebrows." She almost laughs. "Even if you were hideous as a hag—which you're categorically not, by the way—you're still *you*. You're the best friend anyone could ever ask for, and being a hag will never change that."

For a horrible, heart-stopping moment, I think she's going to cry. Instead, she flings her arms around my neck and buries her face into my shoulder. My heart skitters into my throat.

"Em," Carla says, her voice muffled. "Thank you. You're the best."

In the past few minutes, my stomach has been a rock and ruins, but now, it bursts into butterflies, a shimmering spectrum of comfort and false hope.

Carla withdraws from my shoulder and takes my hands in hers. She flutters magnificent eyelashes, and for one, glittering moment, I let myself believe this is *my* fairy tale and I'll get to kiss the princess.

The moment passes. Carla squeezes my hands and releases them. "We should go. Will you bring the crown?"

Carla sweeps out of her bedroom, out of my fantasy.

I grab the plastic crown, silently seething at whichever lucky bastard will get to cram this piece of crap on his head.

Our moms take a million pictures before Carla and I climb carefully into the backseat of my dad's car. Carla holds my hand in the vacant middle seat, squeezing too tightly, her mouth set in a thin line. She's terrified, and there's nothing I can do. I clutch the prince's crown in my other hand, fingers pressing painfully against its plastic points.

"Midnight," Dad confirms our pick-up time before driving away, a fairy godfather in a minivan.

I wish I was wearing comfy clothes and eating pizza somewhere quiet, but it's too late to back out now. Swallowing my trepidation, I escort the princess into her kingdom.

Forest-green lighting casts an eerie glow that complements thorn-patterned drapes concealing tables and windows. An origami rat or two explores each table, and countless fairy lights twinkle over absolutely everything. Haunting panpipe music heightens the mystical atmosphere, more Grimm than Disney.

Carla's teeth press nervously into her lower lip as she surveys the room. I want to smooth away her frown and whisper words to ease her worries. I want to cast off her curse and bring back vibrant, carefree Carla, the girl everyone voted to be their Fairy-Tale Princess.

But only a prince can do that.

"You should check in with Toby," I suggest. "To make sure the swing band has everything they need."

"Good idea." She weaves artfully between clusters of tables adorned with battery-powered tealights, their flames flickering like real candles inside colorful glass spheres—some poison-apple red, others pumpkin orange.

I follow awkwardly in her wake, cosmetics clinking in my purse, gold crown slung over my wrist. Clumsy and self-conscious, I make an unconvincing princess. Two steps ahead of me, Carla is perfectly poised, her tiara glittering in the green glow, Snapper the frog perched obediently on her shoulder.

An army of paper rats scampers across the stage toward the swing band, as if summoned by their melodies.

Carla calls, "Toby!"

His head emerges from an open saxophone case. "Hi!" Toby grins like a Cheshire cat with furry, ginger ears protruding from his black curls. His otherwise unremarkable suit is rendered extraordinary by the cat ears, a matching tail sprouting from the back of his pants, and bright red Doc Martens.

Toby bows. "Puss in Boots, at your service."

"Cute tail," I say.

Carla asks, "Everything going to plan?"

"Yep. The band is setting up, and the sound system is working." He gestures vaguely to the room at large, panpipe music pouring from the speakers. "Have you picked a prince yet?" Toby leans forward conspiratorially. "Leo Kinser is here without a date." He looks over his shoulder at a short boy in a brown blazer.

Jealousy cuts through me like a woodcutter's axe.

Carla glances at Leo, then at me. If she's asking for my opinion, it's that she should kiss any random prince right now just to break the curse, then run away with me and leave this fairy-tale nightmare far behind us.

I shrug. "Your call."

With a stilted smile, Carla tells Toby, "I haven't made up my mind."

Yesterday, she was considering Yusuf. The day before, she preferred Matteo. The crown hangs heavy on my wrist, despite its flimsy plastic.

"Speaking of princes," I say, "let's find somewhere for this crown. I don't want to carry it all night."

"I'll look after it," Toby offers.

I toss him the crown, relieved to be rid of the drain on my emotions. Carla watches it go, as if she's pinning all her hopes and dreams on this single, pathetic object.

With gritted teeth, I accompany Carla to a long buffet table. I glower at toadstool cupcakes, their red frosting and white buttons generously sprinkled with glitter. Front and center sits a masterpiece gingerbread house, heavily embellished with M&Ms and gumdrops. It's so perfect, yet so pointless, a waste to make something look beautiful only to destroy it that same evening.

"Naveen did a great job with that," Carla says.

"I don't care about the stupid gingerbread house!" I snap.

"Em—"

"Just kiss someone," I hiss. "Put the crown on a boy, kiss him, break the curse, then you can stop worrying about it and we can salvage this evening."

Ugh, I'm such a selfish ogre.

"I want it to be *right*," Carla counters.

"We're running out of time for *right*."

Her eyes flash, sharp as a sword. "This isn't how I imagined spending my senior prom, scrounging for any boy who'll have me."

I throw my hands up. "What difference does it make?"

"I haven't kissed anyone before!"

"But..." I'm disoriented, as if a tornado has picked me up and carried me away. "I always thought..."

I thought she'd kissed someone because she's popular, and goes to parties, and dances with boys.

"You thought wrong. I want to kiss someone who actually *likes* me," Carla says, close to tears. "So..." She delicately swipes beneath each eye to save her makeup. "I'm going to see if Naveen needs my help, then I'll talk to Yusuf, Matteo, and Leo and choose whoever I like best. I'll break this curse on my terms, not yours."

I'm having the worst night of my life.

Carla sparkles in the arms of a boy, then another, then another. My insides feel sharp and hot, my organs replaced by burning coal.

Toby is busy with the music, then equally busy with his boyfriend, so I'm sulking in the dark when a ghostly figure appears beside me. Naveen is dressed in chef whites, hat and all, with a gingerbread person poking out of their pocket. "You look like someone's eaten your porridge all up. You okay?"

"No."

They occupy the chair beside mine. "Want to talk about it?"

The hall blurs out of focus, becoming a bubble of light and movement as my eyes swim. "I ruined everything." A tear burns a river of fire down my cheek before disappearing into the folds of my skirt.

Gently, Naveen says, "I don't think it's possible for one person to ruin everything, even you."

A strange, wet laugh escapes me. It's a mortifying sound, half chortle, half hiccup.

Naveen asks, "Can I do anything?"

Bravely, I say, "I'll be okay." It feels like a lie.

"You will," Naveen agrees. "But you're not there yet. Wait here."

Baffled, I watch them walk away. Green skirts swirl on the edge of my vision, and I can't resist the temptation to glimpse Carla in her emerald gown, Snapper still perched precariously on her shoulder.

Naveen returns, carrying a paper plate in each hand, heavily laden with toadstool cupcakes and gingerbread.

I beam. "I needed this."

Summoned by sweet treats, Toby appears and snatches a cupcake. "Delicious," he declares through a mouthful of frosting. "Did Carla try any yet?"

Hot coals have burned a gaping hole in my insides. I'm empty without her. I need to find her and apologize before the evening is completely ruined for us both. Lifting my head to search the hall, I discover her mere feet away, staring right at me.

Carla tilts her head toward the doors. For a pulse-quickening moment, I think she's indicating that she wants to talk to me privately, but then, I remember I have her makeup and tweezers.

"I'll be back," I mutter, brushing cake crumbs from my skirt.

As usual, I scurry behind Carla, tripping over my own feet while she strides serenely ahead of me. Less usual is the tense silence that stalks us like a shadow.

We go into the girls' bathroom, empty except for the two of us, and warily meet each other's gaze. Under the harsh fluorescent lighting, Carla's eyebrows are clearly much bushier than earlier. Deep pouches hang beneath her eyes, and her hair is dull and lifeless.

I want to cradle her in my arms and tell her it'll be okay. Instead, I say, "I'm sorry."

"I'm sorry," Carla says at the exact same time.

We blink at each other, surprised.

"You don't need to apologize," I tell her.

"I was such a bitch."

I shake my head vigorously. "I've been selfish."

"You're not selfish! You came with me, and I've been completely ignoring you."

I swallow hard, forcing hurt and guilt down my gullet. "I just want you to be okay."

Then, we're hugging, arms wrapped tightly around each other. I inhale vanilla perfume. I feel her pulse against my chest, and I cling to her with everything I have. My brave, beautiful, kind Carla.

She whispers, "I'm glad you're here," and her fingertips trail gently down the back of my neck. I never want her to stop doing that. My heart trips over itself as I tilt my chin to look at her flawless face.

My breath hitches.

On her cheeks and forehead, small pimples erupt from smooth skin. My eyes widen, my jaw drops, and in horror, I watch warts form across her face.

"What?"

"Nothing." I hastily rearrange my expression from abject horror to mild alarm.

Carla's enlarged eyebrows curl into a threatening scowl.

"It's fine!" My voice is strangely high-pitched. "We just need more makeup, which we have." I hastily empty the contents of my purse onto the sink unit.

Carla's hand darts to her eyebrows. "Are they that crazy already?"

Yes. "No. It's... something new."

It's Carla's turn to look horrified. She's in front of a mirror before I can stop her, aghast at her reflection. "I'm hideous!"

"No. Never." Thankfully, my voice has resumed its usual pitch, and conveys a reassuring finality. "You're beautiful. You're also cursed. But you're going to break it, if that's what you choose. If you don't want to kiss anyone, you don't have to."

"If I don't kiss a prince, I'll be stuck like this."

"Either way, I'm not going anywhere." I take her hand in mine.

Two girls in ball gowns reflect back at us, scared but resolute.

"I want to break the curse," Carla says. "I don't want to look like this."

"Okay. Have you picked a prince?"

A crinkle appears between her oversized eyebrows, and I know she hasn't. I'm not even annoyed. She's in a terrible position, and she's handling it with all the finesse of a fairy-tale princess.

I love her so much.

She tells our reflections, "I imagined that when I finally kissed someone, it would be magical. Romantic. Not a last resort in a room full of people."

"Maybe it doesn't count," I say. "It doesn't have to mean anything."

"If it's meaningless, maybe it won't work."

"Your curse doesn't need to be broken by true love's kiss," I remind her. "Just a prince's kiss."

"But—"

"Enough!" I pin her with a steely gaze. "You're a princess. And you're crowning a prince. Then, you're kissing him, and the curse will break. That's what's happening, okay? It's going to work."

She turns big, brown eyes on me, batting eyelashes so splendid that Shakespeare would have written sonnets about them, if eyelashes were his thing. She's so close. My stomach butterflies are back, fluttering up a storm.

Kiss her.

Then, Leo or Yusuf or Matteo won't be her first kiss.

But Carla doesn't want me. So, I hold her gaze until she squares her shoulders and says, "Okay."

While Carla tends to her eyebrows, I sponge generous amounts of foundation over her blemishes. The fluorescent lights are merciless.

"Back in the hall, they'll hardly be noticeable," I say.

"You're sure?"

No. "Positive."

"Good." Carla licks her lips. "I've made my decision."

My world tilts. I hold onto the sink for balance. "Oh?"

"Leo Kinser asked about my plans for summer and college. Yusuf and Matteo just told me I look hot."

"Well, that's great," I say, words spilling anxiously out of my mouth without my permission. "Maybe Leo won't even mind that you're a hag."

"Em!"

"What? It doesn't bother *me* that you're a hag."

I *must* stop talking.

"Of course not." Carla rolls her eyes and adjusts her bodice. "Let's get this over with."

The moment we get back into the hall, we're accosted by Miss Anderson, gray hair frizzing frantically from her ponytail.

"Carla!" she exclaims. "Are you ready to crown your prince?"

"Yes." Carla manages a convincing smile.

"Great!" Miss Anderson claps in delight.

The vertigo I experienced in the bathroom doubles its efforts, and I have to clutch Carla's arm so I don't join the rest of the world as it crashes down around me.

"Now, hurry along, Carla. Toby has the microphone ready for you."

Our heads snap towards the stage where, sure enough, Toby waves at us, microphone in hand, beckoning us toward grim inevitability.

I force myself to release my grip on Carla's arm. It feels like I'm letting her go forever.

"Oh, God, I'm really doing this. Don't leave me," she pleads.

"I won't." My heart is breaking, but I won't abandon her.

The walk to the stage is the longest of my life. By the time we climb the steps, everyone is watching us. I try to blend into the shadows while Carla basks in the spotlight. Toby hands her the microphone and joins me at the side of the stage.

"Hello, everyone," Carla says. Several boys wolf whistle. "Thank you for coming this evening, and for voting for me to be your Fairy-Tale Princess." The wolf whistles are joined by scattered cheers and applause. "I know you're all dying to know who I picked to be my prince."

From my shadowy refuge, I see Yusuf—easy to spot, since he's a head taller than everyone else—watching Carla from the middle of the room. A group of boys surround Matteo, ruffling his hair and elbowing his ribs. It's harder to find Leo, cowering near the stage, looking up at Carla like she's the girl he's been waiting for, the one whose dainty foot fits that precious glass slipper.

I kinda hate him.

"So many of you have princely qualities," Carla continues, captivating her audience. "Courage, confidence, compassion. But I only have one crown."

Crap. "The crown, Toby," I hiss. "Where is it?"

"Oh! I put it backstage somewhere." He dithers off to find it while I chew my lip over this impending catastrophe. Without the crown, we have no prince, and this whole debacle will have been for nothing.

"So, without further ado," Carla trills. "I happily announce—"

"Found it," Toby whispers gleefully, shoving the crown into my shaking hands.

"—Leo Kinser is the Fairy-Tale Prince!"

A smattering of polite applause follows Carla's announcement, building to encouraging cheers as Leo clambers onto the stage.

"Here. You wanted her to pick Leo." I try to foist the crown back on Toby, but he won't let me, dodging away with his hands behind his back. "Come on. I don't want to crown him."

Toby—the coward—takes the microphone from Carla, and Leo stands beside her. They spend a strained moment gazing awkwardly into each others' eyes. I swallow hard, determined not to cry in front of the entire senior class.

I'm still holding the crown.

Damn it.

It takes everything I have to step forward and jam the pointy golden plastic down on Leo Kinser's undeserving head. Everyone cheers. Leo flashes a nervous smile at the crowd, then turns his attention back to Carla.

This is it.

Carla leans toward him.

Leo leans toward her.

I've been turned to stone. I can't run. I can't hide.

I can't look away.

I think of all the times I could have told Carla how I feel. I could have told her when we were getting ready in her bedroom, or when she first showed symptoms of being cursed, or back when we decided to go to different colleges.

I could have told her any time, any day, for the past four years.

Now, I'm about to watch her first kiss with a boy she barely knows.

I can't look away.

So, I don't miss the moment when Leo's expression darkens. The stage is more brightly lit than the rest of the hall. There's no way Leo can miss the warts growing like toadstools on Carla's face. He takes a step back, his jaw dropping in horrified revulsion. Hurt and confusion cloud Carla's eyes.

A thought sprouts in my mind, growing thick and fast like a magical beanstalk. Maybe I've had it all wrong. Maybe I'm not the ogre—the villain. Maybe I'm the true prince, here to rescue my princess in her moment of greatest need.

Before I can talk myself out of it, I'm charging forward to plant myself between the couple, crushing origami rats underfoot.

I bellow, "I'll be your prince!"

Shocked silence floods the hall. I don't care. I don't care that my limbs feel stiff and wooden, that my stomach's playing leapfrog with my lungs, or that my mind is whirring faster than a spinning wheel. If the curse is fickle enough to be broken by a pubescent pleb in a plastic crown, gender shouldn't pose a problem.

I glance at Carla, and her smile shines brighter than the second star to the right. My heart leaps. She's not embarrassed that I've declared myself her prince. *She's smiling*. I wrench the crown from Leo's head and place it majestically on my own.

Carla reaches for my hand. I grasp it like a tether.

The silence is stifling.

Then, from the back of the hall, Naveen calls out, "Long live Prince Emily!"

Toby speaks into the microphone, "Long live Prince Emily!" His words surround us, magnified.

I laugh. I have the best friends in the whole world, ever.

Our classmates finally applaud, and Leo gallantly bows out. He pats me awkwardly on the back as he passes, but I barely notice. Carla's hand is in mine, and I only have eyes for her.

"You didn't have to," she tells me. Her painted lips curve into a shy smile.

"Agree to disagree."

She smiles again before dropping her gaze.

"Um. We should leave the stage," I suggest. My wooden legs have turned to jelly, but I manage to steer us toward the steps.

Carla walks with me, down the stage steps and onto the dance floor. "We should find some privacy."

Yes. I shoot her a smile, aiming for flirty but landing on nervous, and lead her to the darkest, most deserted outskirt of the hall. Away from the crowds, the lights, the music, there's just us. Carla and Em. And a couple of origami rats.

Thoughts bubble in my brain, as if my skull is a cauldron. I have so much to explain, so much to apologize for, and I'm not sure where to start. "Carla, I—"

She presses her soft, beautiful lips against mine.

I'm so surprised, I freeze, a rigid ice sculpture, and Carla hesitates.

But no, I don't want her to stop. I've been dreaming about this for years. I'm kissing Carla, and I won't mess it up.

I catch her lips before they've moved too far from mine, and I kiss her.

I kiss Carla.

She steps closer, and we're still kissing, and it's like waking from a hundred years' sleep. It's true love's kiss.

Like all good things, our kiss comes to an end, but Carla is still close enough for me to inhale her perfume.

She says, "I've wanted to do that for ages. I thought you didn't like me that way."

Finally, and far too late, I blurt, "I've liked you for years!"

She laughs. "Seriously? You've spent weeks pointing out boys for me to kiss."

"Yeah, because you were looking for a prince, not another princess."

"*Em.*" Carla is still smiling, but with a desperate, burning hope in her eyes.

Oh, right. The kiss. The crown. The curse.

I step back to sweep my gaze over Carla's limp hair, her eyebrows—where new growth is already visible beneath layers of foundation—and across her cheeks, liberally scattered with warts and pimples.

I try to swallow, but my mouth is too dry.

The hope dulls from Carla's eyes as they focus on her hand, on the gnarled nails extending from her fingertips.

"It didn't work." Her voice is flat, hollow.

I've never heard her so defeated. Carla steps away from me. Her hand slips from my grasp. Panic thuds through me in time with the beat of the music.

"It's gonna be okay," I tell her.

She laughs, but it's choked, and empty, and sounds nothing like a laugh at all. "How? I'm stuck this way forever."

Because of me.

I ruined her chance to break the curse. She's the cursed fairy-tale princess, and I'm the villain.

"I really believed that kissing a prince would work," Carla whimpers. "But look at me!" A tear travels down the uneven terrain of her cheek.

"I am looking at you." I see my kind, courageous best friend. I see the girl I've loved for four years. Slowly, cautiously, I step toward her. "You're beautiful to me. Warts and all." I gently smooth my thumb over her cheekbone, wiping her tear away. "I especially love your eyelashes."

Carla closes her eyes. Another tear drips from the end of her nose. Quietly, she says. "They are my best feature."

"One of your best features," I correct her.

I want to say more to comfort her, but I'm all out of words. Except, "I'm sorry. So sorry that I took the crown, and kissed you, and ruined your life."

"You didn't."

"I think I did."

"No. You didn't ruin my life. I'd rather be with you and be a hag than be without you."

Her words are a beacon in the darkness, drawing me in. I let myself believe her. I tilt my chin up to kiss her again, and the second kiss is just as good as the first.

"I'm glad it was you," Carla says. "My first kiss."

"Me, too. Sorry you had to wait so long."

"You finally get me, and I'm a hag."

I manage to not roll my eyes. "You're not getting this, are you? I don't care that you're a hag. I'll keep saying it until you believe me." She raises oversized eyebrows. "I don't care that your legs are hairy. It'll make me feel better about all the times I can't be bothered to shave mine. I don't care that you've got long nails. I bet we could paint them and make them sparkle." She starts to smile. "I don't care that you've got bushy eyebrows. They balance out your ridiculous eyelashes. I don't care if you've got warts on your face. They won't stop me from kissing you."

To prove it, I kiss her again. Her hands wrap around my waist as her lips move against mine. I hold her close to me, knocking Snapper out of the way to rest my hand on the back of her neck.

When I pull away, I blink, then stare. There's no sudden burst of light, no crackle of energy, no fanfare. The change isn't immediate—it's gradual, and so smooth that I must have missed it just now.

Her smooth cheeks. Her perfect eyebrows.

I laugh. "Oh my God."

Carla jerks away from me. "Is it gone?" She presses her hands to her cheeks, eyes wide.

I'm so surprised, so relieved, it takes me a moment to say, "Back to normal."

Carla doesn't believe me until we've run to the bathroom where she can admire her restored reflection. She checks her legs for hairs, flashing me silky smooth expanses of golden skin that make me want to abandon the ball and take Carla back to my bedroom.

"You did it, Em! You broke the curse."

Finally convinced, she celebrates by kissing me senseless.

Once again, I find myself clinging to the sink unit, dizzied by all the kissing. No complaints.

Carla wants to reapply her lipstick before we go back into the hall.

"There's literally no point," I tell her. "I promise you I'm going to kiss it off again."

Carla laughs. I love her laugh. I love the way she tilts her head back and exposes her beautiful swan neck. I love the way she shyly reaches for my hand before we leave the bathroom. I love the way she squeezes it before we go back into the hall, both of us shivering with nerves and excitement.

I love that I don't have to keep secrets from her anymore.

And we're going to be with each other
Happily

Ever

After.

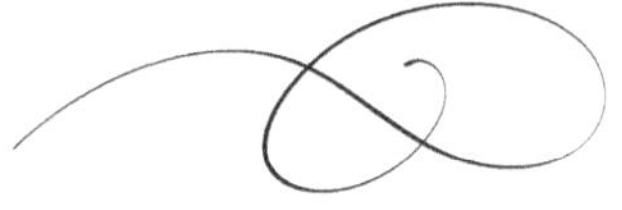

FLARE

BY TOSHIYA KAMEI

A SPOTLIGHT FALLS ON Max and me as our principal announces this year's homecoming court. Applause drowns out the pounding beat of "Stayin' Alive" by the Bee Gees. A disco ball sparkles from the ceiling, and fractured light flickers on the decorated gym walls.

A resonant crack makes me jump, and confetti showers down. I glance at Max, and her smile radiates like it'll last beyond the end of the world. She looks so handsome, her olive skin more alabaster than usual against her black tux.

Tears cloud my vision as the previous king and queen place crowns on our heads. I beam and pinch the hem of my pink dress in a curtsy.

Then, someone shouts and points. My smile drops.

The disco ball shatters, spitting out gleaming shards, and thick liquid *drips, drips, drips* down on us. Blood?

My scream deafens me as my dress turns crimson. Jeers erupt around us. Scanning the crowd, I catch sight of Angie's mocking smile on her fake-tanned face. I turn to Max, but she's despondent, staring at the red floor. Her handsome tuxedo, ruined. Her hair.

Our night. Tonight is supposed to be *ours*.

Fury shimmers from me in visible waves. My fingertips glow red like embers, and I shoot a snake of fire toward Angie. She screams as flames engulf her. The stench of burning flesh turns my stomach. Robbie removes his jacket and covers her with it, trying in vain to put the fire out. The fiery serpent devours Angie until she collapses.

Pandemonium ensues when the crowd stampedes. I stumble off the podium, trip over the principal's prone body, and fall. I crane my neck, searching for Max, but everything blurs in a haze of smoke and incandescent burning.

When I recover enough, the charred ruins of the gym loom around me. Max peers into my face with concern tinged with horror. Regret swirls in my head before giving way to resignation.

Max grabs my hand and gives it a reassuring squeeze. We hobble toward the exit. When we step outside, the chilly night air hits my blood-caked cheeks. Moonlight glistens off the rain-soaked pavement. Sobs and groans waft in the breeze. We walk toward the other survivors seated on the asphalt, and they scatter—presumably out of fear—and make room for us.

The full moon glitters like the disco ball. The wail of approaching sirens grows louder. With trembling lips, I hum the refrain from "Stayin' Alive."

Max removes her jacket and drapes it over my shoulders. Her kindness, along with her scent lingering on the jacket, soothes my frayed nerves. I mumble my thanks and rest my head on her shoulder, snuggling closer. I imagine ourselves hitting the road after a small breakfast in a dawn-lit diner. Fire will repel anyone who comes after us, and we'll drive until we reach a safe haven. A safe haven just for us.

Everything will be alright, and the world will be ours again.

GODDESSES AND CHERRY POPSICLES

BY RAE EVANS

I KICK MY PINK comforter to the floor, and the breeze from the fan hits my bare legs. How is it so freakin' hot in April? And why won't Mom turn on the air conditioner? I'm dying.

"Hey, Alexa..." I strain my voice. "What time is it?" I hope she can understand the croak that's supposed to be me.

"Good morning, Goddess of Manifestation. The time is 9:20 a.m."

I grin because laughing is impossible right now. Best thing I ever did was change my name on my account. My little brother screams my name enough. I don't need to hear it from Alexa, too.

Feeling slightly more empowered, I glance at my phone to see several messages from Mickie. I scroll to the first and read them in order.

10:15 p.m.: Hello? Helloooooo? Did u fall asleep?

I absolutely did. In the middle of our text exchange last night. I'm sick. What did she expect?

Then...

*No problem *smiley face* Rest up. TTYL *heart emoji**

*1:25 a.m.: BIG NEWS!!!! Call me when u wake up. I mean text me—ur throat... but OMG!!!! *shocked face emoji**

What now? Mickie always exaggerates everything. I text her back.

What's up?

She replies instantly.

Calling now.

I groan. Taylor Swift's "Peter" starts playing, and I answer. "Hey." It's barely a whisper.

"Reece! You sound awful, but hey, listen," Mickie says before I get another word out. "I know you can't talk, but you'll want to know this. I swear." She pauses for dramatic effect. "They broke up last night."

I try to swallow, but the dry tacky morning crud gets stuck in my inflamed throat. "What? Really?" I squawk.

"Yeeesss! It's all over his socials. Apparently, hers too, but I'm not friends with her anymore so, you know."

I inhale, trying to take it in. Colton is single.

"Oh, gosh, I should have asked. I'm such a loser friend. How are you feeling?" Mickie's a great friend, but she always says stuff like that ever since she came out, and her friend group dumped her. Well, except me.

"Smokin' hot. I might spontaneously combust at any moment." I open the warm water bottle that sat on my side table all night and sip at the remaining few ounces.

"Well, ten bucks says he'll be hitting you up to go to prom." Her voice is cautious.

"He won't. No time. It's a week away."

"Doesn't matter. Colton's too proud to miss his senior prom, and you don't want to miss it either. Go stag if you have to."

"You won't be there, and I'm not going alone."

Preparing for prom takes too much effort—the hair, the nails, the shoes, makeup. Not when it feels as if someone is holding a blowtorch to my throat.

"You've got your dress," Mickie reminds me. "Just sayin'."

"Don't remind me." That's five-hundred dollars down the toilet. Two and a half months of baby-sitting the terrible trio, and for what? Strep throat and my twentieth viewing of *Pretty Woman* with a side of cherry popsicles. Nice.

Mickie sighs into the phone. "Listen, I promised Taylor. She put up with last year's Gatsby theme to be with me. I owe her."

It was just bad luck or stupid planning that our schools chose the same date for prom. Mickie will be an hour away with Taylor. Am I supposed to sit by myself while Colton performs the Jerk and Sponge Bob, wearing the Prom King Crown? To a cheering, adoring senior class? I don't think so.

"No worries. Have fun, Mick." I meant it, even if my voice was weak.

"If Colton asks you, what will you do? You two made an adorable couple, but he hurt you. I haven't forgiven him for that. My butt is still paying for that quart of ice cream I ate in support of you. The sacrifice," she says with breathy exaggeration.

"I know, Mick."

"And I know he's still into you. I can tell by the way he complimented that ugly medusa sculpture you made in advanced art."

"I worked hard on that."

"Just sayin'. Sending you a picture."

My phone dings. It's a pair of gorgeous sparkly heels.

"Listen, those shoes will match your dress perfectly, and I'm never going to wear them. They're too big for Taylor, although she would rock them."

"Thanks, but I won't need them," I tell her.

"We'll see. Promise me you'll think twice if he asks you."

I'm not as weak as Mickie thinks. "Promise."

Mickie hangs up, and my head spins, only partly from the fever.

Colton broke up with Alyssa.

Wow...

Part of me is glad he doesn't have a date for prom. He can go single, like me. The other part of me misses him too much to wish him any bad luck. Mickie knows me well. If he asks, it will break me to say no. Colton was mine for seven months.

"Rrrrrrrreece!"

I flinch so hard, my toes hurt. "Jesus, Rocco."

"Rrrrrrreece," he says again, trilling his r's like the annoying bratty brother he is. He's learning Spanish, and it will be my undoing. He ballet spins into my bedroom, colliding with the foot of my bed. "Rrrrrrrreece."

"What?"

"Mom wants you downstairs rrrrright this instance."

Instant, I think, wanting to correct him. *Right this instant.* "Why?"

"She has yourrrr medicine frrrrrom Rrrrrite Aid."

"Can't she…" I push myself up. "Never mind." I need some ice water, which I can't trust an eight-year-old to get, not when he doesn't walk in straight lines. I tousle his hair as I walk by. Glad he's better, even though it's his fault I'm sick.

Mom is in the kitchen washing vegetables for her weekday lunches. Eggs boil on the stove, and chicken cooks in the air fryer. She always meal-preps on Sunday.

"Your medicine came in." She dries her hands and pulls the thermometer free from its plastic container. "Open your mouth."

I groan but obey. My body aches, and it takes a great effort to stand upright.

Mom pushes the medicine toward me, then sprinkles salt in a glass before adding warm water. "You have to gargle."

The thermometer beeps, and she looks at it. "To bed. Wait." She empties two ibuprofens onto the counter. "I'll bring you something to eat when I get a chance. The doctor said you'll start feeling better in a couple days. But you need to stay home until Wednesday at least."

That's four days' worth of make-up work, since I missed Friday. Burdened with responsibilities, medication, and another cherry popsicle, I head back to my room.

Once the routine of gargling and attempting to swallow the pain med is done, I collapse on my bed. I fall asleep and wake to my phone dinging.

The popsicle has melted inside the paper wrapping. I lift it by the corner and drop it into the salty glass.

I pick up my phone.

It's a message. From Colton.

My heart beats into my throat. Why am I panicking? But my hands shake as I tap the screen to open his message.

Hey Reece. How's it goin'?

Great! And you? I cringe and consider erasing it and typing another. Maybe it's best to be honest from the get-go in case Mickie's right.

I send the message. The dishonest one.

That's good. So do u hav a date for prom?

There it is. Should I lie? I think about my promise to Mickie.

Not sure I'm going. I'm under the weather right now.

Oh.

Yeah. I started meds today, so maybe??

Want 2 go with me?

I don't answer right away. He sends another text.

Alyssa and I broke up. I've got my tux and all. Just a thought.

Yeah. Sure. Yes. Sounds like fun. I grimace at the stupid message I just sent him. My heart thumps so hard, I can't hear myself read his reply.

Awesome. Catch u later, beautiful.

I kick my legs. I'm giddy. I message Mickie. *You were right...*

Her reply dings fast and loud. *AND?*

I said yes. Have to get better now.

*You will *prayer hands, fingers crossed, four leaf clover, heart emoji**

*I feel like *poop emoji*. What about the shoes?*

I'll bring them this week. Are you sure?

upside down smile emoji

✎✎✎

By Wednesday morning, the body aches are gone, and I sit eating cereal and looking up hair tutorials on YouTube. It's too late for a hair appointment. Every salon in a thirty-mile radius is booked.

I pull my dress out of the closet and hang it on my door—scarlet sequins, spaghetti straps, and an open lace-up back. Worth every torturous second with Rocco and the neighbor twins to earn enough for this dress, now that Colton is my date!

I practice my hair and makeup all morning, then hop on my computer for school work. Senioritis is a real thing. I've had it since October, so attempting Physics in April equals babysitting the terrible trio for fifty hours straight.

Colton sent me a picture of his tux—a classic black and white—and I told him the color of my dress, deliberately hiding the other details. I want to surprise him.

His texts are sparse, but since it's baseball season, I don't press. Also, I'm in resting mode and manifesting good health. It's working. I can feel it.

I go back to school on Thursday, so I don't fall further behind. I use the excuse of a raspy throat to avoid talking in class. It works, and the teachers don't ask too many questions.

I spend lunch getting my Econ notes for a test the next day. The resource room is empty, except for the usual group of AP history students who are always cramming for an exam.

I'm just about to finish when Alyssa, Colton's ex-girl-friend, joins the study group. I move to the far back corner and hide.

I'm stuffing my papers into a folder when Colton walks in. He motions for Alyssa, and my chest grows cold. They stand close, about a foot between them. Her hands are shoved in her jacket pockets. I can't hear them, but Colton reaches out and touches her arm. His hand rests there for a long moment, and I shrink back into the shadows. Alyssa shrugs, then walks back to her table, leaving Colton alone by the magazine stand.

Mickie meets me by my locker at the end of the day. "It could have been worse. They didn't kiss. Or hug. Maybe they had some unfinished business, and it's all over with now."

I appreciate her positive outlook, but I've struggled to concentrate all afternoon, imagining the worst.

"You know I'll tell you the second I hear anything," she says.

I nod. "I know."

"Okay. So, here are the shoes." She hands me a floral drawstring bag.

"Fancy." I open it and pull out a silver, sparkling three-inch heel. "Thank you." I grin, dangling it by the strap.

Mickie crosses her arms and faces the lockers. "There's Alyssa." Mickie lowers her voice. "No one will say who she's going with on Saturday."

"I don't care." I want to believe that. Alyssa and Colton dated for three months, four months less than we were together. But I have loved Colton since my sophomore year, so there's something to be said for that.

Alyssa adjusts her backpack and exits through the side door. I ignore the jealousy that surfaces and force the shoe back into the bag. "Thank you. Are you sure you don't need them."

Mickie's smile is crooked. "Taylor's wearing a dress. I'm wearing a suit."

"I expect pictures."

"Listen, I expect a text every ten minutes with details and recorded evidence. Don't make me come here."

I scoff. "Please don't. You'll be at the Hilton. Don't ditch a posh event for a prom in the gymnasium."

"It's not where you go, it's who you're with." Mickie squeezes my shoulders.

Colton texts me late Friday night. *Pick u up at 4.*
   *Perfect! Looking forward to it *heart emoji**
When he doesn't rapid fire a response, I panic.
Me too, beautiful. C U then.

Between the mixed emotions about Colton and the medication, I'm buzzing. I'm sad we haven't had a chance to talk since Sunday. He always sits with the team at lunch. And Mickie promised me her English notes, so I sat at my usual table.

It's Friday, though. Colton doesn't have a game or a job. I try to shrug it away. I want to chat with him, and I'm jealous of whoever or whatever is getting his time, even if it's his couch and ESPN.

I take another dose of my medicine, wishing it was the last one, but I still have five days' worth. I switch off my bedside lamp and close my eyes.

When I wake up tomorrow morning, it'll be Prom Day. And I'm going with Colton.

I dream of golden crowns and cherry popsicles, silver stilettos and fancy hair updos. When I wake up, my nose is stuffy. I rub the sleep from my eyes.

"Alexa, what time is it?"

"Good morning, Goddess of Manifestation. The time is 7:45 a.m."

Awesome. There's lots to do, and I run through the list in my head. Shower, dry my hair with lots of products so it has body. Paint my nails—all twenty. Exfoliate, shave, hydrate. Add shimmering oil at the last minute. Oh, and only eat salad so I don't bloat. Finally, makeup. I need at least ninety minutes for my face, which feels tight. I sit up and bury it in my hands. I need to get some circulation going. Maybe a long walk on the treadmill.

Rocko thumps down the hallway and stops outside my room. "Rrrrrreece!"

I drop my hands. "What, Rocco?" I sigh.

He stops cold and stares at me, then squeezes his eyes shut and opens them again.

"What?"

"What's wrong with your face?" He starts giggling.

"Very funny, punk."

"Your face." He points, laughing hysterically. "It looks funny!" He doubles over, clutching his belly.

I'm annoyed, but the longer he laughs, the more I think he might not be joking. I look at my hands. What? My arms... Oh no! My chest... I panic and run to the bathroom mirror. My face...

"Moooooooom!!!!!" I scream. I bend over and splash cold water, then look again. This is a nightmare–please tell me it is. My eyes are tiny slits above chubby cheeks. More cool water. I dare to look at my reflection. It's red, pimply, fat. My whole torso is dots of red. "Mom!" I yell louder, tears accumulating. Rocco is still hooting.

I hear Mom come upstairs, talking to Rocco. "Settle down." She pokes her head into the bathroom. "Oh, my God!"

"What is this?" I point at my face.

She blinks several times, as if she's not seeing clearly. "Oh—Oh no. How's your throat?"

"Okay."

"How are you feeling otherwise?"

Other than wanting to die right now? "Fine, but–it's prom. I can't go—" I burst into tears, and Rocco stops giggling.

"It's not so bad. Honestly." Her fingers are cool on my cheeks as she holds my face between her hands. "It..." She screws up her mouth. "Might be an allergic reaction.

I'll call Doctor Newman. He'll know what to do." I know she's trying to make me feel better, but it's not working.

"It's Saturday. They're not open," I remind her.

"Well," she stammers. "Tina will know. I'll call her."

Mom grabs Rocco and disappears. I take off my night-gown. The rash starts at my forehead and runs to my knees and peppers my calves. I vary from bright red to pink, swirled and patchy. My skin, once fair, now resembles a strawberry. My face is almost unrecognizable from the swelling. I can't go to prom like this.

I jump in the shower and blast cold water. I'm shivering when I step out. Mom shouts from the hallway.

"I'm going to the drug store! I'll be right back!"

I pick up my phone and collapse on my bed, screaming into a pillow. Rocco eyes me from my bedroom door, then dashes away when I yell, "What?"

I text Mickie. *This is the worst day of my life.*

She replies instantly. *What happened???*

Instead of explaining my nightmare with words, I snap a selfie and send it.

WTH???

Mom thinks it's an allergic reaction.

*I'm soooo sorry *cry face emoji* *horrified face emoji**

I call her, sobbing. "What should I do, Mickie?"

There's silence on the other end as she struggles to find the right words. "Maybe it'll go away. It has to, right? I mean, it's prom, the most important night of our senior year. Memories for a lifetime."

I snort, which is easy to do with the collection of snot in my sinuses.

"Don't cry, Reece. It'll be okay."

"Will it?" I wipe my face. "Will Colton want to be seen with me when I look like this?"

"He will if he cares," Mickie says. "And he better not be mean to you, or he'll have me to deal with."

The thing is Colton likes pretty girls. Alyssa will look gorgeous tonight, no doubt. And then there'll be me, permanently embarrassed inside and out, and red all over to prove it.

"Listen, maybe Colton knows he made a mistake when he broke up with you. You said yourself he had no real reason. He just wanted space. Maybe he got his space and now realizes he misses you."

"Or he just doesn't want to go alone? And I'm the only one available."

Mickie is silent for a moment. "Then, he's a jerk for leading you on."

"I don't know, Mick. I think I should cancel. This is humiliating."

"I wish I could be there. It's too late now. We don't have tickets."

"I know." I'm dragging her down to the pity pit with me. "It's okay. I'll be fine. You go have fun."

"You sure?"

"Of course," I lie. "Hey, Mom's back from the store. I should go. Thanks for the shoes, even if I don't wear them."

We hang up, and I run downstairs.

Mom sets a bag on the kitchen island. "Here's the plan." She opens the bag and pulls out an antihistamine. "Tina wasn't sure what to do since you're taking the antibiotic for strep. So, I called the twenty-four hour nurse on the back of the insurance card, and she said to stop it for now and call the doc first thing Monday morning."

I shake my head. "I don't care about that. What do I do about my face?" I'm exasperated.

"This." Mom holds the box of medicine and shrugs. "Hopefully, it'll reduce the swelling and redness. It's our only shot."

I press my palms against my eyes. Of all the bad luck.

"Crying will make it worse. Just take this and lie down."

I force down another pill and collapse on the couch where Rocco is watching cartoons. Despite squeaky voices from the TV and his sporadic laughter, I fall asleep.

When I wake, I run to the bathroom and look in the mirror. No change. Frustrated, I find Mom in the laundry room.

"Should I call Colton and cancel?"

"Honey." Mom hugs me. "I understand this is a big day, but it's not all about how you look."

My shoulders fall. Really? Funny, I thought it was. "Isn't that the definition of a formal?" I pull away from her.

"I think," she starts. "The swelling has gone down. You can take more medicine in an hour."

"It's knocking me out."

She tilts her head in sympathy. "How about an early lunch?"

We eat chef salads, then I grab the hand mirror from my room, take the antihistamine, and hit the couch with the TV remote. Later, Mom wakes me with water and a pill.

"It's time. Take this."

I obey, look in the hand mirror, and close my eyes from the horror. My hairline is wet from crying, and I vow to stop. If this round of medicine doesn't work, I'll text Colton and tell him.

When Mom wakes me again, it's 1:30. "You need to start getting ready."

The hand mirror is on my chest where I had fallen asleep holding it. I look at my reflection. The swelling is almost gone, but the red rash is as vibrant as before. I groan, then pick up my phone and text Colton.

Hey.

What's up, beautiful?

Small problem.

Nothing we can't fix.

I work up the courage. *It seems I'm allergic to my meds. I have a rash.*

Oh,...are you contagious?

No!

No prob. C U at 4.

I force myself up. Does he have any idea? I consider sending a picture but then decide to think positively. The rash could fade. Manifestation Goddess, let's do this! I run upstairs and start the whole process.

Mom helps by giving me her expensive primers and heavy concealers to reduce the redness. I do my best to ignore the minimal effects and concentrate on my hair. It has to look stellar because everything else is a disaster.

At 3:30, I slide into my dress and look in the mirror.

Mom stands beside me, biting her lower lip. "You look beautiful."

"Thanks, Mom." I scrutinize myself. The scarlet dress just makes my skin redder. I left my lips nude and used dark eye makeup. "My hair looks good."

"Oh honey. Colton is lucky to have you as a date tonight. Go have fun."

When the doorbell rings fifteen minutes later, I'm perched on the edge of the couch, terrified.

"Hey, Mrs. Woods."

"Hi, Colton. Reece? Colton's here."

When I see him standing beside Mom, looking like a taller version of Tanner Buchanan, I'm glad I mustered the courage. I forget about my unsightly appearance, until I see his reaction.

He blushes and stammers, then holds out a corsage. "I have, uh, this for you." It's a large champaign rose with a gold ribbon and baby's breath. "It's for your wrist."

"That's so pretty." I slide it on, and Mom hands me the boutonniere. I pin the small red rose bud to his lapel, noticing our flowers don't match, but not caring.

Colton avoids my eyes. "I like your dress."

My cheeks warm. "Thanks."

When it gets awkward, Mom chimes in. "Pictures. We need lots. Your dad wants to see how beautiful you look."

We stand in front of the fireplace, then on the front porch, then with Rocco, then a selfie with all four of us.

"We better get going. Thanks, Mrs. Woods."

"Sure thing, Colton. Be careful and have a good time." Mom kisses me on the cheek. "You're stunning," she whispers in my ear.

I'm nervous in the car, but Colton turns the radio on and talks about his baseball scholarship to South Carolina, the coach, and his dorm mate. I listen, so self-conscious that I forget my own plans after graduation. But it's okay because Colton doesn't ask about that.

When we arrive at the school campus, groups of students are getting pictures under the large oaks and we join them.

A few people wave and say hi, and I immediately miss Mickie. We join in a few pictures, and I make sure I'm in the back for all of them.

Inside, the gymnasium has been divided in two for the Fire and Ice theme. Half is decorated in red and black, and the other in silver and blue.

"Let's get punch." Colton points to the red bowls on the fire side, and I follow him, glad for a distraction. I glance around at my classmates and wave at a few.

"Everyone looks amazing."

Colton is talking to Spencer and doesn't hear me. I join them, touching Colton's arm.

"Hey, Reece," Spencer says. He never smiles, unless it's at his own joke. "Nice dress. It matches the room. Actually..." He leans in real close to me, and his gray eyes scan my chest. "I can hardly see you on this side of the gym." He cracks a brilliant smile, and my skin heats. "You blend right in."

Colton laughs. I look at him, trying not to cry.

"Ha ha, Spencer. Turns out, I'm allergic to some medicine."

"Well, don't be surprised if Colton can't find you later."

I roll my eyes for lack of a better thing to do.

"Hey, bro. Catch you later." Colton and Spencer do some fancy baseball handshake, then the two of us find a seat at a table with blue streamers and balloons.

"Where's Mickie?" Ryan, who was voted most likely to meet a famous person, flops down beside me.

"She's with Taylor at her prom. Same night, remember?"

"Oh, how could I forget. But that suuucks."

I nod.

Colton nudges me. "Hey, I'm gonna say hi to Nick." He points to a group near the cookie table.

"Okay." I watch him go. Colton has always been popular. His back retreats, and is then swallowed up by hands and glitzy dresses.

"Has to make his rounds, right?" Ryan asks. "Say, you can sit with us."

I smile at Ryan, who has always been genuine in every situation. "Thanks, but I'll stay here for now." I scan the room for Colton.

Ryan shrugs. "We can sit here with you. Hey, giiirrrl!" Ryan motions a group of four over, all band geeks. We say hi, no one comments on my rash, and we nibble on chips and carrots.

Chloe, the best flutist in the school, leans toward me. "Your hair is on point. How'd you get it up all swirly like that?"

I confess to the wonders of YouTube, hair gel, and dozens of bobby pins.

"Well, you look like a goddess."

Before I can complement Chloe on her stunning black gown, her eyes grow big at something behind me. "Whoa! Look at Alyssa's dress." She nudges those around her.

When I turn, I see Colton and Alyssa. He's looking at her. The whole gymnasium is, and it's with good reason. Her gown is shimmering gold over a champagne skirt. It's perfect against her dark skin and black hair. She's mesmerizing, and none of us can stop looking, including Colton.

Alyssa, in a trio of laughing girls, walks right by him and to the fire side.

"Word is, it's a triple date. Candace has been single since last year, and Jenna's boyfriend is at basic training," someone says.

I realize two things.

First, I could be having fun like that with Mickie and Taylor. Being a third wheel is better than being deserted.

Second, my corsage matches Alyssa's dress perfectly. Colton didn't even have the decency to order a new one for me. I got Alyssa's reject.

I turn back to my table, determined to have a good time. I'm not surprised when Colton never comes back over. I catch glimpses of him on the dance floor, but Ryan and Chloe keep me distracted well enough.

At nine o'clock, I get a text with a picture of Mickie in a dark green pants suit and Taylor in a long, flowy, cream-colored dress with big pink flowers scattered on the skirt. I show everyone at the table, and they oooh and ahhh.

Later, Spencer and his friends harass us, repeating crude jokes and poking fun. "Why aren't you dancing, Reece?"

"Because cherry popsicles melt when they get hot," his friend says. "That's why she's sitting on the ice side."

"Ohhh!" Spencer pretends to understand. "I thought she was already a fire cracker." He laughs.

I turn my back to them.

"Get lost," Ryan says. "Weirdos."

"For the record," Chloe says to me after they leave. "I think it took a lot of courage for you to come to prom. I wouldn't have because I'm too vain. But I think you look fabulous, and who cares what those dimwits think, anyhow?"

I blink back tears. I'm at the best table here with the best people, except Mickie of course. It hurts that Colton totally abandoned me. I never thought this would be my senior prom memory.

"Let's take some pics!" Ryan's camera is out in an instant. We huddle around and snap one.

"I can take it for you." Alyssa is standing beside us with her hand out. Her cheeks and decolletage glisten dewy gold.

"Cool, thanks!" Ryan hands her the phone.

"You all look gorgeous!" Alyssa smiles from behind the phone. "Say seniors!" She snaps several pics and hands the phone back to Ryan, who shares them with all of us.

I take a moment to send a picture to Mickie. She replies, *3 flame emojis* *Where's Colton?*

No idea.

Gggggrrrrrrrrr!

I look up laughing in time to see Alyssa, still standing beside me, awkward and unsure. "I know we don't talk a lot, but can I ask a favor?"

I swallow, knowing I can't take any more teasing or mean drama tonight. I shrug.

"Will you give Mickie a message for me? Tell her I miss her." Alyssa's eyes are watery. She swallows, and a vulnerability touches her expression. "And that I'm sorry for being an awful friend to her."

I nod. "Sure, I can do that."

Her face lights up. "By the way, you look like a goddess in that dress."

I smile, and some of the resentment I've clutched all night slides away. "Thanks." My voice quivers. "That's nice of you to say."

"I think we should be dancing. Let's go." Alyssa motions, and we all follow her.

Candace and Jenna join us, and we form our own little group, dancing the rest of the night. My memories aren't what I expected at all. Actually, they might turn out better.

Keeping a Promise

By Jessica Lee Minneci

Ginnette Young's last moments involved whispers of how much she was loved and the slow beeps of a heart monitor. Her chronic myeloid leukemia took everything from her. She left this world wishing for peace.

Except Ginnette didn't go toward a light like the movies suggested. Instead, darkness claimed her.

Now, she floated in a pitch-black place. If she had a body, she couldn't feel it, and if her eyes worked, she couldn't see. The only sense she had was her hearing. Yet, the silence rang as loud as any bell.

Ginnette had to be in Purgatory. She believed Heaven would be a bright place, and Hell more painful. Purgatory was like becoming a can on a pantry shelf, saved for use whenever it was needed. Hopefully, the judge would come soon.

Time stretched on as Ginnette worried about her sister, Makayla, and Makayla's boyfriend, Holden. They were the ultimate trio of friends, and now, there would only be two because she left them behind.

Greetings, child, a gravelly voice said in Ginnette's mind.

If she were alive, Ginnette would have jumped.

To respond, just think about your answer and direct it toward me.

Like this?

Yes.

That was easy. *Can I communicate with other souls this way?*

No. You're in Purgatory, and I am your Judge, Spyros. Only I can talk with you. All souls are on their own, individual journeys.

Okay, so what's my verdict? Am I going to Heaven or Hell?

Neither. You need to stay here for a bit longer.

Why?

You tell me.

This was ridiculous. He was the judge. Shouldn't he know why she had an extended stay?

Come on, child. I don't have time for hesitations.

Then, the lightbulb flicked on in her head.

What day is it on Earth?

May 18th.

Ginnette had been dead for almost two months. Still, she thanked the powers above that she wasn't too late.

I have unfinished business. I want to keep my promise to Makayla and go to prom with her and Holden.

There was a pause.

I don't grant these requests often, but since you died young, I'll allow it. On Earth, you will wander like a ghost. Your loved ones won't be able to see, hear, or even feel your touch.

This would make her interactions harder, but Ginnette could do it.

How will I know when your unfinished business is successful? Spyros asked.

Ginnette hesitated. She didn't know the situation back home, but she did know her sister's prom fantasy, and if she could make it come true, she could shake Makayla out of the grief she was most likely feeling after Ginnette's death. She deserved the night of her dreams.

It will be successful once I get my sister and Holden to slow dance and kiss at the prom.

Fine. Ginnette Young, you have from sunset to midnight to fulfill your unfinished business, and you may only do so in the same location as your sister. If you succeed, you will move onto Heaven. If you fail, you will remain a sad soul, haunting Purgatory for the rest of eternity.

No pressure or anything.

Begone!

A gong sounded. Ginnette was thrown out of darkness and into light.

Sunset colored the horizon in oranges, blues, and purples.

The sky! She was back on Earth!

Ginnette floated as she had in Purgatory. Chestnut brown hair drifted around her shoulders as the entirety of her body appeared translucent in the evening light. She also wore the hospital gown in which she had died.

Ginnette clapped her hands but couldn't feel the sensation.

Then, she realized where she was: her home in West Ridge, Illinois. The blue house with the white shutters loomed in front of Ginnette, whose ghostly form hovered over the driveway.

Little Bradley from across the street whooped when he sunk a basketball into the net he shared with his older brothers.

If Ginnette could make a sound, she would join him. Instead, she jumped in place.

Ginnette considered flying up to her sister's room, and her ghostly body obeyed.

The window was open to the springtime air, but the interior was dark. Ginnette went inside, hoping she hadn't missed her sister getting ready for prom.

Makayla lay fully clothed on a purple bedspread, her unbrushed brown hair askew on the pillow. Tissues surrounded her.

Oh, Makayla. This was supposed to be her and Ginnette's night, but now, it was Makayla's and Holden's, and Makayla was too grief-stricken to move. Since the sun was setting, Makayla was already late.

Ginnette maneuvered to her sister's side, but before she could do anything further, a bright ethereal woman floating next to Makayla shot light toward Ginnette. It burned like hot coals.

A breeze pushed Ginnette close to the window.

She frantically motioned to her sister, then to her eyes, and then hugged herself, miming to the woman that she was here to comfort Makayla.

Evil spirit, depart this room, or I will force you to go.

The clear voice must have belonged to the woman.

I'm not an evil spirit. I'm Ginnette, Makayla's sister. Don't you recognize me?

You do look familiar, but you have a black stain over your heart, which indicates you must be malevolent. So, your shape could also be a trick.

Ginnette wanted to dance because she could at least talk to someone on Earth, but then the woman's words sank in. The stain on Ginnette's chest was the color of charcoal. *Please, I swear it's me. I died from leukemia. My unfinished business is to help ensure Makayla has a memorable prom night.*

I don't believe you.

Ginnette clenched her fists.

It's true.

Even if it is, I can't let you go near Makayla or harm her. I'm her guardian angel, Celeste.

Suddenly, the woman's presence made sense. She was translucent like Ginnette, wearing a long gown and a halo to match. She also emitted light so bright, Ginnette's eyes would have watered if she were alive.

At least let me see Makayla tonight. I love and miss her.

I will if you tell me something about Makayla only Ginnette would know.

Makayla claims her first kiss was with Holden, but I always joked that it was with the pillow she practiced on for weeks before the real thing happened. Ginnette grinned. She teased her sister a lot, but they were best friends.

Celeste nodded. *You can stay, but I will blast you if any harm comes to Makayla.*

Understood.

Ginnette wanted to crumple to the floor and cry. She needed some alone time with Makayla and Holden, and if her sister had a guardian angel, Holden would have one, too. Nevertheless, she had to stay positive if she was going to help her sister and get to Heaven.

Makayla stirred and rose from the bed.

This was her chance. Ginnette floated to the closet and thought about a breeze. Wind whooshed through the window and opened the door.

If only she had realized she could do this sooner, Ginnette could have defended herself.

"Stupid wind," Makayla said.

It was me, Ginnette wanted to shout. *Go to the Prom. I love you and want you to have fun. Forget about the grief for one night, and just be your happy self.*

Even though she hadn't heard Ginnette, Makayla moved to the closet.

The sisters stared at the dress. It was a salmon pink with a corset top and a long, ruffled skirt. Ginnette and Makayla had picked theirs out together, and the gown was as stunning as the day Makayla tried it on for the first time.

"I can't go without you, Ginnette," Makayla whispered.

Yes, you can. Ginnette summoned more wind. The dress flew off the hanger, and Makayla caught it with a yelp.

Smooth, Celeste said.

She has to go.

I know.

Then let me help.

Celeste considered for a moment. *Okay, you may come closer.*

Tears cascaded down Makayla's cheeks as she held the dress. Ginnette knelt in front of Makayla and looked into her sister's glistening green eyes.

Please, go, Kayla. Go for me.

Makayla nodded and stood. She laid the dress out on her bed before leaving the room.

Did she hear me?

No. You just influenced her by looking into her eyes, Celeste said as they followed Makayla to the bathroom. *That's why I didn't want you near her. Evil spirits can convince people to do terrible things.*

Evil spirits, meaning people from Purgatory like me?

No, beings that travel Earth, convincing others to do malevolent deeds. Why do you think everyone has a guardian angel?

I guess you have your purpose.

Ginnette pretended to raise the roof as her sister disappeared into the shower.

Later, Makayla descended the glossy wooden stairs in a stunning prom dress that matched her freshly painted nails and toenails. Her hair was curled. Her makeup was perfect, and silver jewelry sparkled on her ears and wrists. She was radiant, and despite her grief, she smiled.

Even though Ginnette couldn't physically attend the dance with her sister, it was a victory to see her now.

"Oh, honey, you look magnificent."

Ginnette turned from her post at the base of the stairs to find the speaker. Mom grinned at her daughter. "John! Come see Makayla."

Dad emerged from the adjacent living room, also smiling. "You look beautiful, pumpkin."

Ginnette wanted to wrap her arms around her family members. This would be the last time she saw them together. But they wouldn't be able to feel her embrace, and their guardian angels were glaring at her. Each wore gowns like Celeste, but both were the same gender as their person.

"Thanks," Makayla said to her parents.

"We're happy you decided to go," Dad said.

"Dinner will be over soon, but you can still enjoy the dance," Mom said. "I'll be your chauffeur."

If Mom was driving Makayla to the prom, that meant Holden wasn't picking her up. The prince and the princess were supposed to go together!

Where is Holden? Ginnette asked Celeste.

They haven't spoken for weeks.

Why?

Because Makayla pushed him away. She wants to grieve alone.

Ginnette shifted from foot to foot. This was awful. Holden should at least be trying to coax Makayla out of her shell. That's what she would have done, but Holden was nothing if not respectful of others' wishes. He'd wait for her.

Makayla's tears earlier must have been for both her and Holden. She was brave to go to prom alone now.

"Thanks." Makayla slipped something sparkly into a clutch purse that matched her dress and followed Mom out the door.

About twenty minutes later, Ginnette hovered above the carpeted seats in the back of her mom's car, as it slowed to a stop in front of Westside High School. White LED light glowed from the gym's windows.

"I'm sorry you're on your own tonight," Mom said. "I know your sister would be happy you went to prom. It'll turn into a magical night. These events always do."

"Maybe. I miss Ginnette, but I know she's with me in spirit. I couldn't let her down."

Makayla's words were sincere. If she were in Makayla's place, Ginnette would say the same thing. Plus, maybe humans were more aware of spirits than Ginnette thought. It was comforting to think Makayla believed Ginnette was with her.

"I love you." Mom leaned over and kissed Makayla on the top of the head, careful not to mess up her curls.

I do, too.

"You, too."

As Makayla stepped out onto the sidewalk, Ginnette chose to believe the sentiment was also directed toward her.

"Ticket, please." Ginnette's geometry teacher, Mrs. Conway, held her hand out to Makayla as she approached the door.

Makayla pulled a crumpled-up strip of paper from her purse and handed it to the older teacher.

Mrs. Conway nodded and beckoned Makayla inside. The teacher's guardian angel glared at Ginnette as she trailed behind her sister.

I bet she thought she would never use that ticket, Ginnette said to Celeste.

You have no idea.

Ginnette skipped into the gym beside her sister. She was going to prom.The theme was "Out of This World," and the decorating committee had outdone themselves. Chains of multicolor paper stars hung from the ceiling. Interspersed among them were papier mâché planets, moons, comets, and asteroids. Dark blue crepe paper covered the ceiling and walls. The disco ball emitted the flashing white light that Ginnette had noticed from outside. It must have been meant to look like moonlight. Tables draped in blue cloths were set up throughout the gym and contained lit centerpieces shaped like planets. A large dance floor dominated the middle of the gym.

If Ginnette had been physically there, she might have giggled at the corny theme, but based on all the guardian angels that hovered next to each student, the topic was more relevant than the humans realized.

Makayla wandered to the right side of the space where a camera man was taking photos of students in front of a painted backdrop of the Milky Way. Tentatively, she stepped into line behind a couple. Ginnette floated close to Makayla to avoid bumping into any guardian angels.

When it was her turn, Makayla put one hand on her hip and smiled the way she, Holden, and Ginnette always used to during selfies.

Ginnette couldn't resist. Before the flash went off, she drifted to her sister's side and struck the same pose.

"There appears to be some fog beside you, although it could just be a trick of the light," the cameraman said after snapping the picture.

Ginnette smiled. The fog was her. Makayla wouldn't know, but maybe she would suspect.

"Probably," Makayla said.

"As soon as the photo develops, I'll send a copy to the school, and they will make sure it gets to you."

"Thanks."

Frowning, Makayla walked to the refreshment table. She grabbed some punch and a star-shaped cookie.

Ginnette had gotten her sister here, but without Holden, this night was going to be a bust. She drifted through groups of students in search of her friend but came up empty. Meanwhile, Makayla sat at one of the tables by herself.

Time wore on. Ginnette wrung her hands. She couldn't leave Makayla, but if Holden never showed, she wouldn't achieve her goal and go to Heaven.

Can you go get Holden, Ginnette asked Celeste.

I can't leave Makayla's side.

Ginnette stomped her invisible foot. *Me either.*

But you can wander in the same place as your sister.

What are you getting at?

If Holden is somewhere in the high school, you can go to him. But if he's not, you're out of luck, and if you're gone from your sister and she leaves the prom, you'll return to Purgatory.

Why are you helping me?

Because I see now you're the real Ginnette, and we both want Makayla to be happy. Now, go. I'll keep Makayla here.

It was a huge risk, but Ginnette had to do it for her sister.

Ginnette floated as fast as she could through the familiar halls of the high school. She checked Holden's locker, dodged teachers and their guardian angels by passing through classroom doors, and entered the changing room where Holden put on his football uniform. While it was exhilarating to see the boys' locker room as a girl, it didn't matter because he wasn't there. Ginnette maneuvered up the stairs and down all the corridors but came up short.

In a final effort, Ginnette zipped into the art classroom. Clad in a tuxedo, Holden stood facing away from her. He looked like a lost boy with a paintbrush in one hand. His guardian angel spotted Ginnette and waved his arms in a shooing motion, but Ginnette didn't move.

I come in peace. I'm Ginnette. I need Holden to go to the gym. Makayla is here, she said to the angel.

Let Holden be, or I'll make you leave.

Ginnette didn't have time for this nonsense. She blew a gust of wind toward the angel, and he countered the strike. The winds wrestled together until Ginnette strained from the effort.

She came to Holden's side and beheld his watercolor painting. It was all dark shades of blue, red, and purple, probably mirroring his mood. The angel pushed her away from Holden. She countered his attack.

Ginnette had to be quick. Makayla could leave at any time, and this would all be over.

She wiggled her fingers. The paintbrush flew out of Holden's hand. As he bent to pick it up, she gazed into his eyes.

Holden, Makayla is here. She needs you. Please, come to the gym with me.

The angel knocked Ginnette aside as Holden shivered. He picked up the paintbrush and set it down before leaving the room.

Ginnette twirled in the air. On some level, both Makayla and Holden had to have known she was there.

If she breaks his heart, you and I will resume our fight from before, the guardian angel snarled into Ginnette's mind.

She won't. You'll see.

Ginnette and the angel floated behind Holden as he thanked the teacher outside the room for letting him work on his painting and walked to the gym. He hesitated, then strode to Makayla's table.

Thank you, Ginnette said to Celeste.

You're welcome.

"Hi," Holden said to Makayla.

Makayla raised her head. Her eyes were puffy from crying. "I thought you wouldn't be here."

"Same."

"Why did you come?"

"I was hoping I'd run into you, but after you didn't show up for the dinner, I hid in the art room. I figured I'd try to find you one more time before I left."

"I'm glad you're here. We need to talk."

Holden swallowed. "I'm sorry about Ginnette. Please, don't keep pushing me away. I miss you."

Go, Holden. Makayla needed to hear this.

"I know." Tears cascaded like shooting stars from Makayla's eyes.

"Are you breaking up with me?"

Makayla hugged herself. "I can't be with anyone right now."

Yes, you can. I came all this way to help you heal from grief and attend your perfect prom. Stay with Holden, Ginnette told her sister, but Makayla didn't look in her direction.

The two guardian angels hovered nearby. They couldn't prevent this conversation from turning any more than Ginnette could.

With a wave of her hands, Ginnette blew Makayla's purse open and upended the contents on the floor.

Makayla turned from the tense moment. She knelt to pick up her fallen stuff. "Shit. I must have left this open earlier."

Makayla grabbed some lipstick, her wallet, a compact, her phone, and then paused.

"Are you okay?" Holden joined Makayla on the ground.

Ginnette got closer to see what Makayla was holding and fist pumped.

"I'm fine," Makayla said, but her voice quavered.

Holden took the object from her hand. "Why did you take off your locket and put it in your purse? You always wear it."

"I can't anymore."

"Why not?"

"Open it."

Holden did.

Inside the necklace was a picture of Ginnette and Makayla with their arms wrapped around each other. Ginnette had given the locket to Makayla for her birthday last year.

The inscription glinted in the light of the disco ball. It said, *Sisters, forever and always.*

"She wanted you to be happy like you are in this picture," Holden said. "If being with me makes you happy, she would want that for you. Don't break up with me."

Finally, someone understood Ginnette.

Makayla considered Holden and nodded. He gently moved her hair aside and put the locket around Makayla's neck.

With a gust of wind, Ginnette spun a record on the DJ booth to a slow song. The young disk jockey removed his headphones and looked around but soon swayed to the music.

"May I have this dance?" Holden asked.

"You may."

Makayla took Holden's hand and stood with him. He placed her purse back on the table and led her to the dance floor.

The couple held each other close. Ginnette drifted over in time to hear Holden say, "I love you, Makayla, and I promise to help you get through this."

"I love you, too," Makayla said.

I love you both.

Somewhere nearby, a clock struck midnight. Holden kissed Makayla on the lips as the disco ball pulsed like a heartbeat. Then, Ginnette was swept away into another luminescence that could only be described as heavenly.

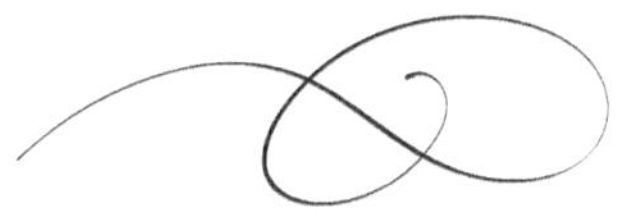

LAST DANCE

BY JESSICA K. FOSTER

last dance
colors ricochet across the dance floor
blue
       red
green
       yellow
like Christmas lights, the end of an era

wall to wall, bodies drenched
in too much cologne
                sweat
                   tension
grind unceremoniously against each other
taffeta against tweed, a precursor to parties later

this is what I came for

I am the succubus of prom-night passion
the music writhes within me
its sharp talons scraping against my loins legs bent,
arms hypnotic as
I caress the hot air above

I want to lose my mind
          taste possibility poured into punch
                    and never think about tomorrow

LIMBO HIGH

BY KATE DEMAIO

CASSIE COULDN'T SHAKE HER headache. Her chest tightened under her thrifted vintage tee shirt. She reminded herself to breathe as she stepped out of the car. She tried to convince herself that this town, this school, would be different. But the building's facade wasn't convincing. She'd thought her last high school was decrepit. This place looked like it should've been condemned years ago. Cracks snaked up the concrete columns at the entrance. The door handle shook under her grasp as she entered the unfamiliar building.

It was her fault she was here. She could blame her mom for making them move, but Cassie knew what she was doing when she stormed out that last night.

"Ditch the smoking buddies, or we're leaving town," her mom had said, though *buddies* was a bit of a stretch. Cassie wasn't sure she'd classify the people she hung out with as friends. They were just people she spent time with that weren't the absolute worst. She wasn't going to miss them.

Her mother's supposed threat was actually exactly what Cassie wanted to hear. She would give anything to leave the small town she grew up in, the place where everything reminded her of Daphne. Each morning, Cassie passed the playground where she had broken her wrist falling off the swings. She didn't remember the pain now. What was burned into her mind was Daphne trying like hell to distract her while the ambulance came. Somehow, broken bones had become happy memories.

As they grew older, that same playground had become their nightly escape. Daphne was the only one who could make Cassie smile through her parents divorce. They'd sit at the bottom of the slide tossing M&M's in the air, only catching the candy in their mouths about ten percent of the time. Daphne would laugh, and Cassie's worries floated away in the wind.

If switching schools at the worst possible time was how she stopped the memories replaying in her head, then so be it. She made sure her mother's threat wasn't an empty one. Cassie slammed the door on her way out of the house before leaving to hang out with the "smoking buddies".

Headphones in, Cassie kept her head down as she moved to her assigned locker. Someone had taped a flier to it.

Limbo High's Senior Prom
A Night Among Spirits
Dress Your Unearthly Best

Cassie's lip curled. This town really leaned into the whole "Limbo" thing. Just because you're named for the afterlife's waiting room doesn't mean everything has to be ghost themed. The deadly theme was only slightly better than the Snowball Prom her old school was hosting. A snow theme in spring didn't even make sense. Cassie pressed a flat hand onto the flier, and in one swift movement, crumpled it into a ball.

"Not into prom?" a boy said to her right. A denim jacket with tombstone patches sewn into it hung over his broad shoulders.

Cassie jumped. He'd appeared out of nowhere. He leaned on the locker next to hers, seeming oblivious to the fact that class started in a few minutes. Cassie was aware of the time though. Not because she particularly liked Spanish, but because she wasn't going to be late on her first day. She didn't need any more attention than she'd already have being the strange new girl. She was sure rumors would abound as to why someone would need to switch schools this late in the semester.

"Not into dressing up and dancing half-heartedly," Cassie replied. The idea of exchanging her sweatpants for a dress with thin fabric and straps that didn't fit right already had her squirming.

"So you go all out? I'd like to see that." The boy's smirk touched his gray eyes. They seemed to glimmer under the school's harsh fluorescent lighting.

Cassie rolled her eyes, forcing herself to break eye contact. "I'm going to be late." She closed her locker and turned to walk away, but the boy managed to get in a few last words.

"I'm Zo, by the way." His voice grew louder as Cassie retreated. "I'll get to work on my promposal."

Something inside Cassie warmed. She tried to push the feeling down, but heat forced its way into her cheeks. She was glad to have distanced herself from Zo. He couldn't see her blush.

When Cassie saw the neon locker from down the hall, she prayed to all that was holy it wasn't hers. The closer she got to it, the more sure she became that it was her locker, and the more she wanted to run. She could turn around, never return, drop out of school. Cassie scrunched her eyes closed. She dragged her feet until she was moving in slow motion. Bright pink post-it's covered the locker like fish scales. Bright yellow ones spelled out *Prom?* And suddenly, there Zo was again, wearing the same denim jacket from the day before.

"Don't you own any other clothes?" Cassie peeled post-its off her locker, starting with the yellow ones. She was sure other girls would've started filming the second they saw the proposal, but Cassie would rather shut herself inside the locker than be part of some viral promposal video.

"I like this jacket." Zo shrugged. "So, what do you think?"

"I don't like the jacket," Cassie retorted.

Zo gave Cassie a playful nudge. His touch sent goosebumps down her arm. "What do you think about prom? Will you go with me?"

Cassie paused. She could go with him. She hadn't gotten out of the house much since she'd moved. But then she'd have to find a dress and shoes. She'd have to do something to her perpetually flat hair. She found herself frowning.

Zo seemed to read her mind. "Come on, it's one night of torture for a lifetime of memories. And I worked really hard on that." He nodded at the post-its in Cassie's hand before breaking into a wide grin. "Look, I won't even make fun of you if you wear sneakers with your dress."

Cassie's head dropped to get a better look at her well-worn shoes. They were more scuffed than she remembered. Maybe she couldn't judge Zo for his jacket. "When is it again?"

Zo put a dramatic hand over his heart. "Is that a yes?"

Cassie rolled her eyes. "It's an *I'll think about it.*"

It had taken Cassie an ungodly amount of time to select her prom dress. Mostly, she scanned racks and racks of floral dresses, not wanting to touch any of them. She'd finally found a no-frills navy blue dress. She was surprised at her reflection when she tried it on. Did something pretty actually fit her well? There were no straps to worry about, which left her feeling a little exposed, but the way the fabric hugged her waist almost made up for it.

Still, Cassie gave herself a moment to confront the dress in her closet on prom night. What if it didn't look the same as it did in the changing room mirror? She pulled the gown off the hanger and slipped it on feet first. So far so good. Cassie reached around for the zipper and yanked. Too hard. There was an earth shattering sound of ripping fabric. Cassie's eyes widened.

Well, that was it. She wasn't going to prom. She sat on her bed and fell back onto it.

The ceiling fan spun endlessly. Somehow she was jealous of it. She wished life could be that simple, that some electrical impulse could tell her what to do. Eat. Drink. Dance. Smile. Maybe it had been like that once. But after Daphne died, Cassie was made to feel things she didn't ever want to feel again. It was like all the pieces of her heart that Daphne had mended together were sliced back open. The remaining, barely-beating scraps only held grief.

She pushed the thought away. Daphne would laugh if she knew Cassie was envious of a ceiling fan, anyway. There was a knock on the door.

"How's it going in there?" Cassie's mom asked.

"Not great," Cassie replied in a sarcastic, sing-song voice.

Her mother entered the room without warning.

"I didn't say you could come in," Cassie said sternly.

"You're right. I'm sorry. I just... I had to check on you. Make sure you're okay. I know this year has been tough." Cassie's mom sat on the bed beside her. "You look great," she said, ignoring the fact Cassie was clearly spiraling.

"My dress ripped, I'm not going."

Her mom put a gentle hand on Cassie's forearm. "I'm sure we can fix it."

"By moving away again?" The words came out harsher than she meant them. Her mother's gaze fell to the floor. Cassie tried retracting her statement. Maybe it was time to let her mom know how she felt, how she'd been feeling for the past year.

She inhaled a small breath. "It's like I lost everything when I lost Daphne. I'm not even sure who I am without her." As she said the words aloud, the tight feeling she'd been holding in her chest loosened just a bit.

"I know." Her mother nodded slowly. "But I'm here. I'm not as cool or as funny as Daphne was, but I'm still here. I know who you are."

Cassie let her mother's words sink in. Her mom was probably the only person who could know Cassie as well as Daphne did, and she'd always been there for her. It was her mom who drove Cassie to Daphne's funeral, her mom who made sure her friend's headstone always had flowers.

"Maybe I can sew your dress back together. Let me take a look."

Cassie took a moment before sitting up. As her back lifted off the bed, there was a distinct breeze on her skin where the fabric had ripped. She put a hand behind her to assess the damage.

"Or maybe you can wear one of my dresses," her mother said, coming to the same conclusion that the dress was too far gone.

Cassie groaned.

"One of your brother's suits then?" She was trying to be supportive, but it wasn't working.

Cassie fell back onto the bed.

"Let me see what I have." Her mother stood, and Cassie continued staring at the ceiling fan. "I promise they're not all old-people clothes."

Cassie couldn't help it. Her mouth tipped up at the corners. "Thanks, Mom." She meant it in more ways than one.

Cassie arrived at prom in a black bridesmaids dress. It wasn't anything like her mother's style, and thank God for that. Cassie tried to not be bitter about the fact that her date couldn't meet her at home. What if it was all part of a plan to stand her up? She didn't have any other friends. She'd walk home if he didn't show.

Cassie stepped into the historic building. She had to admit it was the perfect venue. It seemed like the prom committee had convinced the 1800's house to decorate everything in midnight hues. Thick velvety curtains hung over floor-to-ceiling windows. A glimmering chandelier was draped in black lace, and a full moon, which they had almost definitely stolen from the theatre's props department, hung over the fireplace.

Cassie handed her ticket to the overly smiley junior at the entrance. She raised her dress so as not to trip on it. Fresh high top shoes shined up at her. Being new, they weren't that much more practical than heels. She might still get blisters. But they were at least much more Cassie.

Large round tables dotted the main room. Cassie hesitated. She hadn't gone to junior prom, so she didn't know how this worked. Were there assigned seats? Or could she sit anywhere? And if she could sit anywhere, which table would be the least horrible? She cursed the formal atmosphere for making her feel even more insecure than usual. She turned, avoiding the tables altogether and moving to the refreshments.

"You made it." Zo sidled up to her. "And in sick shoes I might add."

Cassie wasn't used to boys taking notice of her shoes. She wasn't used to boys taking notice of her in general. "Yeah, I... My mom was saving them."

Lame, she chided herself.

"I'm glad the occasion warranted breaking them out of the box." Zo leaned in closer. "Do you want to dance? I heard you have the best moves."

Cassie nearly choked on her drink. "No, I'm good. Have to hydrate first, ya know?" Hydrate first? When had she turned into her grandfather? This whole *be nice to the boy who asked you to prom* thing was not going well.

Zo guided Cassie to a mostly empty table. A couple sat across from them, though they were more interested in the inside of each other's mouths than the newcomers.

"They're announcing King and Queen soon," Zo said, a little too excitedly.

"*Prom* King and Queen? You actually care about that?" Cassie hadn't expected her less-than-fashionable date to give a single thought to some outdated tradition.

"It's an important rite of passage," he said earnestly. "Part of the high school experience."

"Right." Cassie's eyes rolled of their own volition. At least Zo had resumed his role of being the cheesy one.

Thumping pop music faded away into silence.

"Excuse me," another smiley girl said into a microphone at the front of the room. A few prom goers stopped to listen, though most ignored her completely. She continued, "We have the results for Prom Court." She shook a beige envelope in the air and paused for an uncomfortably long time to build anticipation that wasn't there. Cassie didn't know any of these people. And she was sure everyone else already knew whichever popular couple was going to win. Two other members of the prom committee carried out an easel covered by a thick linen tablecloth. It looked like the winners had a full-sized poster of themselves printed. What was the point of the envelope then?

Smiley finally opened it. "This year, the title of Prom Queen goes to someone incredibly deserving, an inspiration to us all whose life was cut too short." Cassie's heart stopped. Daphne had only made it to sixteen. She would've loved to be Prom Queen. She deserved it, too. Cassie could almost see Daphne waltzing on stage in an overly fluffy yet somehow timeless pink dress.

The prom committee members beside the easel pulled the tablecloth off. Cassie reeled at her own headshot staring back at her. She whipped around to face Zo. "What's going on?"

"You won," he said encouragingly. A weak smile rose on his face.

Cassie shook her head in disbelief. "Why are they talking about me like I died?"

Zo reached for Cassie's hand.

She pulled it away. "This is a disgusting prank."

"It's not a prank, Cassie," Zo said gently. "Limbo High isn't a normal high school. It's where spirits go to move on. I'm your guide to the afterlife."

Cassie stood, infuriated. "You think this is funny? I thought you were my friend."

Zo shook his head. "It's not funny, Cassie. It's the truth. What's the last thing you remember before you arrived at Limbo High?"

"I was... We moved." Cassie furrowed her brow. She couldn't actually remember moving. She couldn't remember packing or renting a truck. Had they flown? "But my mom..." Cassie gripped the dress her mom had lent her.

"I'm sorry about that," Zo said. "I had to make it feel real. So you could be at peace. If it means anything, she got to experience the moment, too. You visited her dream."

Cassie was aware of the dozens of eyes around the room waiting for a reaction. And then, suddenly, she wasn't. Everyone was gone—the smileys, the lovebirds. Cassie and Zo were alone in the old house. It seemed smaller now, and it felt like everything that remained—the tablecloths, the curtains—were all holding their breath with her.

Someone grabbed Cassie's hand, but it wasn't Zo this time. She turned to see Daphne, her smile sweet as ever. "Want to see how it happened?"

Cassie froze. Daphne was here, looking just as rosy cheeked as she remembered. So... this was really happening. The room began to spin. Cassie squeezed

Daphne's hand to steady herself. Would seeing her last moments help her understand?

She didn't have to answer. Her final moments flashed before her.

Thick snowy flakes slapped against the windshield. She should've been home by eleven, but curfew was the last thing on her mind. Curfew was something normal teenagers worried about. Cassie had lost her ability to be normal the day she lost her best friend. She was alone in the world. Nothing was how it was supposed to be.

Sometime after midnight, the temperature dropped. The roads became slippery. A blinding light shocked her system. A screeching sound rang in her ears. The semi-truck couldn't stop in time. Cassie swerved. She shrieked. "Sorry, Mom."

It wasn't how she expected she'd react. But Cassie was sorry—sorry for slamming the door, sorry for ditching her family to be with people that didn't care about her. *I'll be better. I promise.* Cassie pleaded with the universe. She would try to see joy the way she used to. She'd try to care again. She wanted to leave town, but not this way, not this permanently.

It was too late.

There was no pain. Maybe that was Zo's doing. Or maybe Daphne shielded her from the hurt the way she always had. The lines between memory and reality blurred. Was anything real anymore? Cassie clung to the memory of her mother sitting with her on the bed, offering to sew an unfixable dress. The lights in the car dimmed as the ones at prom faded.

"Get home safe," someone said as Cassie was escorted into the afterlife.

Lucky Penny

By Kelly Kandra Hughes

Normally, I would revel in going to prom as a single person. But as I'm now going as a dumped-one-week-before-prom single person, my outlook is entirely different. Especially the way I got dumped.

I stop sliding dresses down the sales rack at Diamonds & Pearls Consignment Shoppe and pull out my phone. I re-read Sophia's texts for the three hundred and twenty-seventh time.

OMG!

Casting loved me!!

Offered Role!!!

Starting immediately!!!

Mom & I leave for NYC in a few hours!!!!

Been thinking...

I want a fresh start here.

So...

we should break up.
Okay?

No, Sophia's suggestion is *not* okay. But what am I supposed to say? *Skip your life's dream to go to prom with me*, or *can't you wait a week?* Both responses are ridiculous, given the circumstances.

What about my dress? It's bad enough I no longer have a date or a girlfriend. But not to have a prom dress? I should have insisted I take Sophia's dress home with me after she said I could borrow it.

Instead of any of those responses, I texted back a solitary letter.

K

It's adequate and summed up how I felt about our relationship at that moment. Or the demise of it, to be more accurate. Sophia never responded. I can't blame her. That one letter says a lot.

"Cass, what do you think of this one?" Jayden holds up a dress. It's a gorgeous summer-green color with a gathered bodice, criss-cross pattern on the sides, and a mermaid skirt. This dress sparkles, both literally and figuratively. But it's not for me. I'm sure the whole school knows by now what happened with Sophia. My dress needs to be spectacular if I'm going to show up alone *and* dumped.

I shake my head and slip my phone into my back pocket.

"I'm going to try this on." Jay holds the dress up to her body.

"You already have a dress! Please, Jay, there's no time for that. Prom is in five days. I need you to keep searching. If I can't find the perfect dress, I'm not going."

"Fine." Jayden returns the dress to the rack and pulls off another. "How about this one?"

The dress is slinky with pink sequins. My stomach flip-flops at the sight of it. The dress reminds me of something, but I can't remember exactly what.

Just as I'm about to ask Jayden if the dress seems familiar, someone comes up behind her and snatches it out of her hands.

"Hey!" Jayden whips around, ready to fight for the dress, but I'm stone still. Of course, I would run into Sophia's other ex-girlfriend here, the one who may still have been dating Sophia when I asked her out. In my defense, I didn't know at first.

"Pepto Bismol pink. Perfect for someone like you, Cass." The look on Bree's face makes it clear she hasn't forgiven me yet.

She's not wrong. About the color, that is. Thanks to Bree, I now know why the dress seems so familiar. Chugging Pepto Bismol is how I coped with being bisexual in junior high. How nice to have those memories flooding back to me now.

As for calling me a crappy person, which I assume is what Bree's implying, that's just rude. I ignore her and slide a few more dresses down the rack.

My heart stops as I take in the most beautiful dress I've ever seen. This dress also seems familiar but in a very different way. And, once again, I can't figure out why.

Okay, calm yourself. Poker face on. Don't let Bree see your interest. I face her with what I hope is an annoyed look.

"I'm surprised to see you here. Aren't you too good for a second-hand store?" I make air quotes around the words, *too good*. Shoot. Is that the right use of air quotes? It's too late now. I chalk up the mistake to losing my mind over the dress in front of me.

An evil grin spreads across Bree's face. "Not at all. Especially when I'm here to help out a friend."

"Okay, so why don't you go do that and leave us alone?" I try to make it clear I'm completely disinterested in whatever Bree is doing here, but it's so freaking hard knowing I am *this close* to my dream dress.

"I already did. I dropped off a bunch of Sophia's stuff for her. She asked me on her way out of town. Came over to apologize for the way she treated me. Said she wanted a fresh start." Bree smirks as she makes air quotes around the words, *fresh start*. "I'd tell you more, but I'm not one to kiss and tell."

The word, *kiss,* pains me like a stiletto stabbed in my chest. Did Sophia tell Bree about how she dumped me? Did she kiss Bree goodbye? Did they do more than kiss? I steel myself. I will not give Bree the satisfaction of responding.

Bree's smile gets wider. "If I'm not mistaken, the dress you were supposed to wear was in the pile I just dropped off."

Despite my best efforts to stay calm, I sway as the store goes blurry. Why wouldn't Sohpia give me the dress if she was planning to get rid of it? Did my *K* text response upset her that much? Does she hate me now? I move closer to my dream dress for support. I *will* get through this.

Jayden comes over and hooks her arm through mine. She might be five feet tall, but with her confidence, she makes one heck of a support.

"If you're done with your good deed for the decade, why don't you get out of here?" she says to Bree.

"What, and miss all the fun of Cass trying to find a last-minute prom dress? No thanks. In fact, let's see what she's trying so hard to hide from me."

Damn it! I never did have a good poker face. Before Bree takes more than two steps forward, I break free from Jayden and snatch the dress off the rack, holding it close. "Forget it, Bree. This dress is mine."

Bree rolls her eyes. "So dramatic. Maybe you should have been the one to go to Broadway. Can't you take a little joke?" Her gaze moves up and down the dress in front of me, and her face momentarily betrays her vindictive sneer with a flash of awe. I clutch the dress tighter. She will not get this one. I can't explain it, but somehow, I know this dress is meant for me.

"Whatever. That dress is gaudy. It suits you perfectly. Enjoy your find." Bree makes air quotes again around the word, *find*, and I feel sick to my stomach. What I wouldn't give for my trusty junior high bottle of Pepto Bismol now.

"You okay?" Jayden turns to face me after Bree leaves us. She must see something awful on my face because she says quietly, "Don't let that bitch get to you. Come on, let's see this dress you've found."

I watch Bree slither out the front door. She turns around to look at me again, but it's not me she's looking at—it's the dress I'm holding. This isn't over between us, not by a long shot. It isn't until the door has shut firmly behind her that I hold up the hanger so Jayden can see the dress.

The color is a deep gold that reminds me of butterscotch. The top is sleeveless, with embroidered flowers across the bodice, and the neckline and back are open. There's an embroidered flower collar that wraps around the neck, which is my favorite part. The dress is belted with a ribbon above a perfect tulle, knee-length, A-line skirt. Flowers identical to the ones on the neck circle the hips.

"Cass, oh, my God. That dress..."

"I know, right?" I grin at her, even though I can't get Bree out of my head. She totally knows how Sophia dumped me. And for Sophia to see her before she left town, especially with the dress she said I could borrow? And that they kissed? Devastating. I force myself back to the glory of my hopefully soon-to-be prom dress. Please let it fit.

Jayden strokes the flowers. "I've seen this dress before."

"Yeah. I know what you mean. It seems so familiar, right?"

Jayden's eyes go wide. "No, Cass. I mean, I've *seen* this dress before. So have you. So have millions of people all over the world."

My mouth drops open as my brain connects the dress with a memory of a movie we saw a few weeks ago. "This can't be the original. Surely, it's a copy." I hold the dress out as far as my arms can go. "It looks just like it, though."

"Try it on!"

I don't need to be told twice. Within seconds, my jeans and sweater are discarded on the dressing room floor. The dress exceeds every expectation I have. It's like a fairy godmother whipped up this dress for me using sunshine, gold, tulle, and a tape measure. I half expect to float away with the magic of it all.

Jayden beams at me. "I guess you're going to prom after all?"

"I wouldn't miss it for the world. Not with this dress." I can't wait to get home to post about it on my Vizion social media account. I'm going to tag every single second-hand style influencer I follow to show off my find.

After I take the dress off, I carry it to the cash register like I'm holding Cinderella's glass slippers. This thought reminds me I also need a new pair of shoes.

The owner of Diamonds & Pearls appears out of nowhere. "Cass! I have the perfect shoes for that dress in the back. Just your size."

I should feel startled, but instead, I lean into the magic of the dress. Something tells me prom will be a night I'll never forget.

Mrs. Embry brings out a pair of glittery pointed-toe stiletto slip-ons. "Size seven and a half."

Jayden takes the dress from me and we make eyes at each other. These are the same shoes from the movie! I'd know them anywhere. I kick off my shoes and socks and slide on the stilettos. Wow. My feet look like they could walk a Hollywood red carpet.

"You're right," I tell Mrs. Embry. "Perfect."

She claps her hands together. "Penny will be so happy her dress and shoes have found the right home."

"What do you mean?"

"Penelope Jordan. The actress who stars in those vampire movies you kids love so much. The latest one came out two weeks ago." Mrs. Embry gestures to the dress and shoes. "She wore these in that infamous prom scene."

I shake my head slowly. My ears hear what Mrs. Embry is saying, but my brain can't believe it.

Jayden puts a hand on my shoulder. Since we share a brain cell, she knows I'm in a state of shock.

"How do you know?" she asks on my behalf.

"She told me!" Mrs. Embry winks, and there's a twinkle in her eyes that rivals the sparkle of Penelope's shoes. "I can't tell you all my secrets, but let's just say I have connections. May I?" She gestures towards the dress.

Jayden looks at me, and I nod. She holds it out, and Mrs. Embry takes it and runs her hands along the bodice lining.

"Ah, there it is. Can you feel that?" She offers a section of the dress to me.

There's something small, round, and hard sewn into the material. "Is that a penny?"

"Yes," Mrs. Embry says. "For good luck. Penny often asks a costuming assistant to sew one into her most important dresses on set. Usually right over her heart if the dress can manage it. She says that's why her movies are so successful."

"If that's the case, why didn't she keep this dress?"

I wouldn't think it possible, but Mrs. Embry's smile widens. "Penny is a firm believer that her success should be shared. Today, my dear Cass, is your lucky day."

She's not kidding. Here I was, worried about going to the prom as a dumped person, and now I'm going in a dress worn by a famous teen actress in the most popular movie in the country right now. I should thank Sophia for dumping me the way she did.

But I'm not going to—final decision. In the time it takes me to buy the dress and shoes and get back home to my bedroom, I've gone back and forth ninety-seven times if I should text Sophia how grateful I am that she dumped me. Jayden says absolutely not, under no circumstances am I to let Sophia know that I'm even thinking about her. She's right. So, I do what I planned.

I take multiple photos of the dress and upload them to Vizion. Not the shoes, though. I want there to be some element of surprise with my prom ensemble when I walk into the ballroom. The only thing left is to tag Penelope Jordan. Just as I'm about to post, I hesitate. Something inside me wants to keep the dress's previous owner a secret. I delete Penelope's tag and change the post to how grateful I am to have found such a beautiful dress at Diamonds & Pearls, especially since I'm going to prom single.

Let's hear it for secondhand style, I write. I post it before I can change my mind again.

I usually scroll through Vizion while I wait for others to like and comment on my posts. The magic of this dress is that I don't care what anyone else thinks—it's beautiful, stunning, and absolutely perfect for me. So, instead, I head to the bathroom to play around with my hair and makeup until I have the absolute right look for prom night. The one thing I don't want to do on my own is my nails. I deserve some pampering before prom. I pick up my phone to make a mani-pedi appointment for Saturday afternoon when I know Jayden will be there, too.

Since I already have my phone in hand, I open up Vizion to peek at my dress post. I'm shocked at the number of likes it already has. Secondhand style influencers commend me on such a good find. Friends say how beautiful I'm going to look. Some comment on how the dress looks exactly like the one worn by Penelope Jordan in her latest movie.

Then, I see the comment from BreeZee123: *Is this your "fresh start?" It looks like a cheap knockoff.*

I lose my self-control at the quotation marks. I might have been able to restrain myself otherwise. Without thinking, I whip off a reply: *Takes one to know one. You and Sophia deserve each other.*

The satisfaction lasts for approximately seven seconds. That's when I glimpse the dress reflected in my vanity mirror. A dress worn by Penelope Jordan deserves better than Bree and me taking cheap shots at each other online. I delete the comment. What's better than a cheap shot? How about a single letter?

K.

The utility of this letter continues to impress me. I close the Vizion app. I have better things to do with my time.

For the rest of the week, I don't even look at my Vizion account. This dress deserves to be drama-free, and so do I.

Jayden, however, is not happy with my choice. She complains as we soak our feet at Heavenly Spa & Nails. Her hair is intricately braided in an updo, and her make-up looks so natural, I'm convinced she's not wearing any. Prom is now a mere five hours away.

"I've sent you a bazillion DMs this week that you haven't responded to. I feel so unloved."

I roll my eyes. "My love for you is completely unrelated to unopened DMs, and you know it." I grab her phone out of her hand, being extra careful not to drop it in the foot bath.

"Say corsage!" We pose for a pre-prom selfie. I take the liberty of posting it to her Vizion account with an update on where we are and how we're going to get smoothies after this. I show it to her when I'm done. "Now, do you feel loved?"

"Yeah, I do." Jay smiles and reaches out to squeeze my arm. "I'm so glad you're going to be there tonight. I would have missed you so much."

We spend the rest of our time at the spa gossiping about prom, graduation, summer, and college. When Jay drives us home, we're ready to take on the world. For me, that means killing it solo at prom in my Penelope Jordan dress and shoes. I'm still glad I kept who the dress belonged to a secret.

I walk through the front door, and my parents wave at me from their respective positions in the family room.

"Lookin' good, Cass," Dad calls out, and Mom blows me a kiss before she goes back to her webinar.

Nothing can spoil my mood. I don't care if Sophia and Bree appear at my door, hanging all over each other. Tonight is all about showing up and having a good time, even if I don't have a date.

The moment I enter my bedroom, something's wrong. My eyes zero in on the dress—or what used to be the dress. Scraps of fabric lay in a pile on the floor. Jagged edges and frayed threads call out to me in distress.

No!

I'm on my knees by my closet, picking up the scraps and examining them. *What happened?* It looks like someone attacked the dress with scissors. I'm too dizzy to think coherently, and tears are already streaming down my face. That's when I hear the bird. The *chirp, chirp, chirp* is so loud, I can't help but turn my head towards the sound. My window is open a crack. It's just enough to allow the sound to penetrate my room. But I closed my window before I left for the spa this afternoon.

As the bird chatters away, I stare at the open window. With every *chirp, chirp, chirp,* my brain puts the pieces together of what must have happened. How many times did Sophia sneak through my window when she was my girlfriend? She knows the trick to get it open from the outside. She must have told Bree how to get in here. They did this to me, to the dress.

Tears fall onto the torn-up material. Thank goodness I didn't get my makeup professionally done. It would have been a complete waste. Just like this dress—this beautiful, magical, spectacular dress. It didn't deserve to be butchered like this. I'm not crying because of what Sophia and Bree did to me. I'm crying because of what they did to the dress.

I sit crisscross on the floor and pull all the scraps into my lap. That's when I see it. There's writing in black eyeliner on what's left of the belt.

You and this dress deserve each other.

My heart pounds away at the memory of what I said on Vizion. Even though I only kept that rude comment posted for seven seconds, it was enough time for one of them to see it. Destroying my dress is their revenge.

Anger bubbles through my veins. They may get away with this, but they won't get the final word. I wipe the tears from my eyes and take stock of my situation. That's when I see them sitting there, tucked away in my closet. Penelope's shoes. They're still perfect. Bree didn't know about them, so she wouldn't think to destroy them, too.

I jump up from the floor and push open my closet doors as far as they go. I dig out my basic black strapless dress that goes with everything and give it a sniff. A spritz of some peppermint vanilla body spray will do.

I rush into the bathroom and jump into the shower. My hair is washed and dried in record time while my curling iron heats up. Soft waves soon fall down my back.

Now it's time for my makeup. I have to breathe deeply a few times so my hands stop shaking. When they finally do, I go for a much subtler look than I practiced. Penelope's shoes will be the star tonight.

When I finish getting dressed, I slip them on and check myself in the mirror. Not bad. Not bad at all. I'm jazzed at the idea of going to prom anyway as *my* act of revenge. How dare they take away the magic of Penelope's dress?

I check myself in the mirror again. My look isn't yet complete, so I add small black earrings. Something is still missing. What else is in my jewelry drawer? My stomach twists at the sight of the perfect necklace, a shiny gold locket attached to a wide black ribbon. Unfortunately, it was a gift from Sophia. Can I really wear something that she gave me? I open the locket and stare at Sophia's senior class photo.

"Like I would take *you* to prom," I say with disgust as I rip her out.

Inspiration strikes. I dig through the fabric scraps still on my floor until I find the piece that holds Penelope Jordan's lucky penny.

Snap! The penny is now safely enclosed in the locket. I tie the ribbon around my neck and look at myself in the mirror again.

The magic of the dress still lives in the penny. I *am* beautiful. Prom date or not. Penelope Jordan's dress or not. Tonight is prom, and I'm going to love it because my best friend in the world will be there and I'm graduating soon and want these memories. To hell with anyone else who tries to ruin this moment for me.

There's a knock on the door. When I say, "Come in, " Dad pops his head into my room.

"There's someone here for you," he says. He's wide-eyed and nervous, and it takes him a moment too long to recognize how spectacular I look. As he belat-edly showers me with compliments, I raise my guard.

"Who's here?"

He shakes his head. "You better come see."

"Is it Sophia? Because you can tell her to—"

Dad holds up a hand. "It's not Sohpia. Seriously, Cass. You need to go downstairs. Now."

He leads the way out of my room, and I follow. Surely, it's not Bree. She wouldn't dare show her face here. Maybe Jay has come as a surprise. But why would Dad be acting so weird if it's her?

With Dad in front of me on the stairs, I can't see who's in the entryway until we're practically face to face.

"Holy shit," I say. My eyes flick to my parents. "Sorry, Mom. Dad."

"I think it's appropriate in this situation," Mom says. "We'll be in the kitchen if you need us. Come on, hon." Mom grabs Dad by the arm and drags him down the hallway.

I'm left with a tall, beautiful young woman standing before me. She's wearing a draped white satin dress with a deep v-neckline and high slit. She looks slightly confused as she holds out her hand. "Cass? I'm Penny Jordan. Sorry for intruding. I saw on Vizion that you bought my dress at Diamonds & Pearls." Her brows knit together further. "I thought you'd be wearing it to your prom tonight."

My heart jumps into my throat as I shake her hand, making it impossible to speak. I manage to swallow it back down after two gulps. "I wanted to wear it tonight. Something unexpected happened." I bite my lip, reluctant to say more about how my petty high school drama ruined something so beautiful.

Penny laughs. "I don't suppose this has anything to do with those incredibly rude comments by someone named BreeZee123 or SophiaTheStar?"

I could kick myself. "Probably. I haven't looked at my account all week."

"I'm impressed." Penny smiles at me, and my guts nearly fall to the floor. Who knew standing in my hallway having a simple conversation could feel like a spin on a tilt-a-whirl? Thank goodness my dress is tight enough to keep everything in place. "It can be so hard to ignore Internet trolls. You must have a lot of restraint."

"Something like that."

We stare at each other. It's not lost on me that one of the biggest teen stars on the planet is standing in my hallway looking like she's ready to go to prom. Would it be rude to ask why she's here?

"Do you want the dress back?" *Please say no.* How can I tell her the dress is now scrap material?

Penny shakes her head. "Let's just say I was already impressed before I got here. Mrs. Embry told me you knew the dress was mine. I was intrigued when you posted about it but didn't mention my name."

I don't know what to say, so I tell her the truth. "I wanted to keep it a secret. That dress is... was ... special. It seemed like the right thing to do."

At my use of past tense, Penny frowns. "Is the dress okay?"

"I'm so sorry. No." I extend my leg. "Your shoes, however, remain perfect."

"Ah, well. My lucky penny wasn't so lucky for you, after all."

My hand flies to the locket on my necklace. Penny gives me a curious look, and I open it up to show her.

"I don't know," I tell her. "I feel pretty lucky right now."

"Me, too." Penny holds up a corsage, a slight flush to her face. "I saw on Vizion that you didn't have a date tonight. Would you like to take me to your prom?"

I knew that dress was magic the moment I saw it.

I say the only thing I can think of.

"K."

My Girlfriend and Her Demon

By Arwyn Sherman

It's not every day one goes to prom, or every day one sacrifices someone to a demon. Ezra is more concerned about the latter, but the former is also a point of anxiety as he drives his girlfriend to the gymnasium.

"It needs to be perfect, or else it won't work." Grace looks at Ezra meaningfully, her golden eyes rimmed with glitter so they look like jars of honey in sunlight.

The dress she chose is stunning, the beadwork making her bust glow like whorled pearls, a soft rose and lilac-sheened lace pushing against her chest. It's a color he's never seen before, each twist revealing a different side of the purple/pink tone. It doesn't match the red orchid corsage he bought under the instructions to match *pink,* and he assumed she meant her usual vibrant hot magenta. She doesn't seem to mind, so he doesn't either.

"Everything will be fine," he says with feigned confidence. He doesn't normally disagree with Grace, but he decides reassuring her is more important than his usual deferring.

"You're too relaxed." Grace looks into the car mirror, fixing the flower-laced buns atop her head.

"I am the opposite of relaxed. Everything is fine *because* I'm the most not-relaxed person you could have tasked with this, so can we just enjoy prom?"

"Such a romantic." The eye roll is so thick in her tone, he doesn't even have to look at her to know it's happening. Her predictability is reassuring, and a smile twitches at the corners of his mouth.

"You didn't start dating me for romance."

"No, it was because my best friend was banging your best friend, and I was bored."

Ezra cracks a smile, and when their eyes meet, they both burst into a fit of giggles.

The joke is an old one, flippantly made without thinking by Grace. For a moment, they laugh like their respective best friends aren't missing. In a quick snap, they remember, sober up, and finish the drive to prom in silence.

Ezra wants to hurry up and find someone to sacrifice, so their friends can come back and they'll stop encountering these moments of ice and discomfort. The city rolls by them, birds hopping in the cold spring, clustering by trash cans, and screaming into the burgeoning night.

Meredith and Jonah have been missing since a romantic weekend trip to the city in December, and everyone is already done talking about it. If only Meredith alone had gone missing, it may have kept their interest longer. Meredith is the type of beauty that would make for a famous missing girl. Her senior photo would be up everywhere, her red hair glinting, green eyes bright. They'd probably do a podcast about her at some point. But she's eighteen and her boyfriend is missing too, so everyone assumes they ran off together, like some kind of cursed lovers into the sunset.

If this were true, Grace and Ezra would know about it. And since they don't, it means Meredith and Jonah haven't left on their own accord.

This is why Grace started looking into the occult, and how the whole demon-sacrifice thing came into play.

Since, you know, none of the other avenues of information gathering were working.

Ezra doesn't anticipate how awkward it is to decide on who to sacrifice. Grace says they should pick at prom. That if they choose someone beforehand and they don't show up, it would throw them off so the best course of action is to wait until the actual night to make their selection.. Ezra is inclined to agree, but he tends to agree with everything Grace says, which is how they've dated for so long.

Prom falls on the correct moon cycle for this particular demon they're trying to summon. Grace says the demon will tell them what happened to Jonah and Meredith, then they can go help them. All that it requires is one human life. Which, in the scheme of things, is actually a pretty good deal. Ezra is reluctant to offer up his own soul, so it was somewhat of a relief that he would just have to kill someone—not that he is some kind of rampant serial killer in the making. But for how intertwined Meredith is to Grace, Ezra is to Jonah, a type of passionate devotion that can only come from being friends at such a young age you don't remember a time without the other. Ezra didn't have to think about what his life was when he was with Jonah. They were a unit. And even when Jonah met Meredith in middle school, it was a readjusting that felt natural. They went from a unit of two to a unit of four.

Every day after school, he'd spend time with the quartet, until Grace's super strict step dad made her go home, then he'd go to Jonah's house for the rest of the night. He eventually slipped into his aunt's house at such a late hour, they didn't have to exchange anything but basic pleasantries before going to bed.

Listless doesn't even begin to describe Ezra without Jonah.

He sighs as they walk inside. A sparse pathetic clutch of balloons bop against the ceiling of the gymnasium. Clusters of awkward teens group together like they do in the lunchroom, but instead of the usual day to day dress, they're in various degrees of glittering formal wear. Ezra's aunt let him wear the same suit his father had worn to prom. It would have been sweet, but Ezra just feels weird that he's wearing his dead father's clothes. He also doesn't have the money to *not*, so he fabreezed the ever-loving shit out of it and hopes Grace doesn't notice it smells like it has been sitting in a closet for over two decades.

If Jonah was still around, he'd probably have "found" an extra suit for Ezra and pretended like it was no big deal to loan him. But he isn't, so moldy dead dad suit it is.

Grace isn't noticing anything about his suit. Ever the predator, she glides amongst the groups with a roving gaze, like she's picking a prized cut of meat from the butchers. The lights make her dress glitter, and she's put golden dust in her hair to make it glimmer as well, her dark brown curls streaked with tiny infinitesimal stars.

Eventually, like always, she returns and tastes like cotton candy lip gloss when she kisses him. Her skin is warm and smooth as their cheeks brush against one another so she can whisper in his ear.

"Sasha Browning," she says in a voice so low, it's barely there.

"She's an only child. I'd feel bad," Ezra responds in a murmur.

"But she's a total mean girl."

"She might grow out of it. You never know. She's like mean but not *mean* mean."

"No, you're right," Grace sighs. "She does do volunteer work, so she might end up nice."

"Well, I don't know about that being a metric." Ezra's eyes flutter in not-quite a roll. "Plenty of horrible people do volunteer work."

"Are we sacrificing her or not?" Grace snaps.

"No, we gotta find someone else."

Grace nods but stays by his side, her elbow brushing against his and making his heart ratchet up. She smells like cherries, and he wants to nuzzle the crook of her neck and inhale every speck of her drugstore perfume. Her eye shadow starts to droop under the technicolor lights but still makes her look becoming.

Before they can continue discussing who to murder, the principal gets on stage to announce this year's Prom King and Queen. The likelihood of him and Grace getting into the court is the same likelihood of his aunt buying him his own suit to wear. Ezra is too quiet to be of note to anyone, and Grace too disliked.

Everyone begins to whisper. Fierce giggles rip through the larger bunches of people. The hackles at the back of Ezra's neck go up. There's something about the snickering that sounds wicked.

Brigette McClane's boyfriend gets crowned king. That's expected. He's tall and into sports and has curly hair that fits neatly under a wide trucker's hat. Brigette McClane has a smug grin on her face, like she knows exactly what is going to happen and is loving it. She knows she is going to be queen. She knows her boyfriend will put the crown on her head, and it will be warmed by his freakishly hot hands, and this will be her pinnacle. This will be what she thinks about for years in the future.

So when the principal calls out Grace's name, everyone is confused. Or most everyone is confused.

Brigette is not. She still looks pleased with herself. The group she's with also doesn't look confused either.

Ezra doesn't like that at all.

He tries to stop Grace from going to the stage, but she shrugs him off. She isn't eager to get up there, more a luscious curiosity. He can tell by the way she walks up the stairs, shoulders rigid and alert. Neck ever so still. Brigette McClane's boyfriend—Ezra thinks his name might be Tyler—moves Grace into position on the stage.

She softens slightly as the crown goes on her head, a small hopeful moment that makes Ezra wonder if her antisocial tendencies are born out of necessity rather than want. But before it can fully form on the creases of her face she's covered in blood.

Tyler had put her right under the landing spot for a bucket precariously positioned somewhere in the rafters. The principal, completely oblivious to this plot, jumps out of the way with a screech. Laughter titters through the crowd.

And then there's Grace, completely drenched in what Ezra assumes is animal refuse.

As he starts to push his way through the crowd toward her, Grace's eyes meet his. They're glowing honey and vibrant. A sly grin creeps up her face, her teeth shocking white against the sea of red around them. She slowly, ever so slowly, reaches her tongue out. The whole gymnasium takes a breath, a ripple of confusion at Grace's demeanor, how she looks like a fox that found a bowl of cream rather than a victim of gore.

Grace smiles and, to everyone's horror, licks the blood off her hand.

Ezra knows then she's decided who they are sacrificing tonight.

Prom ends early after this stunt, the chaperones moving in like dogs herding sheep away from a predator. Grace is left soaking and alone on stage, as though she were the one that is dangerous, not the ones who dumped blood on her. The principal approaches like he didn't run screaming, an apology in his open palms.

With the rush of teenagers leaving, their window to find a sacrifice folds to a close.

Ezra has to move quickly. He slips into the flood of bodies as they flow out into the night.

***

Brigette is the kind of girl who brags about needing to shop in the children's section due to how tiny she is, which makes it really easy to kidnap her. Shockingly easy. So easy, Ezra almost doesn't think he's doing it right, until she's tied up in the trunk and they're heading to the warehouse.

Grace reapplies her lip gloss in the mirror to the cadence of Brigette's frantic thumping. She's wiped as much of the blood off as she can with the towel the principal gave her, but she still glows pink with ridges of dark red at her hairline, clumps of strands that are still dripping with blood.

Ezra picked the warehouse after weeks of scoping out the best place to have a demon sacrifice. He wanted the best intersection of decent location and lack of cameras or curious eyes. Being in the middle of nowhere means they won't get back before Grace's curfew, but too close, they're the next viral paranormal activity caught on

CCTV footage. He'd scoured this one for security cameras, and it is bonafide abandoned. The once immaculate cement wall partially crumbled so it slopes against the hillside, and the place has a rotted wooden door. Even though Ezra knows it's perfect, he still waits a beat for Grace's beam of approval before he feels completely confident about his choice.

Grace holds Brigette in one hand, her fingers clutched around the corded bonds around Brigette's wrists, and Ezra in the other. Brigette struggles, but Grace has about a foot and fifty pounds on her and likes to toss her stepfather's kettlebells around for fun. The swath of fabric Ezra tied as a gag around her head is drenched in spit, and Brigette tries to talk through it, her throat making a *glug glug* noise as she sucks in wet air.

The air of the broken-down warehouse is damp and heavy. Grace drags Brigette to the center and forces her to a seated position. Brigette's eye makeup is completely ruined by her crying, leaving her with big bold raccoon eyes and clownishly smudged cheeks.

"Where's the stuff?" Grace asks.

Ezra goes to what he thinks might have been a chimney and sticks his arm up it, grabbing at the backpack he placed there last week.

Ezra sets everything out piece by piece. A set of long candles. Pouches of herbs that took him two weeks and many hours driving to acquire. A jar of cow liver.

"Where's the valerian root?" Grace asks.

Ezra points to one of the baggies.

"Not fresh?"

"They said store-bought was fine," Ezra says defensively.

Grace nods after a moment and continues parsing through everything, organizing the assortment into a system only she can follow. When she's done, she reaches into her bralette and pulls out a very bloodied folded paper with the demon-summoning spell she photocopied from the library.

Ezra is suddenly worried their plans are thwarted by Brigette's prank. "Can you even read that?"

"Yeah." She waves her hand dismissively. "I have most of it memorized, anyway."

Brigette starts a flailing attempt to scoot towards the door, her body scrunching and un-scrunching against the dusty ground like a worm. Without looking at her, Grace snaps her hand out and grabs Brigette by the hair, dragging her to Grace's thigh.

"I would say nothing personal, but you did dump a bucket of gross shit on me," Grace says mildly as she threads her fingers through Brigette's hair. "Ezra, can you hold the paper so I can do the candle part?"

***

The demon shows up after the first incantation and only one round of herbs. Which, according to Grace's research, is unusual. The protective sigils Ezra painted the day prior keep it from rushing them. Although, from the relaxed way it lounges against the eight-pointed star, it doesn't seem like it particularly needs to be caged.

"We're offering this girl in exchange for information," Grace says with the kind of audacity that only Grace seems to be able to pull off, like she already knows things are going to go her way.

The demon eyes Brigette and does a very obvious once-over of her trembling frame. It looks like a classical demon—broad shoulders, black horns, beady eyes. Everything Ezra thinks a demon would have, and he really hopes he painted the sigils right.

It cleans out from under its fingernails and makes a show of flicking the dirt off before responding.

"She's...not really my type."

"Your type?" Grace says incredulously, the dried blood crinkling under her raised eyebrow. "You're going to eat her, you have a type for that?"

"I am absolutely not eating her. I'm not a degenerate." The demon looks genuinely offended. "I'd be taking her to my realm as an assistant I would eventually seduce, and frankly, she's a bit of a boring rude girl for my tastes. You're spicy enough, but a little too sociopathic, unfortunately."

Grace says, "I'm not up for grabs," at the same time Ezra blurts, "She's not a sociopath, she just has low empathy."

"Which just leaves the boy, and he's a bit too long and feminine."

"I'm not into men," Ezra says.

"Oh, sweetie, you're into everyone. I guess you haven't figured that out yet. My bad," the demon says.

"Okay yes, Ezra is bi and in love with Jonah, we've known this for years," Grace snaps. "But how is this going to work if you don't want our sacrifice?"

"I am not in love with Jonah, I love *you*," Ezra tells Grace, his heart getting weird and fluttery at how flippantly she said this.

"Well, you're in love with both of them. That's totally fine. It happens to a lot of people." The demon speaks in the same cadence as the really nice guidance counselor Ezra was forced to see after his parents died. "Some people actually argue non monogamy is more natural than monogamy, but I'm a demon and don't really do relationships, so I wouldn't know."

"Can we get back to sacrificing Brigette?" Ezra whines, severely disliking where this conversation is going.

"Right. Sorry. Didn't mean to upend your world before you had a chance to go to college and naturally discover your affection for men." The demon doesn't sound sorry at all, and he turns to Grace with the air of a corporate businessman who, like Grace, is used to getting what he wants. "I have a proposal."

"As long as Ezra and I stay here, we're open to it."

Ezra warms at the fact Grace has included him in this caveat. For a moment, he wasn't sure she would. Brigette sputters against the gag in her mouth and looks at Ezra with wide eyes that, despite her only ever being rude to him, seem to implore his sympathy.

"And I want to keep my soul," Ezra adds.

The demon doesn't dignify that with any response.

"So, the underworld is boring," the demon says to Grace. "I want to be up here. But I can't without a human anchor."

"What does being an anchor entail?" Grace asks a little too quickly for Ezra's comfort.

"You would just be responsible for me. I'd turn into a cute little dog, and you'd just have to take care of me."

"Deal," Grace says before Ezra can tell her that's a really bad idea.

"So, what happened to Jonah?" Ezra asks, because if Grace is going to offer up herself as an anchor, he's going to take full advantage.

"Oh, them? They're dead." The demon says this casually, and Ezra's ears fill with rushing blood.

"I'm sorry, what?" he stutters.

"Yeah, there's a serial killer active in the city." The demon does a flippant hand wave. "They picked the wrong weekend to visit."

"Meredith too?" For the first time tonight, Grace's voice is weak, almost a whisper. The slight wiggling at the corner of her mouth tells Ezra she's trying very hard not to cry.

"Well then." The demon claps his hands. "Shall we? I am so very excited to not return to that hell hole."

⁓ ℓℓ ⁓

The dog that the demon turns into is not cute at all.

In fact, it's so the opposite of cute that it's painful to look at. It's small enough that Grace can wrap it up into her arms and almost hairless, but not quite. The snaggletooth at the bottom of its lip competes with the giant wart above its beady eye as the ugliest thing on its face. Luckily it's dark, which hides the rolls against its protruding ribs.

Grace coos and makes kissing noises at the thing. It makes a sound that could be a little bark but sounds like the squelching of a slug getting stepped on. It licks her cheek and wiggles its gremlin little tail. Brigette whimpers loud enough to remind Ezra she's still there.

"What are we doing about her?" He thumbs towards Brigette.

Grace seems to remember they've kidnapped someone, her head cocking slightly as she considers Ezra's inquiry. She thoughtfully strokes the demondog's hairless head, curling her finger around the one curling tuft between its ears and making it more pronounced.

"I don't think anyone will believe her if she says we kidnapped her then summoned a demon," Grace finally declares.

Brigette nods frantically, making incomprehensible noises under her gag. Ezra sighs and kneels by her, slowly tugging off the strip of fabric.

"I promise," Brigette wails. "I won't say anything. I'm sorry. I'm so sorry I played that stupid prank. It wasn't even my idea. I don't know why I did it." Snot comes out of Brigette's button nose, her entire face red from the pressure of crying.

"Oh, my God, I'm murdering her myself if she doesn't shut up," Grace hisses, which is Ezra's cue to release Brigette.

Brigette is happy to exit the minute he pulls the binds off, running in her bedraggled dress that looks like muddied strips of chartreuse. She is incredibly loud, and they listen to her thumping away, her hiccuping sobs almost as noisy as her pounding footfalls, until there is nothing but silence.

Ezra has decided the demon is lying. Maybe not about him being in love with Jonah, but definitely the part about Jonah being dead.

Grace believes the demon, and by the murderous look in her eye, Ezra knows how they're spending the rest of their senior year. They are going to go hunting. Grace for vengeance, Ezra for more answers.

"We're going to have so much fun," Grace whispers into the demondog's ear.

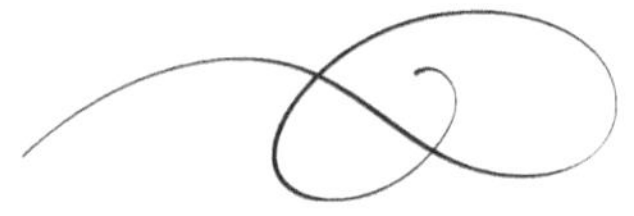

Mystery Prom Date

By Misty Middlebrook

This is crazy.

I must be crazy.

Prom unfolds around me, but I'm blind to it. Tuxes and poofy pink dresses surround me as I stare at my hand and squeeze the well-worn piece of paper in a death grip. Its creased edges are both oddly comforting and nerve-wracking, like one of those cute plush dolls at the dentist with real teeth.

I slowly unfold the paper to read it again, though I don't know why. It's seared into my memory. I could probably recite it backwards if I really wanted to.

Hello Julia,

Do you have a date for the prom? Word around school says you don't.

If not, would you consider going with me?

If your answer is yes, meet me at prom. I'll wait for you under the stars with a single rose until 8 p.m.

If you don't show up by then, I'll know you're not interested.

I know this is wild, but I'm not sure if you'd take me seriously if I asked you in person. I've had a crush on you forever, and graduation is coming. I can't leave school without letting you know how I feel.

Your hopeful prom date.

I scan the sea of people, searching for my mystery prom date. I see pinched faces and puffy faces, hopeful faces and disgusted faces, faces ravaged with acne and faces that wouldn't look out of place on a porcelain doll, but nowhere do I see the kind of face that says, *You, it's me! Your mystery admirer!*

They could be anyone. I quickly rule out those who already has a date. It's prom, so that's most of the room. I sneak a quick look at my phone. It's seven o'clock. I have one hour to find them. Sixty whole minutes! Enough time to have a good meal, to watch some TV, to take a long walk. Plenty of time. Right?

I close my eyes briefly, half-hoping when I open them again, someone will be standing there with a sign reading, *SURPRISE, IT'S ME!* All I see is a gaggle of people standing by the punch bowl.

You know what? This is dumb. What the hell does *I'll be under the stars* even mean, anyway? Is my mystery date hanging out in the parking lot, smoking it up with the burnouts?

I squeeze my way to the punch bowl. The potion inside is a sickly blood-red ooze with irregularly shaped ice cubes that make me think of knucklebones. It wouldn't be a high school dance without generic brand

Faux-Aid from the dollar store. Throwing caution and good sense to the wind, I reach for the ladle but find only fingers.

Peter jerks his hand away and shyly backs away from me, his eyes fixed on an unidentifiable stain on the floor.

"Sorry, Julia. You go ahead," he says.

I look at him curiously. "Who did you come here with?"

"Nobody." He leans in conspiratorily, beckoning me closer. I lean in. "Actually, I'd rather be home playing video games."

Ah. I can't help but smile. Peter is like a puppy that hasn't quite figured out its motor functions yet—all gangly limbs and shy, furtive movements. I didn't know he was also a gamer. It's funny how you can grind day after school day away with someone, only to know so little about them.

"What do you play?" I ask.

His eyes widen as his breath quickens. Has anyone ever asked him that before?

"Super Kart Mayhem 2! It just came out. I pre-ordered it, even though I didn't have to, but I wanted to, so I did. Its tracks are way better than the first one, and you can super boost jump." The gleam fades from his eyes as he slowly returns to Earth. "My mom made me come here." He puts on a disturbingly convincing falsetto voice. "Peter! You spend too much time playing games. You need to have fun." He sighs and takes a drink. "She doesn't think video games are fun."

"No, I get it." Now, it's my turn to lean in. "I pre-ordered it, too."

Peter looks like he's about to vibrate straight out of his skin. "That. Is. Awesome! We should play sometime before graduation."

Speaking of games...

"Hey, Peter? If you were to tell someone to meet you under the stars, what would that mean?"

Peter blinks. "Meet me outside at night."

Goddamnit. "Sure, sure, but what about here, at prom?"

"I have no idea."

"Yeah, I thought so. Thanks."

"Other than the star room, there's nothing I can think of."

"The star what now?"

"You know the room they reserve for prom pictures? It's galaxy-themed this year. Looks like you're standing under a shimmering sea of stars." He sighs deeply. "Just like in Stargazer 6."

"Thanks, Peter."

Holy crapballs! The star room! Of course! And there, across the dance floor, kids were shuffling in and out of a doorway decorated with dangling glitter stars. Nobody is ever going to mistake me for Sherlock Holmes, but gosh darn it, that looks like a star room to me.

My shoes clip-clop across the dance floor as I approach, my heartbeat picking up the tempo with every step. Who was this mystery person? Was it someone I knew? Was it someone I *liked*?

I hadn't had a crush on anyone ever since Brayden broke up with me three months ago. Ah, Brayden. *It's not you, Julia, it's me.* Yeah, it was him and Sophia

Reynolds—and Sophia Reynold's boobs, which, to be fair, are killer. Brayden insisted that he'd fallen in love with Sophia in gym class, and using the logic of teenage boys everywhere, that meant he'd done me no wrong. The heart wants what it wants, right?

Brayden's heart wanted what it wanted, all right, and what it wanted just wasn't me. Why not? Maybe I'm unlovable, and that's why he broke up with me. Yeah, that sounded right.

My shoulders sagged as I pushed aside the dangling decorations and entered the star room. Maybe my mystery prom date could love me. Maybe.

My eyes slowly adjust to the darkened room when someone touches my shoulder.

"Julia, I know who wrote the note," they say as they grip my arm.

I draw back instinctively, reaching in my purse for that little pepper spray bottle my mom insisted I always carry on me.

"Hey, girl," Amy says, her face a dimly lit spectre in the star room. "I've texted you a gazillion times. Why didn't you answer?"

Oh damn, Amy. Amy, my bestest of besties. Amy, keeper of my secrets. Sweet Amy, who has no idea how close she came to being blasted straight in the eyes with a gazillion Scoville heat units of hot stinging justice. *My* Amy. She loops her arm through mine and leads me toward the nearest girl's bathroom. Somewhat surprisingly at a prom where the punch, and other non-school approved liquids, are being consumed in quantities that are certainly not FDA-approved. None of the stalls are occupied. That still doesn't stop Amy from checking each and every door for feet.

"Sorry," I say once Amy finally stops snooping. "I've been distracted lately. What's going on?"

Amy looks at me with all the solemn seriousness of a teen girl about to drop only the hottest and juiciest gossip. "It's Brayden. He wants to take you back."

"What?" I back up into the sink. "Brayden wouldn't do that! He's with Sophia! And her boobs!"

"Not anymore. Apparently, Sophia dropped Brayden's ass when she found out he's still not over you."

I shake my head. "This is insane. He told me he's in love with her."

"Sure, that was true... until she found that note of yours in *his* jacket addressed to you, girl."

No. That doesn't sound right. Brayden? "Amy, why would he need to tell me he's had a crush on me for years?" I smooth out the note and point at the last paragraph. "Brayden isn't shy. He wouldn't use riddles to ask me to prom. He'd just, y'know, ask me."

"Jules, he dumped you. He probably realized what a moron he is and wants to beg for your forgiveness. *I couldn't leave school without telling you how I feel!* C'mon. Brayden wants to tell you those three little words you've been dying to hear. Hell, he even wrote he didn't think you'd take him seriously if he asked you in person."

I frowned. Maybe that could be true? After all, Brayden had asked me to be his girlfriend with three heart emojis and a question mark. A modern-day Romeo, he wasn't.

"If it's Brayden, would you take him back?" Amy asks.

"I... I don't know. But I've had this note for weeks. If Sophia found out about it then, why would she dump Brayden now?"

"I couldn't tell you. I only know her date isn't Brayden."

"Well, who did Brayden come with?"

"He flew solo. He's in the star room."

Again with the damn star room. "Then, why did you stop me from going in there?"

"You needed to know what you were getting into." Amy adjusts the sleeves of her dress. "I gotta get back to Sam. He's going to think I ditched him for some jock with Scotch. Are you okay?"

"Yeah, I'm fine. Go find Sam."

Amy gives me a quick hug. "Text me if you need anything." Then, I'm alone in the bathroom with only my thoughts for company.

Do I *want* to take Brayden back? After three months of being Julia the crying, red-eyed banshee, I'm just starting to feel like myself again. Hell, I was finally getting back into gaming. Brayden didn't like that I played video games. He was always more of an outdoorsy type of guy, more prone to run a mile than stomp an evil mushroom. He never seemed to care that he left me behind, out of breath in the dust. Meanwhile, my online game stats were falling further and further in the rankings. My DMs were flooded with people asking whatever happened to GamerGirl2025. Did I ghost? Was I picked up by a megamillion gaming corporation?

I know what happened to GamerGirl. She lost herself trying to become AthleticGirl to hold on tight to her first love and watched as my online persona slowly withered away. No matter how rowdy the chatter about me got on local social media, one account, NeverlandBoy007, always came to my defense. *GamerGirl is probably taking a break! She'll come back!*

NeverlandBoy, I hope you're right.

I check myself in the mirror and leave the bathroom. Amy and Sam are dancing. I try not to be envious as they kiss. #CoupleGoals. I'm truly happy Amy found someone who gets her, and although Sam looks a little like a drowned rat when it rains too hard, he and Amy just fit together like two pieces of a jigsaw puzzle with regrettable facial hair.

Just beyond the lovers cutting a rug on the dance floor is the prom king and queen ballot box. Surprise, surprise, the nominees are Waynesboro High elite. Hey, look, Brayden and Sophia. Will news of their break-up affect the vote? My mind reels at the thought. At the very bottom, I smile as I see Amy and Sam's names. Who knew? I circle their names on my ballot and file it away in the electorally secure plastic lunchbox.

Grabbing another cup of punch, I sit on the gym bleachers and watch kids go in and out of the star room. *Did I want to go in there? Did I want Brayden?*

"Shit," Peter says as his thumbs furiously tap his phone. "I keep getting mutilated in this boss fight."

I peek at his cracked phone screen to see he's playing Dragon Master's Quest. "Did you know that boss fight's glitched?"

"It is?"

"Yeah, if you tap on your HP just before you're KO'D, your HP meter will automatically fill back up."

"No way." Peter loads up his fight again. "Thanks for the tip."

"You're welcome." I sip my punch, watching the star room. "Can I ask you a hypothetical question?"

"Only if you don't mind a hypothetical answer."

I mull that one over for a moment. "Say you were dating someone, and you thought they were the best thing that ever came into your life. Even though they didn't let you fully be yourself, you loved them anyway and you were happy! At least for a little while, until they broke up with you. And let's say you didn't know who you were anymore without this person, and at the same time, you lost who you were when you *were* with them. If you had the chance, would you get back together with them?"

"Whoa whoa whoa," Peter says. "Is this about Brayden?"

"It's not *not* about him."

"I never knew what you saw in that guy. What did you have in common?"

Sometimes, I asked myself that same question. "Well, he was always more into running and being fit, while I was trying to run up my high scores. He always made me feel kinda weird about that. But at first, he made me feel seen, like I was somebody—not just Julia, or Amy's friend. He made me feel like the main character in my own life, like I could actually be loved."

"You *are* loved."

I shake my head. "Nope. I'm 100% grade-A unloveable. I have papers to prove it. Somewhere. Probably."

Peter frowns. "Your parents love you. That's like their job, right? It's written in their DNA."

Oh, sweet, innocent Peter. "They hardly notice me. Double workaholics."

"Well, what about Amy?"

"I love her to death, but she's all about Sam. When we graduate, they're going to go off and live their awesome-people lives in their awesome-people house and forget all about me."

"That doesn't matter."

"It doesn't?"

Peter shakes his head. "No, because you, Julia Harris, are *fucking awesome*."

"Bwah?" I was?

"I've sat behind you in the same class ever since kindergarten. You are somebody. In third grade, you shared your lunch with me when my mom forgot. You are somebody who's always prepared for class. You are somebody who is sweet and kind. Most importantly, you are somebody who *games*."

"You don't think that's weird?"

"No. That's hot as hell."

"Brayden always made me feel weird about it."

"Well, he's weird for dumping you in the first place."

Peter lies back and stretches out on the bleachers in his tux like he doesn't have a care in the world. I smile at him and take out my phone. "What do you say to some Super Kart Mayhem 2?"

"Hell yeah." Peter grins.

Over the next twenty-five minutes, I tap my phone, dodging Peter's oil slicks and red boomerangs. It's not until I cross the first-place finish line that I notice it's 7:45.

I'm still on the fence about whether or not to go back to Brayden, but whatever I decide, it doesn't feel right to leave him hanging. He deserves an answer.

"Thanks for everything, Peter. I'm going to check out the star room."

He gives me a two-fingered salute and goes back to his phone.

Once again, I weave my way through the crowd and push aside the strings of dangling stars, revealing black walls with strings of fairy lights. A mirror ball hangs from the ceiling, refracting twinkles of starlight. Under the mirrorball stands Brayden, but instead of holding a single rose, he's holding Sophia. She pulls out of his embrace with teary eyes. Sophia freezes for a moment when she spots me, and without saying a word, she wipes away her tears and brushes past me. It's at that moment when I realize I don't want to be with Brayden again. And it's not because he's so obviously in love with Sophia. It's because I'm choosing me. I'm choosing GamerGirl.

Brayden lowers his head as I approach. "Julia, she doesn't believe me. I have to get her back. *Please* help me get her back."

"If you want Sophia back, why did you write me this note?"

"I didn't write that! That damn note made Sophia break up with me."

"Then why did you have it?"

"The person who wrote it asked me to put it in your locker for them. They were afraid of being seen. Since my last class is near your locker, it wouldn't be all *that* weird. But Sophia found the note in my jacket before I could give it to you, and she thinks I still have feelings for you."

"Did you *ever* have feelings for me?" I ask, not sure what answer I expect, what answer I *want*.

"God, Julia, do you always have to make this about you?"

"When have I ever made anything about me? I *changed myself* to be with you, and you broke up with me, anyway!"

"I never asked you to change yourself," Brayden says.

"But you didn't want me as I am?"

"Julia, you are going to be perfect for whoever you end up with. You just weren't the one for me. I don't want my girlfriend to feel like she has to change herself to be with me. I saw the person you were becoming and didn't like her. That's why I ended it. Sophia just fits me better than you did."

"You make dating sound like you're trying on clothes."

"Maybe I am, but trust me, the person who wrote that letter is a better fit than I ever was. Please help me with Sophia. That letter is what got me in trouble."

"All right, I'll talk to her."

"Thank you, Julia."

I leave the star room and wander through the crowd, trying to find Sophia. With seven minutes before eight o'clock, I'm not sure if I can talk to Sophia and find my mystery date in time. They aren't in the star room, and I'm out of clues, unless I go outside. There are too many people. I may as well be looking for Sophia in a haystack. I take my phone out and shoot Amy a text.

Have you seen Sophia?

It only takes a second for Amy to respond.

Punch Bowl!

I head straight for the snack table where Sophia is with her date, a squeaky-voiced freshman. Man, she really is trying to stick it to Brayden. "Sophia, we need to talk."

"What is it?" she asks, rolling her eyes.

"You have to talk to Brayden. There's been a misunderstanding."

"There's nothing to misunderstand. He still likes you."

"No, he doesn't. We never made any sense. He's in love with you."

"I read the letter that was in his pocket," she says.

"Brayden didn't write that. He was just the delivery boy. Please talk to him, Sophia. I know you care about him. Hear him out at least."

"If Brayden didn't write that letter, who did?"

With a glance at my watch, I sigh. "I don't think I'll ever find out."

"Whoever wrote it is a secret romantic. I wish *I* was asked to the prom by an anonymous letter. It's like something out of a storybook, one of the good ones with wizards and elves and imps playing bullshit guessing games." She pauses. "I'm going to talk to Brayden." Sophia shrugs at her date and walks away.

I nibble on a cookie and type out a text to Amy.

I convinced Sophia to talk to Brayden.

She quickly responds.

Hang on. We're coming to you.

By the time Amy and Sam arrive, it's eight o'clock. I don't see Peter on the bleachers anymore. I wonder if he decided to go home. I think I'm about ready to go in that direction myself.

"So, what happened with Brayden?" Amy asks, dragging Sam behind her.

"Nothing happened, except I reconnected him with Sophia."

"But what about the note?"

"He didn't write it," I say, taking it out again. "At this point, it's a lost cause. They're not in the star room, and my time's up."

"Can I see it?" Sam asks.

I give it to him and hope he keeps it forever. Hell, he can burn it for all I care. I never want to look at it again.

"I'm sorry, Julia. Do you want to dance with me and Sam?"

Aww. Amy's so sweet. "No, I think I just want to go home. My pajamas and gaming console sound amazing right now."

"Yo, Julia," Sam says after a moment. "This says *meet me under the stairs.*"

"What? No, it doesn't, it says *stars.* I've read it a thousand times."

"You should have read it a thousand and one then. Look, the letter *I* is written closely to the letter *R*. It sort of blends in, but that's an *I*. It says *stairs.*"

I take the note from Sam and read it again. Sure enough, there's a dot of an i written super close to the letter R.

"I'll be damned," I mutter under my breath.

"Hurry, Jules. It's not that much past eight. They might still be there," Amy says.

I book it as fast as I can to the stairs in the main hallway. I burst through the doors, and under the stairs stands Peter, holding a single rose.

"It's you? It's been *you* this whole time?"

Peter nods. "You think every guy wants a Sophia or an Amy, but sometimes a guy wants a GamerGirl."

I blink. What the what?

"NeverlandBoy007?"

"That's me." Peter smiles and offers me the rose. "I've had a crush on you ever since the third grade. Would you like to go to prom with me?"

I smile. "Actually, I've had my fill of the prom. I've got the new Super Kart Mayhem 2 waiting for me at home. Do you want to play it with me?"

"Absolutely," Peter says, offering me his arm. "Are you sure you don't want to find out who wins prom king and queen?"

"Nah, I'm sure Amy will let me know."

"Oh, there's one more thing I want to do before we go." Peter holds up his phone to take a selfie. I stand closer to him as he clicks the button. "There. Now you have a prom picture."

Just then, my phone chimes with a text from Amy.

Sam and I just won prom king and queen!!! Where you at?

I smile and text back.

Under the stairs with Peter.

Amy responds with a smiley face emoji and a heart. The ellipsis appears by her name with another text.

I'm happy you found your prom date.

Never Gonna Dance Again

By Lianne Robinson

I HAD HIGH EXPECTATIONS for Prom 1985 at Sweet Gum High School. Not only was it my senior year, but I'd scored the raddest dress and the perfect date. The seniors chose the theme, *A Night Under the Stars*, and I had to admit everything turned out beautifully.

Well, as beautiful as a high school gymnasium could look with crepe paper streamers and twinkling white Christmas lights dangling from the basketball goals. A banner announcing our theme in glitter glue hung above the drinks. Scented candles flickered on the tables surrounding the dance floor. The overly sweet aroma of vanilla almost managed to squelch the sour sneaker stench that perpetually lingered in the gym.

George Michael crooned "Careless Whisper" through the deejay's speakers as Shane Whitson's hands drifted down my back. His fingertips squeezed my waist, and I leaned my head back, admiring his striking appearance. I could've sworn I was dancing with Adonis in a white tuxedo with tails. The dramatic spikes in the front of his sandy blond hair contrasted with the long locks that lazily brushed his collar in the back. I was the luckiest girl in the room to be there in his strong arms.

I, too, was a vision in a long, royal blue satin dress with silver heels and matching sparkly silver eyeshadow. I teased my permed hair as high as it would go and preserved it with at least half a can of hairspray. I'd never felt so gorgeous in my eighteen years of life.

We slow danced as closely as the teacher chaperones would allow. Even though we'd only been dating for a little over two months, I was almost positive we'd be crowned prom king and queen. I wasn't anyone special at Sweet Gum High, but he was its star quarterback. Everyone knew Shane, and they also knew he'd be headed to the University on scholarship to play football in the fall. I liked our chances to win.

Shane tilted my face towards his with a finger hooked under my chin. "Wanna get outta here?"

"Now? But I love this song! Besides, they haven't even announced king and queen yet."

"Who cares? They're just stupid tinfoil crowns, Jennifer."

I unsuccessfully tried to stop my face from melting into a frown. "I know, but what if we win? It'll be weird if we aren't here. Anyway, where would we go? We're supposed to meet Gina and Robby at Waffle House later."

"I know a place," he said, pulling me off the dance floor and into the shadows. He waggled his eyebrows suggestively and rained kisses up and down my neck until I squealed. A teacher shot a stern look our way as Shane's hands traveled the silky surface of my dress.

Pushing his roaming hands away, I stepped back and crossed my arms. "Look, I know what you're trying to do. I wanna enjoy our last prom a little longer. C'mon, please?"

Before he could respond, a sharp, splintering *crack* exploded somewhere above us.

I never saw the massive scoreboard as it detached from the wall. People screamed and ran in every direction as I spun in my heels to flee, but someone grabbed my arm, swinging me right back into the danger zone. More commotion ensued, and Shane cried out, "Nooooooo!" It happened so fast, I never knew what hit me.

The music faded away to silence, and the lights flickered once, twice before they fizzled into blackness.

All at once, I became surrounded by a comforting warmth, a soft blanket of contentment and unending peace, which abruptly ended with an unpleasant flash of white light. When I opened my eyes, I found myself staring at my reflection in the mirror in the girls' locker room at Sweet Gum High School.

Unsure of what had just happened, I studied the room briefly. Something was off. Disoriented, I peered at my reflection again. Not a hair was out of place. My eyeshadow shimmered with each blink. Leaning closer, I checked my teeth for lettuce or smeared lipstick and found neither.

I glanced down and saw my handbag on the counter next to the sink. I unzipped it and took out my bottle of Love's Baby Soft. I spritzed a little behind each of my ears and dabbed some on my wrists. The gentle baby powder aroma filled my nostrils and made me sneeze.

"Bless you," I heard as a stall door opened behind me. The girl who'd spoken stepped out in a slinky sequined gown.

My head snapped towards her as I took in her style. Her long hair cascaded down her back in ebony ringlets. Her dazzling, floor-length golden gown sparkled under the murky fluorescent lights. I couldn't stop staring at her. She looked like something out of a movie.

"Whoa!" she cried, stopping in her tracks as she beheld me. "That is an *amazing* retro look! You really committed to that whole vibe, didn't you?"

"I'm sorry. What?"

"Your fit is completely off the chain. The vintage dress and the bigger-than-life hair... That's so crazy. Who'd you come with?"

"Um, I'm here with Shane."

"Shane?" Her brow furrowed as she washed and dried her hands. Pursing her lips, she turned this way and that and admired her reflection.

I watched her preen. "Do you go here?"

"Well, duh. I'm a senior. MaKayleigh Bass." She returned her piercing gaze and tilted her head as she studied me.

"Muh- what? I'm sorry, I didn't get that."

"MaKayleigh," she repeated, rolling her eyes. "I thought I knew everybody in school. Guess not."

"Jennifer Parks." I stuck out my hand, but she glanced at it and wrinkled her nose in distaste.

"We should probably head back. They'll be announcing prom king and queen soon."

"Oh, yeah. You're right."

I followed her out of the locker room. An unfamiliar pulsating beat grew louder and shook my insides as we walked down the hall into the gym. I froze when I stepped through the double doors and recognized nothing.

Gold balloons cascaded across the door in a shimmering arch. Wispy, sheer curtains fluttered from tall Grecian columns. Tiny white lights glittered everywhere I looked. The music, if you could call it that, was a befuddling mess of mumbling and loud drumbeats. Further confused, I stumbled out of the room. Where was I?

The drab gymnasium hallway seemed normal, filled with trophy cases highlighting the glory days of athletes who were mostly long gone from Sweet Gum High. I immediately found the 1984 state football championship trophy...but stopped short when I saw another row of trophies underneath it, engraved with years that didn't make sense: *1999, 2003, 2018, 2023*? Was this some kind of weird joke?

In a blur of bewilderment, I set off to find Shane. Maybe he could help me understand this predicament. I charged back into the gym and tried to ignore the incredible decorations. I scanned the couples sitting at the tables near the dance floor. None of their faces were familiar. Where was Shane? Where was Gina or Robby...or anyone I knew?

I did a double-take and shook my head when I read the sparkly banner hanging over the drink table: *If I Could Turn Back Time*. That was all wrong, too. My stomach rumbled as a reminder that I'd only eaten a small salad earlier. Could low blood sugar have caused my mental confusion? I decided to nosh a snack while I searched for Shane.

I wound through the unfamiliar people and decorations to the dessert table. At least it was still in the same spot. I reached for a chocolate cupcake with a swirl of glittery pink and gold frosting until I saw a sign next to the display that read, *Gluten-free*. I snatched my hand back like I'd burned it. What in the world did that mean?

I spun around and found myself face to face with Shane, except it wasn't Shane. The eyes, the sandy blond hair, and the smile were all right; but somehow, he was taller, and his hair flopped lazily across his brow. His tuxedo had also transformed from white to black.

I grabbed his shoulders, dumbstruck. "Shane, help me!"

He laughed and shoved me away to arm's length. "My name's Cole. Who the heck are you? And what's up with your hair? You look like something out of a terrible 80s movie."

I cringed. "What's that supposed to mean?"

"Dude, have you seen yourself? Seriously, go find a mirror. You look ratchet!"

I tripped over my own feet as he pushed past me.

He turned back and shouted above the din, "If you're looking for my father, he's over there manning the punchbowl to keep it un-spiked. You should say hello. I'm sure he'll get a kick out of your...look." He chuckled.

I wandered through the dance floor where couples writhed and twitched inexplicably to the rhythm of the blaring music. People laughed and pointed at me as I dazedly tried to find the place where Cole had pointed me toward the punchbowl. A cackling girl in a strapless dress stuck a small black rectangle in my face and temporarily blinded me with a flash of white light. Surely that wasn't a camera.

The crowd parted as I reached the edge of the dance floor. As I approached, a gray-haired man in a dark suit poured pineapple juice into a punchbowl. I tapped his shoulder while I fought back the tears that threatened to ruin my eye makeup.

The paunchy man turned to face me, and my stomach dropped to my knees.

"Sh-Shane?" I stammered.

"That's Coach Whitson to you, young lady..." He trailed off as recognition crept into his face. His eyes widened, and his brow creased. "Jennifer? It can't be..."

"Of course, it is, dummy. Who else would I be? But why do you look so *old*? And do you have a twin? Please explain to me what the heck is going on!"

All the blood drained from his features, and droplets of sweat beaded on his forehead. He gripped the table with quivering hands. "But you... You're dead."

"And you're drunk, I guess? Did you spike the punch? Dead, really? How original."

His hand shook as he reached toward my elbow.

"Ouch! You pinched me!"

His incredulous expression was frozen. "You're real? You're not a ghost?"

The music grew louder, and the crowd more raucous. "Can we go outside?"

He shook his head and tentatively grasped my hand. Teachers and students alike watched us leave the gym holding hands. Shane continued to swivel his head around to stare at me as we shuffled through the throngs of dancing students. I noted his pronounced limp.

He released my hand and closed the double doors behind us, which helped to muffle the noise. The hallway's dingy yellow lighting did nothing for his sallow complexion when he faced me again, but it did highlight the wrinkles on his skin and the bags under his eyes.

"What happened to your face?" I asked.

"Time. But somehow, you look just the same as you did at prom... Well, except for the part where you were dead the last time I saw you." He put his hands over his face and steepled his fingers on his forehead. "This isn't happening. This isn't real. It can't be. You're dead."

"Hang on, hang on. You keep saying that. What are you talking about?"

He ran his shaky fingers through his noticeably thinner gray hair. "Jennifer, you died at the prom. You passed right here in this gym in 1985. *I went to your funeral.*"

"Very funny, Shane. Seriously, are you drunk?"

"Is somebody playing a cruel joke? Is this like a 'Ghost of Christmas Past' thing? I swear I'll do whatever you ask if you'll just leave me alone."

"What are you talking about?"

The music stopped, and he drew in a deep breath. The gymnasium doors parted, and a petite, older brunette politely cleared her throat. "Ahem. Coach Whitson?"

Before he noticed her presence, he shouted, "Jennifer, you're dead because *I killed you*!"

His voice reverberated through the hallway and the open doors of the now-quiet gymnasium, where a collective gasp resounded.

Intense rage boiled in my soul as his words echoed in my mind. "Explain yourself."

A gathering crowd of students and teachers assembled at the gymnasium doors. More of the absurd black rectangles pointed at Shane and me. Everyone observed in bemused silence.

He didn't seem to notice the audience. "I heard the scoreboard crack as it broke free from the wall. It fell straight down towards me. I had to make a split-second decision—me or you. I was stuck in the corner, and there was nowhere else for me to go," he sobbed.

"What are you saying?"

"I pushed you down to save myself. I... I killed you. It was a direct hit. They said you were gone before you reached the floor." He hiccupped and wiped his nose on the sleeve of his suit jacket. "I jumped over you, but I tripped on your dress and fell. I blew out my knee and never played another down of football after that. I lost my entire future on prom night. So, whatever you hoped to get from this, that's how it happened. Honestly, when I think about it now, it really was kinda your fault. I wanted to leave, but you insisted we stay."

All the memories flooded into my mind at that moment—the pain, the loss of my dreams, and my vanished future all came back to me at once.

I turned my back to him and glared at the wall next to the gym entrance. Only then did I notice the small bronze plaque.

In memory of Jennifer Dawn Parks, Class of 1985

My fury took control. I whirled around and assailed him with quick punches to his face. I hit pretty well—for a dead girl. I would've kept punching if Shane's doppelgänger son hadn't pulled me off him. He held my arms behind my back as I heaved, wild-eyed and ready to attack again.

"Murderer!" I spat.

Blood trickled from Shane's battered nose. "I couldn't let it hit me. I had big dreams of playing in the NFL. I was gonna make something of myself, something more than a high school P.E. teacher. I guess that was my penance, huh? I already paid the price for killing you by living this sad life. But I promise you...I didn't mean for it to happen, Jennifer. Do you understand how bad I feel about it? You must believe me. Please, *please* say you'll forgive me and go away," he blubbered.

Smoke practically hissed from my ears.

Everyone turned when red and blue lights flashed through the windows. Six police officers stormed into the building.

Cole shoved me at the cops. "Here she is, officers. This crazy chick wailed on my Dad. Arrest her!"

"Can I tell you my side of the story?" I asked through clenched teeth as the policeman slipped a pair of tight handcuffs on my wrists.

"By all means," the officer said.

"He murdered me."

The cop looked me up and down, taking in every detail and sizing up my mental state, no doubt. "He... murdered... *you?*"

I pointed at the plaque on the wall. "That's me. I've been dead since 1985. He admitted he killed me in front of all these people."

The stunning girl in the gold dress piped up, "I streamed it live on TikTok, sir. It makes no sense to me, either, but he said it."

All the cops looked at each other with wide eyes and doubtful expressions. One of the officers pinned Shane's arms behind his back. He read him his rights as he placed the handcuffs on him.

Shane struggled and wailed, "But I was gonna play on scholarship!"

The officer holding me turned my body around to face him. "Then how are you here?"

I shrugged. "I don't know. It seems I had a bit of unfinished business."

As soon as the words left my mouth, relief poured over me like a soothing balm. I perceived the immediate release from the handcuffs—and freedom from my earthly body.

For a blissful moment, I was transported back to 1985. I peered overhead because a spotlight's warmth shined on me. I reached my hands to my head and discovered a delicate tinfoil crown perched there. I spun around in delighted surprise and watched everyone clap for my prom queen coronation. Joy filled me as the strains of "Careless Whisper" reached my ears.

As the song ended, I swayed back and forth and smiled, although I sensed my remaining time here was short. My work here was finished. In an instant, this vision splintered, and I soared toward a blinding white light into a place of eternal peace and happiness.

NO ONE EVER NOTICED MARGARET

BY BRITTANY MACK

NO ONE EVER NOTICED Gemma.

She had always blended in with the shadows cast upon the cinder-block-painted walls. Being four-foot-six in the twelfth grade also played a part, she supposed. But Gemma was no longer the four-teen-year-old genius in high school. No, she was now Margaret James, Gemma to her friends, and chief bio-mechanical engineer at Stratford and Harlow to her col-leagues.

Someone prestigious.

Someone worth paying attention to.

Only, she didn't want the attention. She wanted noth-ing more than to bleed back into the crevasses of her high school cafeteria among the party lights and paper mâché flowers. Whoever thought having a prom for a ten-year reunion needed to be taken out back and beat with a fly swatter.

If it wasn't for Gemma's husband insisting she would regret showing all the clowns she graduated with just how much she had overcome, she would still be at home in her pajamas and watching Bridgerton. Her husband always knew how to motivate her—it was one of the reasons she had married him. He never saw her as—

"Mangy Margaret?" A familiar voice from Gemma's right barreled into her like a youthful nightmare. "Oh, my God, you've grown up!"

Caroline Mabe stood in her shimmering gold dress, a look of amusement and something akin to shock coloring her glamorous face. It was clear ten years had not aged her in the slightest.

"I go by Gemma now, Caroline," she replied, trying to keep the distaste out of her voice.

"Well, you know you'll always be Mangy Margaret to me." Caroline smiled sweetly, as if ignorant to her level of stunted maturity. "I heard—"

Gemma turned back to the crowd without giving any more time to the bully who had made her youth nothing short of miserable. Caroline had taken enough of Gemma's joy, and she wasn't about to hand-feed her anymore.

Stories of children and terrible jokes about jobs no one was happy with wafted toward Gemma as she drifted casually away from her high-school foe. It was intriguing how years could do so much for some and nearly not enough for others. Then again, Gemma never held much hope for those who roamed the halls of Sycamore High.

Twelve steps into the entryway and fifteen minutes of socializing had been the agreement tonight, but the sweat pooling at the back of Gemma's exposed knees and the slight rash springing forward along her neck told her she wouldn't make it. At that moment, everyone within smelling distance turned toward Gemma.

Conversations stopped, the music growing louder with their absence. All the insecurities Gemma had left behind after graduation flooded back. A tidal wave of horror and self-doubt covered her like a wet blanket. It wasn't until she recognized it wasn't her everyone was looking at, but behind her, that she turned as well.

He stood in the doorway, talking to Gemma's senior high trig teacher without a care in the world. The weight of the room's stares held no effect on his confident posture. The commandment of attention was obeyed within the silent request she knew the man wasn't aware he gave.

As if sensing something was amiss, his light eyes met hers, and Gemma's breathing lodged in her throat. Spit pooled in her mouth because her body had suddenly forgotten how to perform basic functions, like swallowing.

A lean body rippled underneath the black silk covering the man Gemma had watched from afar since high school. With strides of superiority and control, Jett Hanover had taken over small-town Sycamore as he closed the short distance between them, but not quick enough to evade Caroline Mabe.

A bejeweled paw jutted out from the thickening crowd and stalled Jett's trajectory. He didn't seem the least bit fazed by the unwanted attention the she-hulk gave. The pair's mouths moved in conversation, but underneath the booming bass of "The Cupid Shuffle," Gemma couldn't make out a single word. A burning ember of jealousy lit within the pit of her abdomen and took on a life of its own. When Caroline stepped forward and placed her face too close to Jett's stubbled neck, the jealous jester catapulted into a somersault.

Gemma's feet were in motion before her mind could comprehend what was happening.

"Hi, honey," Gemma cooed, grabbing Jett's arm and linking it with hers.

The shimmer in her husband's eyes at the understanding of what Gemma was doing made it hard not to giggle at the absurdity of it all. They both knew she was on the cusp of grabbing Caroline by the collar and shoving her into a locker to prove her point that Jett was taken.

"My oh my," Caroline tried to rattle with a tone of surprise. "I didn't realize you two knew one another... like that."

Gemma was not surprised. Why would someone like Jett Hanover, football star and high-school heartthrob, ever pay someone like Margaret James, nerd and child prodigy, any level of attention? Gemma had spent the last six months of their marriage wondering the same thing.

With a sarcastic chuckle, Gemma said, "Don't sound so surprised, Caroline. If only you—"

Before Gemma could finish her sentence, Jett had pulled her away by the arm. With a full belly laugh, he said, "Seriously, Gem?"

"What? You act like that old stuck-up priss doesn't deserve a taste of her own medicine."

"I never said that." Jett stopped them at the edge of the dance floor, next to the dessert table. His sweet tooth was always in the driver's seat. "Caroline put you through a lot in high school. I can understand you wanting to rub your sexy husband in her face just a little bit."

Gemma's eyes rolled as Jett gave her his Oscar-winning smile that caused all women to swoon—all women except for Gemma, but that was before she was forced to oversee him during clinical rotations at Stratford and Harlow.

Gemma crossed her arms in feigned annoyance, both of them knowing it was well worth it to see the look on Caroline's face, even if Caroline's Botox and eye-lifts attempted to ruin it all.

"Do you want to dance, Mrs. Hanover?" Jett asked, setting his piece of icebox key-lime pie back onto the paper-covered tabletop, and holding out his hand.

"That wasn't part of the deal. The deal was I would come to this travesty of a shindig to show my face and prove to this town I'm not breakable, and then we could go home." Gemma wasn't whining—she didn't sink that low. But... this was more of a pinched plea, which is what she would refer to it as later when Jett tried to rub her unwillingness in her face.

"Well, my beautiful, strong-willed, stubborn mother-to-be, what is it you say to me all the time?"

Gemma's eyes bulged at her husband's comment, her head swinging around wildly to see if anyone heard. Not even their parents had been told about the news yet. They wanted to keep it a secret until Thanksgiving. It was cliché, she knew it. But it was so cute how excited Jett was, and she couldn't say no to him... ever.

With a failed attempt to place her small hands over his mouth, she grunted, stepped back, and placed them on her hips instead. "That life will try to shake you off its back, but you must cling to your greatness like a flea."

"That's right." Jett closed the small gap between them. He gently centered her face between his large hands and leaned to place a soft kiss on her full lips. "Be the flea, Margaret James-Hanover. Or better yet, be the tick and suck all of the air out of the room while I spin you around and show you off."

"Can we stop talking about parasites now? Your attempt at a pep-talk is failing miserably."

The melody of "Closer "by Ne-Yo began to play as Jett grabbed Gemma's limp hand from her side and strutted them out to the center of the cafeteria floor, her feet following blindly like a moth to the flame of its demise. Jett pulled her close, his six-foot-two frame towering over Gemma's much smaller one.

As Jett did as promised, holding her close and turning them in slow circles around the perimeter of the dance floor, Gemma absorbed the wide-eyed and thin-lipped looks of disbelief with relish. She had overcome her situation, determined to make something of herself amidst those saying she would always be the freak. The lesser. The unwanted.

She was wanted.

She was loved.

She was exhausted and needed to get her long-legged hunk out of this flashback and back into their present, preferably on the couch with their favorite movie.

Not So Perfect Prom Proposal

By Shuba Mohan

I ALMOST HAVE ENOUGH to tie around the pole, but the balloons keep popping, just like my hopes that Nik Patel will strut over with his soft brown eyes, begging-to-be-run-through, wavy, black hair and deep voice, and offer to help me blow up balloons. Maybe he'll be dazzled by my five-thousand-dollar megawatt smile and ask me to Prom at the last minute. I have a dress ready.

I know Nik hasn't asked anyone. All the girls do. And Archana Gandhi's using her stupid list, that has every detail for Prom color-coded and alphabetized, to hold his attention a little too long.

I inhale and blow, and blow, and blow. *Pop!*

Nik and Archana turn and stride toward me, their long, lean runner legs in perfect synchronization. At least they're not looking at each other anymore.

"Is this job too much for you, Priti?" Archana's perfectly threaded eyebrows lift in smug superiority.

Nik smells like cedar, leather, and mint. If I say yes, will he stay, or will I be stuck with Archana?

"Your valuable time would be put to better use somewhere else, Archana." I spread my lips wide. Here's my chance to get my parents' money's worth of three years of expensive braces. "Nik can help me." Yes! The pearly whites are drawing him in.

Archana looks down at her clipboard and then at Nik. *Come on. Admit defeat. Walk away.* I offer Nik a balloon. He takes it with his infamous crooked grin that, like me, earned him a Best Smile nomination in the yearbook. I'm crumbling.

"I'll need your help later, Nik." Archana lays her hand on his arm. Oh, she's good. I've got to remember that move.

"I'll tie them to the bottom, and you do the top?" I say as he squats.

"You're so chill about everything." He swipes his bangs off his forehead and peeks up at me. "I really like that about you." *Those eyelashes!*

I bend and rest my hand on his arm. "Thank you."

"Done." his head launches up and crashes into my chin.

"Oh, my God. I'm so sorry." He clasps my face. He's staring at my mouth. He's going to kiss me. He's going to kiss me! The world spins. Fireworks flash in front of my eyes. It's the happiest day of my life. Warmth floods my mouth. I'm melting.

"Archana!" Nik screams.

No, no, I'm Priti. I'm Priti, the girl of your Prom dreams.

Liquid is filling up my mouth. I cough.

Archana picks up two glistening pearls from the floor, her eyes bulging like anime characters.

"We've got to hold these back in before they dry out." Her hands are in my mouth before I know what's happening. I liked his hands better.

"Bite down, gently." Nik rips off his shirt and stuffs it between my lips. I feel woozy and lay my hand on his perfect hot-rolls-fresh-out-of-the-oven abs.

"My car is out front," Archana says. "We'll take her to the dentist down the road."

The ride is a blur other than resting my head on Nik's broad shoulder, taking in the scent of him. He smells different. Metallic and salty. But I don't care. I'm cocooned in his arm as his longish hair brushes my forehead. It's as soft as I imagined.

The dentist says she's impressed that we knew to put the teeth back in right away. What teeth? She gives me some anesthetic and hovers over my head with a bright light. "Great job staying calm."

I want to call out for her to stop. Archana and Nik are too close sitting in those chairs, but the dentist's hands are in my mouth.

"Is she okay?" Nik's eyes glisten. Archana places her hand over his.

No! I want to scream.

"You'll be done in no time," the dentist coos.

My parents' furrowed brows are staring at me when I wake up. I reach for my mouth. It feels like my braces are back on.

"Don't touch your teeth," Amma says, stroking my hair. "Your front two teeth are bonded with wire to your other teeth."

"It's a good thing your friends reacted so fast." Appa's voice is deeper than Nik's. He helps me sit up, and it all comes flooding back. "The dentist said we can go home once you woke up."

Archana and Nik are standing near her car. There goes my prom dream, but I guess I can't be jealous. The dentist said their quick thinking dramatically increased the chances of my teeth reattaching.

"Thanks, Archana and Nik!" I call and wave them over.

They turn and stride toward me, their long, lean runner legs in perfect synchronization. After flirting the whole year in English and History, I really thought Nik and I had something, but they make a cute couple. Nik carries a white poster board, and Archana holds a bouquet of beautiful flowers.

"We're glad you're okay," Nik says.

"Yeah," Archana adds. "You were so out of it before." She nudges Nik like they share a big secret. Her smile is pretty, even if she didn't get a Best Smile nomination.

Nik's big brown eyes turn to hers and soften.

"These are for you." Archana hands the flowers to me.

"You didn't have to." I mean it. "Thanks for everything you did."

"You're welcome, but the flowers aren't from me." She rests her hand on Nik's arm.

Nik turns the poster board around. In big letters, it says, *Shall we sink our "priti" teeth into prom together?*

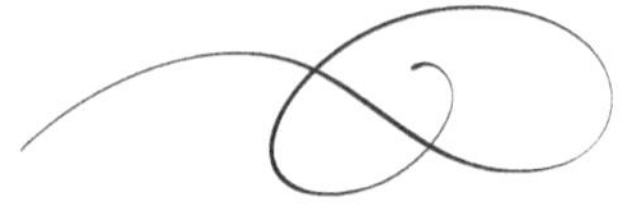

Note to Self

By Jinxie R. Thorne

Who am I?

The class book worm.

It's not like anyone would ask me on a date. I don't talk to many people. Half of me wants to be on this little shopping trip to please Mom, while the other half–wants to go home and curl up with a good book.

Note to self: Smile, and try to enjoy today. Natalie read her note and sighed. It was going to be a long day. She clicked send. The message whooshed as the bubble appeared in a personal chat. Personal chats were the best way to go in her honest opinion. If anyone looked over her shoulder, it made it look like she was talking to a friend, instead of leaving herself notes. She didn't want to be here. Hell, anywhere was better than dress shopping.

It's a memory you'll never forget. Natalie's eyes rolled to the back of her head. Mom's words were like a broken record. An audible sigh fell from her lips. *Sure,* she thought.

What was so special about prom, anyway? Natalie grappled with an answer and came up with nada. The question nagged her for weeks. Prom was only a popularity contest. Natalie just didn't get it. In ten years, prom wouldn't matter. The only people going were those who had boyfriends, and *they* were probably going to be under the bleachers.

Granted, it wasn't the event that bothered her. It was the preparation. More specifically, dress shopping, which was the worst. So far, they had been to at least four boutiques, but only this one carried dresses her size. For most girls, finding the perfect dress was a wonderful experience. Or it should have been. But Natalie *hated* her plus-sized body. A formal dress would only highlight her insecurities.

Natalie stuffed her phone into her back pocket. If her mom, Lynn, found Natalie on her phone while they were supposed to be shopping, she'd never hear the end of it.

Out of sight, out of mind. She cast a wary gaze to the side. Her Mom was busy checking price tags.

Good, Natalie thought. *She didn't see.*

Quietly, she resumed thumbing through the sea of gowns.

"I saw that," Lynn said slyly. Her eyes never left the price tag, yet somehow she knew what Natalie was up to. One of the benefits of being a parent is having eyes in the back of your head, she liked to say.

Natalie plucked a random gown off the rack. "Saw what?"

"You were on your phone, weren't you?"

Natalie twiddled her thumbs while her gaze drifted around the room. "Just some notes for English Lit."

"Mhm, I've heard that before... Come on kiddo, be present! You can't always have your nose in a book, or your phone."

Plastic crinkled with every moving garment. Mermaid Fit? Hell no! That would show every curve and roll on her body! Tea length teal? The dress was plain. Maybe a little too plain. Her head swayed side to side. The next dress was a black A-line. She held it out to observe. Rhinestones glittered under the light. The chiffon ruffles were really pretty. Natalie held the garment bag up to her curvy figure. A soft smile tugged at her lips.

Note to self: Maybe prom wouldn't be so bad.

"Mooooom!" a voice called from across the boutique.

Natalie's gaze darted as she searched for the voice.

A middle-aged woman sat in a cushioned chair scrolling on her phone. A girl around her age stood before a trio of mirrors with her hands on her hips.

"Mom, you know I wear a size five! I'm swimming in this!" the girl shrieked.

Without looking up from her phone, the mother shrugged her shoulders. "We'll try another place, Tasha. This isn't our first stop today."

Natalie's smile faded. Size five? Natalie wished she could go down a few sizes just to fit in a dress, and this girl was complaining of dresses being too big? She quickly turned her attention back to the racks.

Pink, blue, forest green? Yards of material meshed together like rainbow hell. Oh, it was no use! No matter what Natalie picked would make her look like a whale!

Natalie's cheeks flushed. Her face was no doubt as red as a tomato.

Note to self: Busted.

Lynn always seemed to know when something bothered her, even if she didn't say so.

"Don't worry about her," Mom said. "You're beautiful just as you are."

Like usual, Mom knew just what to say. Natalie was grateful for her. Especially because she didn't have to be such a good mom, considering she was her step-parent. When Natalie was younger, Mom was just Lynn, her dad's best friend for fifteen years. Who knew Lynn would marry into Natalie's crazy-ass family?

Their first dinner as a family was burned into Natalie's memory—*Fire in the Hole* Pork chops. The sheer thought still made her laugh. Those damn chops were so spicy, a dragon would have been jealous. Natalie could still taste those over-seasoned chunks of bacon. They went out to dinner that night, and Dad never bought pre-seasoned meat again.

But their engagement, now that was a really special memory, one that her father was still miffed about. The day Cory told Natalie about his plans to propose, shit hit the fan because nine-year-old Natalie blabbed the secret to everyone in the family, *including Lynn.*

Laughter bubbled through her chest. She tried to hold it back, but the memory was too funny. Natalie burst into snorting laughter, unafraid that her laughter rang through the shop.

Lynn's face shifted from concerned to confused. She arched an eyebrow. "What's so funny?"

"Remembering," she said through giggle snorts.

"Oh, lord, what now?"

"When I ruined Dad's engagement surprise."

She chuckled. "Yeah, your father was pretty mad, wasn't he?"

"Yeah. Now he won't tell me jack-shit."

"Don't blame him, Miss Blabber Mouth, and watch that language."

They laughed together and continued to look through gowns.

"So," Lynn began. "Do you know what your theme is?"

Theme? Weren't they just looking for a gown? Natalie immediately stopped. The bulk of a tulle ball gown felt heavy against her.

"Uhm?" Her mind drew a blank. "Theme?" Natalie stared off into space. She didn't know there was a theme. "Oh!" Natalie said. "You mean the Prom theme. I think Night in Paris or maybe Enchanted Forest, I can't remember."

"Use your head for more than just carrying your pretty hair, Missy."

Natalie touched the blonde bun piled on her head. "Hey!" Natalie exclaimed.

Just then, two gowns caught her eye. The first one was a canary yellow beaded gown with a full ruffle skirt. Natalie wasn't keen on yellow, but this dress was beautiful.

The second was a pink strapless gown with a lace up corset.

"Double jackpot." Her voice was almost a squeak. Natalie didn't want to admit this, but pink was one of her favorite colors. The gown looked big enough, but formals were cut differently. She hoped it would fit.

Note to self: This is actually kinda fun.

"Imma go try these on," she said quickly.

Natalie flopped the garment bags over her shoulder. Her gaze darted around. There had to be a dressing room somewhere.

Easy Nat. Don't get too happy, they might not even fit, she thought. No way in hell could someone see her getting giddy over puffy princess dresses.

Tulle pooled from the bottom of the dressing room. The door nearly swung open from sheer force of the full skirt. Natalie barely caught herself from falling out the door. Thankfully, Lynn rushed over.

"I got you, kiddo. Let me help."

Getting into the dress was easy. The corset was the real challenge.

Natalie gasped as her mom pulled the corset laces tight. She drew a deep breath and held it. "This dress hurts!"

"Just wait till you get married," Mom said. "You'll need a team to get dressed."

Oh, great, wasn't it early to be thinking of that? She didn't even have a date for prom, let alone a prospect for marriage. Most of the boys at school were into sports or video games. Intelligent conversation was difficult to come by.

"When the time comes, remind me to elope," Natalie muttered.

The corset boning felt like knives cutting into her skin. Natalie read so many books where women would wear these things. Her only question was *how?* Layers of petticoats added to the struggle. Walking to the pedestal was half the battle.

"A person could build muscle walking in these full skirts!" Puffy pink tulle surrounded her.

Natalie clutched fistfuls of fabric just to step up. She steadied herself on the pedestal. Her fingers uncurled to release the material. The heavy skirt felt like dropping cement dumbells on the ground.

"I look like Barbie threw up." She grimaced. This dress looked so much better on the hanger. It washed her out completely.

Lynn stood to the side. The smile tugging at her lips was clear. She stifled her laughter. "Oh, Natalie, you're so dramatic. Next one then. You know what you like and don't like."

Back in the dressing room, Natalie leaned on the wall. *Note to self: This is a lot of work.*

The canary yellow dress was next. Natalie couldn't wait. Excitement fluttered in her belly like a thousand butterflies. Barely able to contain her happiness, joy radiated on her face. This was such a beautiful gown. *It had to fit.*

Mom helped cinch up the back. Natalie took a deep breath, trying to 'suck it in'. The corset on this one cut worse than the pink dress. The structure imprinted harshly into her side. All Natalie could do was sigh. The yellow gown was a size too small.

Lynn quickly released the laces. "Hold on, I'll be right back." She closed the door behind her.

"I'll just wait here," Natalie mumbled.

Feeling disappointed was an understatement. *Crushed* felt more accurate. Natalie had been so excited seeing this dress on the hanger. She pulled it off her body, avoiding looking at herself in the mirror, and shoved the massive thing under the door.

Her knees buckled. Slowly, Natalie sunk down onto the floor. She reached for her jeans that lay crumpled beside her.

"C'mon, where are you?" she whispered.

Natalie shook her jeans. *Thump.* The phone plopped directly into her lap. Natalie opened her messenger and began to type.

Note to self: Why? Just why? I deserve to feel beautiful too.

There was so much more Natalie wanted to write, but she couldn't find the words. She leaned against the cool dressing room wall. Why were they here again? Couldn't they just go?

A knock at the door made her jump.

"Natalie? Hon? You ok?"

This was embarrassing, sitting on the floor feeling sorry for herself. She just wanted to go home and hide. She wiped a tear from her cheek.

"Yes, I'm fine. I'll get changed and be right out. When are we meeting Dad?"

"Soon as we get done here, sweet pea," Mom replied. "But I have another dress for you."

Great. One more dress—and one more chance to embarrass herself. She had two options:

One, try it on to make Mom happy.

Or two, ask to leave—and risk sounding like a spoiled brat.

Reluctant over either option, trying the dress on was the better alternative.

"All right," she said.

The dressing room door creaked open. Rather than seeing Mom, layers of Cobalt blue blocked her view.

"Holy marshmallow man! What am I about to be stuffed into?" Natalie exclaimed.

The skirt was big and poofy, and crystals adorned the bodice of the gown, each one precisely placed to catch the light. It'd be like wearing a thousand midnight stars. Natalie had to admit—it was a whole lotta dress, but it *was* pretty.

Lynn laughed. "We lucked out. The sales woman said this dress just came in. So, if this is the one, you'll be the only girl wearing it."

Lynn helped Natalie step into the gown. Natalie kept her eyes squeezed shut, afraid of how she might look, afraid to be disappointed again. Soft fabric pressed against her skin.

Suddenly, her mind reeled.

What if it broke? Wardrobe malfunctions were *not* cute, especially on plus-sized girls. Broken zippers were bad enough. A broken corset meant risking full exposure. *Yikes!*

Rising nerves sent her stomach into nauseating waves. Natalie couldn't relax, even though the dress melded to her curvy form.

Please let it fit, she thought.

Nothing cut or hurt. Relief washed over her like a gentle tide. It actually fit! Despite the corset, this gown was surprisingly comfortable. She couldn't believe it.

"Ready to take a look? I really think you're gonna like this one," Mom said.

Natalie kept her head down. She curled her fingers nervously around fistfuls of tulle as she walked out of the dressing room to the pedestal and mirrors. The pedestal gently wobbled underfoot as she stepped onto it.

Natalie took a deep breath and held it for a few moments. Her nerves were at an all time high. She slowly craned her head up.

"Wait!" Lynn exclaimed.

Natalie froze in place. She kept her head down. From the corner, she could hear Mom get up. Light steps closed the gap between them.

"Let me take your hair outta that bun," she said and snatched the scrunchie from Natalie's hair.

"Um, ow?" Natalie muttered.

"Oh hush, child. Gimme a minute."

Lynn's fingers ran through Natalie's wavy tresses, hitting every knot and tangle until her mane was smooth. Then, a couple tight twists pulled at her temples, and bobby pins pricked her head.

"You brought bobby pins?"

"A mom comes prepared."

Natalie's heart melted.

"Now," Lynn said.

Natalie looked up. The plus-sized class book worm was gone. She gazed long into the mirror. Too stunned to speak, she stood in silence. The person staring back wasn't her. It couldn't be. Tears welled in her eyes. Her heart felt as if it were going to explode.

The gown fit like a glove, as if it was made just for her. Joy radiated from Natalie like the sun shining on a clear day. For the first time, she felt beautiful.

"Natalie?" Lynn said. "Whatcha think, lovebug?"

She hesitated. What could she say? *Perfect* was an understatement. Natalie felt just like Cinderella.

"I..." She paused. Then, after a long moment, she finally said, "Wow."

"You look gorgeous, kiddo. Do you think it's safe to say 'Yes' to the Prom dress?" Lynn smiled.

Natalie nodded happily. "Absolutely."

The rest of the appointment was a blur. Natalie was too overjoyed from finding the perfect dress to think about anything else. When Natalie emerged from the dressing room, Lynn was waiting at the check out. She threw her arms around Mom's neck.

"Thank you for making today amazing, Mom," she said, hugging her tightly.

"Thank you for being you, even if you are a blabber mouth sometimes."

They laughed and hugged once more for good measure.

Across the way from the boutique, the local bookstore had a sign in the window. *Tenpenny Dreadfuls: Tales as*

Hard as Nails was in stock, a book Natalie had been dying to read.

Natalie squealed in pure delight. "Mom!"

Lynn nodded. "Go on, I'll catch up."

Natalie didn't need to be told twice. She bolted from her Mom's side, bound for her happy place. As she was busy looking at books and feeling very satisfied by how the day turned out, Natalie's phone buzzed.

The incoming text, followed by the name, *MOM*, flashed on her screen.

Natalie read the text,

I told you it would be a day you'd never forget.

Note to self: I'll treasure our bond for all my life.

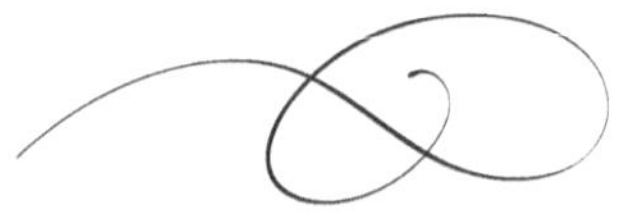

On Midnights Like This

By Jennifer L. Cilia

ALL EIGHT MEMBERS OF the prom committee of Lowell High School piled into their principal's tiny office, speaking simultaneously.

Kate Mendoza squeezed her eyes shut and willed the ringing in her ears to stop. "Wait, what?"

Kate had imagined her perfect senior prom as soon as she entered high school. The event was always very intimate, and this was her second time on the committee. Lowell High School's junior and senior classes usually decorated the activities center of the building in bright colors. The last few years were themed appropriately, with the past year being "Floral Embrace". All they needed were mixed color flowers, whether fake or real, woven with string lights to make it very soft and welcoming.

This year, however, Kate didn't envision any prom at all.

Everyone in the room argued with Principal Larson, and he whistled to quiet them.

"Prom is canceled this year," he repeated. "I'm sorry. We can't get the area cleaned up in time and fix the pipe that burst. There's too much water."

As the head of the prom committee, Kate was the one who usually handled crises like this, but the prom was in three days, and exhaustion had set in.

He pulled a file out of his desk drawer and handed it to her. "These are other locations that we have scouted for prom in previous years if you want to see if you can find something last minute, but getting one in by Saturday may be nearly impossible. Otherwise, I'll have to cancel everything. We can use the same theme and decorations for the next prom."

"But most of us won't even *be here*, since we're gradu-ating!" Kate exclaimed. "We raised so much money this year, and now, we can't even go."

The door behind her slowly opened, and his assistant Mrs. Cole stepped into the room. "Principal Larson, your last appointment is here."

Kate started to object, but she kept her mouth shut. This was out of her control. And she became the head of the prom committee to feel more *in* control.

The committee members left the room, but she stayed behind. Maybe she could try and persuade Principal Larson to throw a more casual event.

"What about—"

"Kate, there's paperwork involved with everything. It's better that we cancel now, rather than on Saturday." His eyes drifted to his office door. "Ah, yes. Come on in."

Milo, Kate's best friend, and Principal Larson's son, appeared in the doorway.

"You're his next appointment?" she asked.

"Milo, what can I do for you?" Principal Larson asked. "Don't you have to be at the rink?"

"Not for another hour." Milo was an elite hockey player who played for the Lowell Stars, training with his team at the local ice arena. He turned and saw Kate sitting in the opposite chair. "What are *you* doing here?"

She gestured to Principal Larson. "Milo, your dad said that we can't have the prom where we want it on Saturday."

"What?" Milo gasped and snatched the folder from her. "Really, Dad, why not? Are you trying to ruin senior year for me, just as you've done since the beginning of the semester?"

"A broken pipe in the wall and the activities center flooding wasn't in the plan." Principal Larson shuffled some papers on his desk into a neat pile and placed a stapler on top. "I know this is your senior year and this shouldn't have happened, but it did."

Kate pressed her lips into a straight line, then smiled. "What about the cafeteria?"

"Yeah, the cafeteria. Or, or, the, uh, library," Milo quipped.

"We can't fit three hundred people in the library at one time." Principal Larson stood from his chair. "And the cafeteria is being used for a school function for the freshmen." After reaching over to pick up his cell phone, he started for the door. "I'm sorry, Kate. We can't manage to have it here this year. My hands are tied."

When he left, Milo sat in his dad's chair across from Kate, who racked her brain thinking of things that she could do to have a prom. She could get the freshmen to move their event, but it was too late to even have them consider.

This was the worst timing. Stressing about finals, graduation, waiting to see if she got into NYU, and finding out her ex-boyfriend Brayden was back in town with his girlfriend wasn't helping either. Brayden would have told her that it was too bad.

Kate's eyes wandered outside. Her grip on the chair was so tight, her knuckles were as white as the magnolia trees through the window of Principal Larson's office.

"Hey, Kate?" Milo's hands waved in the corner of her view, and she blinked back to focus on him. "Hello?"

"Hmm?"

"We should have the prom at Lowell."

She scoffed. "At the rink? No. No way."

"Why not? It's the perfect place to have it."

"You don't know if everyone can skate," she pointed out.

"That's the beauty of it. No one has to skate if they don't want to. We can roll out the carpets, decorate the ice, the snack bar, everything. We'll hopefully get the deposits back, refund everyone, and use the money in the petty cash for snacks and decorations."

"I don't know..."

"We don't need a whole lot. It will be like having skating parties like we used to do when we were in junior high."

Kate's eyes lit up. She loved those ice skating parties at Lowell. "That's not a bad idea."

"And we can have it after hours," he continued. "The—"

"Why would we have it after hours?"

Milo looked behind her, probably to make sure he wasn't overheard.

"Milo?"

Leaning in, he whispered, "Let's just say I am not my dad's favorite person right now. Can you be at the rink at 8:30 to go skating? I'm working tonight, then we can talk. Me and Jesse will be there."

"Jesse and *I*," she corrected him.

"Oh geez." His eyes rolled. "Please?"

She didn't know what Milo had up his sleeve, but it was probably something awful.

"Fine," she muttered through clenched teeth. "But if it involves us getting into some kind of trouble, then I don't want any part of it. It's hard enough having the school breathing down my neck. I don't really need to have my parents and your dad finding out what we did, if I agree to whatever you're proposing."

"So, it's settled. Secret midnight prom," he replied. "You good?"

Kate nodded. Her stomach flip-flopped.

"Good." He hastily rose out of his chair, paused, then faced her. "You know, you can't let last fall go, can you? Can you not see that he moved on? It's been six months."

"I'm totally over Brayden."

"*Lies!*" he exclaimed, pointing at her as if they were in a courtroom. "He *has* moved on. You know that, and you should too. He's at NYU. You've been accepted to three—no, four—colleges, including Penn State. If you're holding out for NYU, you may be waiting forever."

At her blank stare, he turned and left his father's office.

He may have been right.

⌇⌇⌇

At 9:00 p.m., Kate pulled into the parking lot at Lowell Ice Arena, where Milo's elite hockey team played. Milo's truck was the only one in the parking lot.

This prom is such a bad idea, she thought. *What if we get caught? Will my college recommendations be revoked? I may not be able to walk at graduation.*

After taking a breath, she parked her car and walked toward the entrance. *Milo doesn't know what he's talking about.* She shook her head. *Brayden hasn't talked to me in four months, why would he even care about why I haven't talked to him?*

She backed up when she saw a dark figure wearing a black hoodie jiggling with the lock on the front door. When the figure turned, the word, *Staff,* was written on the back.

"Milo?"

Milo pulled back the hood on his sweatshirt, shone a flashlight on her face, and gasped. "I expected you a half hour ago."

"Hey, watch it!" She raised her hand and shielded the light from her eyes. "Sorry I'm late. Where's Jesse?"

He unlocked the doors and followed her into the arena. "I let him go early. It's dead here tonight."

Lowell Ice Arena was a popular place in the springtime in their small town of Old Orchard, Georgia, as everyone enjoyed a break from the heat to go ice skating. Milo's parents grew up there with Kate's parents, then after living in Boston, they moved back to Georgia when his dad got a teaching job at the high school. Milo and Kate met in kindergarten and had been inseparable ever since.

Kate shivered and headed for a picnic bench near the snack bar, and Milo followed. "So, what are you thinking?"

"I can put a carpet on the rink there, and then we can decorate with balloons. Wait, are you agreeing to do this?"

She tilted her head, her eyes rolling. "I'm hearing you out first, and then I'll make a decision."

"Well then, Kate, let me show you." He took her hand and led her to the side of the rink behind the glass.

"What am I looking at?"

"You can really picture it if you see it completely in the dark ."

She cocked her eyebrow at him, but obeyed and closed her eyes.

"Now, imagine the glow of Christmas lights hanging over sheer navy and black tulle above us. We step out onto the red carpet, like we're going to the Oscars."

He went on to explain there would be a carpeted section on the ice with chairs for anyone who wanted to sit. He already persuaded some of his friends to bring food and drinks, and they would be at the snack bar. One of the other hockey players agreed to set up speakers and control the music with his phone.

Milo also promised he would have his dad on speed dial in case anything happens. "So, what do you say? Sounds wicked, right?"

The overhead lights shone bright and Kate squinted as she opened her eyes. "You have three hundred pairs of skates?"

"Three... hundred... pairs?"

"Well, yeah. We have to invite everyone. Total, there's two hundred and ninety-five in the junior and senior class. And I'm not counting anyone else who will bring a date that doesn't go to our school."

He inhaled, then slowly let his breath out, as if he was trying to relax. "Our rink isn't an NHL arena, Kate. I don't think we can invite everyone."

"What? We have to."

"I don't care. We don't have time, and I think this should be your friends, and my friends, exclusively. That's what, thirty or forty people, tops, including dates? I'm drawing the line at the liability. I can't have the entire junior and senior classes causing trouble here."

Her face fell. "Then, no. We can't do it." She pushed him away and started walking back to the picnic table.

"Listen!" He cut her off, slowing her down. "Kate, my point is, we can still have a party, but it won't be for everyone. We can still get dressed up and have fun like it was prom, but it won't actually be the *school's* prom. And no one would know but us."

She stared at him for the longest moment. Milo was acting unusual, insisting that she agree to this wild idea. He never cared about school functions, and she had never seen him this excited before. "Us? As in, no adults that can break up any fights or if someone gets hurt? Or, what if something goes wrong?"

"School is a half mile from here, and we can all put our cars in the upper parking lot where no one will even see them. And Dave Fox said his brother, Declan, could swing by every hour and see if we were okay. If we all keep this quiet, and everything goes off without a snag, then you can have your perfect prom. We'll have it at midnight and be here for a few hours. Trust me, I've thought of everything."

Could they put on a prom with less than an eighth of the senior and junior classes, and still fly under the radar? The more he talked about it, the more she wanted to do it, and risk getting into trouble. As long as he had a backup plan for his backup plan, it would be a great night.

"What do you say?" Milo asked, his eyes sparkling. "Will you plan the prom with me?"

The only thing preventing Kate from saying yes was the fear of getting in trouble. But if this could go off without any problems, they could have the perfect prom. She wasn't sure what would happen, but she was ready to find out what could.

"Yes. Let's do it."

At 11:15 on Saturday night, Kate swiped her eyelashes one final time with mascara and put on her favorite pair of earrings, ones she received from her mom for her eighteenth birthday. She pulled her new teal-colored tulle dress out of the closet and hung it up on a hook fastened to the door. The layered ruffles sparkled in the moonlight. Since her prom was canceled, Kate's parents went away for an early anniversary night. The anticipation of Milo's arrival had Kate's stomach in knots.

A photo of her and Brayden at last year's prom stood on her vanity, hidden by the original prom invitation. She was so happy back then and thought they'd still be together if he hadn't broken up with her. Maybe Milo was right. Kate sighed and dropped the frame into her trash can.

She slipped into her strapless chiffon cocktail gown with glittering tulle ruffles that billowed from her waist.

She paused in front of the mirror and twirled, loving how the dress swirled around her.

Kate's watch dinged with a notification.

"This is Peanut Butter," she answered, indicating the code name Milo had given her in a spy game they had played outside when they were seven.

"So, what, am I the only person who's in front of your house dressed like a penguin? Let's goooooo."

She rolled her eyes, pressed the button on her watch, and said again, "This is Peanut Butter."

After a silence, he whispered, "PB, this is Jelly, here."

She smiled, glad he remembered the secret code. "Happy prom to you, too. I'll be right down." She stepped into her Converse sneakers, grabbed her jacket from the hallway, and slipped it on as she descended the stairs. After locking the front door and dropping the keys in the pocket of her dress, she walked carefully down the sidewalk, the skirt brushing lightly against the concrete.

"Kate."

Her heart skipped a beat when Milo opened the door of his dad's bright blue restored 1973 Dodge Charger. He didn't wear a typical prom tuxedo, though, just a suit and a tie. "A secret midnight prom is exactly what I wanted to do on a Saturday night. Stealing my dad's car wasn't, but a thrill it was. You didn't want to see me try to get this baby out of the garage."

It triggered a memory from when she turned sixteen. Milo's mom taught her how to drive that year. Mrs. Larson preoccupied herself with Kate as an escape from the cancer. Kate thought of her as her bonus mom.

"I never asked you to do that." The car was his dad's prized possession. "You're not going to get into any trouble, right?"

Laughing quietly, Milo slipped a beautiful corsage with white roses and turquoise daisies around her wrist. "You look, uh, nice, I guess," he stumbled over his words. "I wanted to pretend we were going to the real prom, not the fake one." He opened the passenger door, took Kate's right hand, and let her slide into the seat.

He always was a southern gentleman. He learned that from his mom, who said, *The woman you love should always be treated with respect and dignity.*

His mom was right.

"It's not a fake prom." She smiled. "It's our prom."

A lot of cars were in the parking lot behind the school when they arrived. Some of Milo's friends were heading toward the entrance to a path in the woods that led them to the rink, and they followed. With his help holding up her dress behind her so it wouldn't get dirty, she gathered it up and gingerly walked down the path.

"Are you doing okay?" he asked. "Almost there."

"I am."

When they emerged, a makeshift walkway with flickering battery-operated candles lined the grass to the side door, which was propped open.

She glanced at Milo, excited to be experiencing this with him. "Let's go!"

They walked down a long, dark hallway, and she reached for his hand. He held it tightly, and she prayed he felt the same spark she did.

Her hand never left his as they glided into *their* senior prom.

The rink was exactly how they envisioned it. The glass walls were draped in black crushed velvet cloths, and strings of lights above the tables made it very warm and inviting. On the carpeting were four tables set with thirty-six chairs, and there were four or five boys over by the speakers arguing over what Kate assumed what the next song would be. Others were already ice skating. The line for a photo booth was about ten people deep.

Kate's eyes lit up. "Oh, my gosh, you got one of these! Wanna take a photo?"

"Absolutely!"

They waited in line, which moved quickly. He pulled aside the curtain and let her inside first. The seat was big enough for two people, but Milo's muscular body took up most of the area.

"Here," he said, pulling Kate into his lap. "Ready?"

The camera started snapping, and with each photo taken, they changed positions. One of them was silly, one was serious, one was of them switching sides, and the last one was of them gazing into each other's eyes.

"Kate," he whispered.

Kate could feel his heart beating against hers. His face was so close, she could see the gold flecks in his green eyes. Her breathing slowed as she relaxed in his arms. It felt wonderful being close to him.

When the bulb flashed and the photo was taken, he blinked and looked away.

He grabbed the photo strips from the disposal box and handed one to her. "To remember our senior prom."

One of Kate's friends called her from the rink's doors and she walked over. "Come on! You need to get out onto the dance floor. Thanks for everything. It seems like everyone's having fun!"

"You're welcome! It looks amazing here."

Someone nudged Kate's shoulder. She whirled around, and Milo stood behind her with two pairs of skates. She looked at him quizzically.

"Like I didn't know your size," he said. "May I?"

They walked to the picnic benches, and he laced up her skates first, and then his. A slow song began. Almost everyone paired up, and a group of singles skated together in a long line. Kate grabbed Milo's hand, and they glided for the remainder of the song. When it ended, they removed their skates and joined their friends on the makeshift dance floor, which felt cold underneath Kate's feet.

"Are you enjoying tonight?" Milo asked her. "This was a great idea."

Kate agreed with him, but suddenly, she had a feeling something was going to happen. She looked around and made sure everything was in its right place, until she spotted a group of people near the snack bar that she didn't know.

Milo apparently noticed, too, when she saw him staring behind her. "Who are those guys?"

She groaned after recognizing one of the boys. "Oh, my gosh. Brayden?"

"Brayden, as in your ex-boyfriend?"

She nodded.

"Do you want me to take care of him?"

"No, I can handle him."

She headed to the snack bar to face her past.

Brayden's friends pushed him in front of Kate. He wore his letterman jacket from high school and her favorite baseball cap that she returned to him.

"No, guys. I... Hey, Kate," he said nonchalantly.

"What the hell are you doing here, Brayden?" she shouted over the music. The boys behind him smeared chocolate on the glass and had broken the soda fountain. Butter dripped down the counter in front of the popcorn machine.

"I, uh… I wanted to talk to you. I broke up with Erica and came back home to go to college here. I figured we could pick things up where we left off."

She stood in front of his face, and could smell alcohol and weed on his breath. "You're drunk, Bray. Go home or I'm going to—"

"Going to what, Kate? Going to go home to cry? Cause that's what you did the last time. I… missed the way we were together. Our late night talks like we would do tonight."

Kate's face flushed. "I did not, because I moved on. Seriously, can you just not do this? I don't want you here. You weren't invited."

"Come on, man." Milo appeared beside her. "I don't want to have to get the police involved."

"Yeah, because no one else knows you're here. Well, except your dead mom."

Before Kate knew it, Milo had thrown Brayden a single punch, a bruise forming on his right cheek.

"Milo, stop!" she shouted.

The music ceased, and everyone gathered, their phones lit, recording the argument.

"You need to get out of here, and take your guys with you." Milo faced Kate. "Are you okay?"

She nodded, a bit scared, and tears fell on her cheeks. "Please, Milo, I have this handled."

Brayden struggled to stand up and wiped his nose, blood dripping from it. "You know what? Take her. She didn't put out anyway."

Milo whirled around and hit Brayden again so hard, he knocked him out. "Get him away from here," he said to the group. "Before *you all* end up like him."

Brayden's friends dragged him outside and threw him in a car, apologizing to Kate and Milo, leaving them standing together alone in front of the arena.

Milo turned to Kate standing next to him, as she watched them drive away. "Are you alright?"

She glared at him. "Why did you do that?"

"What?"

"Milo, I told you I had it handled. You don't need to swoop in and save the day like a hero. You're my best friend. Friends support each other." She wiped tears from her eyes and dragged mascara down the side of her face. "I'm so tired."

"Tired of what?"

"I'm tired of you teasing me, of feeling like you have to stick up for me all the time. I'm *not* your little sister!"

The sticky, humid Georgia air clung to her like a wet blanket. Her hair had fallen out of its updo. Long tendrils of her wavy locks dangled square around her face. Milo had never hurt her like this before. And he needed to fix it.

The reflection of lightning illuminated the windows of the arena, and thunder rumbled in the distance. When Kate looked down at her dress, rain droplets started to stain the ruffles.

"Kate, you don't understand. I've stood in the background all this time and said nothing while that jerk strung you along. Watched when he broke up with you. Held you when you discovered that he had a girlfriend while he was still dating you toward the end of your relationship." He took a deep breath. "You were there when my mom died. You made me laugh when I wanted to cry. You are the most beautiful, affectionate, bold, clever person I've ever known, and I love you. I've wanted to tell you for the longest time. My God, I love you so much."

She froze, unsure of what just happened, and stepped back, almost tripping over her dress. Opening her mouth, she closed it for fear of saying something she would regret later.

"I know this is crazy, but—" he continued, then was interrupted by a car racing into the parking lot. As it got closer, Kate realized it was Milo's. It screeched to a halt at the bottom of the stairs.

The person driving kicked open the door, and his dad appeared.

"Milo!" he screamed. "Where is my car?"

Milo's face turned white. "Oh, shit."

The storm blew over, and so did the prom. Milo's dad sent everyone home, except for Milo and Kate, who he made stay behind. It was almost six in the morning, and Kate hadn't said anything to Milo since his dad left, but she desperately needed to discuss what happened.

"I seriously hate you right now." Kate wiped the popcorn butter off the floor in front of the snack bar. "We didn't need your dad finding out."

"After I gave you the perfect night, we had one snag and got caught. If my dad hadn't discovered us, our night would have been so much better." Milo closed the door to the stock room that held the skates and locked it.

On her hands and knees in her dress, she scrubbed the floor in frustration. Milo emerged from behind the counter and grabbed a sponge, dipping it in the bucket.

After she finished cleaning one tile of linoleum, she threw the scrub brush back into the bucket and wiped her forehead with her hand. "The least you can do is—"

"Apologize," he finished. "I know. I'm so sorry."

Starting on the next tile, Kate swore that after tonight, she never wanted to see Milo again. However, he was her best friend, and he *did* profess his love for her. That's one good thing that came from the night. She stopped and grabbed his hand.

"What?" he asked.

"Let's take a break. The rink needs to be scraped and cleaned, right?"

Fifteen minutes later, the Zamboni emerged onto the ice, with Kate behind the wheel in her prom dress, Milo instructing her on how to operate it. She started to clear the snow off the rink and disperse water onto it, leaving a clear sheen behind them.

"We've been coming here for forever, and you've never asked me to ride this," Milo said.

She shrugged. "I've always wondered what you would have said if I asked you."

As she drove around, making sure the ice smoothed, Kate didn't know what else to tell him. Here she sat with

Milo, her best friend, who finally told her how he really felt about her, and she had no idea how to respond.

"So," he started. "About what I said outside..."

She pressed on the brakes and turned the key to the OFF position on the enormous monster they sat upon. "I'm really flattered, Milo. Thank you for everything that you've ever done for me."

His face fell. "Oh."

Kate wanted to tell him how she felt, about him being the first one she thought about in the morning, and how she prayed for him at night before bed. She willed the hurt that Brayden caused earlier to disappear. This could be the start of something that it seemed like they both wanted.

She didn't know what else to say, so she did what she usually did when she wanted to hide.

She ran.

Making sure she didn't slip on the ice, Kate crossed the rink to the entrance of the makeshift tunnel and pushed the emergency exit door open, hot air whooshing into the hallway.

"Kate! Stop!"

"Milo, leave me alone!" she shouted behind her, but he caught her at the exit and pulled her into a kiss, their souls finally connecting. Every tensed muscle in her body relaxed as she melted into him.

Oh, my stars.

As the emergency exit door closed, leaving the hallway completely dark except for the twinkle lights above them, they could see each other clear as day. When Milo deepened the kiss, Kate's arms squeezed around his neck, then she let her hands roam around his torso. When he let go, she didn't, and wanted more. She hadn't felt this type of chemistry with anyone else.

"Milo," she whispered.

His face hovered over hers. Their friendship had always been platonic, and she was so happy he had finally told her how he felt.

"About earlier..." She ached to taste his lips again. When he didn't answer and glanced away, she lightly touched his cheek with the back of her hand. "I'm right here. What's wrong?"

He leaned his head down and pressed it against her forehead. "I needed to tell you," he whispered, his breath heavy. "I had to tell you before it was too late. It doesn't matter how you feel. As long as I told you before we left this place and I didn't have the chance. I love you, Kate Mendoza."

"I love you, too, Milo Larson," she murmured.

He wrapped his arms around her waist and picked her up. "On midnights like this, you are the best thing that's ever happened to me."

"I've always been yours." She smiled. "And you've always been mine."

ONE NIGHT

BY S.J. KORZELIUS

I turn and twirl and wish I was anywhere else
but they asked and she's dying so how could
I say no   I never would   one of my many
just like her traits I've heard since I was six

"You can't just *not* go to your senior prom!"
mom said, buying a breast-accentuating dre$$
we   couldn't afford   compounding my guilt
after hers surgically removed without success

I planned to come out to them the very day
they sat me down   the very damn day to tell
me her prognosis, the   brittle air   tasting too
much like dirt to breathe sweet Aria's name

Aria who understands and teaches me not to

succumb to heteronormative sh!t   but will be
in her own heels and dress with a date in a tux
maybe we can sneak away

for
a
kiss

I smile one last time before Dad pockets his
phone   hesitantly   tears slithering from eyes
we pretend not to notice like we getting paid
memories saved but not her not us not ever

Eli'zah at the door, no rusty Nissan pumpkin
tonight it's his auntie's tricked out Jeep for us
and a wristful of red and white carnations no
baby's breath   he knows what tonight means

"Have fun, kids! Stay out all night! Be Safe,"
they wave while we walk down the stairs into
a future devoid of joy   but I can pretend   for
her   for one night.

Partners in Crime

By Avery Timmons

I sigh as I draw a big red X through May 3.

Which means tomorrow is the fourth, which means tomorrow is my senior prom.

Which *also* means—unless a miracle happens in the next twenty-four hours—I'll be going alone.

I look over at the back of my bedroom door, where my dress hangs, just like it has been for the last month. Erica and I went shopping over spring break. She found this gorgeous dark-blue dress that hugs all her curves perfectly, and I settled on one with a poofy, floral skirt that makes me feel like I'm finally living out my childhood dreams of being a princess. We were both so excited that day, so optimistic, talking over Panda Express in the mall food court.

"I can't *wait* to see Noah's face when he sees me in this," she had said, cracking open her fortune cookie. "I worry sometimes he forgets how hot of a girlfriend he has."

"How could he forget?" I had grinned at her. "But I feel like Dominic might ask me. I don't know. We've been talking more lately. Should I mention in pre-calc when we get back to school that I bought a prom dress and hint that I don't have a date? Or is that too much?"

But Dominic never asked me. He asked Anna, the girl who sits behind us in pre-calc. And no matter how many times Erica has said it's okay if I tag along with her and Noah, I can't bring myself to be their third wheel on one of *the* most important nights of high school, especially with this being their first prom together, after they started dating last summer.

But now my phone is vibrating with a FaceTime call, and I know it's Erica even before I pick up, dragging my gaze from that big, ugly red X on my calendar, and all the others I drew before it.

"Hey." I don't manage to sound very enthusiastic.

"Hi." From the curt way she says it and the tight purse of her lips on the screen, I immediately know something's wrong. "Guess who won't be joining us for prom tomorrow."

"Oh, no." I instantly forget all of my own woes and pathetic single-ness. "What's going on? What happened?"

Erica smiles, and it's a smile I recognize well. I like to call it her *I'm-about-to-kill-someone* smile.

"*Well*," she says. "You know how I've been telling you about Sydney, and how she's been a... sore subject, I guess, in our relationship? And how I've been, like, *hey, I feel like you've been hiding something about your friend-*

ship with her, like you might not really be just friends, and he's been all, *no, you're crazy?* Yeah, well, I'm not."

"No," I breathe.

"Oh, *yes*," she continues, talking faster and faster. By the way the background is moving behind her, I can tell she's pacing around her room. "They've been texting. Pathetic stuff, really, like *why won't you just break up with her already? I love you so much,* and, *oh, it'll be so much easier if we just wait until after graduation, and then we never have to see Erica again, and then we can be together forever.* And guess what? I only found out because he let me look up boutonnieres on his phone. And she texted him in the middle of it."

"*No,*" I repeat. "Erica, I'm so sorry."

She smiles again, and her eyes get all squinty, but I know what this one is. It's her *I'm-trying-not-to-cry* smile.

"Y'know what? Come over. Right now. I have stuff for milkshakes."

I have two Oreo milkshakes and two gigantic bowls of popcorn ready by the time Erica gets to my house ten minutes later. I warned my parents and my brother ahead of time, so we're able to sneak down to the basement with our treats without much questioning. But Erica's back to anger, kicking the big bean bag chair we keep in the corner.

"I'm. So. *Stupid.*" She emphasizes each word with a kick.

"*No. He's* so stupid," I say firmly, as she finally surrenders, flopping down onto the bean bag chair and sipping her milkshake. "You didn't do anything wrong. *He's* the one who's been cheating on you and lied to your face about it. That says so much more about him than you. You've been nothing but good to him."

Her shoulders sag in defeat as she drains her milkshake, slurping until she's just pulling air through the straw. It kills me to see her like this, my normally bright, bubbly best friend. But now, it's my turn to return the favor from every time she's listened to my rants about boys who don't like me back and cheered me up in junior high after my boy best friend dropped me and started dating the girl I hated—two separate times.

"But you know what we're gonna do?" I ask, waiting for her to look at me before I continue. "We're gonna get all dressed up tomorrow, and we're gonna have a great dinner, and we're gonna go to the dance and show these boys what they're missing."

After a brief pause, Erica sets her cup down, slowly nodding. "Yeah. *Yeah.* We're gonna have a great time."

I smile encouragingly. "We're gonna have a *great* time."

"And we're gonna key his car."

"And we're gonna– Wait, wait, hold on." I stare at her for a moment, trying to figure out if I heard her right. "We can't key his car. That's vandalism, Erica. That's a crime."

She sighs, but a twitch of her lips tells me she's feeling better already. "Yeah, yeah, okay, whatever. Can we *egg* his car?"

I stare at her again, letting a few beats pass as I think. I feel a sudden flash of anger at stupid Noah. My prom was never going to be perfect—not in the little-girl dream way, with a handsome date to slow dance with while I wear a pretty dress. But Erica should have been able to have that experience with her boyfriend who *supposedly* loved her. But now, she can't, and it's all his stupid self's fault.

And I'm not *that* good of a person.

"I'm pretty sure that's still considered vandalism," I say. "But I won't tell anyone."

For the first time since I picked up the phone earlier, Erica breaks out into a huge smile: her *let's-do-this* smile.

We decide to leave the dance a little early to do it.

Erica shows up to my house around five the next day with her mom, looking as beautiful as I expected her to. She got her hair professionally done. It's twisted into an intricate blonde bun at the nape of her neck, specks of glitter peppered throughout, making her head glimmer each time she steps under a light. It reminds me of how she'd glitter her hair for performances when we took dance classes together in elementary school.

I don't think I look half as great as she does, but I still feel just as princess-y as I hoped I would, my skirt *swooshing* each time I move.

"Look at your *hair*," Erica coos, reaching out to trace one of my ringlets that I only achieved with Mom's help. "So pretty."

Our moms also make plenty of comments about how pretty we look and about how grown up we are as they take pictures of us in front of the fireplace, my brother and dad being supportive by sitting in the room and nodding, but clearly bored out of their minds. Whenever Erica's eyes start to gloss over or her smile falters, I squeeze her arm. I can't imagine what she's going through. All of my heartbreak has been because of guys who never promised me anything—I just got way too into my head about them. But Noah... Well, he's a whole 'nother story. My chest tightens with anger and pain as I remember when Erica texted me *months* ago, giddy, because he told her he loved her.

I hope he'll like the three dozen eggs we bought for him.

After about twenty-minutes too long of pictures, pictures, and more pictures, Erica and I manage to escape and make our way to dinner. I drive us to one of the more fancy restaurants in our small town, a Japanese restaurant we save for special occasions.

I push the conversation, but halfway through the meal, Erica grows quiet and serious.

"I'm sorry," she says finally. "I know I haven't been very good to you tonight." She pushes her noodles around her plate, avoiding my eyes.

"*What* do you mean?"

She heaves a sigh. "It's your senior prom, too. I've been gloomy all night, and that's not fair to you. So, I'm sorry. You shouldn't have to spend prom night trying to cheer me up."

I reach out and grab her hand that's not holding her fork. "You know I'd rather spend prom night cheering you up than with some stupid boy who I probably won't remember the name of in twenty years anyway, right?"

She finally looks at me, her eyebrows lifted in surprise. Or maybe, like she's realized something.

But whatever it is, she doesn't voice it aloud. Instead, she just says, her voice kind of small, "Really?"

I squeeze her hand. "*Duh.*"

She smiles gratefully, and soon after, we head for prom.

We arrive a little after seven, so the parking lot is already almost full. While it's still light out, we take a long stroll through the lot and spot Noah's maroon Honda Civic with the dented bumper, parked in one of the more secluded back rows, which works in our favor.

"He probably parked back here so they could make out in his car and not get caught," Erica grumbles as we head arm-in-arm towards the school, where we can see the flashing lights of the dance through the darkened windows.

My stomach flutters with anticipation. "Well, then I hope he enjoys the moodsetter we're giving him later."

A smile crosses Erica's face, but it quickly drops as we stop at the crosswalk, waiting for a few cars. "Is it bad I miss him?" The front, curled tendrils of her hair blow lightly in the breeze as she turns to look at me. "Part of me is still angry like I was last night, but most of me is just sad now. Like, I obviously blocked him like you told me I should, but... I don't know. It's like I want to unblock him in case he wants to explain himself. I just... I don't understand. I would've *never* done something like that to him."

Even as the passing cars die down, we continue to stand still on the sidewalk. I stay quiet, letting Erica dump her feelings out before we have to walk in the school and see him.

"And I love him still. I think that's the worst part. He hurt me so bad, and yet I still love him. That's pathetic, isn't it?" She laughs humorlessly, her eyes glassy.

I take a quiet minute to think about my answer, the distant sounds of music, laughter, and passing cars filling the silence.

"No," I say. "No. I think that's normal. Like, if you weren't hurting, and you didn't miss him and you didn't still love him, I think it'd just mean you stopped caring about him a lot earlier. I wouldn't expect you to feel okay about it overnight." I offer her a small smile. "Literally."

Erica scoff-laughs, rapidly blinking her unshed tears away. "*Literally.* God, I can't believe it." She shakes her head, and a bobby pin clatters on the sidewalk, but neither of us bothers to pick it up. "But whatever. I'm not gonna let him ruin the night—*our* night. Do you think they're gonna play the same music they did for homecoming? Because that sucked."

She tugs me across the street as if nothing happened, the two of us still arm-in-arm. Being this close, she smells like vanilla, and I know Noah got her a vanilla perfume she'd been wanting for their six-month anniversary.

It'll take time. I know that. But I'll be there for her every step of the way—even when that includes egging his car while she's wearing the perfume he bought her.

Whatever works.

The dance is already in full swing when we get to the cafeteria. We enter by a little area with circular tables where some people are sitting, but most are either on the crowded dance floor by the DJ setup or on the other side of the cafeteria by long tables covered with plates of various snacks and appetizers. Everything is bathed in the glow of lights changing colors—pink one second, yellow the next, then blue, and so on, and so on. The bass of the music pounds in my chest, my heartbeat seeming to sync in time with it. Erica's staring off into the distance, toward the food tables. And I know who she's looking at even before I spot him.

He's alone, which is somewhat of a relief to me. I feel a smug sense of satisfaction when he turns his head enough for me to see his troubled expression, his tight-knit brows.

But then I see he's wearing a dark blue bow tie—the one he bought to match Erica's dress, and my smugness quickly hardens into anger. Who does he think he is?

"C'mon, let's go dance." I tug on Erica's arm, wanting to pull her away into the crowd before he spots us. I don't know if he'd have the audacity to approach Erica here, in front of everyone, but I don't want to risk it.

As we walk to the dance floor, I lean close to her, getting a whiff of that vanilla perfume again.

"Remember at our eighth grade end-of-the-year dance when everything with Julian was going on?" I practically yell over the music.

"How could I not?" she yells back, starting to smile. "I chewed him out in the bathroom for dropping you the way he did. Best day of my *life*."

I laugh, and her smile grows.

"Just think of it as me repaying the favor. But I'm not gonna yell at Noah tonight, and neither are you. He's not worth our time. Well, later, maybe, but for good reason." I pause, grinning. "But neither is this music. What *is* this?"

"Didn't I call it?" Erica says, grabbing my hands. "But, whatever. Dance with me!"

The dance floor feels like it's about fifteen degrees hotter than the rest of the cafeteria, and everyone's bumping elbows and shoulders. When some junior accidentally stomps his dress shoe on Erica's exposed toes, we agree to try something different.

"Photo booth?" I suggest, pointing past the tables to where there's a little curtain-clad photo booth, reminiscent of the ones Erica and I always begged our moms to give us money for when we'd go to the mall as kids. And I think Erica might be thinking the same thing, because she smiles wistfully as she tugs me towards the booth.

But as we duck into the darkness, her smile seems to dim a bit. I'm sure she's thinking of all the cute pictures she could have taken with Noah in here, so I'm quick to grab a comically large pair of sunglasses from the prop bucket and put them on her, careful to avoid snagging her hair.

"Fine!" She laughs, placing a glittery, pink cowboy hat on my head. "Here ya go then, partner."

We keep up the awful Southern accents as we pose for our photos, standing back to back with finger guns, smiling with our arms around each other, and making funny faces, giggling and scrambling to think of a new pose before each take. Despite graduating in a few weeks, I feel like we're those ten-year-old girls in the mall again, and by the time we exit the photo booth, I realize I definitely wouldn't have rather been asked by some boy I barely know and have to worry about not looking ugly or acting silly in front of him all night. There'll be plenty of time for that when Erica and I won't have this anymore, instead having to FaceTime each other from our colleges, miles and miles and miles apart for the first time in our lives.

And for once, I'm the one more in my head. Erica is pointing at us in the photo strip, laughing about how ridiculous we look. I take the moment to peer around for Noah, and I end up finding him on the dance floor, but he's just standing, surrounded by some of his guy friends.

Our gazes lock across the cafeteria. His eyes seem to light up, like he was looking for us—for Erica. But I shake my head, hoping he gets the message:

If you ever really, actually cared about her, don't you dare come over here.

And, to my relief, he doesn't. He just looks away.

We don't stay for much longer. After picking at some of the food and saying hi to a few friends, we quietly slip out. As soon as we step into the cool, late spring air, we take off as fast as we can in our heels to my car, where the eggs are awaiting us in the trunk.

"I can't believe we're doing this," Erica whispers as we walk over to his car. "What if he decides to leave now, too?" She freezes a few feet away, holding the first carton of eggs close to her chest. "Is this the right thing to do? Or should I be the bigger person?"

Her voice is low and timid, so I know she wants a genuine answer. I take a minute to genuinely think about it. The night is quiet now, with it being late enough that barely any cars are out and about, and everyone is inside the school still.

He knew what he was doing. He knew how badly it would hurt her, and yet, he still did it, and he didn't own up to it until he was caught.

I think about us walking away and taking our eggs back home. I think about school on Monday morning, and the possibility of Noah coming up to Erica's locker while I'm not around, asking her to talk or apologizing. Maybe asking her to give him another chance, now that he's realized what he's lost. And it infuriates me.

"No," I say. "As in, don't be the bigger person."

Erica pauses for so long, I think she's changing her mind, and I'm a little disappointed, my shoulders sagging. But then I hear that crackle of the egg carton opening. Slowly but surely, she takes out a single egg, turning it in her hand like it's a softball and she's twelve again, mentally preparing herself for the first pitch of a game.

I jump when the egg cracks against the windshield.

Both of us stare as the slimy yellow yolk slowly slides down the glass.

She makes a noise, and at first, I think she's crying, but no—she picks up another egg, and this one cracks against the other side of the windshield. She lets out another laugh.

I start to grin as I watch, just letting her do her thing, with the occasional glance over my shoulder to make sure we're still in the clear. After about half of the carton is empty, she starts to attach a reason to each egg before she slams it against the car—on the windshield, on the back windshield, on the door windows.

Soon enough, she's opening the next carton of eggs.

"And this," she says. "*This* is for every time you called me crazy when I had a gut feeling something was going on!"

One by one, she takes each egg out and throws it against the car with an impressive amount of force, until finally, she's left with another empty carton. Her eyes are filled with a feral sort of joy, and she's smiling. And this one is her *I'm-having-the-time-of-my-life* grin.

I start to laugh. And I can't stop. Which makes Erica start giggling, and then, we're both gasping for air, only to stop, look at each other, and break out in laughter all over again.

"I can't believe this," she giggles. "He's gonna be *pissed.* How many do we have left?"

"One more dozen." I open the carton, holding it out to her, and carefully study our work so far. "Do the handles. He won't be able to get in without the eggs covering his hands that way."

Erica just looks at me for a beat, grinning.

"You evil genius," she says slowly. "I knew you had it in you. And our moms always said *I* was the bad influence."

Once all the door handles and windows are covered in egg, we book it back to my car, laughing hysterically and nervously the entire way. Erica barely has the passenger door closed before I take off, wanting to get as far away from the school as possible before Noah sees what we did. At every stop light, I look behind us, my heart pounding, as if Noah—or worse, a cop car—is following me.

"Relax!" Erica laughs, rubbing her hands over her arms. "You're making *me* nervous!"

We end up safely back at my house (though I did speed... a little), still giggling as we walk through the door. The house is quiet, so I shush Erica as we sneak up to my room, but not before grabbing some snacks.

After changing into pajamas and turning on a random movie, we talk about the night—how everyone looked, who was with whom. I don't say anything about Noah, and neither does she, but it doesn't feel like he's the elephant in the room for the first time all night, or like we're dancing around bringing him up.

But I know that tomorrow, she might be sad again. And that the next day, she might feel okay. And the next, she might be angry. Her feelings will change each day, but I'll be by her side through it all, because she's done the same for me.

After a long pause, she says, "Y'know what?"

Her words are slow and slurred, and sure enough, when I look over at her, she's fighting to keep her eyes open. Her eyelids droop, and then fly open, only to droop again, but she manages to get the rest of her words out. "Noah and I would've broken up at some point any-way. And then I'd just have mem'ries of a prom I went to with some stupid boy. But this one..." She pauses for so long, her eyes closed, that I start to think she fell asleep.

But then, still with her eyes closed, her lips curve into a slow smile. "This is one I'll be able to tell my kids about. And they'll never believe it, that I egged a boy's car with Auntie Amber. But we'll know. We'll remember."

When her breathing slows, I know that she's finally fallen asleep, curled up on my bed, still with that small smile on her face.

And I smile as I walk over to the calendar and draw a big red X through May 4.

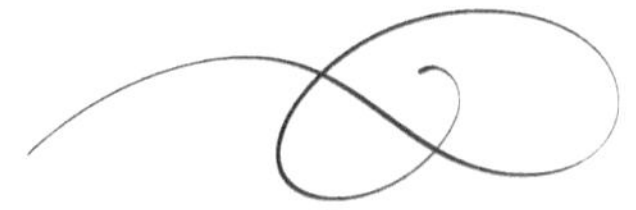

Perfect Promposal

By Kristi McManus

"Yes! Of course I'll go to prom with you!"

The small crowd that had gathered broke in to cheers, whoops of excitement accenting the scene as Sarah jumped into Justin's arms. With a nod from me, rose petals began to fall from the trees, raining down soft waves of blush, pink, and peach, courtesy of my team. Another cheer rose from the crowd at the grand finale, and I couldn't help the smile that stretched across my face.

As Sarah and Justin's retreating forms disappeared across the courtyard of the school, the small crowd dispersing with them, I shifted gears and began the next phase of my process: the cleanup. Pulling my long brown hair into a messy knot on top of my head, I popped the trunk of my car and began breaking down the scene we had created.

I had to admit, I wasn't sure I was going to be able to pull this one off. When Justin had asked for a Disney themed promposal because his girlfriend, Sarah, loved everything Disney, I was anxious. How did I pull off the magic of Disney in the middle of an Ohio high school courtyard? Thankfully, my best friend and artist in residence, Marija, had created a stunning backdrop of Cinderella's castle to be draped between the two towering oaks that dominated the courtyard. Balloons and flowers blocked out the school, and of course, the music of "When You Wish Upon a Star" came from hidden speakers. Everything turned out perfectly.

Marija joined my side, pulling her beautiful painted backdrop from the tree. "That was awesome," she said, a smile breaking across her tan face. "Maybe the best one yet."

"You say that about all of them," I pointed out, collecting the final speaker and popping the last of the balloons.

"Because you consistently outdo yourself." She blew a strand of her black hair from her face before handing me the corners of the backdrop. "You've pulled off successful promposals for more than half the school this year, and we still have three weeks until prom."

Before I had a chance to respond, a tall figure appeared from the sky beside me, and I yelped. Ethan's broad smile was the first thing I noticed as he uncoiled from his crouch on the ground.

"You scared the hell out of me," I scolded, slapping his arm.

His grin only widened, pride shining in his blue eyes. "Then I, too, have had a successful day."

I rolled my eyes. "You could have broken your neck jumping down from that tree, you know."

"You're the one who told me to get up there to drop those rose petals. Although, if I had hurt myself, I would have gotten workers' comp benefits since it happened through my job, right?"

I laughed, reaching into my pocket and pulling out a twenty dollar bill. "I don't know what kind of business you think we're running here, but all I can offer you is this."

Ethan's full lips pursed, the wind toying with his light brown hair as he rose to his full height. He towered over me, the sun silhouetting his muscular frame as if the heavens themselves shone down upon him. Warmth crawled up the back of my neck. Butterflies escaped the cage in my stomach and forced me to avert my gaze.

With a lift of his shoulder, he accepted my offer, sliding the money into his own pocket. "I guess beggars can't be choosers."

Once the last of the items were loaded into my trunk, the heat of the late spring sun causing sweat to bead on my forehead, I leaned against the side of my car. "Good job, team." I smiled, scrolling through my Perfect Promposal app on my phone. "Now, we only have..." I paused to count. "Three more promposals to finish."

Marija wiped the back of her hand across her forehead. "That's not much time. Do you think we'll get them done?"

"Yeah, I think so. I've got the one at the theatre this Friday. I already received confirmation from Mr. Baker that we can get in to the theatre before it opens to the public for the evening showings to set up."

"Did he agree to free popcorn for the setup crew?" Ethan leaned against my car next to me, nudging me with his elbow.

"Yes." I laughed. "You can have free popcorn as long as you don't make a mess before people show up."

Ethan feigned offence, but I ignored him as I continued through our list. "Then, we have the scavenger hunt on Sunday for Graydon and the baseball team Thursday for Mike." I gnawed on the inside of my cheek. "It's close, but we can pull them all off with a week to spare."

"Good thing we work well under pressure," Marija said, pushing off my car and earning a laugh from Ethan.

"Good thing I closed requests a month ago, you mean," I added. "Otherwise, we might still have them pouring in."

"That too," she said, glancing at her phone. "We gotta go. I have to be at work in fifteen minutes."

Looking at the time, I jolted. "Crap. I have to be home. Mom's working this evening, and I have to stay with Grandpa."

Offering Ethan a wave, I climbed into the driver's seat with Marija in the passenger side. Pulling out of the school lot and onto the quiet road, our windows down and the warm breeze filtering through the car, I let the residual tension from another promposal ease from my muscles.

We drove in silence, Marija bobbing her head to the music while I tallied our income for the millionth time. What started as a favor for my brother when I was a sophomore and he was a senior had developed into quite the side hustle. It was only supposed to be one time for him to ask his long-time girlfriend, and now fiancé, to senior prom. Then, his friends started asking me to do the same for them, offering me money for my service. I made a lot of money that year and had a blast doing it. Junior year, not long after winter formal, I had people approaching me to ask if I could do their promposals. It hadn't even occurred to me to do it again, or for so many people, but again, offers of payment followed, and I couldn't turn down the opportunity.

Calculating the numbers again, the tension returned to my shoulders. Nerves released in my gut, my teeth gnawing on the inside of my cheek. The deadline for tuition for Ohio State was the week after prom, and I was still short on the amount I needed.

Marija had told me over and over to ask my mom, but I refused. She worked too hard already, picking up extra shifts at the hospital just to keep us comfortable. Once Grandpa moved in with us, our already strict budget became stretched wire-tight. Mom gave me a little, all that she could, when she learned I had been accepted to my dream school. I saw the guilt and worry in her eyes as she handed over the small check, wishing she could have given more. The sight broke my heart, and I promised her I had the money already, that I had saved, and was working and could do this on my own. The sadness lifted from her face, and I refused to be the reason it returned.

I had to figure this out alone, hence the promposal business, recruiting my best friend, Marija, and childhood crush, Ethan, as my team, to make people's dreams come true, including my own.

Turning down Maple St. toward Marija's job at the grocery store, she glanced toward me. "So, Ethan seemed flirty today."

I rolled my eyes as my cheeks flamed. "You say that every day."

"Because every day, it's true," she argued, turning to face me. "I swear, Mia, it's like you two are the only ones who don't see how much you like each other."

"Ethan doesn't like me. Not like that." I didn't miss the hint of sadness lacing my tone, even as I tried to sound unaffected.

"And you say *that* every day," she said. "Which only proves my point."

Pulling into a spot, I put the car in park and tried to keep myself from pushing her from the vehicle. "Your point doesn't even make sense. Now, go before I kick you off the promposal team."

Her laughter echoed as she pushed out of the car, slinging her bag over her shoulder. Instead of leaving, however, she stuck her head through the window. "You know, you could just ask him to prom."

I shot her a glare. "I swear, I will run over your toes if you don't leave."

She merely laughed again, throwing me a wave over her shoulder. I returned the wave half-heartedly, then headed home.

"Your Gran and I used to do that," Grandpa said, his voice distant as if the words were more to himself than to me. His pale gray eyes, just like mine, were trained toward the screen, enthralled by the movie we had watched more times than I could count.

"That's sweet," I said, just like I did every time he brought it up, glancing toward him with a soft smile. There was no point in reminding him he had told me the same thing over and over. Or that he had watched this movie with me several times a week for the last year. Or that every time a scene appeared with Carl and Ellie enjoying time together, whether it was reading books, taking a trip to the zoo, or dreaming of travel, he would say, *Your Gran and I used to do that.* As much as his mind failed him at times, watching *UP* seemed to bring back the memories that had escaped—memories with Gran, of their years together, and the things that made him happy.

And every time, my heart would break just a little bit more, for myself, because I missed my Gran so much, but more for him, for losing the love of his life. My mom didn't understand why a man in his eighties would want to watch a children's movie over and over, but I did. Because it wasn't about the movie, but the life it depicted, and the adventures to be had even when you thought those years were over. So, every time he asked to watch *UP*, I obliged him, making popcorn and sitting on the couch, stealing every moment I had left with him as if they were my last. Because I knew, just like in the movie, eventually they would be.

Tossing a piece of popcorn into my mouth from the bowl between us, my phone chimed in my lap. Grandpa didn't seem to notice, his attention latched onto the movie.

Perfect Promposal: New Message

How was that possible? I had closed the inbox ages ago, once our schedule filled up. Huffing quietly, I opened the message, convinced it was a glitch.

Anonymous: Hey! I know your app says you're closed to new requests, but I'm hoping you'd be willing to do just one more.

My brows furrowed, before I began to send a reply.

Perfect Promposal: Hi there. Unfortunately, we are not accepting new requests at this time. We are fully booked for this year. Sorry.

Setting my phone back on the couch beside me, I turned my attention back to the movie. It only lasted a moment before my phone chimed again.

Anonymous: I know, and I'm sorry for reaching out so late. But I'm hoping you'll make an exception.

Hitting reply, I began to type another declination, when another message came through.

Anonymous: I'll pay five hundred for the inconvenience.

I almost dropped my phone as I read over the message again. Five-hundred dollars? For a promposal? It had to be a typo. I usually charged between one hundred and two hundred, depending on how extravagant of a promposal the person wanted. But five hundred? That was crazy and probably meant they wanted something way out of my reach.

But that would give me enough to pay my tuition.

The realization sent a chill down my spine. My fingers flew across the screen.

Perfect Promposal: Five hundred? Are you sure?

Anonymous: Yes. Completely sure. I know you normally charge less, but you'll be doing me a favor. And the girl is totally worth it.

The corners of my lips kicked up at that.

Perfect Promposal: What do you have in mind?

Anonymous: Well, that's the thing. I don't really have any ideas.

Perfect Promposal: Well, tell me about the person you want to ask, and we will go from there. I can't promise we will take the job, though.

Anonymous: She's incredible, although I'm sure all your clients say that. But this girl really is. I've known her for ages, and we're friends, but I'm too chicken to tell her I want to be more. A friend recommended that I use prom as my chance to shoot my shot and said you're the best in the business. She's been so focused on everyone else lately, I want to do something that is about her, you know?

My cheeks began to ache at the sweet description on the screen.

Perfect Promposal: I do know. That's really sweet. What does she like? What kind of promposal would be her style?

Anonymous: I'm not sure. What would you like if it was you?

I was startled by the question, my mind wandering.

"Your Gran and I used to do that." Grandpa's voice broke through the bubble that surrounded me, and I turned to find him smiling softly at the television. It was the scene where Carl and Ellie were simply sitting beside each other, reading, Carl stealing glances at Ellie quietly. Grandpa's eyes glistened, a look of longing setting his features, and my chest ached again.

I always dreamed of having a love like theirs, one that made memories, lasted years, and extended beyond separation. As much as watching *UP* was for Grandpa, it had become just as much for me.

My phone chimed again.

Anonymous: Are you still there?

Perfect Promposal: Yeah, sorry. Still here.

Anonymous: What would your perfect promposal be? It might give me ideas. LOL!

This time, I didn't shy away from the question.

Perfect Promposal: This might be silly, but I love the movie, UP. I watch it all the time with my Grandpa. It's a way for him to remember my Gran, who passed a couple of years ago. But it's also for me to spend time with him, and fantasize about a love like theirs.

Anonymous: That sounds amazing! The girl I want to ask is really close with her Grandpa, too. I think she would love something that incorporated him. Do you think you could do it?

Perfect Promposal: Incorporate her Grandpa? Probably, if he was willing.

Anonymous: No, I mean all of it. An UP promposal.

I grinned. It was senior year. Perfect Promposal would end in just a few weeks as I moved on to the next chapter of my life. If I wanted to end on a memorable note, this would be it. It would be a lot of work, and would either be incredible or a complete disaster.

Only one way to find out.

Perfect Promposal: Yeah, I think I can.

———

It was the week before prom, and all of our promposals had gone off perfectly. The grand movie themed spectacle at the theatre, complete with an audience, had won a standing ovation. The scavenger hunt that had Ethan out until after midnight laying the trail of clues and texting me threats of filing a workers' compensation claim if he ended up with poison ivy on his ankles from traipsing through the treeline of the park, ended with an enthusiastic yes. Even the final event, a promposal by the captain of the baseball team for a girl in his history class, which involved the entire team, and even the coach in the middle of the final game of the season, thrilled the school.

I had been thanked, congratulated, and clapped on the back for closing out the year with such originality and a perfect *yes* record. And while I was proud of all we had accomplished, I couldn't help but be distracted by our final, and by far grandest, promposal of all. Not to mention that I had spent just as much time messaging with the anonymous client as I did planning. Even now, three days from the scheduled ask, I didn't know their name or the one of their love interest. Yet, we messaged every day, well into the night, going over every little detail.

Perfect Promposal; Do you want to include the dog?

Anonymous: Of course! Can't have UP without Dug.

Perfect Promposal: Where do you want this to take place? Can you get permission to use a property?

Anonymous: She lives near you, actually. And your house looks similar to the movie. Do you think you could do it there, and I could walk her by for the big reveal?

Perfect Promposal: Are you going to dress up like Carl?

Anonymous: As epic as that would be, I kind of have another idea. Do you think your Grandpa would like to play along?

Normally, I would never involve my friends or family in my business. But this one was different, and I couldn't help but ask. Grandpa was thrilled to be a part of our plan, laying out suits in his room and asking which one looked most like the movie. All week, he had been brighter, steadier, counting down the days to his *new adventure*.

The more I talked with my mysterious client, the more I felt like I knew him. Not his name or what he looked like, but that he was funny and caring, and willing to go the extra mile to make someone he cared about happy. And I couldn't help but feel a hint of jealousy for this mysterious girl he was going to these lengths for. So, I was putting everything I had into this promposal just as much for myself as for this lucky girl.

Sitting on the porch step of my home, Marija cross legged beside me as she put the final details on Dug's collar, I started going through the plan again in my mind just as a thud sounded on the walkway, and a tall figure appeared.

I yelped, jumping back. Ethan began laughing as he wiped his face with the hem of his shirt. Exposing his toned stomach caused a flutter in my chest, but thankfully, he was looking at the roof he had just descended. "Well, I did as you asked, mistress. The roof has been fitted with clips for more balloons than I think is humanly possible. I fear if we pull this off, your house might actually lift off the ground."

I smiled. "Then, we really committed to the plan."

"And I didn't even fall off the roof."

"Surprising," I replied as he flopped onto the step at my side.

Brushing his hair from his eyes, he looked out over the yard with a soft grin. "This is going to be a great final promposal, Mia. You've really outdone yourself."

"Thanks," I said, warmth climbing up the back of my neck.

Ethan was quiet for a long moment, then his voice turned serious. "Do you think she'll say yes?"

"I hope so. I mean, if she doesn't, I think she's crazy. If a guy is willing to do this much just to ask me to prom, I couldn't imagine saying no."

He nodded thoughtfully, the shadows casting along his sharp jaw. Again, I was struck by how handsome he was, how much he had changed from the playful, round-faced boy I had met in second grade to the striking, strong lacrosse guard he was now.

"What are you staring at?" His voice broke me from my thoughts, only to find his blue eyes crinkled in the corners, a teasing smirk on his lips.

"Nothing," I muttered, cheeks flushing at the realization I had been staring at him.

He said nothing more as Marija's voice interrupted our tense little moment.

"Done!" she cried, holding up the collar, complete with a voice translation box and nametag with *DUG* across the front.

"It's perfect," I said, taking the collar and turning it over.

"We're officially all set," Ethan said, looking at the collar before stealing a glance at me. "The balloons will go up on Wednesday, and then, we have nothing left to do."

"Except wait for her answer," I said with an exhale.

"The scariest part," Ethan added before standing to help Marija tidy up the porch.

Pushing through the front doors of the school, I wove through bodies in the courtyard, practically pushing my way toward the parking lot.

"Marija, you better be back," I muttered under my breath, hitching my backpack higher on my shoulder. Anxiety dug at my chest as I rounded the corner, eyes scanning the lot in search of my little blue Civic. When I came up empty, I cursed, pulling my phone from my pocket.

Mia: Marija, where are you?! You promised you'd be back before school let out.

I knew I shouldn't have given her the keys to my car. But when she cornered me outside the cafeteria before lunch saying she had one more thing to grab for the promposal today, and the only chance was her free period at the end of the day and she needed my car, I had no choice but to hand them over.

Only now, she left me stranded, apparently not able to answer texts.

"Mia," Ethan called out.

I turned to find him jogging toward me, dressed in a white polo and khakis. He looked unnervingly good, but I pushed the fluttering butterflies aside to focus on more pressing matters than my unrequited crush.

"What's wrong?" I asked, immediately worried. "Where's Marija? She said she needed my car because she forgot something for the promposal, but she's not back yet, and—"

"Everything is fine," he interrupted, hands raised as if approaching a wild animal.

Looking him over again, I gasped. "The balloons! Ethan, are the balloons—"

Gripping my arms gently, he gave me a calm smile. "The balloons are done. Everything is ready. Don't worry."

"But my car! Marija—"

"She finished what she needed to. Everything is set up at your place. We're all good."

Slowly, he turned me toward the street. "But—"

"Marija just got tied up with something else and asked me to walk you home. We'll be there in plenty of time. Don't worry."

"Ugh," I groaned, twisting the strap of my backpack anxiously. "We better hurry then."

He snickered. "You live only a mile away. We'll be fine."

Setting a brisk pace, I threw him a scowl. "If you're wrong and we run into an apocalypse and we're late, I'm blaming you."

He laughed now, rolling his eyes. "Fine. If we encounter an apocalypse on the walk to your house and are late for the promposal, you can entirely blame me."

We set off down the street, Ethan's long legs easily keeping up with my scurrying pace. The light afternoon breeze did little to cool the sweat that began to bead on my neck, both from the heat and from fear of messing up the biggest event of my career.

Turning down a treelined street, shadows stretching across the road and offering shelter from the sun, I finally faced Ethan.

"Why are you so dressed up?" I asked, eyes raking over him again. "You weren't dressed like that this morning."

He rubbed the back of his neck. "Lacrosse thing. Coach wanted us to dress nice."

I grinned, knowing how much Ethan hated dressing up. "You clean up well."

The corner of his lip curved upward. "Wow. Was that a compliment?"

"Don't get used to it."

"Wouldn't dream of it," he said, slowing his pace a notch.

"Come on," I urged, waving my arm at him. "We—"

"We have plenty of time. You don't want to show up all gross and sweaty, do you?"

"Did you just say I'm gross?"

Throwing his head back, Ethan groaned. "I said you don't want to be gross, not that you *are* gross."

Narrowing my eyes, I followed his now natural pace, choosing not to bicker any longer. It didn't take long before he broke the silence again.

"So, are you sad this is our last promposal?"

I lifted a shoulder. "Yes and no. I mean, I'm glad we pulled it off and that this hectic season is done. But I'm kind of sad that our little business is over, you know?"

He nodded. "I get it. It's been fun working for you, even if the benefits were lacking."

"You wouldn't need benefits if you weren't such a hazard." I nudged him with my elbow.

"I wouldn't be such a hazard if you didn't put me in hazardous situations for the sake of your 'vision.'"

"You could say no."

He paused for a moment, a pensive look on his face. "No. I couldn't."

I was about to ask him why not, when he continued.

"I'm going to miss the promposals," he admitted. "I liked watching you create all these incredible things for people, the way you got so excited about them and worked so hard to make them perfect."

"That was my job."

"It was more than that," he continued as we turned down my street, my driveway coming into view in the distance. "I liked working with *you,* spending time with you. When you asked me to help you, I thought I'd be nothing more than your sexy muscle to do all the heavy lifting."

I snorted, and he threw me a narrow-eyed glare before continuing.

"But it was fun watching them come to life, especially this one, because it's so personal to you. You finally got to do something for yourself, even if it was supposed to be for someone else."

"It was fun," I admitted as we approached my house. "I just hope she loves it and says yes."

"Oh, I know she'll love it," he said before rubbing the back of his neck again. "I just hope she says yes, too."

Walking up the driveway, the full scope of our creation came into view, and my heart stuttered. Hundreds of balloons of every color rose from the roof like a kaleidoscope against the green backdrop of trees. My attention immediately fell to Grandpa, sitting on a rocking chair on the porch in his brown suit, mimicking Carl's scowl to perfection. Before I had a chance to say anything, a streak of golden fur came barreling towards us. It collided with Ethan, tail slapping against my leg as he crouched down to pet his dog, Steve, who was our Dug stand-in.

"It looks amazing," I said softly, taking in all the features, everything we had built.

"It does," Ethan agreed, joining my side as Steve aka Dug bounded around the yard.

Glancing at my phone, my chest tightened. "It's five o'clock. They're going to be here any minute, we should—"

Before I had the chance to hide, Ethan grabbed my hand. "Actually, they're already here."

I stalled, eyes wide as I scanned the yard again. "What? Where are—"

He pulled me closer, taking my hands. My mouth opened to protest, until I saw the smile on his lips and softness in his eyes. "They're right here."

"What..." It was then that it hit me like a tidal wave. Why I never learned the name of the client or the girl he wanted to ask. Why he was so adamant that the promposal be exactly as I would want, all the details I dreamed of, with my own Grandpa watching on.

Ethan was the client.

He was Anonymous.

"Mia, I know we've been friends forever. I know I've had a million opportunities over the last decade to do this, but I always chickened out. I knew this was my last shot, and it had to be big to make up for wasting so much time."

Tears burned in my eyes as he released my hands and called Steve, aka Dug, back over. The dog obeyed eagerly, coming to sit by Ethan. Reaching down, Ethan pushed the button on the speaker, the collar Marija had designed working perfectly.

I half laughed half cried as Ethan's voice emitted from the speaker. "Mia, will you please go to prom with me?"

I nodded through my tears. "Yes."

The smile that broke out across Ethan's face stalled my heart as he pulled me into a hug. Steve, aka Dug, joined in, jumping on us while Grandpa and a now revealed Mia cheered from the porch. I buried my face deeper into Ethan's chest, excitement and embarrassment and every other emotion coursing through me.

Pushing me back, Ethan looked down at me with a crooked grin. "Does this mean Perfect Promposal is officially closed?"

I laughed, lifting onto my toes to press a kiss to his cheek. "Yup. And we saved the best for last."

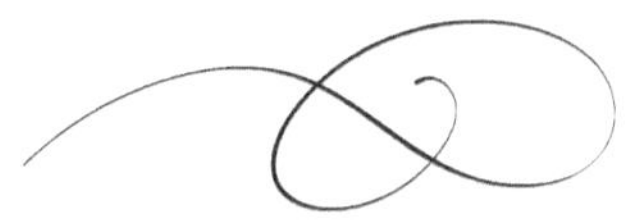

Prom Memories

By Lynn Katz

I REMEMBER THE YEAR: 1971

I remember his old-fashioned name: Elmer, like his father's, like his grandfather's

I remember his face: kind, sweet

I remember my dress: backless, paisley, muted reds and yellows

I remember the flowers: wrist corsage roses, baby's breath, wilted and cold

I remember our ride: the cab of his brother's garbage truck, me tucked in the middle, laughing, gleeful

I remember the smirks, the jeering, the catcalls, the sneering...

And no matter how hard I try...

That's all I remember.

PROM QUEEN . . . PRETENDING

BY STEPHANIE HENSON

I'M THE PROM QUEEN!
The tiara that sparkles on my head says so.
So does the sash draped with a smile across my chest.
On the outside, I'm the picture of perfection.
But all is not what it seems:
Honey highlights through thick hair mask my natural color.
Curls have been straightened and smoothed.
A spray tan gives the appearance of a golden goddess.
New nails applied and finished with care.
Have starved myself for a week to fit into this dress.
A designer frock that we really can't even afford.
Makeup caked, skin glowing with glitter.
Red bottomed heels of superiority that allow me to tower over everyone else.

Nice to your face while plunging the knife into your back.

This is me.

Or who you want me to be.

It's all about perception when you're a Princess or a Queen!

Fake it until you make it. . .

And I made it!

Presenting your Prom Queen . . . Pretending.

Promquest

By Lissa James

Junior prom was such a human tradition. Girls spent too much money and time on shiny dresses and overdone hair and makeup while guys had to—he didn't actually know what guys did, but the whole thing was stupid, and the worst part was that he, Nicholas Warburton, son of the High Wizard and heir to Cloudcoven Castle, did not have a date. He had, in fact, *never* had a date. During his year at Westhaven High School, human girls had proven shockingly unimpressed by his Warburtonian charm and good looks, and he was forbidden to use his magic, except in an emergency.

"Do I have to go?" he whined to his mom during their almost-daily phone calls.

"Of course not," she said in her usual sympathetic tone.

"Great, then I won't—"

"But your father won't consider your training complete until you've participated in all the rituals significant to humans your age."

"So, if I don't go to prom, there's no chance he'll let me go back to being homeschooled next year?"

"That's correct."

"Can't you talk to him? I've done my homework, attended football games, bowled, and sung karaoke at a classmate's party. Isn't that enough?"

"Nicky, find a nice girl. Go to prom. Get your receipts, as the humans say. Then, I'll talk to your father."

He was too mature to stomp his foot. "I don't wanna!"

"Then... stay... senior year." Her voice faded into static, then came back stronger. "Who knows? You might even have fun."

Ha! Double ha! What could *possibly* be fun about a ritual as idiotic as junior prom?

Static crackled again. Maintaining a cell-phone link between realms was tricky, even for a white witch as strong as his mother. "Nicky, I've got to go. Miss you."

"You, too."

After the call ended, Nick flung himself onto the bed, which creaked dangerously. He wanted to stare moodily at the ceiling, but since his bed was the lower bunk in the spare room of the Sullivans' house, where he was spending the year as a foreign exchange student, all he could see were the doodles the Sullivan children had etched into the bedframe over the years—initials, a blob that might have been a skull, *Go Tigers*, and a series of lightning bolts.

He sighed. He didn't want to do it, but he needed help.

The basement door was locked. He knocked three times, paused, and knocked again. The door opened immediately.

"Nick! Come in!"

Pete motioned for him to enter and closed the door behind him. His ginger-brown hair stood up, and his eyes were bleary from his late-night gaming sessions. As always, he looked thrilled at the company, and Nick felt guilty that they hadn't become the best friends both their parents were clearly hoping for.

"Want to play Cosmic Castle Quest? I've reached a new level."

It was hard to share Pete's enthusiasm for a video game when he'd explored real castles and performed actual quests. Nick shook his head. "I need your advice."

Pete's eyes widened. He patted the seat beside him on the worn leather sectional that occupied most of the basement's central room. "Come, come, Dr. Pete is in session."

Dr. Pete? Nick knew better than to ask. "I need to go to prom."

"Prom?" Pete's face brightened further. "You want to go? It shall be my mission to help you with Promquest."

Pete could turn anything into a quest. Right after Nick arrived, he'd launched Pizzaquest to find Nick's favorite pizzeria in town. It was a short quest, since there were only three. Then had come Shoequest, for sneakers to replace Nick's hand-tooled boots. Pete was currently on Licensequest, so he could quit riding the school bus, but so far, he'd failed the driving exam twice.

"You'll need a tux," Pete told him. "So retro, but school rules. I'll show you where to rent one. You can ride with us—Domino, Casper, and me. We're going to—"

"Don't I need a date?" Nick interrupted.

Pete's smile dimmed. "Sure, ideally. But going with friends can be fun, too."

"For the full experience, I should have a date, right?"

"Yeah, I guess."

"How do I decide who to invite?"

Pete shrugged. "Pick someone you find attractive, and—"

"Kelsey Cameron is very pretty! I'll ask her."

Pete's eyes widened. "Kelsey? You think—"

"Do I call her? Text? What's her number?"

"You think *I* have Kelsey Cameron's number?"

"Then, where do I get it? Online?" Nick headed for Pete's desktop computer on the table beside the TV.

Pete grabbed his sleeve. "You can't ask Kelsey."

"Why not?"

"For one thing, she's almost certainly got a date already. For another..." Pete flopped onto the sectional's sagging cushions and pulled Nick down beside him. "Remember when we discussed social levels in American high schools?"

"Yes." Pete had been annoyingly persistent in explaining them.

"I'm a geek. I know it, and I own it." He waved at Nick's star-patterned shirt and black cargo pants. "You fall into the Artsy group. They're geek-adjacent. Maybe one rung higher."

Nick nodded. The explanation was unnecessary, but he'd learned it was quicker to let Pete talk than to argue with him.

"Kelsey is a cheerleader. I don't know how they do things in Estonia."

Nick's cover story was that he was a foreign exchange student from Estonia. Since no one in small-town Tennessee had ever met an Estonian, they didn't question Nick's accent or unfamiliarity with American customs.

"In Estonia, no one cheers," Nick said gloomily, just to mess with Pete.

"Okay, well, here, cheerleaders are the highest tier of the female social hierarchy. They date boys at the top of the male social ladder, which, despite all the supposed progress of the twenty-first century, still means athletes—football players, mostly."

"I can become an athlete."

"Remember when you tried athletics? We joined a game at the park, and when someone tackled you, you threatened to have him beheaded."

"Yes, although I would never actually have anyone beheaded. My country is very civilized."

"Estonia used to behead people?"

"Estonia, yes. Many years ago. But you were explaining about a prom date?"

"I'll be honest, even if she didn't have a date, Kelsey wouldn't go with you. She might even laugh or insult you if you ask her."

Nick bristled. In Clouddesmesnes, girls at court were *thrilled* when he invited them to dance. They lined up to talk to him. Their mothers advised them how to capture his attention, and they gossiped about what he said, wore, and ate. The idea that a mere cheerleader was worthy of his company would be laughable.

But he wasn't in Clouddesmesnes, was he?

He forced down the magic that was making his fingertips tingle. "If not Kelsey, then who?"

Pete shrugged. "I'm not the best person to ask, given my ongoing lack of female companionship. Maybe try my parents?"

"I just select a girl and ask her to accompany me to prom?"

"You can. But there's also this thing called a promposal."

Pete explained, in great detail, every human prom tradition he could think of. By the time he finished, his parents had gone to bed, and Nick had to wait until breakfast to talk to them.

When he went downstairs, Pete's dad was pouring orange juice into small carton-printed glasses. "Smurf or Scooby?"

"Scooby," Nick chose at random. "Mr. Sullivan, how do I determine which girl I should invite to prom?"

Mr. Sullivan handed him the glass. "Greg, remember?" The Sullivans kept reminding Nick to use their first names. "That sounds like a Meg question."

Meg stood at the stove, scooping up eggs with a plastic spatula. She smiled at Nick. "You're going to prom? Wonderful." She set a plate of eggs on the table. "It'll be an experience to remember."

"Yes, but I don't know how to choose a date."

"Hmm." She put one hand on her hip and held her spatula in the air. "The prom's in two weeks, so you don't have much time. Your best option is to see if anyone is giving you signals."

"Signals?"

"Watch the girls you're around. Notice who smiles or stares at you. See if she twirls her hair or looks down and then back at you, or if her cheeks turn red when you talk to her. Those may be signs she's interested."

"So, if I find a girl who does that, I just ask her to go to prom with me?"

"Sure."

"What if she says no? That would be embarrassing!"

"It's a risk you'll have to take. No one else needs to know."

Unless he did a promposal, as Pete suggested. Did girls expect such a gesture? Nick ate his eggs and picked up his Scooby glass. Promquest was more complicated than he'd expected.

The redhead who smiled at him on the bus did the same to everyone, so it probably wasn't a signal. He thought a girl said hello to him in math class, until he realized she was talking to someone behind him. When he picked up the notebook a tall blonde girl had dropped, she thanked him without even looking his way. All day, he watched the girls around him without seeing the signals Meg had described. He was debating whether or not he could convince his parents going with friends constituted a full prom experience when he walked into the art studio.

Art was his favorite class. His teacher, Ms. Sun-strom—Sunny, as everyone called her—did her best to make the art studio a happy place. This week, she was letting them pick their projects, which, in Nick's case, meant ink drawing and watercolors.

He had finished a watercolor of a sailboat, and he picked up his blank sketch pad while considering what to draw next. Sunny was always complimenting his ink skills, not surprising, considering he had begun lessons at the age of four. Drawing sigils, letters, and diagrams precisely and correctly was a crucial wizardly skill. Tobin, his father's court scribe, called Nick his finest pupil ever.

Without conscious decision, his hand began to move. Nick looked down to see that he was creating not a sketch, but a Gothic letter *P*, entwined with a vine of roses. He glanced around to see if anyone was watching him. Across the room, someone was.

Lilith Morales.

Her skin was pale copper. She wore sparkly eye makeup, and at the ends, her brown hair turned into a bright, purple-pink. She waved her paintbrush, and he raised his pen in response.

Meg hadn't mentioned paintbrush-waving. Was it a signal? Lilith's cheeks weren't red, but he was afraid his were. Why hadn't he thought of Lilith as a prom date?

He knew the answer—he was *very* good at not thinking about Lilith and the flutter in his stomach whenever he saw her. A relationship with a human couldn't last. He was going back to Clouddesmesnes, and the last thing he needed was to, as his mother would say, catch feelings for a human. Not that he wasn't human. Wizards might consider themselves superhuman and better than ordinary humans, but biologically, they were the same.

His cheeks grew redder at the thought of biology, and he ducked his head. Maybe, subconsciously, he had already decided what to do, because what word started with *P* and ended with *rom*?

He changed pens and drew the roses in red, with a gold-inked box around the *P*. He spent the rest of the class meticulously inking each letter, with an artistry that would make Scribe Tobin proud. He was finishing the hook of the question mark when a shadow fell across the page.

"Whatcha working on? Another sailboat?"

Jasmine wafted up his nose, and he didn't need to look to see who was beside him. "Not a sailboat."

"What is it?" Lilith peered over his shoulder. "Pr—oh! Nice! I'm sure she'll love it, whoever she is."

She stepped back, and Nick froze.

Do it, part of his brain urged, while the other part thought, *What if she says no?*

He spun around and held the paper out. "It's for you."

Her mouth dropped open, and she made a noise somewhere between a gasp and a squeal.

"I mean, if you don't already have a date—"

"I don't."

"And if you want to—"

"I do."

"Maybe we could go to prom together?"

"Yes!"

Her hands were clasped in front of her, and she bounced once. Hopefully, he'd read the signals correctly. At least she hadn't laughed.

He took the page back and wrote his number in one corner. "Text me your address. I'll pick you up next Saturday at seven. Okay?"

"Yes. Great. Perfect."

He thought she was going to say more, but the bell interrupted them. Nick was thankful they didn't have any other classes together, because he didn't know what to say to her now.

"I got a date," Nick told Pete after the school bus had dropped them off.

Pete paused outside the front door. "You did? Who?"

"Lilith Morales."

"The hot art chick?" Pete nodded in approval. "Cool."

"So, now I need a tuxedo?"

"Yep. Tuxedoquest! Guys night at the mall! I'll text Domino and Casper."

Guys nights with Pete were never as exciting as they sounded, but Nick couldn't risk making the wrong clothing selection. "Okay."

At the mall, they found a black tux that paled in comparison to the blue silk robe embroidered with magical symbols that Nick wore in Cloudcoven, but Pete assured him it was appropriate. "Tuxedoquest complete!"

As thanks for their help, Nick ate pizza with the guys, then went back to the basement to play videogames. They were progressing nicely through a castle's levels until they found a treasure chest with strange carvings.

"Stop!" Nick yelled, but it was too late.

Before Nick could warn him to check for booby traps, Pete opened the lid and released a cloud of poisonous green gas. The group had to do a side quest to find a healer before they could resume their main quest of locating a power jewel to save the kingdom of Ranevar.

Nick could've told them the premise was ridiculous. A single power jewel couldn't save a whole kingdom. King Hervay of Larsland had *three* power jewels, and they hadn't helped when the swampsluggers invaded his kingdom. Although, to be fair, Hervay was ninety and never the most skilled wizard.

They played until late, and Nick spent the next week watching music videos and practicing his moves. After twelve years of dance lessons, he considered himself pretty good, but human dances were different. He practiced until Pete called him "super cool," which wasn't the confidence boost Pete had meant it to be.

In art class, Sunny assigned group projects. Lilith wasn't in Nick's group, so they barely talked. By the next Saturday, he was worried. Had she changed her mind? Forgotten? She'd texted him her address, but he'd heard nothing since. Should he have reminded her?

"No way is a girl going to forget about prom," Pete said when Nick had asked. "Although, maybe you should've texted her."

"Should I do it now?" Nick asked. He was wearing his tux. Meg had helped him, and Pete put on their bow ties and made them come downstairs for pictures.

"Don't worry. That girl will melt when she sees how handsome you are." Meg positioned him beside Pete and snapped several shots.

Greg leaned against the doorframe and nibbled on a protein bar. "You two handsome dudes have fun, you hear?"

"But not *too* much fun," Meg said. "Remember your curfew."

"Call me if you need a ride." Greg finished the bar in one bite.

"Nick, don't forget your corsage," Meg said.

"Corsage?" Nick froze.

Meg frowned. "A flower for your date to wear? Pete said he told you about it."

"I did," Pete said.

"I forgot," Nick said—or, more accurately, hadn't been listening. "Can we stop and buy one?"

"None of the florists will be open now," Meg said.

Nick's stomach churned. He might have ruined his date and failed Promquest.

No, it was just a side quest. Corsagequest. He didn't have flowers, but maybe... He turned and ran up the stairs.

"Where are you going?" Pete called. "We're leaving in ten minutes!"

In his room, Nick grabbed his art supplies and pulled out a sheet of heavy paper. He began sketching a simple script letter *L*, entwined with roses. Scribe Tobin wouldn't approve, but he had likely never had to ink his way through a prom emergency. He cut a circle around the letter and frayed the edges. Not his best work, but given the circumstances—

"Nick! Time to go!" Pete called.

Nick rummaged for a safety pin and ran downstairs. A black SUV was waiting in the driveway. The Sullivans waved goodbye, and Nick and Pete hurried outside. Casper's brother was driving his father's enormous black SUV, and he was wearing the uniform of the car service he worked for. Not a limo, but, as Casper pointed out, free.

The guys teased each other about their looks. Pete's and Casper's tuxes matched Nick's, but Domino's was deep red with a ruffled shirt. Nick gave Casper's brother directions, and in minutes, they reached a small 60s rancher. The door opened before they stopped, and Lilith ran outside, waving goodbye to someone inside the house. Before Nick could get out, she climbed in beside him and slammed the door closed.

"You look beautiful," he said, which he was almost sure was true. He'd only glimpsed her for a second, and the car's interior was too dim for him to see her clearly.

"Thank you." She arranged her skirt over the seat, and Nick smelled jasmine.

They rode in silence until Casper's brother stopped at the high school entrance.

"Be back here at eleven," he said.

Meg had told Nick what to do. He hopped out and extended a hand to Lilith, while the guys piled out the opposite door. Lilith stepped down, holding her skirt in one hand. A red carpet stretched from the school's front doors to the cafeteria, which was decorated with banners and fake torches. A photographer stopped them for pictures beneath a sign that read, *Welcome to Ye Olde Westhaven Prom.*

When Lilith let go of her skirt, it billowed around them. The dress was made of a shiny fabric in the same shade as the tips of her hair. It had a ruffled neckline and a skirt so full that Nick couldn't get close enough to put both hands on her waist like the other couples were doing.

Lilith saw him step back, and her face turned red. "Sorry."

"No problem."

Nick took her hand, and they smiled for the camera. While they posed, Kelsey Cameron in a gold sequined dress, and two of her cheerleader friends, joined the line.

One of them said, "Check out that dress."

"Probably an old bridesmaids dress from some nasty thrift shop! Either that, or she thinks they're remaking *Gone with the Wind*," Kelsey said. They talked over the music, as if they wanted Lilith to hear. "Why'd he invite *her*, anyway?"

"I know, right? She's so weird! Always has been. Does she use her hair as a paintbrush in art class?"

They all laughed. Nick was guiding Lilith toward the cafeteria, but suddenly, she broke away, ran around the barrier that roped off the classroom wings, and disappeared down a dark hallway.

Pete and his friends had finished their photos, and Pete stopped beside Nick. "What's happening?"

"Some girls were talking about her."

"Where'd she go?"

"She ran off."

"Go after her, man." Pete nudged him, and Nick took off.

The only illumination was from the emergency lighting. Nick followed the hallway until he spotted her where he should've guessed she'd be—her favorite place, the art studio.

She hadn't turned on the lights, and she sat huddled on one of the tables. Nick walked over to her.

She started speaking before he could. "I'm sorry. You shouldn't have invited me. Just go. Have fun. I'll call my dad to come pick me up."

"No, I don't—"

She raised her head, and her tears glinted in the dim light. "Kelsey's right. I did go to a thrift store because prom dresses are really expensive, and this one was the best they had. I thought it'd be okay, but now, I know it's all wrong. I've ruined my prom, and I don't want to ruin yours, too."

Nick patted her arm awkwardly. "It's okay."

It was not okay. He couldn't leave her here alone. Should he call Greg to come pick them up? Or hide out here until Casper's brother came back? But then Nick wouldn't complete his Promquest, and his father wouldn't allow him back home.

"It's dark in the cafeteria. No one will notice what you're wearing."

"Kelsey and her posse already noticed." Lilith dabbed her eyes. "I'm not going back out there. They're probably telling everyone about my ugly dress."

Another side quest. How did he fix the problem? Nick looked around, but there were no spare dresses hanging in the art studio. Anyway, he wasn't sure the dress was the real problem.

"Why does Kelsey care what you're wearing?"

Lilith sniffled. "It's not the dress—I mean, not just the dress. Kelsey has been kind of bullying me for years."

"Bullying you?" He'd thought Kelsey would be the happiest person in the school, with her golden hair and high social status.

"Yeah." Lilith hunched her shoulders. "We were never friends, but in fifth grade, I got the part she wanted in the school play, and she's hated me ever since."

"She bullies you over something that happened in fifth grade?" Ridiculous, but no worse than the ambassador of Larsland, who refused to speak to Sir Egglebert Swannington, because Sir Egglebert had stepped on his foot twelve years ago and never apologized.

"Why? She's not a friend of yours, is she?" Lilith looked up at him.

She's the first girl I thought of taking to prom.

Nick stopped himself before he could utter the words that might doom his Promquest. Thinking before speaking. His diplomacy tutor would be so proud.

"No. I just don't understand why she would mistreat someone over something that happened so long ago."

"It's not just me. She and her friends talk trash about everyone. They're mean girls." Lilith's hands clenched into fists. "Sometimes, I fantasize about revenge. I'd like to punch her or rip up her pompoms or spray-paint bad words on her sparkly dress."

She looked around as if suddenly realizing she was in the art room with a supply of spray paint conveniently available. Nick squeezed her arm gently.

"What if we find a way to get revenge that's less likely to get you expelled?"

"Like what?"

"Will you trust me and go back to prom?"

"You have a plan?" Lilith blinked at him with hopeful eyes.

He did not have a plan, but he was sure he could think of one to get Promquest back on track. "Trust me. Kelsey Cameron is going to regret she ever bullied you."

She thought for a long moment before sliding off the table. "Okay. I guess things can't get any worse."

"One more thing." Nick reached in his tux pocket for the substitute corsage he'd made and offered it to her. "A Nicholas Warburton original."

He half-expected her to laugh or reject it. She stared at it, then looked up, eyes shining. "It's beautiful. Thank you." She pinned it at her neckline and reached up to hug him. The scent of jasmine filled his nostrils again, and he was almost too dazed to hug her back.

They crept through the dark halls back to the cafeteria. By now, they'd missed almost half the prom. The cafeteria lights were on, and Principal Billings, a slender Black woman with silver-white hair, was on the raised area that served as a stage.

"I hope everyone's having fun!" she said and received cheers in response. "Will the nominees for prom king and queen please come forward?"

The crowd parted to allow three couples to make their way to the stage.

"I bet Kelsey will win," Lilith said through gritted teeth. "No one would've voted for her if they heard the things she says."

"Like about your dress?"

"Like about everyone."

The candidates lined up onstage. Kelsey's dress sparkled brighter than the other two girls' gowns, and she was smiling as if she knew what was coming.

"Your new prom queen is..." Principal Billings paused for dramatic effect. "Kelsey Cameron!"

Kelsey put her hands to her face, as if shocked, then stepped forward to get her crown. She looked so happy, and she'd made Lilith so sad. Everyone *should* know the mean things she said.

She waved to the crowd and leaned toward the microphone. Nick flicked his hand to invoke a speech-remembrance spell his father had used to uncover a spy posing as a traveling merchant.

"It's such an honor," Kelsey said.

At the same time, from somewhere else in the room, the same voice spoke. "Did you *see* Mitzi's makeup? She must've watched a YouTube tutorial for a clown school!"

Kelsey leaned back, confused.

"Lauren kept bragging her father was buying her a Mercedes, but she got a Kia instead. Park with the poor people, Lauren!"

"Dougie's breath always smells like sandwich meat. I hate it when he kisses me."

The whole room had gone quiet.

Kelsey looked around. "What's happening? Was somebody recording me? I mean, I never said those things! It's obviously a fake."

The voice continued, spewing comments about teachers and students. Kelsey stepped back from the mic, and her face crumpled.

At first, Lilith laughed, but then, she tugged on his sleeve. "Nick, are you doing this?"

He shrugged and didn't answer.

"Make it stop."

"Why?" Kelsey's face had turned red, and she was edging off the stage. "I thought you wanted everyone to know what she was like."

"I did, and now they do."

He looked at Lilith. "Aren't you enjoying revenge on a mean girl?"

"*She's* a mean girl. I'm not. That's enough. Make it stop."

He flicked his hand, and Kelsey's amplified voice fell silent. After a pause, the principal proceeded with the announcement of prom king—quarterback Dougie Sawyer of the meat breath, who looked unlikely to kiss his date, Kelsey, anytime soon. Applause was muted, and Principal Billings signaled for the music to resume.

"What now?" Nick asked.

Lilith stretched her arms. "I just want to dance like no one's watching."

When they started dancing, Nick understood why she didn't want anyone watching. Lilith was a *terrible* dancer. She'd find the rhythm for a few beats, and then lose it again, floundering between moves. Nick cast a curtaining spell to create a bubble of shadowing around her and did his best to not embarrass her with his own proficiency.

When the song changed to a slow one, he discovered there was one type of dancing Lilith was good at. They stood close together and shuffled in circles. It felt wonderful. Lilith looked up at him, and he leaned down to kiss her. Her mouth was soft and coconut-scented, and a blue light burst behind her back.

She turned around. "Fireworks? That's the only thing that would make this night better!"

He gestured, and multicolored explosions filled the air around them.

"How? Inside the building? Oh, it's just images!"

"Sure. Images."

They watched the lights until the spell ran down, then they danced some more. Too soon, it was eleven, and they had to go outside to meet Casper's brother. Pete and his friends were all in a good mood, since they'd danced with some girls from their gaming club. Casper's brother stopped at Lilith's house first, and Nick walked her to the door. They stopped on her porch.

"Thanks for taking me to prom," Lilith said. "And thanks for this." She touched the *L* pinned to her dress. "I had a great time."

"Thanks for going with me."

Nick leaned forward, and when Lilith didn't move away, he kissed her again. After they broke apart, she looked down, then up again.

A signal?

"Would you like to go out again? Like to a movie or something?" he asked.

"Sure."

"I'll call you."

He squeezed her hand and walked back to the car. As soon as he got in, Pete high-fived him. "Way to go!"

"Dude!" Casper and Domino high-fived him, too.

Nick was still grinning when his phone vibrated. He glanced down to see if Lilith had already messaged him. Instead, it was a text from his mother.

Urgent! Call me ASAP!

Once he was in his room, he slipped off his tux jacket and sat on the bed to make his call.

"Nick, are you alright?" his mother asked.

"Yes, why?"

"We received warning alerts for magic use in your area. You must evacuate immediately! Do you remember the protocol?"

"Mom—"

"Proceed to the exit point, and—"

"*Mom*. I'm not in danger."

"You don't know that. Magic usage indicates—"

"It was me, okay? *I'm* the one who used magic."

There was a pause, and when his mother spoke again, her voice had changed. "Were you in danger?"

"No."

"Then why did you use magic?"

Nick shrugged helplessly. "For my prom date."

"Did anyone see?"

"Maybe." Definitely.

His mother sighed. "I'll let your father know. He'll send a mage to wipe any memory of magic usage. Breaking a rule like this won't help your argument to come home early." She paused. "Did you at least have fun?"

"Yes."

"Then, I hope it was worth it."

Nick lay back on his bed and closed his eyes. The scent of jasmine lingered on his skin, and he pictured Lilith gazing up at the fireworks.

Yes, it was worth it.

Promquest complete.

ROYALE BLUE DANCE

BY JACQUE VICKERS

DONNING A ROYAL BLUE dress,
At midnight, playing a game of chess,
Ruby, a playwright,
Decades on, recalls her senior prom night.
Streamers with glitter upon the ceiling,
The school gym all abuzz, a magical feeling,
Greeted by her peers with welcoming smiles,
Seeing everyone all dressed up, the music beguiles.
Ruby, who thought of going to the prom on her own,
Until being asked out a few days before the prom by
Tyrone,
Tyrone who'd enjoyed reading a play of which Ruby had
written,
He asked her out after she beat him at a game of chess,
clearly smitten.
At the prom, Tyrone wore a tuxedo with a royal blue
bow tie,

Ruby wore a long royal blue dress, others awestruck passing by,
Ruby, her long red hair out, her eyes a glow aquamarine,
Tyrone's dark hair luxurious, the prom, their first date on the dancing scene.On the dance floor, the music started off played upbeat,
Ruby and Tyrone, preciously light on their feet,
A playlist of songs from the 1990's, seniors rehash,
Couples and groups of friends dance with panache.
Tyrone, his brown eyes sparkling, dancing meeting Ruby's gaze,
Their dance moves in sync utterly amaze,
Slow dancing perfectly in tune,
Wishing it'd never be over soon.
Arranging a date for the next night,
Ruby's aquamarine eyes shone bright,
A time before photos were taken on a phone
Ruby recalls her first dance with Tyrone,
The long royal blue dress from the prom, Ruby still wears,
She a Queen, Tyrone a King, they play chess in the park on giant chess squares,
The tuxedo and the royal blue bow tie from the prom he'll still don,
Ruby and Tyrone now a long time married, their love blooms, continues on.
Playing chess, Ruby quite often winning like their first game
With love, it seems that some things almost stay the same,

On giant chess squares, slow dancing perfectly in tune,
Outside, seeing reflected a glimmer of the moon.

Something Original

By Dana Hawkins

I. Am. Fabulous.

Charlie swirled in her peacock teal blue dress, poofy shoulders the size of her head, and tulle so scratchy the government could classify it as a weapon. She tugged the thick sash across her waist, tied a monster bow, and pirouetted in the cracked mirror. The '80s had *nothing* on her. When her aunt Rosie wore this gown to her own prom, she danced to Madonna and Duran Duran. Tonight, she'd flex her moves to Ed Sheeran and Taylor Swift. She needed to channel her inner goddess. Because tonight was the night. She was making her move.

Jess.

The prettiest, smartest, most fun girl in the entire Junior class. Charlie pretended she didn't give a shit, but Jess *really* didn't give a shit. She was the most unaffected human Charlie knew. Two years ago, Jess stomped in mid-Freshman year as a transfer, wearing knee-high boots, ripped jeans, a studded leather jacket, and a Ramone's t-shirt. She was all sass and lips, and Charlie's knees quaked in her presence.

For weeks, Ben, Charlie's bestie and default prom date, helped devise a scheme for Charlie to talk to Jess. She couldn't just pop over to the goddess with a simple "hello" like some amateur. She needed something cool, something clever, something *original.*

Last week while creating a homemade iced salted maple syrup—using Ben's Abuelita's yard-tapped maple syrup—Ben said Charlie should bring Jess a mocha. "Girls love coffee," he said.

Charlie rolled her eyes. "Everyone loves coffee." Someday, she was gonna have her own coffee shop. And when she did, she'd create the yummiest, spiciest, drink with chocolate, cayenne pepper, and cinnamon and call it Jess's Inferno.

Or something like that. She didn't flush out the details, yet. Point was, to catch Jess's attention, she had to do something bold. Something brave. Something totally not Charlie-like.

An engine outside sputtered to a stop, and Charlie peeked through the dirty windows. Ben stepped out of the car and tugged on the bottom of his bulky, two sizes two big tux, loaned to him by his cousin. Didn't much matter, though. His megawatt smile against his golden brown skin proved Ben looked good in anything.

"Damnnnn!" He put two fingers in his mouth and whistled, rattling the walls in her single-wide trailer. "You are rockin' the shit out of that gown. Only you could pull off something so hideous and make it spectacular."

"I accept that compliment." She tugged on his floppy bow tie. "Remi let you borrow her car?"

"Not exactly." Ben flipped the car ring through his fingers. "I had to pay her twenty bucks, and she said she'd kick my ass if I didn't bring it back in pristine condition."

Charlie warmed. His foster sister, Remi, had a unique way of showing she cared. "Ah, she loves you."

"I know." He grinned and held out his hand. "Well, come on, my little lesbian Cinderella. Your broken-down 1992 Ford Escort chariot awaits."

⁓ℓℓ⁓

Bumping through Ballard on their way to Seattle South High, Charlie's stomach twirled so much, she almost puked. The radio provided a little reprieve when her favorite Macklemore song popped on. She cranked the volume and breathed out the nerves.

Ben killed the engine in the parking lot. His boisterous, highly annoying self, turned unusually quiet. "Listen."

Oh no. He just cleared his throat.

"Whatever happens tonight with Jess..." He tugged his lip between his teeth. "She's got nothing on you. Got it?"

Tears prickled beneath the surface. "You're the best."

He grinned. "I know."

Inside, the gym smelled like latex balloons, perfume, and teenage nerves. Streamers, paper-clothed tables, and dangling miniature disco balls adorned the space. Charlie tiptoed inside, holding Ben's arm, sure she was going to pass out. Because, there she stood. *Jess.* In a black frayed bottom cocktail dress, glittered ankle boots, and fresh shaved lines on the side of her head. The white strung lights cast a glow around her, and she looked like a dark angel. *Perfection.*

"Go." Ben nudged Charlie with his elbow. "You look incredible, your make-up is on point, and its less creepy to actually talk to the person you're ogling."

"I'm not *ogling.*" Fine, she totally was. But what was she supposed to say? All her one-liners fell out of style in the sixth grade, and she'd come up with nothing original. She tugged on her silver bangles when Ben poked her arm, then slid away. *Oh God, she's coming this way.*

The gym narrowed. Lights, dresses, and the click of heels against the floor faded. The music pumped through the speakers, but the words blurred. The ringing in her ears mirrored the thudding in her chest. She smacked her tongue to the roof of her mouth, begging it to retain moisture.

Jess's gaze traveled Charlie's dress.

Charlie felt that look directly to her toes.

"Your dress is cool as hell. The retro vibe is awesome." Jess grinned. "Totally unique."

Nailed it.

Charlie lifted the side and curtsied. "This old thing?"

Didn't nail that.

But Jess laughed anyway. A real laugh, and Charlie melted.

Jess held out a black nail-polished hand. "Wanna dance?"

Charlie's chest soared. She gripped Jess's hand, tingles spreading up her arm. "Absolutely."

This. Was. Fabulous.

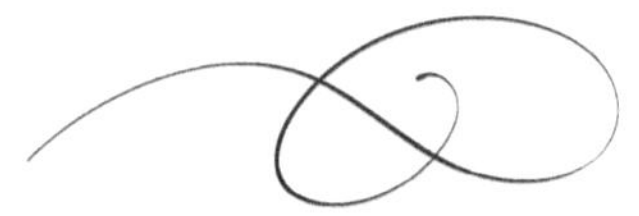

Sovereign of the Promenade

By Adele Liles

Alone in the crowd, she reigns supreme,
In secret misery, lost within her dream.

Her smile a mask,
Sparkling over her face,
Veiling the sorrow of her solitude.

A crown of jewels,
Fake as her friends,
Hides the shimmering tears upon her cheeks.

Every hollow waltz swirls her,
Twirls her,
Among strangers she's known for years.

Her laughter rings,

Bright like a diamond,
But the crown weighs heavy and cold.

Beneath the glitter and the gleam,
In a kingdom of admirers,
She yearns for a confidante.

But through the night, she'll play her part,
With a fractured smile and aching heart.

Stupid Prom

By Erica Duarte

May 1997

Linda

Sleater Kinney's recent release raged in Linda's ears as she made her way to her mom's classroom after last period. Demon-kids jostled her in the halls, making the CD skip. Four more weeks, and this place would be history. She had survived, endured four years of high school under the radar, holed up, and camouflaged. Four more weeks would be a breeze.

She passed a couple of cheerleaders putting up a poster advertising the world's worst idea. *Prom under the stars, a night to remember!* A night Linda Monroe would happily forget once all the painting was done.

For four years, she had helped her mom, the one and only Art teacher, and chairwoman of décor and design, paint huge eight-by-eight murals depicting whatever that year's theme was. This year, it was Night. Not one of her mom's grander ideas, but this year her mom was also going through her third divorce, and as such, didn't seem to have the same lovelorn, hopeless-romantic sparkle that usually imbued her beloved event. All fine by Linda. Her step-dad was no one to lose sleep over.

Prom was all hype anyway, and Night was easy. Dark brooding sky was actually a favorite of Linda's. Today, her mom had her working on Perseus and Andromeda constellations, a love story about a guy who saved a girl. *So* not original.

Settling in, brush in hand, fumes of paint thinner and oil pastels making her wonderfully light headed, the door to the art room opened and in walked the new boy. Linda hadn't been able to discern yet if he, like the other demon-kids at this hellish school, despite his angelic name and rather lovely messy black hair, hid horns and cloven hooves.

Angel

He recognized her immediately. The only girl at this school who never seemed to talk—not stupid, since she was in the same honors classes he was in, just quiet. Always listening to music in her headphones, alone instead of wildly chatting like the other girls, all girls, every girl he had ever known, including his two sisters. Her hair was a short pixie cut, brown and shiny. He itched to touch it to see if it was as buttery smooth as it looked. She outlined her eyes in black like she wanted them to stand out, but it kind of gave her a scared look. More like she knew she was prey in a world of predators. Always wearing too big clothes, baggy jeans paired with oversized flannel shirts, armor, even though it was May and the temperature was turning to spring. Flowers were actually blooming in his yard; something he'd not noticed happening at the last three places his dad, a Marine, had been stationed.

The girl looked at him with a scowl on her otherwise pretty face. He scowled back, wondering what her problem was until she abruptly turned her back to him and he was floored by what she was painting. At first glance, it looked like a big black canvas of nothing, but the more he looked, the more he saw it was far, far, eons away from nothing. It was dark, yes, a night sky of blue-black, violet, and indigo swirled into a storm with glittering fireflies, butterflies, grasshoppers, beetles, moths, and among the chaos, dots of stillness, stars, two careening constellations.

A woman's voice startled him, "Hello, Mr. Sanchez."

He turned to see the art teacher, Mrs. Painter. Her name was too perfect for her profession. He figured it was made up. "Yes, mam." He stood straighter, sort of towering over the tiny, tiny woman, easy to do since he was close to six feet tall and still growing.

"Thank you for volunteering to help with prom decorations, I always need a hand," she said, even though volunteer was not the right word, more like coerced after she saw his work in class. He kept his mouth shut. If his dad found out he was anything but polite to a woman, he'd kick his ass. "Come meet my daughter, you'll be working together."

Daughter? So, the dark, brooding girl was a teacher's daughter. It made total sense and he saw the resemblance now that she'd said it. Mrs. Painter motioned for her daughter to remove her headphones, and Angel caught the slight wail of a woman's melodic voice before she hit pause. He stepped closer.

"Angel Sanchez, meet Linda Monroe," Mrs. Painter said.

Green eyes flecked with amber fire, he'd never gotten close enough to notice before, caught him off guard, and he sucked in a breath.

Linda

What was this BS? She worked alone. Always alone. She had never had a helper before. What was different now?

"I don't need help, but thanks anyway," she said quietly, making an effort to unclench her teeth so as not to appear as mad as she was with this ridiculous situation.

"Nonsense," her mom waved her off like the tiny mosquito she'd just painted and continued on. "Prom is three weeks away, and we need all the help we can get. Angel is tall, strong, and a good painter."

Linda looked this so-called "Angel" up and down. Good painter was yet to be seen. Tall was indeed accurate, but not lanky, not too thin like other boys, and strong, well... He did have muscles, not bulky but lean, and where his waist tucked in, his jeans hung enticingly low on his hips. He caught her staring, and warmth crept up her neck. She quickly turned away.

"Over there." She motioned to a large blank canvas propped up against the wall, needing to be primed. "Start with that one. Mrs. Not For Long Painter will give you your orders." And with that, she turned back to her own painting, put on her headphones, and turned up the volume.

Her hand shook slightly as she started working on a cloud of bats hunting in the night sky. Four weeks, four weeks, and this would all be over. Then, one short summer and she'd be on her way to the Art Institute of Chicago. A new city, a new life, a whole world of wonderful, not at all terrifying, opportunity.

Angel

Every day after school, working in the art room with Lovely Linda, a name he absolutely kept to himself, always brought a new surprise. She was definitely not a talker, but he liked that. He liked watching her work. The way her hands moved and how she never cared that she was constantly covered in paint. He finished nailing together the last frame and started stretching the canvas like Mrs. Painter had shown him. It was easy work. Stretch, staple gun. Alternate sides. Repeat. At home, his mom and dad had him doing way harder work—changing the oil in the car, minor plumbing, fixing drywall. When his dad was gone, he became his mom's maintenance man.

Finished with everything assigned, he looked for Mrs. Painter to ask what he should do next, but she wasn't in the room. At the opposite wall, Linda was swaying to a song as she painted, singing quietly. He pressed his lips together to suppress a grin. She was in her happy place.

The first time he caught her doing this, her voice was so sweet and low and she was so zoned in, it made him feel like he shouldn't be there, like he was invading her wondrous, extraordinary, private world. He couldn't bring himself to leave though, and needless to say, that quickly became her most endearing quality. Especially since the only other side of her he saw was resting bitch face.

His sister's liked to use that expression a lot. Like to do it a lot too. To him, it was another one of those strange and utterly confusing girl things. Girls could be brutal. Only, Linda's wasn't genuine. It was more like a mask she put on so as to blend in, to hide, or save herself from *this* world. He tapped her shoulder, and she jumped.

Sorry, he mouthed as she removed her headphones, her cat eyes looking startled.

"It's fine, what do you need?" she asked, her voice soft like velvet.

"I'm all finished, what should I do next?"

Looking over his shoulder, she eyed the stretched canvas. "I guess you can start priming."

He nodded, and she put her headphones back on.

Priming was the very first thing they'd had him do, so he knew where everything was. He pulled out all the supplies and quietly set himself up close enough to hear Linda if she started singing again.

Linda

What was he doing? There was a whole room, and he put himself right next to her. Did he know nothing of personal space? What the hell? It was distracting to say the least. She tried to ignore him by turning up the volume and focusing on painting, but in her peripheral vision, she saw him continue to intermittently stare at her.

"What?" she asked, pulling off her headphones.

"What are you listening to?" He dipped the brush and pulled it across the canvas, his too handsome features carved into a careful expression, his eyes darting away.

"Nirvana," she said.

He grinned. "Which album?"

"*Nevermind*, it's my favorite." She sounded skeptical, suspicious of him and his ulterior motives, because everyone had ulterior motives and cute Angel Sanchez was probably no different.

"Me too," he said, bobbing his head, "I mean of their albums."

Okay, maybe she was just being weird Linda Monroe who spoke to herself in the third person and refused human contact.

"What other bands do you like?" she asked, not wanting to be *that* girl.

"Sublime, Snoop, Dr. Dre, Chilli Peppers. I've been living in Cali for the last two years."

"Green Day?" she asked.

"*Dookie* album, all-time favorite!" He looked down at her beaming, his eyes shining like melted chocolate, and her heart filled with nervous hope that perhaps Angel was more like his name than she gave him credit for.

Angel

The next day, in Calculus, Angel noticed that Linda twisted her rings around her fingers when called on, an adorable nervous habit. Then, at lunch, he watched how the other girls treated her and realized why she never laughed.

Linda

A few days later, in Spanish, Linda noticed how fluidly, how blindingly beautiful he spoke the romantic language. And it was no wonder why all the girls looked at him with stars and hearts in their evil eyes.

Angel

For a week and a half, he'd been coming to the art room after school and doing whatever the Lovely Linda told him to do. She'd even swapped out her headphones for ear buds and would let him listen with her while they painted side by side. Prom was a week and a half away.

"This is my favorite part," she said, becoming animated and playing her paintbrush like a guitar, not caring at all that she was splattering paint all over.

He grinned, pulling a dark indigo paint she had mixed for him across his own canvas. They'd gotten into a sort of routine that he could easily admit was his favorite part of the day.

"So, are you going to this thing?" He asked when the song ended and there was a brief pause of silence. Not a great segue, since she looked confused, so he motioned to the paintings around the room, now totaling five.

Her face hardened into a careful expression, and her eyes looked to the paintbrush in her hand for support. "Prom is stupid."

He shrugged like it was no big deal, even though his palms had gone all sweaty and his heartbeat sped up. "You're a senior, right?"

She nodded, wide eyed like she had no idea where in the hell this conversation was going. Yes, of course, he knew that. Crap. Where had his brain gone?

"So, you have to go."

"Um, no."

"Well, I'm going."

"Good, have fun." She rolled her eyes, and he glimpsed the spark of defiance she kept under tight control. He loved that about her. Wrong, liked that about her.

"Come with me!" he blurted out and wanted to crawl into the deepest, darkest hole the world had to offer and die.

Linda

Her mouth unhinged, dropping all the way to the f-ing floor. What just happened? Did he not hear a word she just said? She turned down Radiohead—a thing she *never* did—and faced him. The move caused his earbud to fly out. Good, and she wasn't going to give it back, either.

"Ha ha, real funny." She deadpanned at his way-too-pretty face. He was messing with her, and that thought, because she actually liked this one person out of all the devil spawn who roamed these halls, made hot tears spring to her eyes. She blinked them back, looked away, went back to painting, and forgot about Radiohead.

"So, I've gone to three different high schools in the last four years. I've only been at this one for a little over a month, and you're the only girl I know." She could hear the shy smile in his voice.

Was he being genuine? She couldn't tell, but it sounded like a pity ask which enraged her.

"Look, even if I *was* interested, saying you want to go with me because I'm the ONLY girl you know does nothing to help your case." Her voice was so thin, so stretched, it seemed as if it might crack like her vocal cords did not get the memo that she was mad. Pull it together Linda. Damn it.

He lifted the brush, dipped it, and painted the canvas. "You're right." He put the paintbrush down and faced her. "Linda Monroe, I don't really know you, but I would like to. You have really pretty eyes and great taste in music. You paint like... I don't know, a really famous painter. Picasso!" He said, jolting with pride that the name graced his tongue. "And I would be honored if you would accompany me to prom."

Angel

Oh, God, dear God, if you really are up there in Heaven and all that, please let her say yes.

Linda

"NO!" she bellowed before her traitorous heart could protest because her mind was in charge here, and he was really taking this joke too far. No boy in his right mind had ever asked her, the school leper, to a dance, not once, not in all four years of high school or even in middle school when the ridiculous dancing started.

But then, the sad, lonely look that crossed his face gave her pause. She stared at him dumbfounded while he fumbled with the paintbrush, got up, took it over to the sink, dropped the brush in some water, grabbed his backpack and mumbled, "Yeah, of course, I totally get it. I don't know what I was thinking. You're right, Prom is stupid." Then, he bolted out the door.

And her heart fell all the way to the deepest depths of the darkest hole.

Angel

For the rest of the week and into the next, he didn't help in the art room after school, opting instead to go to the gym. It was a pastime he could always find comfort in. Every school, no matter where it was, had a gym. He had never gotten into sports, having moved too much to ever fit into a season, but his dad drilled him, made him jog, and lift weights, preparing him to be what he was, a soldier. It was a good profession, a noble career, and the pay was good, if only he could go right now, get out of here, and away from the one person he could not get out of his head. Linda. Crazy, weird, quiet, lovely Linda.

In truth, it was fine. Better even, he'd never gotten tied too closely to a girl before. School was ending, and in a few months, he'd be off to basic, so why start now? That's what he told himself as he took the long way to the gym, walking past the art room. He stuck to the far side of the hall until he heard crying. He peeked inside.

Linda was sitting on the floor, shoulders slumped, her back to him, softly crying. In front of her was the blue painting she had been working on the day they met, only it was messed up, painted over with streaks of red. He went in and sat beside her.

"What happened to it?" he asked, touching her flannel. "Did you do this?"

She jerked her head back. "No! No, someone else did." More tears leaked from her eyes in big black droplets. "It's so stupid, I don't even know why I'm crying. I hate prom, and it's just a dumb painting."

The flannel was soft between his fingers.

"What are you doing here anyway? I thought you hated me like the rest of them."

It was the most she had ever said to him in one sitting. "I could never hate you."

"Yeah, you say that now." She wiped at the black, smearing it under her eyes. He let go of the fabric to give her a tissue from his backpack, and she gave him a look like he'd just performed a magic trick.

"My mom," he informed her, and she smiled the sweetest, prettiest smile he'd ever seen. He wanted to tell her, but how do you say that? "Sorry about the painting. I know it was your favorite. It was mine too."

She wiped her eyes and seemed to forget she was wearing black eye makeup until she saw it on the tissue.

"It's okay, gives you that bad-ass artist look." His heart was beating too fast, dangerously fast. He leaned forward, tugging the cuff of her flannel until her hand was in his.

Linda

A thousand butterflies caught fire in her chest. She dared to meet his eyes. His perfect chocolate brown eyes with enviable lashes were staring at her. He swallowed. Pink rose up his neck and darkened his hazelnut cheeks.

"Angel?" A smile flickered and faded across his face when she whispered his name like a question.

"Don't say it," he said, his thumb tracing the back of her hand.

The sensation was so wonderful, thrilling, heart achingly confusing. She had to know, but bit her lip for fear of what this was.

"Say what?" she asked.

"That you want me to let go of your hand." Then she saw it, a look that mirrored her own, and possibly, just possibly, he *was* an angel.

Angel

His muscles tightened, and flames ignited inside him. His hand was sweating, and he didn't even care, couldn't find it within himself to be embarrassed. He just wanted to keep holding her hand, touch her black tear-streaked cheek, kiss her heart-shaped lips.

He leaned in slowly. A barely perceptible flash of fear flickered in her eyes. He stopped. "Is this okay?"

She nodded and closed her eyes.

Linda

As first kisses went, Linda was sure this was the Mount Everest, the Sistine Chapel, the Mona Lisa. She had nothing to go on of course, but didn't need it. This was fire in her stomach, dynamite in her veins, crackling, scorching, melting her.

Angel

Silence poured into the space between them. And Angel never felt more comfortable. His whole body exhaled.

"Wow. I didn't know a kiss could be like that." A grin lifted his cheeks.

Linda

Barely breathing, nervous, petrified, she whispered, "Angel, what does this mean?"

The corners of his pink, perfectly kissable lips lifted.

Angel

He stared at his hands, opened and closed his mouth several times, before the words rushed out, carefully, quietly. "It means we're going to prom."

She laughed, head back, cracking up completely, and if he thought her singing was endearing, her laugh was utterly, heart-meltingly enchanting. Yes, he was absolutely going to take Lovely Linda to stupid prom.

Linda

The dress was maroon with a black lace overlay and crisscross straps. It was simple but pretty. The fit was tighter than anything she'd ever worn before, and for a minute, she contemplated wearing her red flannel over it, but thought better, opting for her black Dr. Martens instead. All her favorite rings, black choker, light eye makeup, and touch of lip-gloss made her feel more like herself. She was ready. Slightly sweaty, but ready.

A knock at the door brought Mrs. Not For Long Painter—even though she'd told Linda the name was too good to give up—running with the camera. Linda gave her a stern look, and she calmed down infinitesimally. After counting back from ten, Linda opened the door and her chest clenched.

Angel was so beautiful, mesmerizing, unbearably handsome dressed in a black tuxedo. She scanned him from his shoes up and stopped at his face to see him staring at her with his mouth open. For a second, he stood completely still with an absent awestruck look that made her heart speed up. After a corsage, a hundred million pictures, and a few tentative steps, they were on their way.

He opened the door for her, and Linda giggled like a nine–year–old going to the pool.

"You look really pretty," he said, starting the truck.

Linda blushed from the tips of her toes to the tops of her ears.

"Can I kiss you?" he asked, and Linda could fall in love with this hesitant, shy Angel.

"Drive down the street first." She motioned toward her mom still standing on the porch, and Angel's eyes flickered past her shoulder then back again.

He drove down the street. Stopped. Leaned over. His delicious weight pressed against her. He smelled so good, soap and a slight hint of cologne. She leaned in, fingers holding, tongues stroking. He was really, really good at this. Charmingly insistent. Electricity consumed every synapse, and Linda wondered vaguely if he felt it too. A car horn honked, and they flew apart.

"Oops," he said, and they both smiled.

The smiling lingered all the way to the dance.

Angel

Out of breath at the intensity, he had to remind himself to breathe. But she was here, wearing a dress that showed all her curves. He couldn't stop staring, couldn't stop holding her hand, touching the small of her back, her arm, her bare shoulder. Before he knew what he was doing, his lips pressed just there. She sucked in a breath, looked up at him, pressed closer, didn't shy away, and he loved that she didn't. He wanted to be closer.

Hand around her hip, he matched his long strides to her short ones. At the door, she hesitated. Ace of Base blared. Not her favorite band.

"Follow me," he whispered in a rush, knowing the exact place he was taking her. He'd set it up himself after they'd finished with the decorations yesterday and she'd left with her mom.

Weaving through the crowd, she followed him, ducking behind a huge balloon display, and off to the side where he'd angled their favorite painting, restored, to catch the light of a star machine in such a way as to make the small space glow, but stay hidden.

Linda's eyes widened as she took in the small space with a grin. "Did you do this?"

"For you, Lovely Linda, only the best."

She blinked fast and pressed her lips together, suppressing a smile. He brushed a feather-light touch to her hair—yes, it was just as soft as he'd imagined—and her eyes met his. Jenny Berggren *saw the sign*, and the space filled with heavy silence.

Linda

Phish's "Waste" lilted through rented speakers, and when Angel pulled her into his arms, it was the perfect minute of Linda's whole accumulated seventeen-year-old life. She leaned her head on his shoulder as his fingers tightened around her. The song vibrated through him, through her, through everypart of her body that touched his. He spun her at the end, stopped. Stared down at her, lips parted like he was in shock. Suddenly, Linda felt very unsure of herself.

"What? Did I step on your foot?" or maybe she was too sweaty despite using her step-dad's left behind supposedly super odor eliminating deodorant.

"No." He pressed his lips to her ear, sending an outstanding shiver down her spine. "No, I just really, really, *really* like you."

And Linda wanted to cry, to laugh, to bite down hard on his chest where her mouth reached just above his heart, but she held back. Instead, her arms tightened around his back and she hugged him, her beautiful, wonderful, totally unexpected, but absolutely deserved, needed, wanted, angel.

"I like you, too," she whispered back.

He started swaying to the music again. She looked up once, and his eyes softened to a steady solemn melted chocolate gaze and it was not, could never be, a night she would ever, not if she had a thousand lifetimes, ever, ever forget. Stupid poster. Stupid Prom.

Angel

After hours or days or years of dancing in one single spot, and talking softly, the music stopped. The lights came up.

"We should..."

"Yeah."

Both were in agreement and reluctant, slow to let go of each other.

At her front door, a warm lilac scented breeze blew hair across her face and he wanted so badly to brush it away.

"Do you want to come in?" She asked to his utter astonishment.

"What about your mother?"

"She prefers for me to bring people here, rather than going out and being unsafe." She put her finger to her lips and motioned for him to follow.

He swallowed hard, like he was about to get caught doing something he shouldn't.

Off the living room was a den with a door. She closed it behind them and flipped on a lamp. The room had a couch, an easel with a half-finished painting,and double doors that led to a deck. It smelled like her, vanilla and cadmium paint.

She opened the double doors to the porch and showed him over to a swinging couch like bed that was just shy of his own bed in size. He caught her eye and could think of nothing else than laying down with her on this amazing piece of human engineering, but he was suddenly rendered frozen. She touched his hand, and it was like life returning to his limbs. He climbed up next to her. Laid facing her, legs slightly bend, heart thundering in his chest. He loosened his tie to get more than two seconds of breath into his lungs.

Linda

"I'm going to miss you when you're gone," she said.

His heart pounding against her palm matched her own. He had pecks, actual peck muscles. She trailed her fingers down to his abs.

He leaned in and kissed her, clumsy and over eager, and she loved it. Like he couldn't wait. Couldn't get enough. And when he pulled back and looked at her, something vibrated between them, a mysterious pull like the moon and the tide.

"I'm going to miss you too," he whispered, touching her hair, her shoulder, her hip, the small of her back, pulling her closer until she was pressed right up against his chest, his legs, his... Oh my goodness. She sucked in a breath, but not from fear. The feel of him touching her made her pulse spike, vision dot, lungs void of air in the best, most enticing way. Her body had become a crazy wonderland of sensation. It made her not want to stop, but her head did. She pushed lightly against his chest. "You're so beautiful, it's hard to stop." Their eyes met.

"Isn't that what I'm supposed to say?" he grinned a too sunny, awkward smile, turning him into a vision.

"You'll have to write me letters like the soldiers in the forties did for their sweethearts back home."

"I will. And you'll have to send me paintings."

"I will."

She watched him, his eyes full of thoughts. They talked long into the night of their past and dreams for the future. Of how often or unusual people meet the person they will love at seventeen. The stuff of myth, of Greek tragedy, of fate, of destiny, of their shared love for tacos, until the birds began to chirp and a pale-yellow sun rose over the horizon.

Linda pulled a blanket over top of them, tucked her head under his chin, and fell asleep a little happy, a little sad, a little lost, a lot found, not knowing if this would in fact last, but glad for this one night with an angel.

Sweeping Stardust

By Leigh Therriault

"Help, I can't hold the moon!"

I rushed over to grab the other side of the gargantuan monstrosity.

"Thanks," Shyla said. "It almost crushed me."

We hauled the crescent-shaped piece of plaster across the gym as the lights dimmed. Globs of gold glitter dropped onto my borrowed dress. *Great.*

"Remind me again why we volunteered for this." Shyla rubbed her shoulders.

The Starry Night theme of this year's prom beamed across the airy space. I kicked through the celestial confetti cut-outs, being careful not to slip in my scuffed heels.

"It'll be worth it when we get into Columbia next year," I said.

The music pulsed, the lights flashed, and flushed students danced through the cosmos.

By midnight, most of the tinfoil stars had fallen, giving the gymnasium floor an eerie, aluminum sheen. Once the last song faded, the lingering graduates finally left too.

We stretched out on the lowest row of benches, the cool metal pressing into our backs.

"Isn't it wild that something made so long ago is still influencing us now?" Shyla traced the stellar outline glued to the wall. "It's a Van Gogh piece, right? Starry Night."

"He painted it in 1889, while he was in a mental asylum," I said.

We gazed down at the scraped hardwood, which glimmered with sparkles and streamers like an infinite, festive sky.

Shyla whispered, "I'm sorry about your parents breaking—"

I pushed myself off the bleachers.

"Time to clean up."

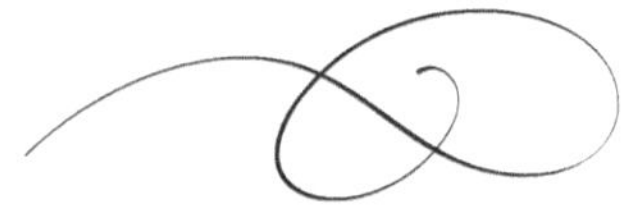

The Anti-Prom

By Michelle Bulsiewicz

Only at an anti-prom would two people named Journey and Genesis be voted king and queen, especially when they're dressed as, respectively, the phantom from *The Phantom of the Opera* and Grizabella from *Cats.*

I suppose Andrew Lloyd Webber was the true winner tonight.

It only fits since the entire drama club ran this event, held in our stage manager, Taylor Gutierrez's, massive backyard. None of us quite belong with, or particularly enjoy, the crowd running the regular prom being held tonight at a swanky hotel. Some of us (especially me), can't quite afford a ticket, let alone a dress, a beauty salon, and a limo. So, instead, we decided to start a new tradition that reflected our quirky selves a little more.

There's a bouncy house, a karaoke machine, and show tunes blaring amidst the twinkling lights strung across the palm trees overhead. The sun has long since set behind the golden San Jose hills. Everyone was told to dress up as someone from a musical, but most of the backstage crew didn't quite comply—myself included. I keep telling people I'm just a high schooler from *Dear Evan Hansen*, but it was only an excuse to put on normal clothes and call it good. I paint sets and shuffle them around in the dark where no one can see me for a reason.

Taylor herself stands on her back porch, flanked by the phantom and Grizabella, giving a speech. "I can't wait to see what gorgeous works of art we all create next year, especially since Mrs. Nguyen said we're going to be putting on *Wicked*!"

Everyone cheers, and I clap, while inside my heart shrivels in on itself.

"Don't you think those sets are going to be absolutely next level to get to make, Morgan?" Mason Liu, my fellow set designer, says from where he stands beside me.

I force what I hope is a believable smile on my face. "Totally."

"And to think, for our senior year. So epic. I'm so glad we didn't have to miss out on this."

I can't take much more of this kind of talk, so I slip away from Mason's side, claiming I need a drink. I wander over to the refreshments table.

There's plenty of spiked punch, but I bypass that. After watching my father's alcoholism for the first twelve years of my life, I'm not willing to risk that I might carry the same tendency in my genes. Plus, it smells terrible and makes you act stupid. Not that it's not entertaining to watch all my classmates drunkenly smashed up against each other out on the concrete slab Taylor transformed into a dance floor. They've turned on some Beyonce post-crowning the king and queen, taking a break from show tunes, it appears.

Then my eyes snag on the lanky six-foot-two frame and dark, shaggy hair of Isaac, standing with some other crew guys off to the side of the dance floor. This weird combination of heart-fluttering excitement tinged with heavy, stomach-sinking dread surges through my veins—the same way it has every time I've seen him for the past two weeks, since the day my mom told me we're moving to Sacramento, that I'm not going to get to have my senior year with my friends now I've finally found a place where I feel like I belong in my high school drama club.

But money has been tight for several years now, since my dad left. I should have seen it coming, honestly. We'll be able to afford to live easier in Sacramento. My mom won't have to struggle and cry all the time. We won't have to worry about our lights turning off at the end of the month.

I feel like a bad daughter for being angry at her. But I can't help it. Because now she's making me start all over somewhere new when I only have one year left. I'll be with a bunch of people I don't know, who've all formed their own memories and friendships for years running, and I'll just be the odd girl out, like I've always been, the quiet one who just fades into the background. Except with drama club.

My eyes catch on Isaac again, because they can't help themselves. They're always continuously drawn to him and the way his hair sweeps across his forehead, his dark, soulful eyes, the way his smile tucks up into the corner of his cheek. I think of all the conversations we've had while hanging out backstage, building sets and waiting in the wings between act breaks. We both have messed up dads, though his is actually in prison for drug dealing. Still, it made it easy to connect. That, and our obsession with Terry Pratchett books—for me, the best escape from the lonely ache of my life. Until Isaac.

And I never told him how I feel. I never made a move. I thought I had more time.

My eyes fill with tears. Here at this celebration, where everyone is happy and enjoying themselves, the contrast of how I feel is so palpable. It opens a well inside me, and my eyes start to fill with tears I can no longer contain. My throat thickens, choking me on my emotions, and I turn away from my classmates' joy and make a mad dash for the side of the house.

I have to dodge a few couples making out before I find an empty corner behind the garbage cans to hide and finally let everything out.

And out it comes in wracking sobs. I can barely breathe as my chest shudders with the pain of it, tears streaking down my cheeks and over my chin. I drop my face into my hands and slump against the wooden fence, my legs scraping against a few scraggly weeds growing up between cracks in the cement.

It has been ages since I've cried like this. Since my dad left. Maybe not even then. Maybe only now is it all coming out, now that I'm at a party where I'm supposed to be happy, but I can't be.

"Morgan?"

The sound of my name in Isaac's voice startles the breath from my lungs. I all but jump out of my skin as my chin jerks up to see him leaning over me, peering down at me where I'm crouched in a ball behind the tall, green recycling bin. I hastily wipe at my cheeks, but I don't know why I bother. There's no hiding what I've been doing here.

"Isaac, I..." I look at the garbage, the fence, the cement, my knees—anywhere but at him.

"Are you okay?" He bends down, balancing one hand on the ground, peering into my face that has to be all blotchy and red from crying.

I don't know how to respond. The answer is obvious, but I don't want to confess to it, either. Instead, I search his face for one moment, finding worry and confusion there, then lower my eyes back to my knees without a word.

"Sorry, I saw you run back here and I wanted to check on you. I didn't know if you were sick or something..."

Shit, how embarrassing. Mortified, I try to push to my feet, struggling in the tight quarters. "I'm fine, just..." I don't know what to say when it's such a blatant lie.

Isaac gives me a look like he's no idiot, mixed with concern. "Did something happen?"

"No, just..." Apparently, I've forgotten how to finish a sentence. I give up on standing and let myself fall back to the ground. Finally, I face the reality of the situation and own up to the truth that everyone's going to have to find out about eventually. "I'm moving."

His eyes widen in surprise. "What? When?"

"In two months."

"Where?"

"...Sacramento." I drop my head into my hands, unwilling to see the expression on his face.

After a moment of silence, except for the pounding of the music in the distance, he asks, "How long have you known?"

How does he know I've been holding out on him? "Two weeks."

My head still in my hands, I hear and feel rather than see him shift until he's sitting beside me on the cement, the heat of his body just inches from my side. How many times have we sat like this backstage, lost in conversation while the actors sang and danced for the audience?

"I thought something was up."

I lift my head to look at him. "What? How could you tell?"

There's that small smile, tucked into the side of one cheek. "You got all quiet and sullen. You've been avoiding me. I thought maybe you were mad, that I'd done something."

His words are a lead weight in my stomach. "I'm sorry. It wasn't you. I just didn't want to tell you. I didn't want it to be real."

He wraps his arm around my shoulders, squeezing me into his side, and I'm overwhelmed by his woodsy scent, the warmth of him, the soft fabric of his black cotton shirt. It's not the first time he's hugged me to him like this, but it's different now, knowing how little time we have left.

"I'll miss you," he says.

Damn it. Tears sting the corners of my eyes again. "I'll miss you, too." My voice cracks on the words.

What's the point of all these feelings ready to burst inside me, if I never get to let them out? I held them in for too long. I was too scared to take the risk, to upset the balance of the friendship we'd created by daring to ask for something more. Over and over, I thought he would have done something if he'd wanted to, so clearly he did not want to. But I hadn't either, had I? Instead we circled each other for months and years, and I never took a chance.

And now it's too late.

But is it?

Maybe there's nothing to ruin now. Since everything is ending anyway, maybe now is the time to take the leap, throw caution to the wind and all that. What do I have left to lose? Here we are at the anti-prom, to which there were no dates, and no corsages, and no fancy outfits, and no limousines, and only ironic royalty. Maybe today is the day to try something different.

The very thought sends tremors through my body, like the California fault line I sit on has absorbed itself into my body, always shaking, always ready to explode with release.

I pull away from his side just enough to tilt my face toward his. I can count the dark hair follicles on his chin. He hasn't shaved in a few days, I think. His mouth is mere inches away, full and warm. His honey-brown eyes meet mine, and something sparks between us.

Just do it. Just do it.

And I do. I close the gap between us and press my mouth to his. For a moment, Isaac seems startled, unsure. I'm a fraction of a second from pulling away and running as far from this corner of Taylor's yard as I can and never looking back. I will never live down this shame.

But then, his lips return the pressure of mine. His hand reaches around and cups my jaw, pulling me closer. His tongue brushes the seam of my mouth, and I open. I let him in.

There's a bizarre moment where it occurs to me that I'm making out with Isaac behind a trash can.

Then, I decide I don't care in the slightest.

Because *I'm making out with Isaac.* The amount of time I've spent fantasizing about this exact moment cannot be calculated. It's simply infinite. This moment itself is infinite. I swear it will last forever. All thought vanishes from my mind as I lose myself in the feel of him, the heat spreading low in my abdomen, my hands finding their way around his back, clutching at the fabric of his shirt.

At some point, we come up for air, and he's grinning at me like I've never seen him do before.

"Damn, I've wanted to do that for a long time," he breathes, resting his forehead against mine.

"Really?" My chest heaves, my heartbeat erratic. "Why didn't you?"

"I don't know. I guess I was too scared."

My cheeks hurt with the intensity of my answering smile. "Me, too."

He huffs out a laugh. "I guess we're both idiots, then."

Then, he kisses me again.

I don't know how long we sit back there in our little corner, kissing and talking.

"What now?" I dare to ask at one point.

"What do you mean?"

"I mean, I'm leaving."

He lifts one shoulder in a shrug. "Sacramento's only a couple hours away. We can visit. And phones still work. This doesn't have to end in two months. Not if we don't want it to."

"I don't want it to." The words are too honest, too vulnerable. They hurt coming out, but I can't stop them.

His eyes are bright and all-consuming above me. "Then let's do it."

Eventually, we make our way back to the party. He holds my hand the rest of the night, and I'm walking on air. Nothing can bring me down. Not even as I break the news of my move to the rest of my friends and classmates, who cry and hug me and express all their love in all the best ways. It hurts, facing this, but I feel I'm strong enough to do it now. If I can show Isaac how I feel, then I can tell my friends the truth. I can do anything tonight. I can face anything that's coming my way. I can be brave.

And one thing I know for sure about this next year at a new school?

I'm not going to hold myself back anymore.

THE BOX WITH THE PINK SATIN BOW

BY AMY JOYNER BUCHANAN & BRUCE BUCHANAN

MY DAD IS WHAT some people might call a real wheeler dealer. He's not the kind for one steady job. Not when he can cobble together three side hustles or follow some get-rich entrepreneurial dream to make ends almost meet.

Which explains why we're here digging through an abandoned self-storage unit he bought at auction. Ever since he heard about the guy who bid $480 for a unit and found $7.5 million cash locked inside a safe in it, he's been looking for his own windfall. We haven't come across any real treasures yet, mostly just a bunch of junk you wonder why anybody would save. The rest, we end up selling at the flea market.

I try to make sure I'm scheduled to work my after-school job at Burger Bunker whenever there's a storage unit auction. I don't love digging through the hot, dusty units. It's hard to wash off the smell of mothballs and old grandma—or worse, that clings to your hair and clothes after hours sorting through musty boxes and plastic bins.

But I don't hate everything about it. Sometimes we do find cool stuff, like a stash of vintage Christmas ornaments still in the original packaging. Collectors pay big bucks for those. And it's hard not to imagine the people who used to own these things, especially when you find old letters and mementos they saved. One time, we found a stack of notes a young woman sent to her boyfriend when he was stationed in Europe during World War II. I never knew if they lived happily ever after, but those letters obviously meant enough to him that he kept them for seventy years.

And Dad, to his credit, tries to make the storage locker experience fun. Or at least not too horrible. He's got his lame-as-hell dad jokes. *This storage unit needs to go to therapy, because it's got shelf-esteem issues.* I try not to laugh, but I usually crack.

He also brings along this battered old CD player, so we can listen to music while we pick through junk. Today, he's playing *Foreigner's Greatest Hits* front to back, which isn't as bad as some of his throwback musical selections.

Dad always makes a big deal about it when we find an old trunk or suitcase, like we're going to open it and finally find out what was in the briefcase in "Pulp Fiction."

"Ronnie, girl, I've got a good feeling about this one," he says, eyeing a hot pink foot locker covered in stickers ranging from Barbie to Banarama. "Why don't you do the honors and open it?"

The trunk isn't even locked, so I doubt there could be much of value inside it. Probably just some long ago teenage girl's hopes and dreams.

An oversized white cardboard box, tied in pink ribbon, sits inside. Beside it, a pair of satin heels, dyed baby doll pink, with rhinestone clips attached to the vamp.

"I knew this was going to be good." Dad grins. "Those might even be diamonds."

I don't need a jeweler's loupe to know he's wrong. The clips are costume-quality jewelry, but definitely fakes.

I don't know what's in the box yet, but it was special to someone at some point. There are different kinds of valuable, and you don't tie a perfect satin bow around something that means nothing to you.

I untie the bow and lift the lid off the box. An old ad, ripped from a magazine, rests on top of a tissue-wrapped bundle. The ad features a girl about my age, her expression halfway between innocent and seductive.

She wears an off-the-shoulder prom dress in the same baby doll pink as the shoes inside the foot locker that has a lace-covered bodice sparkling with a scattering of beads. The skirt, made from lace over satin over layers of crinoline, hits just below the model's knees. They liked their hair and their skirts poofy in the eighties.

"She looks like the girls I used to go to high school with," Dad says. "Or how they wanted to look."

"Your 1989 prom fantasy," I say. Dad had hauled out his old prom photos after we watched *Pretty in Pink*. He towered over his date, but she tried to make up for their difference in height with 3-inch heels and bangs teased nearly as high.

"The girl in that ad was way too uptown for me," he says. "So was my prom date, come to think of it. She lived in a two-story house on a cul-de-sac, and I didn't want to tell her we lived in a trailer."

I never know how to respond when he gets serious or reflective. Flighty, cornball or cringe dad is easier to deal with. I start unwrapping the tissue paper, revealing a pristine satin and lace dress identical to the one in the magazine ad.

"I'm guessing the girl who owned this box would have been too uptown for you as well."

⌒⌒

"Wish they would fix these potholes," Dad says.

My head nearly bumps the roof of Dad's truck as he bounces down the entranceway of Lincoln Oaks, the apartment complex where we live. He sighs, be it ever so humble, and pulls the rust-and-primer-colored pickup into a parking space beside a "No Trespassing" sign.

We step out onto the cracked pavement, and he grabs a box from the truck's bed to take to our second-story apartment.

"I'll get the rest of the stuff, Dad. I just want to check the mail."

Fishing a ring of keys from my pants pocket, I open the #215 box and pull out a stack of envelopes. The power bill is down $5 from last month, which is good, since the water bill is $10 more. And don't get me started on Dad's credit card statement, which is stamped "URGENT" in red letters. I'll open that one later.

I tuck the bills under my arm, making a mental note to add them to the "Household Expenses" folder I keep in the kitchen drawer. Wednesday is payday at Burger Bunker, and that night, I'll go through the bills. Hopefully, we found some things today that we can sell quickly to help with them.

Going back to the truck, I grab the white cardboard box tied with a pink ribbon and head up to our two-bedroom apartment.

⁓ ele ⁓

The next day is Sunday, which means a short shift at work, and thankfully, I don't have much homework, so late morning is a good time to catalog and post the stuff we dug out of the storage unit.

Loud snores buzz from Dad's bedroom. Good. I can work faster without his distractions. I swear, living with him is like having a toddler sometimes.

We've sold every decent chair we've come across, so I opt to sit cross-legged on the floor, rather than on our swaybacked, puke green couch. There, I look through the stuff we brought home, sorting the items into separate piles on the dingy beige carpet in our living room.

A couple of heavy brass candlesticks might get us a few bucks, if I clean them up, but nothing major.

A pile of die-cast cars could do okay with the vintage toy collectors on eBay, but some child dinged these up years ago. Besides, everyone knows that toy cars only go for big money if they are still in the original package.

A pillowcase of Beanie Babies? You can find these in the dollar bin at any Goodwill in the state. We might be able to sell them for a quarter apiece at the flea market.

For the next hour, I sort through the rest of the stack, finding more trash than treasure. There's nothing here to pay the utility bills, much less help us with next month's rent.

I blow out a deep breath and slump my shoulders. Keeping it all together is hard sometimes. And it's not like I get much help.

I wonder what my classmates are doing on Sunday morning. I doubt too many are worried about paying bills. Maybe some of them are making plans for the prom next month.

But that's not my life—and no use dwelling on it. I stand and stretch out on my tiptoes to limber up my stiff legs, then grab the white foam board I use as my photo backdrop for small items. Starting with the candlesticks, I place each object in front of the board, then snap a series of photos with my phone.

Within a few minutes, I have everything shot—except the prom dress and shoes. My online research tells me this 80s prom outfit might be the big ticket from yesterday's haul. Vintage Gunne Sax dresses can go for $200 to $300 on etsy, eBay or Poshmark. Add in the shoes and other accessories inside the box, and we might get another $200 or so.

Since it's prom season, we might be able to sell the dress and other things quickly. An extra $400 or $500 dollars could definitely help our budget this month.

I grab the box and start pulling out the accessories. I'll photograph the jewelry first—the shoe clips, a teardrop rhinestone necklace with a big pink center stone, and a pair of matching earrings.

This girl was definitely into color coordination. Pink shoes. Pink dress. Pink jewelry. I wonder what her favorite movie was. Definitely *Pretty in Pink*. Would she have chosen Blane or Duckie? Hopefully neither. Blane was just boring, and best friend or not, Duckie was a borderline stalker. Maybe take no for an answer, Duckie. Eighties movies could be so cringe.

Other than her penchant for pink, this girl didn't leave many clues. I wish she had tucked a photograph of herself at prom inside the dress box, but there's not so much as a Dear Diary page or a ticket stub.

I can't really get inside the head of a girl like this. And it has nothing to do with the dress being from nearly forty years ago. The era, I understand.

I just feel so disconnected from what life is supposed to be like for a teenager, in any era. My classmates are busy worrying about things like climate change, becoming Tik Tok famous, getting accepted at their top schools, making sure their outfits ate, standing up to the patriarchy, but not me.

In my dad's generation, teenagers grappled with the existential dread of nuclear war, fitting in with the popular crowd, losing their virginity before graduation, and making sure their hairspray held their bangs in place all day.

But I don't have time or brain space for any of that. Not the fun stuff, the school stuff, or the bigger world problems. My reality is right here, this moment. Survival mode. The only future I think about is what happens if our money runs out before the next paycheck. I don't dream about going to prom or college or what life might look like in some near or distant future.

And right now, I need to finish taking photos and get these listings ready before Dad wakes. I wish we had a dressmaker's form I could use. I snap a few shots with the dress on a hanger. But it doesn't really show off the details of the dress the way I would like.

I guess I'm going to have to model it and use the tripod and the self-timer on my phone.

Might as well go for the full effect. I gather the shoes, dress, and accessories and take them back to my bedroom. I don't plan to show my face in the photos—the internet is full of creeps, after all—so I don't bother with makeup or doing anything special to my hair.

The dress is my size, or close enough, and I step into the poofy skirt and pull the beaded bodice up over my chest. I'm able to contort my back and arms enough to shimmy the zipper up without needing any help. I put on earrings and then the necklace, which hits mid cleavage. I slide my hands into the matching lace fingerless gloves and finally step into the three-inch satin heels. So this is what it feels like to be tall.

The tripod is set up in front of our blank living room wall. I set the phone camera's timer to 10 seconds to give myself time to get in place and pose. I need to show the dress from all angles and also take some detail shots. With all the back and forth camera settings and posing, I might be here forever. This must be how it feels to be an influencer.

"Mornin', Ronnie." Dad lumbers into the doorway and scratches his belly, his hair going in every direction but straight. Normally, he'd stumble into the kitchen for a mug of black coffee. But today, he stops after a couple of steps. His eyes widen, and he doesn't speak for several seconds—probably a new record for Dad.

I put my hand on my hip and tap my foot, which isn't easy in these heels. "Got something to say? Let's hear it—I look ridiculous, right?"

Dad just shakes his head. "N-No, not at all. It's just... I didn't expect to wake up this morning and see my little girl so...grown up."

We move into the kitchen, and he sits at the table, falling quiet again. I take a seat beside him, easing down into the chair for fear of splitting a seam on this valuable dress.

"Hey, it didn't come out of nowhere, y'know? I'll be eighteen in just a few months."

Dad reaches out a trembling hand and places it on my forearm. "I know, it's just... Yeah, you will be an adult soon. But you haven't been a child for a long time. And that's my fault."

This isn't just Dad being serious and reflective. He's sad. Rather than play it off, I just let him continue.

"Believe me, Ronnie, I wanted better for you. I wanted to be a better father for you. I just told myself, 'You'll do better, starting tomorrow.' But it's been seventeen years of tomorrows. And now, it's almost too late." Dad never cries. But his eyes water, and his voice catches on something in his throat.

I pat his hand. "Hey, it hasn't been so bad. We've had some good times, right? I mean, thanks to you, I was able to sing 'Hot Blooded' in the second grade talent show!"

Dad half laughs/half snorts. "Yeah. We've had a few laughs. But I wanted you to have...a childhood without worrying about all of this." He waves his hands around, gesturing at our apartment.

Now, it's my turn to be at a loss for words. I just stare down at my hands in the lap of this unfamiliar pink dress. Yeah, I have more responsibility than the average teenager. A lot more. And it wasn't always easy. But complaining didn't seem to solve anything, particularly when bills needed to be paid.

Dad smiles and brushes the hair off my face. "I mean, I haven't heard you say a word about the prom. I bet it's coming up soon."

Three weeks from yesterday, to be exact. It's hard to ignore prom when you're in high school. There are posters hanging all over the hallways, and I'd witnessed three elaborate promposals just last week.

But prom is something for the basic and bougie kids, the ones whose parents have real jobs and don't rummage through storage units to pay the light bill.

"Sorry, Dad. Prom isn't on my social calendar."

He shrugs his shoulders. "Why not? You've got a killer dress, and plenty of kids go stag these days. You would have a blast. You deserve a carefree night."

Now he's starting to get on my nerves. He knows damn well why not. We can't afford it! We need every dollar we have!

I stand. "C'mon, Dad. I'm putting this dress back in the box. I've gotta go to work before long."

Normally, he would just nod, smile, and make one of his dumb jokes. But today, Dad looks up at me, his face heavy. "Ronnie, if it's the money, don't worry about it. We'll make it work—no, *I'll* make it work. Let me figure it out for you this once. But it is your decision. You've gotten yourself this far on your own—and done a fine job of it. The dress is yours to do with as you see fit."

I hold in a sob as I rush to my bedroom to change. Instead of putting the dress back in its box, I hang it in the corner of my narrow closet, beside my thrifted Army jacket and Burger Bunker crew shirt. Then, I sit on the edge of my bed and think.

What would one night of being carefree mean in the big picture? Possibly nothing. But it could mean a lot.

I look at the dress. It really is gorgeous.

It deserves to make some girl happy on prom night.

I get dressed for school the following morning, being careful not to wake Dad. After a quick breakfast, I reach into my nightstand. I keep a stash of money hidden there, tucked inside my dog-eared copy of *The Secret*

History. It's meant to be emergency cash in case we need to buy a tank of gas or a bag of groceries when the checking account is light, And Dad doesn't know I have this money.

I check the stash—$25. Exactly the amount I need. Thank you, Donna Tartt.

Most mornings, I get to school right at the tardy bell. But today, I'm here early. I have a stop to make—the main office.

"Can I help you?" The receptionist, an old lady with a side-part hairstyle, doesn't even look up from her crossword puzzle when I push open the office door. But that's okay. I know what I want, and my mind's made up.

I take the money and slap the bills on the counter so loudly, the receptionist gives an involuntary shiver.

"One ticket to the prom, please."

The Crown

By Kimberly Witz

9:00 pm
Rachel

The second the DJ cuts the music and the senior class president appears with an envelope, Emma Clarkson rushes the stage with her squad. Her white-blonde updo bobs across the gym like a planet, each of her clones one of those orbiting moons with the weird mythological names I can never remember.

I exchange a glance with my friend, Sienna. Barring a miracle, this is Emma's moment of triumph.

The senior class president clears his throat. "All right, party people, the moment you've been waiting for! Your prom king and queen." He breaks the seal on the envelope and lifts his eyebrows. "Your king... Xavier Miller, get up here."

A gangly boy in a blue suit strides forward, his bronzed hair bouncing in time with his steps. He bows his head to accept the crown from the principal before mounting the stairs to the stage.

"And your queen... drumroll please... Emma Clarkson!"

Yep, there it is. Inevitable. I roll my eyes as Emma makes a beeline for the crown, jamming it on her head before the principal can move. With an artificial smile, she takes her place on stage next to—but slightly in front of—Xavier.

"Now, a word from your king."

Xavier steps up to the microphone. "So, like, this is one of the coolest—"

He's cut off by a piercing shriek.

My gaze flies to Emma, whose face has gone full deer in headlights, her hands pulling at the glittering crown in her hair. It doesn't move, as frozen in place as her smile has been until now.

It's as if all the humid air has been sucked from the gym. All motion stops, every breath held.

Emma tugs harder at the crown, and her updo tilts, pulling with it, hair and plastic fused together. I clamp a hand to my mouth to stifle a gasp. What's going on?

Near me, Leo King and his girlfriend whisper to each other. Other students murmur and press forward, some breaking out their phones. Xavier, with his front row seat to whatever's happening, bursts out laughing.

The principal climbs the steps and grabs for Emma's arm, but she pulls away and stomps from the stage with mascara tears streaming down her face.

As the gym descends into chaos, Sienna's warm breath tickles my ear. "Rachel, what did you do?"

8:00 pm

Rachel

The coast is clear. Almost.

I duck into an open classroom and wait for a cluster of students to make their way down the hall toward the thumping bass of the music.

As the last flashes of satin and glitter disappear around the corner, I sneak toward the principal's office, where they keep the crowns until the king and queen announcement later tonight.

But my steps slow the closer I get. Maybe Sienna's right. Maybe I shouldn't drag it out and get revenge for something that doesn't really matter.

I reach the principal's door and push it open, crossing the room and staring at the shimmering crowns on the desk.

Maybe I should abort the mission.

But what if *just once* Emma Clarkson gets not what she wants, but what she deserves?

7:00 pm

Leo

Crystal has been close to tears ever since I picked her up for the dance. Now I lean in close, as the camera flashes and we shuffle toward the obligatory balloon arch photo op. "Did Emma do something?"

And those are the magic words, because Crystal's lip quivers. "I don't know why I'm surprised anymore. She knows I need that job at the bookshop. The interview went so well, they said it was practically mine. But then..." She swallows and swipes at her cheeks. "Emma doesn't even *like* books. It's all about who she knows." She gestures around the gym. "And now here we are for her victory lap."

"Maybe she won't win prom queen."

Crystal scoffs. "Of course she will, Leo. Any competition, Emma Clarkson wins. Always."

Maybe she's right. This isn't the first time Emma has pulled something like this, not by a long shot. Figures she'd stuff the ballot box too.

My mind flashes to the boxes stowed in the trunk of my car outside. If Emma is guaranteed to win, maybe it's time to make her regret it.

6:00 pm

Rachel

At the El Tecolote restaurant, Sienna and I scoot our chairs closer together.

"You're obsessing," she says over the clink of dishes around the table. "She's not worth it."

"Emma has it coming." And as my best friend, Sienna should know that better than anyone.

"We don't even know if she's gonna win."

I roll my eyes. "Did you forget she stole homecoming queen from me twice? *Twice!* Of course she'll win."

"But stealing the crown? Do you really think that'll fix things?" Her eyes are pleading now, and fine, maybe she has a point. But so do I.

"She can't win the crown if it's not there to win, can she?"

4:00 pm

Leo

Mom adjusts my tie, smiling at our reflections in the hallway mirror. "There. You look so handsome, Leo."

"I'd be falling apart without your help." Which is totally true—I've had calc exams easier than tying that tie. "I'm glad they let you off early."

"Me too. It was a close call, but once I told them I'd take the extra inventory off their hands..." Her gaze drifts to the leaning pile of boxes on the entry table.

My ears perk up. We've gotten some cool stuff ever since she started working at the candy store. "What is it?"

She pinches the bridge of her nose with a sigh. "Six cases of black licorice gum. This isn't all of it, either—still two boxes in the trunk of the car. I guess the candy store can't even give it away."

I groan. "I'm not surprised. That stuff's disgusting."

"Well, it's all ours now. The price of leaving early. Maybe you can do something with it, Leo?"

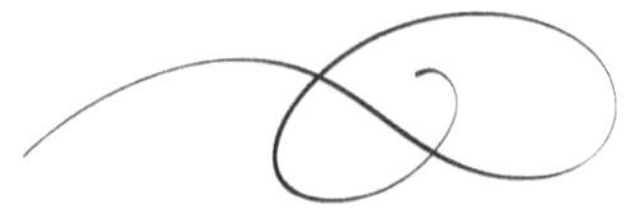

The Dress Thief

By Desirae Gracyn

It was gone!

My prom dress, my senior project, and my ticket out of this dreadful town had vanished. How could this be possible?

Clutching my chest, knees wobbling, I collapsed onto the vinyl floor right in front of the bare mannequin that once held my future. Emmett fell with me, his strong vanilla scent encompassing me as he wrapped his arm around my shoulders. I buried myself into his chest, snot soaking into his Armani jacket.

He played with my brown curls. "Ivy, where did your dress go?"

I jerked my head up and threw daggers at his ocean-blue eyes. "You think if I knew that, I'd be a train wreck right now?"

"Touche. Maybe Ms. Marris placed it in safekeeping?" He stood. "Look, there's a note."

Emmett was right. Our fashion teacher probably set it somewhere safe since the junior high toured our school today. She probably didn't want any of their grungy hands messing with my masterpiece. My anxiety slowly dissipated until I registered his expression.

He was frozen solid, and the note shook in his hand. My stomach lodged into my throat, my lungs collapsing. I wobbled to him, glancing at the letter over his shoulder. My eyes bulged instantly at the message displayed from magazine letter cutouts.

No way it was from the teacher.

I snatched the note from him and read it aloud. "Pride goes before the fall. But I guess in your case, pride causes the fall."

Red-hot anger slithered through my veins. I crumbled the letter, enjoying the crunch of the paper and the ability to destroy something like whoever stole my dress destroyed me. But once it couldn't smush further, the pain seared through me.

I couldn't believe someone would take my prom dress I created with my sweat, tears, and countless sores because of my pride. They had to be messing with me. I wasn't prideful. I noticed my flaws, like how I could've made the dress faster. And I always complimented people on their work, sharing how they almost made it as good as mine. Or, helped them improve by telling them to add a bit of lacy fabric.

I was pure encouragement. Wasn't I?

"Ivy, who do you think took it?" Emmett leaned against the teacher's desk, arms crossed.

"Hell if I know. The real question is, why they'd do this? This is my future they're jacking with!"

"I'm pretty sure the why is in the letter." He raised his eyebrows.

"There has to be something deeper here." I paced around the room, my six-inch heels clacking against the polished floor. "If this were just about the fashion scouts Ms. Marris invited to prom, maybe I'd understand them taking it. They're worried I'd steal the thunder. But that doesn't explain the pride comment."

"Ivy." Emmett gripped my shoulders. His muscular hands bit into them, forcing me to stop moving. "Did you not hear what you just said?"

"Yes, they're worried my dress is better."

"Is that not prideful?" He tilted his head.

"Whatever." I brushed his hands off me. "This isn't fair. Whether or not my dress would outshine theirs, this is worth forty percent of our final grade. I'll fail without it. Or have to go to summer school." I slumped on the couch in the corner, sighing.

I was dead without that dress.

Whoever stole it was going to get a fist full. They messed with the wrong person. How could they be so cruel? Our class spent the last semester on this project. And since we were in the advanced fashion class and Ms. Marris loved our creations so much, she promised ten extra credit points if we wore the dresses to prom.

Emmett pulled out his notebook, a pen, and a cardamom muffin. The sweet spice and cinnamon instantly filled the room.

Though it was our lunch period, the thought of eating made me want to vomit. "How can you eat at a time like this?"

"Um, stress eating. So tell me, who has a fork to pick with you?" He clicked his pen.

"No one." I stared at the cotton fabric ripped hole on the couch, orange fuzz sticking out in several places.

"Ivy, you know that's not true." He bit his lip. "We're not the most popular. We both spend more time closed in with our hobbies than socializing with others. Me always attached to the computer, figuring out new things to hack. And you're always trying to be the best at everything."

I let my head fall back. I hated how true his words were. More than anything, I wanted to tell him there was nothing wrong with either of those things, but our passions didn't make us unpopular—it was the attitude and competitive spirit they brought out in us. Because of that, mixed with our ADHD and autism, we tended to stay in our lanes. We didn't venture out, we didn't make friends, and we didn't talk with others.

Straightening back up, a bulky black dome in the corner of the room, reflecting my brown eyes snagged my attention.

"Emmett! Cameras! Let's ask the groundskeeper if we could see the tapes to learn who stole it."

"That's a great idea!" He high-fived me, and we rushed to Ethan's office.

Hunched over and out of breath, I squeezed my knees and counted to ten. Emmett caught his breath sooner and knocked on the slightly opened door. It swung the rest of the way to reveal Ethan sitting on the back bench, untangling a string of lights for prom and bopping his head to whatever song blared through his headphones—sounded like rock.

His eyebrows arched when he noticed us. He pushed the headphones back. "Something I can help you guys with?"

"Someone stole my prom dress out of the fashion classroom. Can we check the cameras and see if we can figure out who?" I clasped my hands together and brought them to my lips.

"Of course." He stood and moved to his desk. "Sorry to hear that."

He clicked a bunch of buttons on the keyboard, as I tried not to hyperventilate. To help, I fidgeted with my ring.

Emmett noticed my unease and bumped my shoulder. "Vee, it's going to be okay. We'll get the dress back."

I nodded and squeezed his hand.

"Got it!" Ethan yelled.

Both Emmett and I stared at the screen. Images of the classroom sped by with fuzzy static bars. The time in the corner of the screen rapidly changed as he started from 7:15 this morning when the dress was still there. At 12:57, the dress vanished. Ethan rewound it, and I yelped, pushing my hand in front of the screen. "There."

He forwarded to 12:40 when 5th period ended, and we were dismissed to lunch. Sure enough, someone in all black and wearing a ski mask used that passing time to sneak into the classroom and steal my dress. We missed them by seconds.

Tears streamed down my face as I turned and dashed out of the room. I had no idea who it was. Without connecting the dots, there was no way I'd find my dress.

A few minutes later, Emmett came out of the room. "You have to tell Ms. Marris. You can't fail because of this. She'll understand. Maybe she'll give you an extension."

I sniffled. "How is an extension going to help me? It isn't going to give me the answers to uncovering the dress thief."

"But it'll give you time to make a new one." He smiled.

"It took me a semester to make this one," I groaned.

"Ivy, you were born to be a stylist. You can do this."

I looked up at him, doubtful I could fix this nightmare. It didn't matter how great I was. There wasn't enough time.

—ele—

"She's given me a week. A week to make a new dress." I sighed.

"That's good." Emmett walked into the living room and placed our drinks on the coffee table.

"No, it's not." I flopped onto the silk couch.

"I'll help you." He lit the vanilla infuser on the fireplace mantle and joined me.

"Help me find the original." I grabbed my iced latte, the cold glass freezing my fingers.

Emmett grabbed his drink, too, and twirled the straw around, eyes downcast.

"What are you not telling me?" I shot up, turning to face him.

"Uh..." he stuttered.

"Em?" My nostrils flared. We didn't hide things from each other.

He pulled out his phone, almost dropping it due to his sweaty palm. "There's something you might want to see." He gulped and placed the phone in my hand. It was turned on to a video of the camera recording we'd seen in Ethan's office.

I scrunched my eyebrows. "I already saw this."

"Look at the dress thief. What do you see?"

A stealer of joy, a destroyer of dreams, a murderer of my life. Shaking my head, I groaned and rewatched the video. I didn't see anything, so I rewatched it again and again. By the seventh time, my eyes narrowed, and my knuckles turned white from the magnitude of my grip.

I saw it.

Around the dress thief's neck was a 14K rose gold necklace with an emblem of a mannequin wearing a flowy dress. Only one person had a necklace like that. My nemesis and fiercest competition in fashion class—Gesette.

My lips curled back, and the veins in my neck engorged.

Emmett pulled the phone from me and placed his hand on my knee. "Breathe with me." He used his other hand to move my chin to face him. "In. Out. In. Out."

After the hundredth time, an idea struck. A mischievous smile spread on my face. Emmett's eyes widened.

"I need your help." I placed my hand on his.

"I'm not going to like this."

"Please!" I pouted. "I need you to break into the school's files and find out where Gesette lives."

"That's illegal, Vee."

"And it's illegal to steal my dress." I crossed my arms. "Come on, Em."

"Fine. Give me an hour."

◦◦◦

"206 N Union St, Lambertville," Emmet said as he shoved a thin sheet of paper at me.

"Are you going to come with me?" I grabbed my purse from the hook.

"GPS is already set." He pointed to his car. "Are you?"

"Yes. I'm ready to gravel." I placed my hand on his bare tan shoulder, his green sleeveless shirt barely covering anything. "I'll do anything to get my dress back."

Her house was only ten minutes away. During the ride, Emmett blasted our 2022 top hits playlist. His magic trick worked. I couldn't help but sing along, which got me away from thinking about the pit forming in my stomach.

Once we made it up her paved cobblestoned walkway leading to her glass door, my body tensed, and my heart pounded. I stomped the rest of the way and banged on her door with every ounce of strength I had—which wasn't a lot. I didn't stop until a gray-haired gentleman opened it, sending out a gush of wind scented with rosemary. He stared wide-eyed at us.

"May I help you?" he asked, disgusted.

"I need to speak with Gesette." I forced a fake smile. It burned.

"One minute." As he shut the door, my heart thundered louder.

Emmett grabbed my hand and squeezed. I turned to him, and he brushed my brown curls behind my ear. With him beside me, I could do this.

A couple of seconds later, Gesette appeared on the other side of the glass. She opened the door, stared at us with her mouth agape, and slammed it in my face.

Oh, hell no.

I banged on the door again, and this time, even kicked it a few times. Any second, the glass would shatter if she didn't answer me.

She opened it back up. "What?"

"You stole my dress." I ground my teeth.

Her lip trembled. "You don't know that."

I thrust my phone in her face, where I had zoomed in on her necklace that she currently had dangling from her neck. "Explain that."

She gulped. "What do you want?"

"Huh. My dress back," I said sarcastically.

"I can't do that." The color drained from her face.

"If you don't, I'll show everyone the video and let them know you stole it. Ms. Marris will fail you." I shrugged.

"Not to mention the fashion scouts at prom tomorrow won't take kindly to this," Emmett added.

Her hazel eyes widened. "You can't do that."

"Well, you can't steal my dress, but here we are."

She slumped on the doorframe, hand clutched to her chest. "It's too late."

"Too late?" My cheeks turned red hot. She better watch her next words.

She took a deep breath. "I destroyed it."

I lurched forward, knocking us both onto the soft carpeted floor. I pulled my arm back, about to swing, when Emmett grabbed my hand and yanked me off her.

"What the hell?" I glared at him.

"Vee, violence isn't the answer." He kept my wrist in his calloused hand.

I collapsed on the wooden porch, bringing him with me. "She stole everything from me—destroyed every-thing."

Mr. Gei returned. "Everything okay?"

Gesette stood and brushed off her jingling sequence skirt. "Yeah, I tripped."

Mr. Gei shook his head and walked away.

"Why?" I looked up at her. "Why did you take my dress?"

"I wanted to bring you down a peg." She massaged the floor with her ruby slipper. "After all the crap you've put the rest of us through, the amount of bragging you did, and the fact you hogged the teacher's time, never giving her a chance to help someone else or admire anyone else without you one-upping them, it felt justified."

Her words stung. I knew my work was good, even better than theirs. But I didn't realize I bragged about it or stole Ms. Marris's attention. "Once she finds out, you'll lose your chance anyway. You'll have her attention now, but not in a good way. You'll be ruined."

"I never stood a chance against you. No scout will ever notice me if you're present. No matter how good my work is, with your personality, you'll always outshine the rest of us."

I blinked at her. "You..." I choked. "I..." I tried again, but everything I wanted to say didn't sound right. After several deep breaths, I found my voice. "Can I still have the dress?"

She jerked back. "Um... Yeah. One second."

As she shut the door, Em glided in front of me, holding me at arm's length. "I'm so sorry."

I shoved his hands away. "I'm mad at you." He kept me from punching her. She deserved it for what she did. Didn't she?

He rolled his eyes.

The door opened again, and I gasped. She wasn't kidding when she said she had destroyed it. Where it once was a pastel pink, it now looked dirty brown, like she threw dog shit on it. Instead of the glitter body, with real rose petals embroidered in elegant designs from the collar to the waist, it now had tire trecks. The sleeves that used to hang around the arm were now torn.

I yanked it out of her hands and held it close, not caring what was on the dress. This was my baby. And it was destroyed. As I cried, I sniffled, and the scent of chocolate wafted to my nose. Thank God.

I wiped my tears on the dress and turned around to walk towards Emmett's car.

"What are you going to do about me?" Gesette called out.

"I haven't decided." I hopped in the leather seat and shut the door with a thud without ever glancing back at her.

Emmett joined me in the driver's seat. The entire way back to my house, he let me cry. But once I put my hand on the door handle, he stopped me. "Ivy, what are you going to do?"

"I don't know. Prom is tomorrow. I have no time to make a new dress. I have no time to show off to the scouts. I'm ruined. So I'll probably sit in my room and mope, dreaming of what could've been."

"Are you going to tell on Gesette?" His eyes looked misty.

Seriously, that was what he was thinking about? "Wouldn't you?"

"I guess..." He sighed. "She went too far. But I do feel bad for her. Compared to you, no one can shine. Both of us have a bad habit of stealing the teacher's attention."

"You're siding with her. How dare you?" I stepped out of the car and ran to my room.

⁓ ℓℓ ⁓

Laying against my headboard, I wrapped my silk blankets around me and yanked the fur out of my teddy bear. I couldn't believe this. Not only did I lose my chance at everything, but I was being told I was prideful, selfish, and stole the teacher's attention. On most occasions, Emmett would be the first person to hold me and tell me everything would work out and that everyone was wrong. But this time, he agreed with them.

This day couldn't get any worse.

I tried to fall asleep, but when sleep escaped me, I rummaged through my closet and yanked the clothes I made off the hangers, ripping them apart. I destroyed the dress from last year's homecoming to the point of no return. Same with my skirt for my 17th birthday. My quinceanera dress was torn to smithereens.

Once everything I ever made lay in pieces on my floor, I fell to my knees.

What had I done?

A knock came to the door. I didn't answer.

It came again, and this time, when I didn't answer, the intruder walked in.

Mom stood with arms wrapped around Dad. Inside Dad's hands was a card. He held it out for me, but when they saw the disarray of my room, he pulled it back to his chest. And they both stared at me. "Everything okay, Little Dove?"

"What's the card?" I didn't feel like telling them my whole life was over, not yet.

"Umm." Dad gulped.

I stood and snatched it from him.

Congratulations to our Little Dove on receiving acceptance into a prestigeous fashion school.

"Don't tell me you already sent them. I haven't even gotten accepted yet. That's so premature, Dad." I shoved the card at his chest.

"Yes, it's been sent. We have faith in you. We know you're going to wow the colleges tomorrow at prom."

If I even go. I take it back, today could get worse.

"What do you think?" Mom asked.

"I love it." I didn't know why I lied. I should've just told them. But they gave up the last two years of their life, driving me to fashion conferences and fashion weeks across the country. They used my college fund to pay for it, certain I'd receive a scholarship. How could I tell them it was gone now?

"Good." They both hugged me.

"Thanks, guys." I parted from them. "But I think I'm going to bed early. Tomorrow's a big day."

"Okay, let us know if you need anything."

They both left, and I leaned against the wall, pounding my head. Shit.

A ping came to my phone. I pulled it out of my jeans pocket. A picture of the invitation, and *You can make a new one*, from Emmett.

I slammed the phone on the floor. How? I just destroyed everything I ever created. I left the ruined dress in Emmett's car, and I had less than twenty-four hours until prom.

Another string of pings came through. I groaned. But didn't pick up the phone.

A bell chimed, Emmets ring tone. I rolled my eyes and answered it. "Em, I don't wanna talk."

"Please! Or at least, let me inside."

Pulling on the closet door, I stood and looked out my window. Sure enough, he was at my front door, my destroyed dress in his arm.

"Fine." I hung up and rushed downstairs before my parents saw the ruined dress. "Hurry to my room."

I shut the door behind us and glared at him.

"Look." He dropped the dress on my bed and held his hands up. "Next year, we're not going to school together. If you make it into any of the fashion schools, you'll be in upstate NY or London. And I'm going to Berkeley, which is on the other side of the country. You and I both will have to make some friends. To do that, we're going to have to let our light dull so the spotlight can be on someone else. We got to learn to be a team player." He stepped closer to me. "When, not if, we become bosses, we're going to want those under to enjoy working for us." He tilted his head to the side, and I nodded. "We can talk about that all summer and how we plan to be the best team players. But right now, let's deal with this dress."

Emotions flooded me, and I couldn't help it. I wrapped my arms around his neck, shoving his tousled golden hair out of the way, and hugged him. I squeezed so tight, I feared I might pop his head off. He laughed and squeezed me back, lifting me off my feet, his vanilla scent swarming me, soothing me.

"So we're good?" he whispered in my ear.

"Always." I smiled.

"Then let's get to work on this." He placed me back on my feet and pushed the dress into my arms.

"How am I supposed to fix this?"

"I don't know, you're the fashion designer. I'm just the assistant."

I sat at my desk, twirling my feet in eights. Seconds later, an idea sprung. "Do you have anywhere to be tonight?"

"Wherever you need me."

"Great, because I have an idea."

After washing the original and Emmett bringing his prom clothes over, we spent hours combining fragments from every outfit I ever made into one massive piece. Each section told its own story. Once the sun shined through my windows, Mom came in with two steaming coffees and a platter of fresh pancakes. Both our stomachs groaned.

We devoured the food and returned to work. Emmett even surprised me by asking if we could make him matching accessories for his tux. I gladly obliged.

At four in the afternoon, we finished. I stared at our outfits pinned to the mannequins, and my heart melted. It was the best I ever designed.

He got dressed and went to dinner with his family while I headed to my makeup and hair appointment. He promised to pick me up at seven.

But seven came, and he didn't.

When I called, he didn't answer. I wasn't going to prom without him. So I waited for him, and in the meantime, I fiddled with the dress more.

Around 8:30, Emmett knocked on the front door, rainbow corsage in hand, face red, and bangs sticking to his forehead. "Sorry I'm late. It was a nightmare finding this."

"It's okay. It gave me time to spruce the dress more." I smiled. "Close your eyes."

He closed them, and I escorted him to my room. "Open."

His jaw fell to the floor, and he lifted me, spinning me into circles. "This is the best dress I've ever seen in my life. You're going to kill it at prom."

"Go put your tux on, will you?" In the closet mirror, I could see my cheeks turning rosy, amplifying the rose-hue eyeshadow that enhanced my almond-shaped coffee-brown eyes.

We both changed, took several pictures for the family, and headed to prom.

Music blared from the venue. Students mingled on the front lawn. Teachers chaperoned.

I gulped, my breathing turning shallow. Emmett approached my side, holding his arm out to me. "You got this!"

I nodded, and he walked us into the venue through an arch made to look like a heart. Our prom was themed as a lover's paradise. Tables stood to our left, buffet to our right, a dance floor in front of us filled with our classmates, and several teachers hung around the walls. Ms. Marris stood next to two huge fashion scouts. Gesette was in the middle of them, wearing a beautiful one-shouldered multi-texture dress—feather sleeve, leather top, satin pink waist corset, ruffled glitter bottom, and a mesh backing. I bit my lip, jealousy seeping through my veins, but also pride. I shook my head, and Emmett whispered in my ear, "Let them come to you."

"Take me to the dance floor." I held my hand out for him.

"Of course, but first..." He rushed us to the DJ booth, said something to the DJ, then walked us to the middle of the vinyl dance floor.

The strong bagpipe echoed off the walls. Several couples parted and walked off the dance floor. I stared at Emmett, smiling. I couldn't believe he just requested they play our favorite song, "Copperhead Road." We even made up a dance to the chorus. He stood behind me and removed the white leather coat covering my dress. Several gasped beside us.

The original pastel pink dress stayed the foundation, but I ripped the sleeves off and added my teal-blue sleeveless straps from my quinceanera dress and the teal-blue elbow-lengthed gloves that had silk fabric hanging down. I attached my big orange poofy skirt from my 17th birthday to the dress with ribbon bows scattered throughout it and along my waist. Instead of roses, I added pearls and made a mesh rose design on my back.

He smiled, placed the coat on the chair, and started dancing. I laughed and danced with him. When the chorus came on, he grabbed my hands, dipped me underneath his legs, then shot me up. I wrapped my legs around his waist as he flipped me behind him. Back to back, we locked arms, and he flipped me once again, landing me in front of him. I spun out twice, and the second time he pulled me into him, he ripped the ribbon along my waist, and the skirt fell, revealing the original tight-skinned pink dress meshed with a dress from Emmett's eighteenth birthday that added ruffles to the side. A slit carried from mid-thigh to the floor.

More gasps filled the room. He finished the spin, pulled me into a cradle hold, and dipped me to the left. I came up, wrapping my leg around his neck, before he bounced me back to the floor in time for the chorus to end.

As my feet started dancing to the traditional choreography, I noticed no one else was on the dance floor. They were all standing around it and watching us—including several scouts.

After the song finished, I hugged Emmett.

Someone tapped me on the shoulder seconds later, and we parted.

Ms. Maris stood beside us with two scouts. Emmet excused himself to get us a drink as Ms Marris walked us outside the venue.

"Ivy, nice to meet you. I'm Claudette from the Fashion Institute of Technology." She held out her hand for me to shake. I did as the other scout introduced herself from Pratt Institute.

"Nice to meet you both," I said.

"Ms Marris has told us a lot about you. You would fit in great at our school. However, I already offered our scholarship to another student in your class. Next semester, I'd love to offer it to you." She handed me a business card, brochure, and a bag.

"Same." The second scout's lips thinned. "I offered to another student at your school. But the following semester, you have a spot here at Pratt with a full scholarship." She handed me the same things.

"Do you have any questions?" Ms. Marris asked.

Several, like who did they offer it to? Would they have offered it to me if I had arrived sooner? What did I do now?

"So many! Tell me about your fashion programs."

We talked for several minutes before they both left. Ms. Marris stayed behind and nudged me on the shoulder.

"I'm proud of you!"

"Thank you!"

"If I'm not mistaken, underneath all the pieces is your original dress. Where did you find it?"

"A friend took it to their house so we could prep there."

"Well, that's kind of them. Scary. But kind." She laughed.

"Yeah." I shrugged.

"Well, I love the additions, and so would my wife." She flipped out a business card and handed it to me. Huge bold letters read, *Belle Tenue,* a huge French designer.

I raised my eyes to her.

"My wife is one of the lead designers. They'd love to see your piece!" She smiled. "I need to check in on the other students. Have a wonderful prom, Ivy."

I gripped the card tight, jumping in my spot.

Emmett appeared out of nowhere and jumped with me. "I'm proud of you, Ivy!"

"You don't even know—"

"I stood by the wall. I heard everything. I told you that you could do it! And that was really awesome of you for not turning Gesette in."

"I took what you said to heart." I pocketed the card and hugged him. "I hope she was one of the students who got offered the scholarship." I was glad we had come late.

As we walked back into the venue, arm in arm, I leaned into him. I couldn't be more lucky to have a friend like him. And to be honest, his words made me realize this whole time I had been the dress thief by always hogging the teacher's attention, not allowing anyone else to learn or shine.

I could shine without stealing someone else's light.

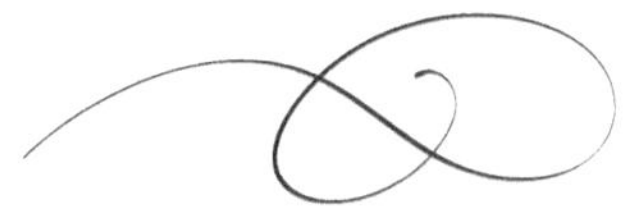

THE MOON & STARLIGHT PROM

BY TRACY TRUELS

SUZANNA WORE A CROWN of flowers—deep red and pale pink broken up by soft yellow blooms. The boy beside her was tall, toothy, and handsome. No one suspected he was a wolf.

"Surely they can tell," he whispered, worry nipping at his voice.

She squeezed his hand, then leaned close to cup his ear. "I promise they can't."

The spring dance was held every April, and just their luck, this year it fell on the full moon. For those three nights each month, his human eyes were full of her.

The hands were tiresome to deal with, especially for someone who preferred the sensation of digging sharp claws into the earth. Still, he was grateful for the chance to get so close, to stroke her face and run his gentle fingers through her hair. They'd spent all last night on the couch watching movies to prepare: *Buffy the Vampire Slayer*, *10 Things I Hate About You*, even *Grease*.

Hand in hand, they wove through the crowd. To her delight, he followed without protest. When they stopped at the border of the dance floor, she grinned. With the flower crown and dark slip of a dress, she was every bit the enchanting forest nymph from his mother's tales.

They didn't notice the couples nearby, who stopped to watch and began to murmur. "Who is that with her? Where does he go to school?"

At the first notes of the slow song, he took her waist, then pulled her close. They swayed side to side, just like she'd taught him in the living room, because above all else, he wanted to make her happy. After all, he could be with her so little. He would refuse her nothing, and he would ask for nothing in return. During those months padding around her back window, he'd seen enough of her father's rages. Now that he was gone, she should be free to do as she pleased.

Despite feeling shy, Suzanna managed to look into his eyes and speak in soft tones. "Kiss me." The song was more than halfway over already.

He blushed. "Right here?"

She nodded. A red petal shook loose from her crown and floated down to the gym floor. He took his hands from her waist and cradled her head, bowing down to her lips. Their kiss was warm, infectious. The couples nearby gasped. Even still, they couldn't see the stardust that fell from her hair, nor the delicate roots that sprouted slowly from her fingertips and wound gently around his arms, piercing his skin.

As usual, after the initial pain, his blood began to sing. The notes spoke to him of a nymph who couldn't feel her own magic. Because of this, the poor creature's soul starved. The nymph forgot she was special, drifted out of the forest, and fell into the human world. Tricked into marrying a terrible man, she birthed a daughter, then died filled with sadness.

But this was only the beginning. As their kiss deepened, Suzanna's roots took hold in his veins and the song became something new. Its melody called out his wolf name and etched itself into his spirit. He was a creature of the forest at heart, after all. What she took from him, he gave willingly. Her very breath provided him oxygen to breathe. It was only natural for his blood to be the perfect nectar. Maybe if she drank enough from him, one day she would feel her magic just as he could—the magic her mother had given her. Or maybe she would think of herself as a human forever.

Their lips parted as the song came to an end. Now it was her turn to blush. They quietly slipped away from the dance. On the long walk home, she linked her arm through his and asked him to hum that song again, the one he always did when they were together. She'd never told him, but she heard it in her dreams, the same one each night since they met.

In the forest behind her house, she stood tall, feet planted into the earth. From her toes to the top of her head, she soaked in the songs of the trees around her. They gave her words of reassurance, of love. "You are special. You belong." Red, pink, and yellow flowers bloomed at the crown of her head. This all felt right, as it should be, and no matter how cold it was outside, warmth flooded her body, for a gray wolf wrapped itself around her ankles and never let go.

The Night the Music Died

By Karla Marie S. Eduardo & Lester N. Linsangan

In the shadow, she hides, feeling small and unseen
In the mirror, she stares; she's neither a princess nor a
queen
The high school promenade she always dreams,
Wrapped in doubt, bursting at the seams.

It's a night of masquerade ball, walking in a grand hall
In a sea of faces, her elegance does enthrall
Even in slick black, she shines like a star,
Diffusing grace and class from near and far.

As their paths collided, a quick gaze, a chance,
Two hearts close, yet in a distant romance
Three years apart, but souls entwined,
In his stare, she felt like a lost piece of a puzzle, finally
defined.

At last, the moment she longed for, finally came,
Hoping he'd ask for her name
One song, one dance, feels like a mere encore
Yet, if she unveiled her mask, would he recognize her as
before?

Through the night, they prance, filled with vibe and
dance
As the sounds harmonize, with tears and cheers, they
take a chance
In the dazzling light so bright, the night is their delight
As they twirl beneath the gym light, lost in the rhythm's
trance, feeling just right.

She wonders if this marks the end, or if tomorrow it will
blend
No matter what unfolds, this moment will eternally be
treasured and held,
Similar to stars that gleam, simple to discern yet tough
to seize
They're akin to fire and ice, never to align, destined for
unease.

As they dance in the rhythm of classic music, craving for
love that would never bend,
But the hopes were like glass slippers, fragile and easily
shattered by the night's end
It was like Cinderella's timepiece struck at midnight,
Marking the end of their mystical night.

She ponders if the sunrise arises, could there be one
more chance?
To clasp her hand and sway to dance
Or will the forthcoming day bring only more yearning
and uncertainty?
The answer lies in the whispers of fate, echoing for
clarity.

Maybe it's the first and last, tomorrow will lead into the
unknown
A dust carried by the wind, leaving behind a path of
memories sown
The melody of the song fading slowly, silence becoming
so loud
One final gaze, as they retreat with quiet steps astound.

In fleeting whispers of doubt, she found her glow
No crown adorned her, no spotlight to show
Yet in the midst of many, her heart and purity soared
high,
Till the night the music died, bidding goodbye.

THE PERFECT PROM

BY M. CHRISTENSEN

THE MOONLIGHT SHINES UPON Conner's striking brown eyes.

"Thank you for coming to Prom with me." His smile lights up his face.

"Of course." I smile back. Today is the epitome of perfection.

He steps closer.

This is it.

He strokes my cheek gently.

"Serenity," he breathes. "Can I kiss you?"

My throat grows tight, and I nod, my lips parting slightly.

Conner leans closer and rests his forehead against mine. His breath tickles my face, mirroring my insides.

He moves his lips slowly over mine then pulls back.

"That was better than I imagined," he says passionately as he leans in for another kiss.

That's funny. It wasn't as good as I thought it would be. Maybe I read too many books because I was expecting fireworks. Or at least a desire to repeat the experience. Instead, disgust builds inside me and I start to analyze the situation.

It's Prom night. I came with a guy I like. I look hot in a bright yellow dress, my brunette curls pinned up just right. After the dance, we came to a romantic spot by the river. A willow tree reaches it's branches around us, and the moon provides the only light.

Everything is ideal for this to be the best first kiss of my life.

What is wrong with me?

I'm doing my best to pretend to enjoy this experience, and I must be succeeding because he seems happy.

This is a not so perfect Prom after all.

THE PIMPLE I TOOK TO PROM

BY VICKI BERGER ERWIN

PERFECT. EVERYTHING NEEDED TO be perfect—the dress, the shoes, the hair, the makeup. The date already was. For three years, I'd wanted a date with Drake Harris, and this year, he was taking me on the biggest date of all—prom.

Okay, so he'd graduated, and I'd asked him. It didn't matter. I told myself seventeen times a day. I had my perfect date.

The first time I'd seen Drake, he was an eighth grader, and I was a seventh grader. He smiled and said hi when we met on the sidewalk, and I knew. All that had to happen was him realizing that we were meant to be. Like I said, I already knew.

My perfect dress was white with red dotted swiss, an unusual fabric for a prom dress. No one else would have one like it because my mom made mine from a design I created. I'd been working on it for four years. And red shoes. I'd found the perfect red shoes with the perfect height of heel. All a good start to the perfect prom.

I dragged a kitchen chair into the bedroom to look at myself in the dresser mirror. Perfect, perfect, perfect.

But wait...

I leaned closer to the mirror. A small red dot, matching those in my dress, bloomed in the middle of my forehead.

What the what? I had flawless skin, the one quality I counted on. Why now?

I jumped down, removed my dress, and hung it carefully in my closet. "Mom, quick, I need you." I leaned into the mirror again.

Mom came running, dish towel in her hands. "Is something wrong with the dress?"

I pointed at the pimple.

"What?" Mom looked puzzled.

"This pimple. This huge red pimple. When I look at myself in the mirror, it's all I can see."

"I have to squint to see it." Mom flicked me with the towel. "If you think there's something there, put a little cream on it. It'll be gone by Friday."

I quickly googled "how to get rid of pimples fast." I skimmed the pages that showed up. There didn't seem to be one good answer. I texted my friends. Some of them had experience with bad skin, unfortunately.

Hemorrhoid cream was the first answer I received.
What??!!!??
Beauty queens use it all the time.
Hmm, bet Dad had some in their bathroom.
Ice was the next answer.

That sounded easy and seemed more logical to me.

Heat came next. *Alternate with ice.*

Alcohol, but sometimes it burns.

Why do you need to know? my best friend, Angie, texted.

Pimple. Prom, I replied. It was almost possible to hear the collective gasp from my friends on the text chain.

Try the skin care aisle at DrugMart, was Angie's advice.

Whatever you do, don't worry about it. Stress will only make it worse.

Brilliant suggestion, since it was all I could think about.

And whatever you do, don't touch it. Bacteria from your hands can make it infected.

I quickly stopped massaging my forehead with my bacteria-laden hand.

Mom shook her head as I filled a sandwich bag with ice and wrapped it in a towel. I stretched out in the recliner and placed the ice across my forehead for twenty long minutes, every one of them spent feeling that pimple growing bigger and bigger. I truly tried to stop worrying, but it was impossible.

When I checked, my entire forehead was so red, I couldn't tell if the pimple had gone down in size or was lost in the sea of ice-burned skin. I soaked a cotton ball in rubbing alcohol and pressed it to the pimple. *Be patient.*

Before heading to the drugstore, I donned one of my brother's baseball caps and pulled it low, then slid on a large pair of sunglasses. Incognito was the name of the game.

There was almost a complete row of skin relief products at DrugMart. I read label after label and chose three; one promised quick action, another redness relief, and one that said, *Poof! It's gone.*

At home, I applied the quick action lotion first. The bottle said it would change "the landscape of my face" within twelve hours. There were moments as I lay awake when my skin tightened, and that comforted me. Other times, the pimple throbbed. Was it trying to tell me something?

I woke up thinking of the pimple and ran my fingers across my forehead, then quickly pulled my hand away. Not only did it feel bigger, but the surrounding skin seemed to have puckered, dried, and was flaking. One look in the mirror confirmed my suspicions—redder with wrinkled edges. And I had to go to school. I applied the redness relief. Perhaps that would at least camouflage my blemish.

"What a time for you to break out," Angie said when I picked her up for school in my Mini Cooper.

"Thank you for noticing," I said tartly, tears burning as I realized the second "potion" hadn't worked either.

I suffered through that Tuesday, feeling like everyone was staring at my forehead. The next cream had better work.

"That spot on your face is visible now," Mom said when I sat across from her at the kitchen table. She had papers spread out in front of her, editing a piece for the magazine she worked for.

"What should I do?" Again, I wanted to cry.

"Don't worry about it."

I'd heard that before.

"Prom is three days away. Plenty of time for it to go away," Mom said.

It was clear she didn't understand. I made another ice pack and took it to my bedroom, where after the requisite 20 minutes, it seemed to do no good at all. Angie suggested heat since the ice didn't work. I dug out a heating pad from the linen closet from the time Dad hurt his back and pressed it against my forehead. Heat felt good. It relaxed me a little, and I napped.

I used the *Poof! And it's gone*! Before bed. It reeked, and I was sure I'd never be able to rid myself of what smelled like a burnt match soaked in rotten eggs.

"What is that smell?" my brother, Chad, asked as he stomped upstairs. "Pee-yew!" He opened my bedroom door. "New perfume? Better not wear that for prom."

I slammed the door in his face.

The door opened right away. "What is wrong with your face?"

I screamed and slammed the door again.

The next day, I wore a hat, pulled low, to school.

That afternoon, I alternated ice and heat, and the pimple had grown every time I checked it. I practiced covering it with makeup. It looked like I was covering a pimple with makeup.

Thursday morning, it seemed slightly smaller, giving me hope. I used the quick action lotion in the morning, then at lunch, I added the redness relief. Even Angie said it was looking better. By the time I arrived at home to institute the cold/hot regimen, it had puffed up again. Had I touched my forehead too many times? Was it becoming infected? And I was worrying. That was sure to make it worse. AACCKK!

It was time for desperate action—the hemorrhoid cream. I dug it out of my parents' bathroom vanity and applied it. It felt nice and cool against my agitated skin. But by bedtime, the pimple had grown even larger and was turning white in the middle. Ugliest pimple ever!

I pulled my hair over my forehead. Bangs, the one thing I'd vowed never to do again. They would cover the darn thing. But I needed help. Angie was good with hair. I texted her with an SOS.

—ele—

Thursday afternoon. Time was short.

"But what if I mess it up?" Angie chewed on her thumbnail as she ran her fingers through my hair.

"Could it look any worse?" I pointed at Mr. Pimple. It had to be male to be making me so unhappy. Perfect dress, perfect shoes, perfect perfume—although I still smelled *Poof!*—perfect nail polish. It would be okay if my makeup and hair were slightly less than perfect, wouldn't it?

I found a pair of scissors that seemed like they'd never been used for food or gardening and handed them to Angie.

"You decide how much hair you want in your bangs and how short." She held the scissors behind her.

"Not too much and not too short," I said, marking a spot mid-eyebrow. I gathered a hunk of hair, kissing the ends. It had taken me four years of high school to grow my hair one length. By college graduation, I'd have it back again.

Angie placed the hair between the scissor blades, took a deep breath, then let go and stepped away from me, my hair flopping over my face.

"You've got to do this. It will hide the pimple. Cut."

"You do it." Angie held out the scissors. She covered her eyes.

I grabbed them, held out my hair, closed my eyes, and snipped before I could change my mind. I looked in the mirror, expecting to see a nice, even set of bangs covering my forehead. But no. How did that one side end up so short?

Angie quickly parted my hair on the side and brushed my bangs in a way that looked... okay. "They'll grow out in no time."

❧

One more day. I practiced covering the pimple with makeup again, as well as every other tool in the tool chest.

On Prom Day, school dismissed early. Administration knew everyone would leave whether or not they approved.

I rushed home to find no positive change in my pimple. Perhaps a bit larger and redder. I'd have to make sure everything else about me was perfect.

As I applied makeup, I wondered if Mr. Pimple made my bangs puff out a little more than they should. The rest of my hair fell in shiny, gentle waves over my shoulders and down my back.

Once I was dressed, Mom held up a silver necklace with a garnet teardrop dangling from it. The perfect accessory.

The doorbell rang. My stupid brother Chad answered, and I prayed he wouldn't say more than "Hi."

Dad caught me by the hand at the top of the stairs. "You look beautiful." His eyes shined with tears. I kissed him and hoped I hadn't messed up my lipstick.

"No one will notice that huge pimple in the middle of your forehead," Chad said as he ran past me to his bedroom so fast, my punch aimed at his arm missed.

"It's fine," Mom said, rearranging my skirt.

Drake had his back to me as I walked carefully down the stairs. I was wearing heels after all, and it would not be perfect to fall head over heels, although that's how I felt when he turned and smiled, holding out a corsage of red roses. Perfect.

Wait a minute.

In the center of Drake's forehead was a pimple that rivaled mine in size and redness. I looked quickly away.

Drake's hand swiped over it. His brow wrinkled. "Is there something..." His voice trailed off.

I pressed my bangs against the pimple.

"Your hair? It's different. I like it. You look perfect." Drake smiled.

It seemed Drake and I would have a double date for prom—with our pimples.

Perfect.

THE PROM DO-OVER

BY: DIANE BILLAS

Prom is supposed to be the pinnacle of the high school experience, a night to let loose and let it all hang out. So why am I dreading the whole spectacle? Maybe because it's the night that will make or break my relationship with my girlfriend.

"Addy, she's here!" my mom calls from downstairs.

The *she* my mom is referring to is Jenna Smith, my girlfriend of six months. I've known her throughout high school, but we never ran in the same social group until last year's musical. We had both been relegated to the chorus cast as town person number one and two respectively. After last year's public spectacle of my ex-girlfriend, Eve, dumping me during her Prom Queen acceptance speech, Jenna was there to help me pick up the pieces, so much so that I fell for her.

Right before Thanksgiving break, Jenna took me to my favorite vegetarian restaurant, gave me a bag of Butterfingers, my favorite chocolate candy ever, and asked me to be her girlfriend. Of course I said yes. I was so smitten and haven't questioned anything, until now. *Will she break up with me at prom like Eve did last year?*

I take one last look at myself in the mirror. My lips are painted red to match my long, sleeveless satin dress, and a red carnation is tucked behind my ear to compliment my ridiculously curly blonde updo. I told my mom to spare the expense of the hair appointment—I could have done it myself—but she insisted.

"It's your senior year and your last prom. You'll never get this day back," my mom said.

I would be fine with never having another prom, but whatever.

I told Jenna we really didn't have to go and could do something else equally as cool, like go to the new roller rink that opened up, but when the light extinguished from her bright brown eyes, I couldn't say no. Who was I to deprive her of that just because I had a bad experience? *This year has to be better, right?*

I slip on my silver heels that I know will come off almost as soon as we arrive. Does any girl with heels ever wear them the entire dance? If so, I want to meet them and ask them how they do it. I can barely even walk down the steps in them, so I hold onto the railing like it's a lifeline.

My mom's mouth opens when she sees me. "Oh honey, you look so beautiful." She throws her arms around me and brings me in for a tight hug. "Tonight will be better. I just know it."

When she lets go, she motions to the window. "Your chariot awaits."

I scrunch my eyebrows and curl my index finger to pull down the blinds. I peer out and gasp, my hand flying to my mouth. I was expecting to see Jenna's fiery red Toyota Corolla, but what sits before me is so not that.

A door opens on the side of a Hummer black stretch limo. The vehicle is so large, it goes past the STOP sign and blocks the intersection. A long, tan leg emerges from the open door. My mouth drops when the individual appears.

Jenna's brunette hair is half up, half in a braided crown around her head. Her floor length, dark blue dress with thin straps has black sequins forming shapes of flowers around the bodice, and her sequined black clutch completes the look. *She's breathtaking.*

My girlfriend holds out a hand, and her mom emerges from the limo, talking excitedly with her hands. Jenna's mom is in her typical athletic wear—black shorts, Under Armor T-shirt, and a pair of bright sneakers. She's the type of mom that always looks like she's about to run a marathon. Mrs. Smith points at our door, and I pull back from the blinds. I don't want them to catch me staring.

Before they can ring the bell, my mom flings open our door. "Welcome! We've been expecting you!" She ushers them inside. Jenna pauses to give my mom a hug, and while she's doing so, her eyes widen as she spots me at her twelve o'clock. She lets go of my mom and slowly walks over to me.

"Oh, my gosh, Addy, you're gorgeous! Red is so your color."

I motion to her outfit. "You're one to talk. You're so beautiful. I don't think I've ever seen you in a dress before except for the musical."

Jenna's cheeks turn pink. "Yeah, I can clean up when I want to."

Her whole family is more on the sporty side. She isn't quite like her mom—she usually just wears a T-shirt and jeans—but on occasion, she can be known to just wear athletic clothes to school. I mean, I don't blame her since her dad owns the local sports store. I'm sure they have all the free athletic clothes they could ever want.

"And you got us a limo? You didn't have to do that," I protest.

She shrugs. "But I wanted to. It wouldn't be prom without a limo. And it won't be just us. We're picking up Mark and Brody on the way."

"Sweet!" I pump my arm in the air. They're our queer BFFs. All of us queers stick together at our school. There aren't many of us, so when we're together, we're loud, out, and proud.

"Don't forget this," Mrs. Smith says, whipping out a plastic box with what looks like a flower inside.

"Right!" Jenna opens the box and gingerly takes out the flower. It's a single red rose flanked by baby's breath and a few green leaves. I hold out my right hand, and she slips it over my wrist.

I stare down, my lips curving into a small smile. The rose looks like it belongs there, a perfect match with my dress. Last year, Eve forgot to buy me a corsage and we certainly didn't take a limo. I had to drive her in my mom's Subaru Forester because her car was out of gas.

I run to our refrigerator and grab the plastic box with Jenna's corsage, sitting on top of a tub of arugula. after we finally scooched into the limo, this sentence. Jenna's mom is hanging out at my parents' place until her dad gets off work—it's kind of cool they all get along.

"And this is for you," I say, placing the white rose with a dark blue ribbon and baby's breath over her slim wrist.

Jenna's face breaks into a huge smile. "Thank you." She pulls me into a hug. As she lets go, she says, "I know this all feels cheesy and cliché, but after last year's prom with me being single and what happened with Eve, I thought we deserved the prom of our dreams."

As long as it's not our last night together.

After the awkward pictures forced upon us by my dad with his extra-large camera trying to get the lighting just right, we finally scooched into the limo.

Our parents wave goodbye as we drive away, and my mom blows me a kiss. I have to say, I won the lottery in the supportive parents' department. When I told them I was pansexual a couple of years ago, my mom threw her arms around me and thanked me for telling her. She also said if anyone gave me any crap, I should let them know and they would take care of it. My dad agreed. *Take care of it? What are they, the mafia?*

When the limo stops, Jenna opens the door and I hear, "It's time to PARTY!" Mark sticks his head in blowing a noise maker. I can't help but laugh. He physically drags Jenna out of the vehicle, and I follow. His parents are already in the front yard, taking action shots, so the four of us stand behind some blooming bushes and smile.

Mark and Brody are wearing bright blue matching tuxes and donning smiles that couldn't get any bigger if they tried, but other than that, they're very different. Mark is gay and Puerto Rican with dark black hair and almond eyes, and Brody is bi and white, with the blondest hair and bluest eyes you'll ever see. Honestly, when he moved here in tenth grade, I had the biggest crush on him, but then once I got to know him, he became more of a brother. Jenna and I got close with both of them at last year's musical, and the four of us have been inseparable ever since.

"Time to live it up!" Brody says once we're back in the limo, pulling out a bottle of champagne, and I gasp.

"What? We can't have that, especially in a moving vehicle," I say, backing up as if it were poison.

He waves his hands. "Relax, Girl Scout, it's non-alcoholic champagne. My older sister gave it to me and said it tastes like the real thing."

After confirming from the label that the champagne was indeed non-alcoholic, we all clink our plastic flutes together and shout, "To JAMB!" Yeah, we are that cheesy and made our group name a combination of our first initials.

I take a huge swig from the glass and wrinkle my nose. "Ew, is this what the real stuff tastes like? Why do people want this?" I'm one of those good girls who still hasn't touched a drop of real champagne. Whenever I do even a super small thing wrong, the guilt that follows is all-consuming. Just the thought of doing something actually illegal, like underage drinking, makes my stomach churn.

Mark laughs and pats my leg. "Hon, it's more about what the real stuff does to you than the taste."

And that's when the colorful lights begin streaming. I face Jenna with my mouth open.

"I had to get the party package!" she exclaims, pulling out glow sticks from under the seat. The lights pulsate between a rainbow of colors so wildly, as if you'd need to put a seizure warning on the window before entering this vehicle. Dua Lipa's newest hit is pumping at full blast. Mark lets out a shriek and starts moving his hands enthusiastically, glow sticks high in the air, and Brody's arms are going up and down. I shrug and bump myself into Jenna, grab some glow sticks, and we join in the dance party. *When in Rome, right?*

After a few minutes, the limo stops, causing all the party fun to screech to a halt. The bright white lights come on like the end of the actual prom. At least none of us are sweaty yet with makeup dripping off our faces.

"Are you ready for this?" Jenna asks, holding out her hand to help me out of the limo.

I bite my lip. *Am I?* I take a deep breath and nod. I keep saying, *Jenna's not Eve,* over and over again in my head like a mantra.

Our prom is at the nicest hotel we have in our town, and I feel weird walking in through the automatic doors, even though we're wearing our super fancy get-up. It's the kind of place that has a chandelier with cascading crystals as soon as you enter the hallway, valet parking, a concierge desk, and a spa. I'm used to the bare minimum when it comes to hotels, someone glued to their phone at the check-in desk and rooms that somehow smell like smoke even though it's a non-smoking hotel.

We're directed to go up the escalators into the *ballroom*. We hand over our tickets to a girl who's a junior near the entrance.

"Welcome to Under the Sea," she says, pointing inside.

As soon as we enter, we're enveloped in a sea of blue decorations. To our right is a photo-op station with a 2D towering ship complete with dark sparkly sails. Leaning against the ship is an anchor splattered in glitter. On the ground right near a photographer is a stationary steering wheel that a jock is currently trying to steer, making over the top grunting noises, his date folding her arms next to him with a frown on her lips.

"We will have to get our picture there for sure," Jenna says, clapping her hands.

I mutely nod my head. My senses are overloaded. We move out of the doorway through the arch of blue glitter ballons. To our left is a buffet table of Sterno trays with a crazy long line of people waiting their turn. A whiff of fried food and meat reaches my face and I wrinkle my nose. I've been a vegetarian since ninth grade when I stumbled upon some documentary on the meat industry and haven't touched meat since.

"Come on, we need to stake out a table," Mark says, dragging Brody behind him.

There's a round table by itself close to the dance floor where Mark is already draping his suit jacket over the back of a folding chair. The table cloth is a dark glittery blue with a conch shell centerpiece.

"They went all out, didn't they?" I say, inspecting the conch shell. "Better than last year's ranch theme."

Jenna laughs. "I still think there's hay stuck on my shoes."

I set my red clutch on the table cloth and survey the dance floor. A few people dance among a sea of blue and white balloons. Some blown up mermaid balloons are attached to the white pillars lining the white and black checkered dance floor. This venue must have cost the school a fortune unless one of my classmate's parents work here or something and got us a discount.

Jenna looks down at her Apple Watch and a small smile appears on her face.

"Hey, I'll be right back. Don't get any food without me," she instructs.

Before I have a chance to ask any questions, she disappears. My eyes scoot over to meet Brody's, and I raise an eyebrow. He shrugs.

"Maybe there's a volleyball team picture," he suggests.

As much as she loves the volleyball team, she wouldn't cut out as soon as we got here for that, would she?

"Jenna didn't tell us to wait to get food. Sorry, Addy. I want to scope out the scene before all the good stuff is gone," Mark says waving to the buffet line.

"As if there's anything good."

Mark rolls his eyes. "I'm sure there's something fried and greasy for us meat eaters."

I'm about to sit and play on my phone while I'm waiting when someone taps my shoulder. I whirl around, and Jenna's grinning ear to ear with an outstretched hand holding a brown bag. I take it from her, unload the contents, and gasp.

"Is this Ra's Asian Fusion?" I ask, lifting the lid on what looks like a green curry sauce and sniff. That's definitely green curry with tofu, my absolute favorite.

"Yes! I know that last year the vegetarian option they gave you was pretty crappy, so I didn't want that to happen again."

I wrap my arms around her and pull her into a tight hug.

"You really are the best. I can't believe you got me takeout! Much better than my potatoes three ways last year."

She laughs. "What was the 'three ways?'"

I shake my head. "Fries, mashed potatoes, and tater tots. I thought maybe they'd have pierogies, but that was asking too much."

I take a seat and remove the rest of the bag contents on the glittery table cloth. I hand the other takeout container to Jenna.

"I'm glad you got yourself something too so you aren't stuck with that mess of whatever," I say, motioning my head towards the buffet.

"I couldn't help myself. You got me addicted to Ra's."

After we both stuff our faces with delicious goodness and listen to Mark and Brody gripe how Jenna didn't think about them in her food plans, Jenna springs up from the chair and holds out her hand.

"Picture time before we get all sweaty and gross. Come on!"

She practically drags me down the aisle to the elaborate ship setup.

"Aren't you two cute together," the photographer says, giving us a genuine smile. He's even wearing a black tux with his brown hair slicked back. "I suggest going in front of the steering wheel so we can get your entire outfits in the picture."

We position ourselves leaning against the steering wheel, Jenna behind me with her arms wrapped around my waist. It's just then that the goosebumps show up. *She really likes me. There's no way she'd go to all this effort if she's going to break up with me.*

"Smile!" the photographer says, and I do, much bigger than I ever have in my entire life.

He squints at the camera display window and gives us a thumbs up sign.

"That's a keeper right there."

I turn around to face Jenna and give her a huge kiss right there in front of everyone. When I pull away, she laughs.

"What was that for? I know you aren't much for PDA."

I reach for her hand. "Thank you for everything. It has already been a magical night. I'm so lucky I found you."

She squeezes my hand. "Addy, I feel the exact same way."

"I'm all for a good lovefest, but we need to get our picture so we can go dance," Mark says, pushing us out of his way.

While we're waiting for them to get the perfect pose, a few of Jenna's volleyball friends come up to her and whisper in her ear. Once they catch me staring, they give me innocent smiles and walk off.

"What was that about?" I ask.

She waves her hand. "Oh nothing. There's a volleyball afterparty they wanted to let me know about."

I cock my head. "We can totally go if you want."

She's staring straight ahead, watching Mark and Brody kiss the anchor. "Naw. I'd rather do what we've planned."

We decided to go glow bowling with Mark and Brody and then have some *alone time* in Jenna's car before heading home. I hadn't thought too much about it, probably because I had convinced myself that she was going to break up with me tonight. Then, another thought occurs to me.

"Wait, how are we going to get anywhere without your car?" I ask.

"Don't worry, my parents are bringing it here before the end of prom. Oh, they want us for pictures!" Jenna exclaims.

Mark and Brody are excitedly waving their hands at us. After some ridiculous poses and too much fun, I'm being led to the dance floor.

Everyone else must have had the same idea, because the floor's starting to get really crowded. People are all up on each other, some couples blatantly making out. Jenna pulls me into her arms, and I wrap my arms around her neck to dance as close as possible. Mark and Brody are also dancing uber near each other. I dare the chaperones to say anything to us. It wouldn't be prom without sweaty bodies pressed up against each other, right?

The beat slows down, and all the single people meander off the dance floor.

"Everyone, it's time for our first slow dance of the night. Grab your date or someone who you wish was your date. Time to get cozy."

We didn't really have to make too many adjustments because we are pretty cozy already. With Jenna wrapped around me, her lilac scent reaching my nose, I think back to what led us here and the promposal. It didn't go viral, but it was sure memorable.

There's a rock-climbing wall at her dad's store that we enjoy going to. Hey, free rock climbing, who wouldn't? We have to take turns because it only holds one person. Usually, I go first and then Jenna—I'm not sure why, but it's our thing.

But this time, Jenna grabbed my hand and said, "Mind if I go first? There's something I need to do quick after."

I shrugged. "Sure, that's fine." *What did she have to do?*

The store assistant helped her into the gear, and she was off. She powered up the wall, her long legs moving even quicker than her normal pace, which was already fast to begin with. Right near the top, she turned around, flashed me a smile, and said, "Addy, get ready."

She pulled on a string, and a huge paper banner descended down right in front of Jenna. In big red letters, outlined in black, it read:

Will you go to PROM with me?

Jenna was still wrestling to get out from under the banner, and finally, her head in the black and green helmet popped around it.

"So, what do you say?" she asked, biting her lip.

This was the most Jenna promposal ever. It was super sweet, and even though it wasn't perfect, it felt perfect to me.

"For you, yes," I said.

I heard cheering from behind me and turned around to see her mom holding a phone, making a whooping noise, and Jenna's dad with a small smile on his face.

"I'm glad the rock-climbing wall could be of use during this momentous occasion," he said, coming up and giving me a hug. Her mom put down the phone and also wrapped me in an embrace.

"Thank you for making my girl so happy," she whispered in my ear.

"What's making you smile that much?" Jenna asks, pulling me out of the memory.

I give a little laugh. "Just remembering the promposal and how you got stuck behind the banner."

Jenna groans. "Yeah, not my finest hour, but I really thought I'd be able to find a way to go around it faster. Easier said than done, right? I'm just glad you said yes. I know we talked about going together, but I wasn't sure if you'd change your mind."

I rest my chin on her chest. "I hadn't been sure of the whole prom thing, but I knew it would be with you, so I trusted that thought."

The music changes again, and I groan. "Not the *Cupid Shuffle*. I hate that dance! I'm going to take off my shoes. Wanna come with me?"

Jenna releases me. "Mind if I stay and do this one with the volleyball crew?"

"Go for it."

I head back to our table and sink into my chair, rubbing my feet after slipping off my heels. I'll probably never want to stick my feet back into these things ever again.

"The *Cupid Shuffle* sucks," Brody says, sitting down at our table.

"You said it, although it doesn't help that I'm not really coordinated. I don't know how they dealt with me at the musical for two years in a row."

Brody laughs. "Being your dance partner this year was a challenge. I still think my big toe is black and blue. Hey, at least you have a decent voice."

"But not decent enough to graduate from the chorus and get an actual part with a name," I say, rolling my eyes.

Jenna is dancing her heart out with her volleyball girls. She, on the other hand, is the most coordinated person I've ever met. That's when I see something that makes my heart freeze, and my stomach turns over. Behind Jenna and the volleyball girls, my ex, Eve, dances without a care in the world.

I grab Brody's arm and squeeze like it's a stress ball. "Oh, my God. Why is Eve here?"

Brody's eyes widen. "Woah. She must have come as someone's date."

That's exactly the moment when Eve catches my eye, while my mouth is agape. How can this be happening on my perfect night?

She whispers to the red-headed girl next to her, someone who I thought was straight, then she heads in my direction.

"Oh no. What should I do?" I ask Brody, my voice raspy.

"First off, how about you let go of me?" he says, forcibly removing my fingers from his arm. "I was starting to lose circulation. Second, don't show her you're upset. She doesn't deserve to ruin your night."

As Eve approaches, I rise from my seat and face her head on.

"Addy," Eve says smoothly. She looks gorgeous in a tight emerald green dress, a gold chain with a seashell attached to the end, and gold heels. She has a plastic purple starfish attached like a barrette to her short pixie cut black hair. If mermaids were real, she'd be the epitome of one.

"What are you doing here?" I ask, trying as hard as possible to make my voice not wobble.

She points back to the dance floor. "With my girl, Ray. I'm surprised to see you here."

"I didn't want one bad prom experience to be the one I remembered for the rest of my life. I'm here with Jenna."

"Oh, yeah. I heard you two were together. Good for you. Glad you got back out there," she says, clicking her tongue.

I grind my teeth together. *How did I ever like this girl?* "She, unlike you, is here for me. Every day, not when she feels like it."

Eve puts her hands on her hips. "Come on, Addy. It's not like we were soulmates. We were having fun, and I was leaving for college. How did you think we'd work?"

"It would have been nice to learn this BEFORE you humiliated me on stage at prom last year. Why couldn't we have talked about it in private like normal human beings?"

A hand touches my arm.

"Hey, you okay?" Jenna asks, her eyebrows knitted together.

I nod. "I'm good. I need to do this. Something I should have done a while ago."

I turn back to Eve. "You broke my heart into a million pieces that night. I'm still working on putting them back together, thanks to Jenna and my other amazing friends and family. But you had no right to do that. Are you here to do it again to your new girl? Are you going to destroy her faith in humanity like you almost did to me?"

Eve's mouth drops open. "What? No, that's not what I did. I had been thinking about breaking up with you for a bit, but we kept having more things planned, and I didn't know what to do. So I decided to just rip the bandage off. I didn't mean to do it during my acceptance speech. It just kind of happened. I'm sorry."

"Ladies and gentlemen, now's the time you've all been waiting for, Prom King and Queen!"

"Speaking of," I say, rolling my eyes. I turn to Jenna. "Hey, let's bounce. I don't need to see any more ridiculous acceptance speeches, especially with this one around."

Jenna's eyes turn alarmed. "Can we stay, please? I'm pretty sure one of my friends is going to be crowned queen, and I want to be here for her."

I suck in my breath. I can do this for Jenna. She's done so much for me already.

"Okay, and then can we go?"

"I promise."

Eve slinks away without saying anything else. *Good riddance.* I zone out when they announce the candidates for Prom Queen.

"And the winner goes to...Addy Ward!"

"Wait, what?" I exclaim. "I'm not even on the ballot!"

I had been hoping I would be a contender this year, but when they had announced who the candidates were, I pretended I was totally okay with it, but secretly was super bummed. I thought it could be my redemption story. And now this happens? But how?

Jenna's wearing a huge grin on her face.

"This had to be you. How did you make this happen?" I ask.

She winks. "I have my ways. When you have multiple sports teams on your side, write-in options actually become a legit way to win. This just proves it."

"Oh my gosh, thank you so much. I don't know what I did to deserve you, but you are the best girlfriend in the world," I say, giving her the biggest hug ever. I pull away, and her face is bright red.

"Go get your crown, my Queen," she says, shooing me away.

I hold my head up high and take each step one at a time. As I reach the podium, I see Eve already standing there, holding the golden crown she received last year. Her mouth is in a straight line. I forgot about this tradition. No wonder she's here. She's not one to stray from the limelight.

"I pass the Prom Queen crown to Addy Ward, congratulations," she says into the microphone. As she places the crown on my head, she whispers to me, "I hope this brings you everything you've ever wanted."

She's wrong. It won't. I seek out Jenna in the crowd and wave to her. I already have it.

The Spy Who Took Me To Prom

By Abigail F. Taylor

KELSEY SQUEEZED A SPONGY strawberry off its toothpick and onto a little plastic poker chip plate stacked with fruit and cubed cheeses. She gave an impatient huff, waiting for Eliza to finish choosing between the white and dark chocolate fountains. The finger foods were provided by a local bakery called *Kneadle and Bread,* and Kelsey was interested in trying the pretty ambrosia custards in the frosted glasses. Eliza blocked the display with her lack of decision making.

The prom committee had really gone all out with a *Casino Royale* theme. Even if Kelsey did think it was too on the nose for The Moran Academy of Promising Young Women, she liked the neon palm trees bowing over the three foot tall dice where couples were taking pictures, and the elaborate games were set up through-out the gymnasium.

They were one of the few students who arrived on time, even though Kelsey, in a last minute panic, had changed from a sparkling, form-fitting gown to a flowy, mint-green cottagecore dress. She'd done her eyeshadow to match the delicate peonies stitched into the gauze of her skirts and settled on practical, pink slippers that could be kicked off at a moment's notice.

"So, what is it you were saying?" Eliza asked. She popped a chocolate blueberry into her perfect cupid's bow mouth.

Next to them, an enormous Roulette game flashed, *WINNER! WINNER!* One of the girls on the volleyball team had to use both hands to toss the white ball onto the wheel and cheered when it bounced into a red square.

Kelsey turned her attention back to Eliza. "Mr. Howard and Mrs. Tupling were talking about prom. They don't know that *I know* Lithuanian! So I was just being all casual putting my bag away. They're planning something. I think prom is a test!"

Eliza slowly let out the bubble of air caught in her cheeks. "I thought it was going to be something good."

"This is good," Kelsey said, impatiently pushing a strand of wayward black hair behind one ear. "Prom is a setup!"

"Duh. We're supposed to mingle with the other schools, forge friendships and strong alliances, and figure out who's going to be our biggest competition once we're pushed out into our chosen careers. Dad figures there's going to be scouts here tonight. We have to put on our best Emily Post behavior."

"Not a test like that. A *real* test," Kelsey insisted, turning to watch the gymnasium doors as more junior and senior students filtered in. She recognized some of the boys from Saint Eliot, their sibling academy and biggest rivals. She hoped half of them remembered their tango lessons because she had every intention of dancing tonight.

Eliza arched a brow, and Kelsey sighed. "Okay, so my Lithuanian is tourism level at best, but—"

"You think everything is a test." Eliza picked up a spoon and tilted her chin into the dim reflection, checking the blend of her makeup in various angles. "Anyway, I think I'm going to ask him out."

"Who?"

Eliza removed a fleck of chocolate with her little finger. "Mr. Howard."

Kelsey gasped, spinning in another direction, looking for their gym teacher, like he might have heard them through the throng of laughter and the Top of the Pops blasting through the speakers. "You can't do that! He's old!"

"He isn't even forty."

"But he's our teacher!"

"So? I'm eighteen."

"You're joking."

"Bet," Eliza said, dark eyes sparkling.

Mr. Howard stood by the punch bowl, talking with Mrs. Tupling, Principal Mendel, and the *Kneadle & Bread*'s pretty owner. He was the newest member of the faculty and clearly hired just to make the girls' lives miserable. He put them through rigorous obstacles, full of mud and razor wire. Rumor had it he was a government experiment.

Eliza thought there was "something charming" about his irritability towards the girls' constant failures at various tasks. Kelsey thought he looked one part comic book hero, two parts junkyard dog, and that Eliza had an *I-can-fix-him* disorder.

Some of the other Moran Academy professors got caught up reliving their glory days, interrupting History or Biology lectures with exaggerated tales of espionage, which Kelsey found boring. She was told by Mr. Navarro, the non-verbal communications professor, that people who talked the most, lied the most. Mr. Howard didn't talk at all. He was aloof. Mysterious. A real spy. Exactly what the Moran girls were training to be.

Still, asking a teacher—a *gym teacher*—to dance? Total ick.

Kelsey abandoned her fruit plate and trailed after her friend. If anyone could achieve a goal through charisma alone, it was Eliza. Tall and athletic, she was stunning in her periwinkle, backless mermaid dress. Her strappy heels put her nearly level with Mr. Howard's one working eye.

"Hi. Interesting to see you here." Eliza fluttered her rhinestone lashes.

"Is it?" he asked.

Kelsey realized he wasn't looking at them, they were just in the sightline of the eyeball that couldn't move. She shuttered and searched for a lifeline from one of the other teachers. Principal Mendel had gone off to yell at three Saint Eliot's for inappropriately straddling the giant dice. Mrs. Tupling was asking the bakery owner where she found her dress. This embarrassing display was without an audience. Kelsey chewed the inside of her cheek. Maybe this would be part of the test, too.

"You normally don't chaperone," Eliza said.

"That's astute of you." His thick arms remained crossed over his broad chest. He was using a different accent this evening—French Canadian. The teachers rotated the way they spoke, partly to keep the Moran girls on their toes. It was the chief reason Kelsey wanted to specialize in dialects and languages. At this stage in her studies, she could nail down where half the teachers were born and raised.

"Yes." Eliza plucked her teardrop necklace, a nonverbal cue inviting him to look at her cleavage. "It made me wonder if you'd be interested in a tango later with me?"

Mr. Howard turned to give her a once over and, in a tone that suggested he was discussing the weather, said, "Gross."

Eliza's acrylic nails slid from her necklace to the jewels adorning her dark blonde hair, and she quickly turned the click of her tongue into a self deprecating laugh. "Excuse me?"

They had gym class on Monday, and Kelsey, who hadn't managed to conquer her fear of heights, worried it would be ropes and Mr. Howard would put her on the fifteen-foot platform. So, failing to make things less awkward, she said, "I like your suit. The green matches your... your eye..."

"Ladies!" Mrs. Tupling's attention turned at Mr. Howard's rough, mirthless laughter. "Don't you look resplendent this evening."

"Thank you," Kelsey said, smoothing her clammy hands over the gossamer fabric at her waist. This would be the perfect opportunity for her and Eliza to make a clean getaway.

"At least you think so," Eliza said, her chin turned up with defiance. "Mr. Howard was just telling me I looked gross."

A stone of secondhand embarrassment dropped into Kelsey's stomach, and Mrs. Tupling's thick eyebrows disappeared into her long fringe. "Ted? Now really—"

"Och, fuckin' kill me!" Mr. Howard said, tossing his hands in the air as he strode away from the table. He made it about forty feet before he collapsed.

With the music as loud as it was, no one had heard the thud of Mr. Howard's big body, not even Kelsey who was closest to him. Mrs. Tupling rushed forward, and with some effort, flipped him onto his back. Blood blossomed from the center of his chest, squirting against Mrs. Tupling's hands as she began CPR. It looked like a gunshot wound. But Moran Academy was neutral territory.

Around them, the students began to stop their fake gambling, and the music shut off. Kelsey snatched a cloth from the nearest table and offered it to Mrs. Tupling. She looked into the shadowy rafters. "What can I do?"

"Maybe it came from over there?" Eliza suggested from behind Kelsey.

"The angle's wrong. It might have been..." She glanced from side to side, still pumping vigorously against the gym teacher's chest. "We don't have a pulse. Kelsey, switch out with me. Eliza, call–"

The lights went out.

Screams echoed through the gym as they were enveloped in darkness. Kelsey continued to work on Mr. Howard, whispering the lyrics to 'Stayin' Alive' so she wouldn't screw up. She couldn't see more than two feet in front of her but thought she heard another teacher whisper, "I don't remember this part," before her words were drowned out by Eliza.

"I'm going to call the emergency!" For a brief moment, Eliza's diamond-cut face was beautifully illuminated in the shine of her phone screen. A figure rushed forward, knocking into her, and the phone clattered away. She shouted, "Watch yourself!"

The person continued to move with a determined speed.

Right for Kelsey.

She was yanked away from Mr. Howard. Thinking fast, Kelsey dropped her weight forward and flipped herself out of the stranger's grasp, while keeping the offending arm close to her torso. She landed with a thump onto the wooden floor and heard the satisfying smack of another body. Then another. And another. More screams. Crap.

She scrambled to her feet and continued to knock into shoulders, unable to get traction. Rough hands yanked her back by her dress. It was so dark, and there were too many shadows, too many voices. A wet cloth covered her nose and mouth, swamping her with the sickly-sweet odor of chloroform. She thought she heard Eliza shriek her name. Frantic. Searching.

But it was so distant, Kelsey might as well have been at the other end of the world, slipping down a stream and into a gutter where she'd disappear, unnoticed, forever.

Minutes or several hours later, Kelsey slowly regained consciousness. She was zip-tied to a chair, and a burlap sack covered her head. Itchy cotton filled her mouth. She remembered how to regulate her breathing, giving the opportunity of a few precious moments to listen in on a conversation, or scope the surroundings before the abductors knew she was awake. The Moran Girls were often reminded that espionage was rarely like the movies. It was ninety percent paperwork, and the other ten percent wouldn't be filled with villains monologuing their plans.

A soft vibrating caught her attention, and she held an exhale in her nose.

Someone said, "I have her, and if you don't produce the product like we'd discussed, you'll be receiving her thumbs in the mail."

Kelsey swallowed, tucking her thumbs tight against her palms. *Focus. Focus!*

The voice was familiar, a particular lilt to it. She almost shook her head to loosen the remains of chloroform that cobwebbed her thoughts, but stopped just in time. No need to reveal that she was awake just yet.

"...Yes, that's right..." The voice sounded reasonable, soothing, and male. "I know what a bind you're in, but honestly, David."

The exasperated sigh and the way her father's name was said were the final clues. The man was Principle Mendel, using his real voice—that twangy Albuquerque accent, the way it sounded like it belonged to someone safe and lovely to be around. The betrayal cut deep.

Why would Principle Mendel threaten to mail her thumbs? Was this all part of the secret test she'd heard about just that morning? Kelsey swallowed, nearly gagging on the cotton, and tried to figure out how big the room was by the echoes.

She pressed her toes against the soles of her ballet slippers. What did she know about him that could help her escape, other than that he was from New Mexico and favored fake accents from the Adriatic Coastline? He'd been principal of the Academy for decades. He was old enough to have fought during Desert Storm. So, with that knowledge, she could...

Crap. She was stumped.

Unsure if the brain freeze was due to the chloroform or because of panic, Kelsey tried to give herself some words of encouragement, but all that came to mind was, *At least I'm not hanging fifteen feet off a building.*

"Look who's awake," Principal Mendel said, taking on an Albanian accent. He didn't sound pleased at all. "I suspect you've been awake a lot longer than you want me to think."

"Sorry," Kelsey said, unable to stop herself.

"Not your fault. I have a habit of hiring teachers who are really good at their jobs."

He yanked off the burlap sack. The high voltage, neon light struck Kelsey with such force, she gasped.

Principal Mendel paused, gently cupping her chin in his hands. His round face and sharp nose overwhelmed her wavering vision. With a small huff, he dropped her head. "No concussion. Good. We're taking a ride."

"What sort of ride?" she asked as he cut the zip ties free and swiftly replaced them. He hugged her close, leading her across the empty warehouse and toward a set of stairs that went... up. *Oh no.*

"I read in your file you've a fear of heights. I'm happy to give you another dose if it'll keep you from panicking." He was using the tone of a sympathetic leader. *You can't be a principal without being a pal* was his favorite phrase.

"Go to Hell!" Kelsey snapped, driving her elbow into his floating ribs.

She ran. Two thoughts tumbled in her head as she sprinted across the dank, half-lit room.

The first: *Get to the door.*

The second: *Thank God I wore a loose dress.*

Principal Mendel wasn't far behind. Not a surprise. She'd seen him with Mr. Howard running at dawn around the track. But she was faster.

Her tied hands slammed against the metal bar of the exit door. It swung fast back into place, giving her time to scoop her dress between her legs and tuck the ends into her belt. Behind her, the rusting scream of metal meant her time was up.

Kelsey hooked a right, towards the distant street lamps, but she miscalculated and toppled head over heels into a ditch with a dry well half inserted into the ground.

Principal Mendel cursed and swung her into a fireman's carry back to the warehouse. Her pulse thumped in her ears, and she stared at his feet. There were four of them. Blood and dust clogged her nose. Was that her imagination, or was that a helicopter overhead?

"I really wish you wouldn't have done that," Principal Mendel said with a disappointed sigh. "I can't get you medical attention until we're at our next location. There might be a kit on the chopper, but..."

Kelsey squirmed, but his grip tightened around her waist. "I'm not going anywhere, you son of a gun!"

He set her back in the chair and fitted the burlap sack over her head. "You'd make a damn fine field agent one of these days if you weren't so scared of heights. Shame, really."

"The only shame here is you, Arnie!"

Kelsey could hardly process the thick Irish accent before it was replaced with the satisfying sound of metal on bone. The hood was off again, and she blinked against the annoyingly bright neon light strip once more. Mr. Howard's attention was no longer on her, but on Principal Menel's lifeless body. An eight foot rebar pinned his head to the ground. Kelsey turned away from the gruesome scene while Mr. Howard rummaged through the pockets.

"Big breaths, Parrack. Nasty fall back there. Probably knocked your brain a bit."

"Beats... beats... a pole through my head."

Mr. Howard turned back to her and snapped the zip-ties off her wrists. "Sorry I didn't get here sooner."

"It's okay. You were dead."

"Right, so, I'm good at that sort of thing—playing dead." He smoothed down his suit and tie, head tilted upward at the unmistakable sign of a helicopter landing on the rooftop five floors above them. "All right, Parrack. Let's get dirty. We're going south, then west. There's a gap in the fence. My car's there. We can make a clean getaway."

"Why me?" Kelsey asked, reenforcing the fabric of her dress into her belt. Mr. Howard shrugged and led her toward the exit opposite of the one she'd tried to make her escape from.

"Arnie was embezzling apparently. Had a good round of luck by the look of things, and a fake company exporting sawn wood from Croatia to Kuwait. He got loose with money from the wrong sort of Croatians. Yatta. Yatta." He flapped a hand in the air. "Your da's the Canadian Ambassador in Kuwait."

"I was ransom?" She couldn't believe it. "He wanted my dad to pay the debt."

"Right as rain, Parrack."

They were fifty feet from the door. Twenty. Ten. Then, with the roar of an engine, Mr. Howard's cherry red El Camino burst through the walls, sending rubble everywhere. The front bumper of the car wrapped itself around a pillar of concrete, which slammed into Mr. Howard. Kelsey staggered back in time to avoid most of the damage and shielded her eyes from the pebbles of debris jettisoning her way.

"For fuck's—" he grunted, forearms braced against the pillar. His muscles bulged through the various torn parts of his tailored suit, and he tossed the offending concrete to the side with an irritated huff, like it was a feather pillow. The Camino wheezed into a pile of steam, thumping against the desecrated wall that now lay beneath the tires.

Eliza tumbled out of the driver's seat with a shriek. Struggling in her skin tight mermaid dress, she somehow managed to make her way over the hill destruction and into Kelsey's arms, "Oh, my God! I thought you were dead!"

"How did you find us?" Kelsey hugged Eliza back, unwilling to let go of such a friendly face.

Eliza gestured to the tiny sequined purse dangling from her wrist. "I had you on Find My Friends. I knew something was up when Mr. Mendel ran off with you, and suddenly, Mr. Howard was alive again. Mrs. Tupling didn't even look surprised. So, I guess you were right about them planning something."

"It was meant to be dinner theater, like," Mr. Howard grumbled. "Escape room drama. A bit of fun. Ah, Jaysus. My car's toast."

"Sorry." Eliza shrugged, not sounding it at all. "I figured you were a bad guy, and it was my moral obligation to jack you. How are you still standing, anyway?"

Mr. Howard's thin lips tightened, and his one eye roamed over Eliza, like he didn't quite believe that was her only motivation.

The smoke emitting from the hood thickened, and Kelsey tugged them both. "That thing is going to blow, and who knows what else is in here that might catch fire? We need to get out, and fast."

"No way but up," Mr. Howard said. "I heard the helicopter land."

"Do you know how to fly one of those?" Eliza asked.

"Nope." His hand slid to his left hip, and he removed a customized revolver from its concealed holster with a little wild west flip. "But I have a gun."

They ran toward the door, away from the heat. Thin licks of flames jumped around the sides of the dented hood. Eliza paused only once to grab the hem of her dress and rip it up to her thigh. Kelsey was the first to make it to the stairwell, and she swallowed the thick gob of nerves that knotted at the base of her tongue. The stairs were not the issue. It was what she'd face at the other end. Yes, there was the height factor, but she had no idea what sort of adversary they'd meet. Would Mr. Howard, and the training Eliza and Kelsey had the last four years be enough for them to successfully escape?

Mr. Howard clapped his big hands as he sped past her. "Parrack! I know you're faster than me. Don't make me beat you."

Eliza roped her long arm around Kelsey's hip, and the two of them ran together up the five flights. Their footsteps mirrored Kelsey's frantic heart as they clacked against the metal steps.

"We're going to get out of this easily," Eliza panted. "I'm not going to miss prom because of some idiot middle aged man!"

"That's the spirit!" Mr. Howard called. He kicked open the rooftop door, and it vibrated downward, as though to spur the girls onward.

Kelsey clutched Eliza, unsure of how stable this old building was. She picked up her pace the final few steps. No need to spend what was supposed to be a wonderful night buried alive because the warehouse couldn't withstand her gym teacher's vicious kick.

Zinc sulfate dust devils were caught in the force of the propeller. Mr. Howard was able to cover his mouth with his suit jacket. All the girls could do was duck their heads and charge to the back seats.

With a sleek movement that Kelsey didn't think capable of a man his size, Mr. Howard swung into the front and pressed the barrel of his gun against the pilot's temple. "Howya? Plans changed. You're taking us to prom."

The pilot glanced over his shoulder to the two smudged faces grinning in the back. "I don't think that–"

"You want to keep your brain in your skull for future shit you don't think about? Then, I suggest you do as I say. Real smooth," Mr. Howard said.

Kelsey wanted to take notes. Why wasn't there a class about banter in the field? The pilot nodded and began clicking the various buttons into place.

Mr. Howard grinned. "Seatbelts, ladies."

The helicopter barely made it into the air before the growing El Camino fire exploded out of the side of the building. The force of the blast sent the helicopter flying sideways.

Eliza squeaked, her hands fumbling over the buckle she hadn't finished fastening. She slammed against the door, which popped open with a sudden gasp of warm air.

Kelsey wasn't sure if she had screamed, or if the sound she had made was something beyond human. Somehow, she snaked out of her seat and followed Eliza out of the door and into the yawning sky below them. The only thing keeping Eliza from freefall was Kelsey's gripping her strappy heels and the tangled harness buckles wrapped around her own knee.

"Hang on!" Kelsey almost laughed in the mania.

Eliza was half petrified, but her hands were either clawing for safety or desperately trying to keep her torn dress from falling past her hips. The shoe slipped in Kelsey's sweaty palms. She told herself, just as much as she told Eliza, "I've got you!"

From the front seat, Mr. Howard called out, "Hook your legs around the landing skid!"

"I can't reach!"

His encouraging "Yes you can!" was followed by a curse, and Mr. Howard was out of his seat.He twisted as he fell, snagging the landing skid with both hands.

"See? It's not that hard," he stuttered from the shock of hot wind blowing up from the burning building as the chemical fire reached frantically for them. Blood splattered his face, his nose bent from the pilot's punch. Swinging himself toward them, he pushed Eliza back toward Kelsey, who reminded her, "You were always the best at monkey bar crunches!"

Eliza curled into herself and made it into the cabin just as the pilot jerked the helicopter in the opposite direction.

Another string of curses escaped Mr. Howard. He hugged the landing skid, face draining of all color except for the splatter of blood. "Parrack! Do something, and fast!"

"Yes, sir!" she shouted, but she wasn't even sure how to begin. The pilot was turning them away from the burning building, and even further away from Moran Academy.

"In your own time!" Mr. Howard's growl disappeared into the slipstream as the helicopter picked up speed.

Eliza's eyes widened. She pushed her hair and the tangled tiara out of her face. Kelsey followed her gaze.

Mr. Howard's pistol.

Eliza lunged for it, but the pilot was faster. He slapped it out of their reach.

"How long do you think he can hold himself up?" Eliza asked Kelsey, thumping into the back seat with a pout. "Maybe I can make these seatbelts into a rope?"

"How about you both just don't move?" the pilot said, maneuvering the helicopter into several jerks, like a horse trying to rid itself of an annoying fly.

Eliza wrapped herself more tightly into the back. Kelsey strained to hear Mr. Howard. If he was cursing, that meant he was still alive and could save them.

No. What was the point of the Moran Academy if not to teach Kelsey how to save herself?

"Remember that simulator course you signed up for last summer for extra credit?" she whispered in Eliza's ear. Her friend stopped messing with the belts and nodded. Kelsey grinned. "Good."

Before she could talk herself out of it, Kelsey flipped Eliza's strappy stiletto in her hand and rammed the point into the ligaments between the pilot's skull and spinal column. His body slumped forward, and the nose of the helicopter tilted downward.

Eliza scrambled into the vacated co-pilot's chair. Screaming, hands trembling, she began flipping switches. "I have control! I can't believe it! I have control!"

"Hell yes, you do!" Kelsey said. "Oh no! Mr. Howard!"

The helicopter jerked again, and for a brief moment, Kelsey saw the sprawl of the city through the window—the galaxy of lights, the swooping traffic, cars the size of ants. She couldn't help it, she vomited chocolate strawberries, which, of course, made things worse. All the adrenaline flooded out of her, dropping into her lungs like a sharp stone. "Oh, my God. We're going to die!"

"No, we're not!" Eliza called out, her glittering tiara still flopping over the side of her face. "We're going to fucking prom!"

Kelsey nodded. She steeled herself, then crawled to the open door. Mr. Howard was, remarkably, hanging on the landing skids like a three-toed sloth.

Kelsey jumped back into the cabin. "Rope! Rope! He's still there!"

Working quickly, she tied the seat belts together, using the extenders, her own belt, anything within her reach, until she made something resembling a fishing line. Anchoring one end to the dead pilot's chair, she shimmied forward to swing the other end out. The ground below them was so far. So,...so very far.

"Do. Not. Puke. On. Me. Parrack."

Kelsey nodded and screwed her eyes shut. She swung the rope in his direction three times before he snapped at her for not looking. Trembling and swallowing a fresh wave of already-chewed chocolate, Kelsey squinted through her false lashes long enough to aim correctly.

"Got it!" he shouted.

At the same time, Eliza said, "I can see the school! Emergency landing in the soccer field is a-go!"

Kelsey saw it too, dark except for the gymnasium that glowed in strips of red and yellow. The spotlights spinning on the fake *Welcome to Vegas* sign acted as ground control. The buckles in her hands tightened, burning the skin on her palms, threatening to take off the calluses Mr. Howard himself had put there from all the forced obstacle courses. She braced her feet on either side of the open door, her back muscles strained against the considerable weight of her gym teacher. She couldn't do it. She wasn't strong enough. There was too much sweat stinging her eyes.

"We're good." He clambered inside, pulled the door shut behind him, and collapsed into the seat, catching his breath.

Kelsey's head bobbed. Her eyes swam with tears that threatened to spill into her curled, ripped hands. A few moments passed in silence, so Eliza could focus on getting the helicopter on the ground.

Then, Mr. Howard said, "Oh, hey. Is this your first kill? Nice."

And Kelsey vomited right into his lap. Sighing, Mr. Howard thumped her back until the helicopter landed and the engine shut off with a sputter.

The death grip Eliza had on the joystick between her knees loosened. "We just did that! We just did that!"

A wild hoot escaped Eliza as she pumped the air and tripped on her way out of the helicopter, toward Mrs. Tupling, waiting at the edge of the field. Mr. Howard gently nudged Kelsey, and she turned away to wipe her mouth with the back of her hand.

"I'm sorry! I didn't mean... I'm sorry."

"Parrack, it's just chocolate. Try to focus on *every-thing* else that happened tonight."

He gestured to the dead pilot, the blinking controls, and Eliza, who was literally performing somersaults in the field until she landed in an awkward sprawl on her back. Mrs. Tupling tried to help her up, guiding her toward the nurse's assistant, who'd appeared with an emergency kit.

"We did that!" Eliza shrieked, pumping the air again.

"We really did?" Kelsey asked, feeling outside of herself, like she was watching a movie.

"You really did." Mr. Howard nodded, and Kelsey's pride devoured the cotton of fear that had clogged her mouth.

"Yeah," she said. "Cool."

Theme

By Erin Jo Eldry

Teal ribbon corsage
Mermaid dress that shapes my form
I'm Under the Sea

When We Were Young

Jennifer Spurgeon

Sweaty bodies writhed at one end of the dimly lit convention hall. The banner over the DJ's booth read, *Starry Nights*. I scanned the crowd for anyone I knew, but my *date* was off with his partner and all my friends were sulking at home because they weren't juniors or seniors. Prom had a funny way of excluding half the school, even though the age difference wasn't that big. What made someone older better than someone younger? I was actually older than a few of the juniors.

Tonight was a fancy evening for guys and gals, and I sat alone at the farthest table from the dance floor, impatiently fussing with the tulle under my skirt. It was scratching my legs, even though I had on tights. Twisting the material, I tried to rip it, but it didn't even tear.

Sighing, I leaned back in my chair and stared out the opened double doors behind me. *Kori*! I'd forgotten she was here.

"I yelled at her through the doors: "Got any scissors?"

She waved me over. The world outside the underwhelmingly large room was far more themed and impressive. There was the photo booth with a midnight blue backdrop and fairy lights; a snack bar with popcorn, chocolates, and fruit; and the "help" desk with a few members of the student council. Kori wasn't actually a member, but she'd been the closest they could get to a professional stylist. She could do hair and makeup, and best of all, she was relatable. There was nothing off putting about an emo chick who somehow knew everyone's secrets.

Anthony was gay; Shanice was pretending to be dumb; and the lunch lady was sleeping with the janitor. Okay, everyone knew that last one, but no one cared, so it wasn't really a secret.

"What do you want scissors for?" Kori's voice cracked as she spoke. She'd been here for hours, long before anyone even arrived, and her voice was starting to give.

"I have to cut this shit off." Lifting my knee-length skirt above my thighs, I showed her how red my skin was under the black tights.

"If you need to alter your gown, please go to the bathroom," Coach Tiller instructed us from the photo booth as two band kids scooted in close to their drum major. With Kori's help, they had jacked their old marching uniforms and altered them into unique outfits. The duct tape couple waited in the wings. Honestly, his dress and her suit should have won scholarships.

Kori stood from her spot at the greeting table and took off her corsage—a pin cushion. Grabbing the scissors, she led the way to the even more unimpressive bathrooms. The beige stalls screamed, *nineties convention center*, not *night of your life*, though someone was sobbing in the big stall.

"Bella dumped Evie for Ginnifer," Kori whispered in my ear. "But Ginnifer turned her down."

"Makes sense." I nodded as Kori set about cutting the tulle. "How's your girlfriend?"

"That's an odd thing to ask with my head up your skirt," she jested. "But she's good. She's setting up the After Prom booths."

For the briefest of moments, my mind wandered to the sensation of her fingers grazing my thighs. Fire burned along my nerves but cooled when I took a deep breath. The corset of my dress dug into my side. She was my friend.

"You two really need to start an event planning place after school," I said, clearing my head.

"You think we want to stay here?"

"Fair enough." I had no desire to leave this town. It was cozy here. Besides, I'd had two more years before I needed to make plans for any big next moves. Kori, on the other hand, was finishing off her junior year. If it weren't for the fact that she was terrible at math, I probably wouldn't have even known her—she was in my Algebra 1 class last year. I planned to finish Calc by senior year. She just worried about getting Geometry out of the way so she could graduate and move on to a design school.

"Where's Robin?" She set the scissors on the sink and meticulously wrapped up the fabric. She'd never waste a scrap.

My date brought me because I had promised to pay for his ticket. I was a sophomore among the Upperclassmen. His family was in dire straits at the time and he really wanted to go with his partner but didn't want to admit that his family was having money problems. "Come on, you know where he is. Probably smoking out back or making out."

"I know. I saw the two of them duck into a dark corner at the end of the hall when we came in here, but I wanted to see if you knew."

I smiled, but it was obvious I was bored.

"Why don't you hang out with me, and we can head to the after party in an hour?" Kori offered.

Her smokey eyes tempted me. Whenever I hung out with her, it was always super chill, but there was a wall, something I had erected but couldn't explain, as if we were the same person split by a lack of mutual interest. She could have been me in another universe, or I could have been her.

"Maybe I should offer to head back with Bella." The idea came out before I had the chance to completely consider it. Bella may have been a cheat, but we had attended health class together in eighth grade. So, I should help her.

The second I took a step toward Bella's stall, Evie's aquamarine gown billowed past me.

"Bells, I think you're beautiful. I love you," Evie whimpered. She was known for being dramatic, and that certainly was true, but her affections were genuine.

Silence filled the space, but cheering seeped in from out in the hall. When Bella's stall door creaked open a second later, Evie threw her arms around her. I lost interest in them as soon as DJ Casper's *Cha Cha Slide* beckoned from the main hall. Who could resist the magnetic pull of the Hip Hop Line Dance?

"Come on," I invited Kori to grab the scissors and saunter back with me, but my walk was more like that of a newborn deer. My sexy was quite awkward, but I wanted to be noticed, and sometimes, I fell victim to my own jealousy of pretty girls and photoshopped magazine covers. The corset and Kori's compliments did make me feel hot.

Unfortunately, by the time we got back to the greeting table, the song had ended. My disappointment mounted when two girls stumbled out of the convention hall, their boyfriends in tow. The ensuing drama, however, was too much for me to handle, so I disappeared back into the hall, leaving Kori to tend to them.

"I didn't know you would be here," a familiar voice said before Ethan appeared in front of me. His sleek baby-blue tux was the perfect reminder of his airy personality. He wore a smirk, and his sandy-blond hair was slicked back. Drawn like a moth to the flame, I hung on his every word. "It's good to see you."

"Thanks," I mumbled. His eyes trailed up my body, meeting mine. Heat burned my skin. If the room were any brighter, he'd have seen me blush. We'd danced around each other before. Just after school started, he had been hanging out with his cousin, who played second violin with me, and he had snuck us into the rafters above the auditorium.

"Where's Julie?" I looked around for his cousin. She'd joked that he and I would look good together. We were close in height.

"She's a freshman."

"Right." I stumbled over the word, worried I was making a fool of myself. "I forgot there's three years between you two."

"How are you here?" He cocked his head. Gleefully caught in his gaze, I ran my finger over the black beading that blended into my dress.

I muttered something about coming with Robin, but only because he needed someone to buy his ticket. The two of us were friends for a long time, but I didn't want Ethan to get the wrong idea and think I actually came with Robin because I was dating him. It would have been nice if Robin hadn't left me alone the entire night.

"Wanna grab something to eat?" Ethan asked, pushing his hands into his pants' pockets. It was cute he'd rather go peck at the food selection than invite me to dance. His cousin had told me he had zero coordination, even though Ethan's older brother was a legend at the school.

"Sure."

When we got to the snack table, it had been picked clean of the good stuff. So, we nibbled on a few grapes and talked about going to After Prom. The promise of more time with him, and food, was enticing, and I happily accepted his invitation.

On the way out, I saw Kori helping Coach Tiller pack up and made sure to tell her we were heading back to the school for the after party. She would be there once she took care of everything here.

When we got out of his gold El Camino at the school parking lot, my stomach growled. The ride had been quiet—I was too anxious to say anything. As he held the door open for me, I stepped out, surprised by the change in attire. There were still a few suits and gowns, but most people had switched into sweats or jeans and T-shirts.

Near the edge of the football field at the other end of the parking lot, a bonfire grew, and so did the music—Yelloward. The chilly night confronted me as I lost focus of the school grounds and remembered what I was wearing.

Ethan took my hand. The sudden warmth flooded my body, pushing back the cold. When I shivered, he placed his suit jacket over my bare shoulders. I reveled in his body heat and the silky fabric on my skin.

Sliding my arms into the jacket, I glanced over at him and was greeted by his charming smile.

"Thanks," I squeaked. "What should we do first?"

He scanned the activities: cornhole, ring toss, and a small, shabby putt putt course. "The bonfire?"

Before I could turn around to look back toward the football field, my eyes caught on the snack table. I fixated on the sliced up sub sandwiches. If I didn't eat, I wasn't going to make it across the parking lot, let alone the field.

"Let's eat," I said as I walked forward, our hands separating. Doing my best to saunter, I forgot about people and bumped into Dominique, her messy bun in my face. "Sorry."

"No problem." For such a small person, her deep voice always surprised me. In heels, I towered over her, but I was at least six inches taller than her normally. She straightened a few things on the table and said, "I don't see Kori."

"I came with Ethan."

She finally looked up, her emerald eyes staring past me as though I were invisible.

"John is messing with the bonfire again," she complained to someone at the drink table. "Can you please go up there?"

It was less of a question and more of a command. The guy jogged off. Ethan handed me a plate and took two sandwich chunks for himself. I snatched the thickest portion I could find.

"Do you think Kori will be here soon?" The concern on Dominique's face was marred by fatigue. She'd been there for hours and probably wouldn't sleep until noon.

"I think so. She was packing up with Coach Tiller when we left," I said, cramming the sandwich into my mouth. I got shuffled about when a few other people came over to get food. My body pressed into Ethan, who'd been behind me the whole time. He was nearly finished eating. So, I rushed to eat mine as Dominique spoke with me about the setup and her sister's upcoming graduation.

She glared past me and sighed. The bonfire was huge, and the guy was walking back. "They had to put the pyro in charge. I knew John would go hard, but I was hoping he'd have some restraint."

"Dad said they're sending a few guys tonight," Ethan said. I always forgot his dad was the Fire Chief. Right on time, the fire engine rolled up to the emergency road behind the football field.

I managed to choke down the last of my sandwich while Ethan watched the truck park a few yards from the bonfire. Before I could suggest we head up there, Kori strolled over. Her plush hoodie had bear ears and fuzzy ball tassels for drawstrings. I wanted to squeeze her like an oversized teddy bear. She clapped me on the shoulder before she went to hug Dominique.

The two enthusiastically recounted their evenings, making sure to include me from time to time. Their sweet affections were brighter than the bon-fire—brighter than stars. They were the romantic couple proms are geared to, not hapless sophomores who were in it for the fancy dresses and overpriced experience. A pang of jealousy stole the briefest hint of happiness I had for them.

Remembering Ethan, I excused myself from their conversation to focus on him. He'd been by my side the entire time, but he was still focused on the football field. I looped my arm through his and headed toward the bonfire. He gladly followed my lead, playing the charming prince.

When we got to the dirt pit just past the goal post, he allowed me to take a few steps in front of him. He stood behind me and wrapped his arms around my shoulders. As he rested his chin on my shoulder, I caught the subtle scent of his fruity hair gel. His breath tickled my neck under the collar of his suit jacket. I was completely enveloped by him.

My heart raced, and I inhaled sharply, taking in more of his presence. Everything spun, and the world around me faded. Only the light of the bonfire broke into my narrowed vision. All that existed was him.

My chest tightened, and I lifted my hands to his forearms, clutching the only thing that seemed real. I wasn't alone in my spiral. He was holding me to himself.

Careful not to disturb our piece of time, I leaned into him. My wish was that this would last forever, even though I knew it wouldn't. His graduation was coming, and this could only be the beginning of the end.

As he nuzzled my neck, his words barely made it to my ears as they melted into my skin: "I'm so glad I ran into you tonight."

I couldn't speak. My thoughts were lost in the sensation running through my body. The heat on my skin was more than I could take. I let my desires—his desires, burn me.

FINAL WORDS FROM DEMI MICHELLE SCHWARTZ

Dear Wild Ink Prom Guests,

We did it!

We danced the night away—well, read the night away, but you get the idea.

The decorations have been stored in their boxes, glitter has been swept off the floor, and memories have been made. I'm going to take my editor crown—I mean, hat—off for a moment to do my final task as a member of the wonderful prom committee. Every author and poet featured in this anthology poured their heart and soul onto the page. So, it's only fair that I step out from behind the curtain and do the same, right?

Here's my prom story.

Funny enough, this book was published exactly ten years after my senior prom, a whole decade since the night many call a pivotal point in our lives. But it wasn't for me, not really. As someone who didn't get asked to prom, or any high school dance for that matter, I felt like I missed out on a fairy-tale experience, one I would never get the chance to have again.

At least, that's what I thought, until last April.

When S.E. and Abby reached out to me practically at the same time, inviting me to be the lead editor for this anthology, I couldn't believe it. To me, this project is much more than a book I had a hand in bringing to life. In many ways, it became the best prom experience ever, ten years after my graduation. Who knew?

I may not have bought a designer dress, picked sparkly shoes, and did my hair and makeup for a dance, but I had the opportunity to read and edit such stunning works of art. Each story and poem in this anthology is special in its own way, and it was a privilege and true honor to have had the chance to immerse myself into these words that will always hold a meaningful place in my heart. To all the authors and poets who trusted me with their work, I can't thank you enough.

Also, the excitement around *Prom Perfect* has been a beautiful thing to witness. Starting on the day the submission call went live, this anthology came up in many conversations on social media. Everyone celebrated the day I sent out the acceptances, and I loved joining into the festivities as the authors and poets shared their invites to Wild Ink's Prom. Several of them revealed the exciting news that this is their first ever publication. As an author who got my first short story accepted by Wild Ink, these messages and posts warmed my heart the most. I'm beyond happy this book made dreams come true, and now that it's in print, all of us will get to relive the magic over and over again.

Like the characters in this book, we all have our own prom memories, but the coolest part of all of this is that we experienced Wild Ink's Prom together. Stories have been shared, and friendships have been made. So, thank you for being part of this adventure, one even more magical than a fairy tale.

With that, it's time to close this chapter of our literary lives, but we'll always have the memories. I may not have been voted prom queen at my school, but working on this anthology brought me more joy than rhinestones and glitter ever could have.

With Love from Your Editor,
Demi Michelle Schwartz

AUTHORS

AVERY TIMMONS

Avery Timmons is an Illinois-based writer holding a BA in creative writing from Columbia College Chicago. Her short fiction can be found or is forthcoming with Querencia Press, Wild Ink Publishing, Fiery Scribe Review, and other digital and print publications. Her debut novel, Thicker Than Water, is to be published with Wild Ink Publishing.

Abigail F. Taylor

Abigail F. Taylor is an award-winning Own Voices author from Texas. When she's not writing, Abigail spends her time out in nature, practicing aikido, and cross stitching. She lives with four cats, two small dogs, and one sassy rooster. You can follow her on her website abigailftaylor.wordpress.com

Adele Liles

Adele Liles has been a high school English teacher for 24 years. She has been a finalist in the Writer's Workout Fiction Potluck contest and published in the North Carolina Bards Poetry Anthology and Wild Ink's Tenpenny Dreadful's Tales as Hard as Nails horror anthology. Her young adult novel, Among the Whisperings, debuts with Wild Ink in 2026.

She lives with her husband and their "tiny panther" in Virginia.

Amy Joyner Buchanan & Bruce Buchanan

Amy Joyner Buchanan is the founder of Atta Girl Says website, the author of five non-fiction books, and a former award-winning journalist.

Bruce Buchanan is the author of the New Adult fantasy novel THE BLACKSMITH'S BOY (Wild Ink, 2025) and adult superhero novel THE RETURN OF THE CERULEAN BLUR (Wild Ink, 2026).

Andie L. Smith

Andie L. Smith is the author of LUCKY ENOUGH and The Bonded Series. She writes coming-of-age stories are sometimes set in our world or found in a futuristic society. When she's not writing, Andie loves to spend time with her husband and two kitties or hang out at Disney World.

—*ele*—

Arwyn Sherman

Arwyn Sherman lives in the woods of Maine where they tend to their menagerie of animals and write fiction. Their work has appeared in anthologies, on a few stages, and is probably tucked away in the chapbook you forgot you bought at a late-night poetry show. Their debut novel WE, THE MISSING will be released from Conquest Publishing in May of 2026

—*ele*—

B Wheeler

B is an aspiring novelist, passionate about bringing relatable LGBTQ+ characters to teen and young adult fiction. She works in learning support and runs the student LGBTQ+ group. Her short story 'Red Spots' was featured in little living room in 2023. She enjoys musicals, long baths, and trips to the seaside.

—*ele*—

Brittany Mack

Brittany Mack has been an avid reader since before she could remember. After spending a decade chasing a corporate career in healthcare, Brittany chose to pursue her passion with a graduate degree in Creative Writing & Professional Publishing from SNHU where her passion for book editing started. Brittany specializes in editing the genres of romance, paranormal, fantasy (low and high), contemporary, thriller/mystery, and young adult fiction. As a professional editor, she likes to dip her toes in writing the stories that fill her thoughts.

Dana Hawkins

Dana Hawkins is a contemporary romance author of sparkly sapphic stories, including NOT IN THE PLAN, IN WALKED TROUBLE, and SO NOT MY TYPE. When not searching the country for the perfect cup of piping hot Americano, she spends her time chasing her kids and rewatching '90s movies. After living for twenty years in Seattle, she recently trekked back to her hometown in Minnesota. She is a huge romance-genre book nerd and borderline obsessed with happy-ever-afters.

Desirae Gracyn

Desirae Gracyn is a nurse and neurodiverse slash queer writer. Working with patients, she has seen how powerful words are in healing and escaping, and it revived her childhood dream of being an author. She predominantly writes fantasy and hopes to help others escape in the worlds she creates.

Diane Billas

Diane Billas is an award-winning author of the YA sapphic contemporary romance novel *Does Love Always Win?* featured in *Parents* Magazine, and the YA superhero novel *Superficial*, both with Creative James Media. Diane lives in Philadelphia with her husband and son. When she's not writing she can be found reading multiple books at once, performing the French horn and piano, or dreaming of the next country she's going to visit. You can find her at <u>dianebillas.com</u>, Instagram/Threads @dianebillaswrites, and TikTok @dianebillas.

Erica Duarte

Erica Duarte hopes for the privilege of writing stories as a full-time career. When not taking care of her family,or working her paid gig, she is writing, reading or listening to audiobooks––her newest obsession. She has another short story in Uncensored Ink, by Wild Ink Publishing.

Erin Jo Eldry

Erin Jo Eldry is an up-and-coming author from central Florida, dabbling in both poetry and adult fiction. She graduated from Stetson University with a BFA, minoring in Creative Writing, and has previous short works featured in *Bunker Squirrel Magazine*. Her debut novel, *A River Like Mine*, is slated for release in Summer 2026 from Conquest Publishing.

Hannah Brooks

Hannah Brooks is a lawyer living in New Jersey with her husband and their senior rescue mutt.

Jacque Vickers

Jacque Vickers is a graduate of Newtown High School of the Performing Arts. Her writing has been published in Anthology Angels 2023 anthology: Hot Diggety Dog! Tales from the Bark Side, Uncensored Ink: A Banned Book Inspired Anthology (Wild Ink Publishing.)

Jacque lives in Sydney, Australia.

Jenni Howell

Jenni Howell tried out archaeology, linguistics, mongoose herding (known to some as "teaching"), finance, and espionage, but always got bored. Now she writes books, so her entire world changes every six months—and she will never be bored again. BOYS WITH SHARP TEETH, her debut novel, releases April 8, 2025 with Macmillan (US) and Scholastic (UK). She can be found on socials at @byjennihowell or www.jennihowell.com.

——*ell*——

Jennifer Cilia

Jennifer Cilia knew she always wanted to be a writer. A graduate of Seton Hill University in Greensburg, Pennsylvania, she returned sixteen years later to receive her Master of Fine Arts in Writing Popular Fiction. She resides in Pittsburgh, Pennsylvania and loves being indoors curled up with a good book.

——*ell*——

Jennifer Spurgeon

Jennifer's passion for music and languages often finds its way into her writing. Her short story *Entangled* is in *The Aurora Journal's Spring 2021 Issue*. Her vignette *Hello Mello* is in *Full Mood Magazine's Yellow* Issue. Other pieces are on her site *A Rabbit's Stories* einetogicuentos.blogspot.com.

——*ell*——

Jessica K. Foster

Jessica K. Foster is an author of Young Adult Contemporary Romances including *Andy and the Extroverts* and *Andy and the Summer of Something.* She lives in West Michigan with her husband, two boys, and ragtag crew of rescue animals. Find out more at jessicakfoster.com.

———

Jessica Lee Minneci

Jessica Lee Minneci is a young adult fantasy author, living in Louisville, Kentucky. She has a BA in English, Creative Writing and an MFA in Writing Popular Fiction from Seton Hill University. Jessica has had one short story published in an anthology by Dragon Soul Press with another coming soon.

———

Jinxie R. Thorne

Jinxie has always enjoyed reading, and creative writing. She is a loving wife to her husband of eight years, and caring Pet Parent to her furbaby "Baby Fluff".

———

Karla Marie S. Eduardo

Karla Marie S. Eduardo is a second-year college student at NEUST-San Isidro campus, pursuing a Bachelor of Secondary Education Major in English. Karla explores the beauty of language and emotions in literature, expressing her poetic voice for the first time in this piece.

Kate DeMaio

Scientist by day and storyteller by night, Kate DeMaio writes kidlit for all ages. Hermiddle-grade novel, Fiona and the Forgotten Piano, debuts January 2025 through Wild Ink Publishing.

Kelly Kandra Hughes

Kelly Kandra Hughes loves love. And magic. And dogs. As much as she tried, she couldn't fit a dog into this particular prom story, so love and magic will have to do. She's a member of SCBWI and the North Carolina Writers Network (even though she currently lives in Colorado).

Kristen Argyres

Kristen was born and raised in the Midwest. She wrote fan fiction for years before finally making the leap to try publishing her work. Her loves include family, TTRPGs, and chocolate. She lives with her wife and high school sweetheart, Gertrude, their two children, and their clumsy senior cat.

Kimberly Witz

Kimberly Witz is a former high school English teacher who lives in California with her husband and two small children. When she isn't writing, she's walking her golden retriever, haunting coffee shops, or plotting overly complicated scenarios for her next mystery.

Kristi McManus

Kristi McManus is a Registered Nurse by trade, but avid reader and enthusiastic book lover all her life. Her debut novel, Our Vengeful Souls, was released Summer 2023 by CamCat Books. When she isn't writing, she enjoys photography, art, and considers napping to be a form of cardio. She lives in Toronto with her husband.

Leigh Therriault

Leigh Therriault is a writer and analyst from Ottawa, Ontario. She earned a Master of Science in Communication, Behaviour and Credibility Analysis from the Manchester Metropolitan University, and graduated from the Creative Writing Program at the University of Toronto. Her writing has appeared in The Caterpillar, Cricket, Consilience Journal, Polar Starlight, and elsewhere.

Lester N. Linsangan

Lester N. Linsangan is a Filipino writer and educator. He graduated with a degree inBachelor of Secondary Education at Nueva Ecija University of Science and Technology (Got the highest score of 99% in the final teaching demonstration); earned his Master of Arts in Education at the College of the Immaculate Conception (with honors); obtained his 4-year course in ecclesiastical education at the Institute of Religion, and finished his Doctor of Education at Wesleyan University-Philippines (Cum Laude) Additionally, Dr. Linsangan wrote three literary books entitled Litera, Il Vento Sotto Le Mie ALi, and Rendezvous and served as co-author, anthologist, and reviewer for numerous titles.

Lianne Robinson

Lianne Robinson's writing journey began in childhood, sparked by the discovery of her grandmother's ancient Remington typewriter. Recently, she penned two novels and is in the process of writing a third. She resides in Alabama with her husband, three children, and their goofy rescue dog, Piper.

Lorie Wackwitz

Lorie Wackwitz is an author, editor, publisher, and filmmaker with lead editor responsibilities at two micro-presses. She writes from her island cottage in northern Michigan where her family maintains a private nature reserve.

Lynn Katz

Lynn Katz is a retired school principal and full-time writer. Her debut novel, The Surrogate, is a psychological thriller published in 2021. Her middle-grade novel, Chester and the Magic 8 Ball, 2022, received a Kirkus Review, starred review. Her poems have been published in anthologies for adults and children.

Marianna Palmer

Marianna Palmer has lived many lives all in her own mind. Hidden away from the world, she clacks away at her keyboard, penning amazing stories about teens and their love escapades. In reality, she hides away, hoping no one will see her. But at the same time hoping they will.

Lissa James

Lissa James has always loved to read about magic. She is still disappointed the wardrobe at her grandparents' house didn't lead to Narnia. Now she writes young adult and middle-grade fiction about the legendary creatures she's always wanted to meet. For more magical adventures, look for The Fairy Princess Pageant and Winter in the Blue House on Amazon.

Michael Joseph Tharnish Roby

Michael Joseph Tharnish Roby is a fantasy and comedy writer and a graduate of Seton Hill University's writing popular fiction program. One of his great writing loves is to unite the fantastical with the every day, this piece being his latest to find magic in the relatable (and vice versa.)

Michelle Bulsiewicz

Michelle Bulsiewicz has a degree in journalism and formerly wrote and edited for the arts and entertainment section of a local newspaper. She currently resides in California with her husband, two sons, and her dog and cat. On the rare occasion she's not writing, reading, or wrestling children, she is usually practicing yoga, riding her bike, or enjoying a cup of tea.

Misty Middlebrook

Misty Middlebrook resides in Ferndale, Washington, where she writes, cooks,reads, and loves, though not necessarily in that order.

Mogene Christensen

Mogene Christensen is a married 30-year-old with a 3-year-old daughter and one on the way. She loves reading, exercising, and sandwiches. Despite health challenges, she takes on life with enthusiasm and optimism.

Pines Callahan

Pines Callahan is a former geriatric psych nurse and current professional native plant nerd. She typically writes contemporary fantasy or cozy horror, and always makes her "monsters" lovable.Find her on X at @pinesforstories, or at pinescallahan.squarespace.com.

Rae Evans

Rae Evans grew up in the mountains of West Virginia where she spent summers by the lake, often with a book in her hand. Today, she teaches high school English in PA, and spends her free time with her daughters and cheering for the Phillies baseball team.

S.R. Hartley

S.R. writes paranormal romance and dark romantasy when she isn't busy working the night shift as a registered nurse. She's a mom of two kids and two cats and enjoys reading, traveling, and drinking all the best wines. She's currently querying her debut romantasy novel: Claimed by Darkness.

Shuba Mohan

Shuba Mohan's writings explore possibilities. She believes failure makes you smarter, perfection doesn't exist, and continual learning is the only way to say you're living life to the fullest. Her works have been featured by Yellow Arrow Journal, Brown Girl Magazine, and Fairfield Scribes. She lives in Southern California.

S.J. Korzelius

SJ Korzelius attended five proms and seven semi-formals, all with borrowed or hand-me-down dresses. She believes love is the greatest human calling and finds joy in the moment, especially through words, photography, and the great outdoors.

Stephanie Henson

Stephanie resides with her family in West Chester, Pennsylvania, but her roots trace back to Central, New Jersey. She holds a degree in Communications and a

Publishing and Professional Writing Certificate from Rider University. Stephanie is an active member of SCBWI (Eastern PA Chapter) and has achieved recognition as a 2024 SCBWI Virtual Conference Scholarship winner. Her work has been featured in both print and online publications, including several delightful children's poems. Notably, she has published a Children's Poetry Book entitled "In the Right Lane" (Number 1 New Release in Children's Poetry), a Middle Grade Contemporary Novel through Oh MG Press entitled "Share Faire Famous" (Number 1 New Release in Children's Books on Peer Pressure), and a Picture Book through Tielmour Press entitled "No School, My Rules!" (Number 1 New Release in Children's School & Education Books).

Tohiya Kamei

Toshiya Kamei takes inspiration from fairy tales, folklore, and mythology. They attempt to reimagine the past, present, and future while shifting between various perspectives and points of view. Many of their characters are outsiders living on the margins of society.

Tracy Truels

Tracy Truels is a poet and storyteller. Her poems have appeared in the literary magazines *Fugue, Subtropics, and Sentence*. She also penned the libretto for *Cosmic Ray and the Amazing Chris*, a comic fantasy opera produced by Chicago's Thompson Street Opera Company.She also penned the libretto for Cosmic Ray and the Amazing Chris, a comic fantasy opera produced by Chicago's Thompson Street Opera Company. She lives and works in Tulsa.

Vicki Berger Erwin

Vicki Berger Erwin is the published author of 31 books and several short stories.She worked in sales for Scholastic and owned an independent bookstore. Vicki is a member of the Short Mystery Fiction Society, SinC, and SCBWI. She has an MFA in Writing Popular Fiction from Seton Hill University.

www.ingramcontent.com/pod-product-compliance
Lightning Source LLC
Chambersburg PA
CBHW061332310726
48974CB00001B/11